P9-CKN-743

And Still the Wind

345-JEYS

And Still the Wind

Gene H. Jeys

Copyright © 2001 by Gene H. Jeys.

Library of Congress Number: 2001116577
ISBN #:   Hardcover   0-7388-6756-X
                   Softcover   0-7388-6757-8

All rights reserved. No part of this book may be reproduced or transmitted in any form or by any means, electronic or mechanical, including photocopying, recording, or by any information storage and retrieval system, without permission in writing from the copyright owner.

This is a work of fiction. Names, characters, places and incidents either are the product of the author's imagination or are used fictitiously, and any resemblance to any actual persons, living or dead, events, or locales is entirely coincidental.

This book was printed in the United States of America.

To order additional copies of this book, contact:
Xlibris Corporation
1-888-7-XLIBRIS
www.Xlibris.com
Orders@Xlibris.com

Contents

Dedicated to Eve, Betty, and Pauline

PREFACE

There was always someone in my family ready to tell a story, but my father's were the most interesting. Somehow he managed to hold onto his audience until the very end, even though we'd heard most of them many times. If the audience, (usually the neighborhood kids and my mother) seemed to lack interest, he'd change it. At the conclusion of the story, mother would often add, "Joe, if you tell that story one more time, you'll start to believe it yourself."

One family story was about a diary of a family member who, in 1849, took part in the California gold rush. As a ten-year-old, this story really fascinated me since there was more than one version. One way father told it, someone in the family made off with the diary. Another time, father said it might have been lost in a house fire. A lot of homes were destroyed in those days, not many fire hydrants out on the prairie. As an adult, I tried to locate the diary, but was unsuccessful.

My uncle, Sam Jeys, delighted us with stories of his life as a trick rider and roper with Buffalo Bill's Wild West show.

Father embellished many of his stories with versions that included encounters with Jesse James' gang. No good storyteller could pass up the opportunity to tell a story about the James gang, or a shootout involving the death of a close friend, and why my father vowed to never carry a firearm.

It seemed unusual to me that we never had guns in our house. I once asked my father if he had ever killed anyone. It seemed to me that anyone who had captured wild horses on the plains of Colorado, or rowed Frank James, Jessie's older brother, across the Missouri River at night to play poker, would surely have engaged in some gunplay. Father avoided the subject.

I don't know if my father ever did those things, but the idea that those events could have happened, fuels my imagination. This is an important point about storytelling...don't get hung up on the truth. There is always a grain of truth in the most implausible stories, but truth is different for each of us. The good storyteller is able to capture the spirit of the story that carries that grain of truth.

In "AND STILL THE WIND," I've embellished an actual experience of my own to tell the story of the Lightning Horse. As a young man, I was courting a girl whose brother did not particularly like me. He had a horse that wouldn't let anyone but himself ride him. One day, I told him I could probably ride that horse. He agreed to let me try, but clearly he was hoping I'd get bucked off to teach me a lesson and humiliate me in front of his sister. I walked calmly around the horse for a few minutes, talking quietly all the while, before I swung onto his bare back and rode him to the end of the lane and back without incident. To this day, the brother and I are the best of friends.

Mother didn't offer to tell many stories herself. I guess she thought father told enough for all of us, but when we did get her to talking, it was refreshing and often her point of view differed from father's. Like one of the bear stories father told. Mother and father were married in 1902, and went northeast from Nebraska to homestead at the tip of Lake Superior, near Duluth, Minnesota.

Mother accompanied him one day to pick berries while he chopped wood. She placed the baby on a blanket and started picking along a nearby thicket. She and a black bear came to the end of the thicket at the same time. Mother screamed, threw her berry bucket at the bear, snatched the baby and ran to father for protection. He laughed and when he told the story, added, "I'm not sure who was more scared, Lena or the bear. He ran from her as fast as she ran to me."

"It wasn't funny," mother would say, and walk off.

As a child, mother lived in a sod shanty on the Nebraska plains. As I relate this, I can hear her singing a song whose last words were, "my little old sod shanty on the plains."

Mother played the piano and several members of the family had good voices. Many times we'd gather at the Byrd family home on Sunday afternoons and sing all sorts of songs. As I remember, Irish ballads were the favorite. Mother's and my favorite was, "I Will Take You Home, Kathleen." After all these years, I still get teary-eyed when I hear it. I must have been all of seven years old at that time.

Our family was a large one, five girls and six boys, spread out over twenty-five years. There was always room for one more at our table, and if a homeless child was around, enough love and kindness to share for all. There were a lot of tough times, then, especially during the depression years, but I prefer to remember the good things and ignore the bad.

Throughout my life, I've been captivated by stories about Native Americans and the old west. I have had the pleasure of knowing, learning from, and working with many Native Americans in my various careers. I realize that some of the terms used throughout this series are not ones commonly used in much of the popular lore about Native Americans and the west. For example, the lore often fails to make the distinction between the Blackfeet and the Blackfoot tribes.

The Blackfoot Nation comprises a group of Algonkian-speaking tribes originating in Alberta, Canada and the northern plains region of the United States. Among this group are the Kainah, or Blood, the Siksika, or Blackfoot, and Piegan. The southern Piegan of Montana are officially known as the Blackfeet.

The Blackfeet were a nomadic group who live in villages of 'tipis'. Another less familiar word in this story is 'capote', which is a French word for hooded cape or cloak, often worn by soldiers and travelers.

I've been fortunate to have had a diverse background from which to tell stories of my own. I've worked at many occupations that required practical, hands-on skills: machinist, draftsman, construction laborer,

345-JEYS

carpenter's helper, house painter, tool designer, quality engineer and professional counselor. The second book in this series is "FAIR WIND THAT BLEW," which includes many details about steam trains that derive from personal incidents and experience.

My extensive work as a Boy Scout leader brought great satisfaction in sharing practical and spiritual wisdom with the young men. Some of my fiction, as in "FAIR WIND THAT BLEW," reflects the aches and pains of adolescent development and life style.

My formal education came late in my career, but it enabled me to participate in the space program at Sandia National Laboratories. I hold a B.A. from the University of Albuquerque, and an M.A. in counseling psychology from the University of New Mexico and Antioch University. My wife Eve and I now live in Albuquerque, New Mexico.

Gene H. Jeys

CHAPTER 1
A HEAP OF TROUBLE

*(You know how little while we have to stay,...)*III

Jack slid the club toward Charles. "Look out Charlie, he's a bad one," he grunted. Charles' hand tightened on the club. Nodding his head, he surveyed the man in front of him. The tall Blackfeet tossed some skins on the counter. "Whiskey," he snarled.

"No! No whiskey," Charles said, pushing the skins back toward the Indian.

"Takes-A-Gun want whiskey, you give." his voice was insistent. Charles shifted his gaze toward the door where two other Blackfeet warriors hovered silently. He spoke softly in the Piegan dialect. "You want to trade, we trade, but no whiskey." He jerked his head toward the shelves, behind the counter, his eyes not moving from those of the Blackfeet. Takes-A-Gun slapped the counter with his open palm and said something in a low voice. His companions slid away from the door in opposite directions. The trader shifted his position and Takes-

---

Italicized subtitles and verses are from <u>RUBAIYAT OF OMAR KHAYYAM</u> , third edition, 1872 (except where noted in the text), by Edward Fitzgerald, Books, Inc.

A-Gun eased his hand to his waist and lightly touched the handle of his knife.

"I'll take care of them two," Jack growled.

The knife was in Takes-A-Gun's hand. "Whiskey," he snarled. Charles moved swiftly. The club slammed into the Blackfeet's knife arm and the weapon clattered on the floor. In the same motion, Charles vaulted across the counter and jerked and twisted Takes-A-Gun's arm behind him. The red man attempted to pull away and found himself more tightly constrained as Charles' other arm tightened around his neck.

"Nice work, Charlie." Jack motioned toward the door with a pistol, then swiftly pointed it back toward Takes-A-Gun's companions, who with a quick glance at Takes-A-Gun gasping for air in Charles' chokehold, jumped for the door opening. They slammed into each other, tripped, and crawled outside. They ran for their horses.

Charles grasped Takes-A-Gun by his belt and thrust him out the door. The disgraced warrior sprawled in the dirt. Charles ignored his glare and tossed Takes-A-Gun's knife in the dirt in front of him. "Get out and stay out," Charles said.

The tall man brushed the dirt from his legs, gestured angrily, then picked up his knife and stalked to his horse. Without looking back, he rode furiously away.

"Reckon you might have made an enemy there," Jack said.

"Don't much care, his kind we can do without." Charles said, as he placed the oaken club behind the counter.

Jack slowly shook his head. "Almost forgot how quick you were," he said. "You ain't forgot nothing I taught you about the rough stuff neither." Jack's voice was quiet, but his obvious pleasure in the way things had gone was evident in his tone.

"You taught me? I've forgotten more about brawling than you'll ever know." Charles slid his arm over Jack's shoulder. "But I was glad to see that you haven't forgotten what I taught you about using a gun."

"Why you ungrateful whelp, you weren't hardly dry behind the ears when I taught you the whats and wherefores about soldiering. Charlie, you've hurt my sensitive feelings and unless you apologize right smartly, there ain't no predicting how I might act."

Charles laughed and slapped Jack on the back. "I thought I'd bust a gut laughing the way those two fell over each other getting out the door."

Jack placed both hands on the counter and looked at his friend. "You know you'll have to kill Takes-A-Gun some day, don't you?"

"Lots of bravado there," Charles said. "He'll be all right, soon as I return his skins and he cools down some."

"Listen to me. Most of them Blackfeet braves are reasonable fellows, especially the Piegan band." Jack pulled his beard in a nervous gesture. "Them two with him ain't much, but Takes-A-Gun is a big man in the tribe, and you insulted him in front of his friends. He'll try to do the same thing with you on his own territory. You watch yourself around him."

"I'll land on my feet." Charles began to straighten a pile of pelts. "I'll do what I have to when the time comes. What just happened isn't worth killing someone over."

Jack studied his young friend quizzically for a moment then slowly shook his head. From time to time he looked to where Charles was working, then returned to his bookwork. At last he closed the book.

Charles looked up at the sound and Jack smiled at him. "Old Beaver Tail sure lost a lot of his dignity when he fell down trying to get out of here. Hope you're right and we've seen the last of them. But remember what I said, and don't count on it." Jack came around the counter. "Time to close up," he said. He handed Charles the heavy bar for the door.

345-JEYS

CHAPTER 2
LOOK, BUT DON'T
TOUCH

*(Would not we shatter it to bits—and then)*XCIX

Na-Ha-Ki's father always expected her to go to the trading post with him, since she spoke the white man's tongue and could play the role of interpreter. It was considered improper for a Piegan girl to exchange looks with a man in public. However the last time, as they left the trading post, the young white trader, Charles Tucker, had smiled at her, and she looked forward to seeing him again.

Consequently, she was quick to volunteer to help her father on his next trip. Now, as she moved around the post, she noticed the trader watching her. He smiled, and she quickly smiled back, then moved to another area. Again he caught her glance, smiled at her and went on with his activity. A voice from behind startled her. "So, the young trader is interested in you?" It was Crow Woman, the wife of Jack Taylor. Na-Ha-Ki laughed nervously then glanced at the white man again.

"Why should he be interested in me?" she whispered. "He must have many white women of his own where he comes from."

"I do not think so. He does not speak of them. My husband tells me he has talked of taking a Piegan for his wife. Perhaps he is thinking of you?" She added. "But you must have many warriors who have already asked your father for you?"

"No, no one has asked for me." Na-Ha-Ki's heart thumped and she stole another look at the white trader. His long blond hair and blue eyes intrigued her. He sensed her gaze and returned her look. It seemed to her that he must know what she was thinking. She blushed in confusion and turned away.

"So, he does interest you. I will tell him if you wish." Na-Ha-Ki mutely nodded in assent. For the next few days she savored the moment at the trading post when she and Charles had exchanged glances. She was anxious to see him again, but there didn't seem to be any way she could manage it. She, like most Piegan maidens, was closely watched. It would be difficult.

Help came from Crow Woman. She and Na-Ha-Ki's mother, Sa-Ka-Ki, were discussing a dance for the trappers and traders, to be held at the trading post. "There will be many Piegan women there," Crow Woman said.

Sa-Ka-Ki glanced at her daughter. Na-Ha-Ki bent over her sewing and pretended not to notice. "I don't know, some of the young women have acted foolishly at those dances," she said.

"Oh come now, old friend. Do you not remember how much fun you and I had?"

"Ah, it is as you say, friend. I have grown old. I have forgotten how much the young enjoy such things. As long as you are there with my daughter, I suppose it will be all right."

Crow Woman laughed. "Hah, we old women make big plans for Na-Ha-Ki and she may not wish to go. Maybe she would rather stay at home and sew."

"I would like to go." The young girl's heart raced and her face felt warm. She awaited her mother's decision.

"Someone will have to go with her to bring her home when the dance is over."

345-JEYS

Crow Woman stood slightly behind Na-Ha-Ki's mother. She winked at the young girl. "She can help me before the dance and afterwards. My man, Jack Taylor, has told me to find someone to help. Na-Ha-Ki is a good worker. We have room for her at the trading post and we can bring her home afterwards. I will have much work to do preparing for the dance. She can help me then as well."

The girl's mother nodded. "She will work hard for you. When do you want her to help?"

"She can go with me now, if you can spare her. I have much to do."

Sa-Ka-Ki patted her daughter on the shoulder. "Get your things. Do as Crow Woman asks." She paused and eyed her daughter. "Have a good time at the dance. It is as Crow Woman says. When I was your age, the young men always asked me to dance first." Sa-Ka-Ki eyed her daughter. "Maybe the white trader will ask you to dance." Na-Ha-Ki smiled, surprised and pleased with her mother's words. She always liked it when Crow Woman visited. She and mother always joked and laughed, and Crow Woman treated her as if she were a woman, not a young girl.

As Crow Woman and Na-Ha-Ki rode away, Sa-Ka-Ki pictured herself dancing back and forth, around and around. She hummed a tune as she went back to the tipi.

The post was located about a half mile outside the adobe walls of Fort Benton on a flat that fronted the Missouri River. A ferry crossed the wide stream, and in the spring, when the ice broke up, crossing was perilous. Before too many years in the future, an iron bridge would cross at this point. There was little Indian trouble any more and the wide gates of the fort were seldom closed. Na-Ha-Ki's family belonged to a band of Piegan who had always maintained good relations with the whites and had a sizable camp, a mile or so up the river from the fort.

When they arrived at the trading post, Crow Woman motioned for Na-Ha-Ki to dismount. "Come, we will speak to my husband and the young trader." She took the girl by the hand and entered the trading post where Charles and Jack were busy sorting hides. They stopped and looked at the two women. Na-Ha-Ki lowered her eyes and suddenly felt her cheeks grow warm.

"This is Na-Ha-Ki. She will help me get things ready for the dance and stay with us afterward for a while to help me with the work."

Charles wiped his hands on his pants legs and grasped both of Na-Ha-Ki's hands. "May I have the first dance?" he said in the Piegan tongue. She nodded, surprised at how well he spoke her language.

Jack slipped his arm around Crow Woman. "Looks like you got yourself a right pretty helper. I think I'm going to have to keep my eye on Charlie. He's sort of taken with her."

Crow Woman smiled at Jack. "We will need these moved." She swung her arm in a semi-circle and indicated several piles of hides and furs stacked about the large rectangular room.

"Honey, Charlie and I will do whatever you want." Jack kissed her on the cheek, then grinned as the woman pushed him away. Na-Ha-Ki had not understood what Jack said, but it sounded friendly and she decided that she liked the big dark haired trader.

"Na-Ha-Ki. What a beautiful name. I will teach you to say it in English." Charles said. "Child of Laughter. Na-Ha-Ki, Child of Laughter, Na-Ha-Ki." She practiced saying her name in English until she finally got it just right. Charles grasped her hand and squeezed it.

"That's it," he said pleased.

"I have learned to speak your language from my friend Crow Woman," she said.

"She has taught you well," he said.

"Charles, I must show Na-Ha-Ki her room," Crow Woman said.

Charles reluctantly released the girl's hand and went back to sorting hides. "Where are we going to put all of these skins?" he asked Jack.

"We can put most of them in the storage rooms outside," Jack said, gesturing at the hides. "Don't get big ideas about that girl. She's Eagle Chief's daughter and if he thought there was something funny going on, he could cause a heap of trouble," Jack said. "Remember what I told you? Look, but don't touch."

345-JEYS

CHAPTER 3
A DRESS FOR THE DANCE

*(—and the Bird is on the Wing.)*_{VII}

The partners had not stinted themselves for room in the trading post. The spacious adobe-chinked structure built in 1866, just after the Civil War, held storage sheds with outside access for hides along the south side. The inside trading area was in one large rectangular room at the front where the dance would take place. Lanterns hung from rafters and the room was heated by two potbellied stoves. Windows with heavy wooden shutters provided light and ventilation. Several bedrooms, personal storage rooms and a kitchen with a cast iron stove were to the rear. Adjoining bedrooms shared fireplaces.

A heavy counter with trade items on shelves behind ran along one side of the trade room. Arrayed in a colorful display were yard goods, trinkets, blankets, capotes, and other items. Pots, pans, axes, and heavier items rested on the floor.

Traders and trappers dances were popular events and the two partners decided a dance would be a good way to make friends with the independent traders and trappers around Fort Benton. White women were non-existent in the territory, except for a few army wives and some hurdy-gurdy girls in the mining camps of Virginia City and Helena.

Crow Woman had arranged for several of the Indian women to attend. They could be counted upon to be fine dancers and would provide the female company.

Jack Taylor played the fiddle. He was anxious for the festivities to begin. The big room was cleared, scrubbed, and fresh sawdust was spread on the floor. Bright colored yard goods gathered in the center and tied with a huge bow hung from the ceiling. By early afternoon the women finished their preparations and Crow Woman smiled at the younger woman.

"We have one more thing to do." Na-Ha-Ki looked at her questioningly as she went to the shelf behind the counter and pulled down a roll of red velvet. She dropped it on the counter, then unrolled several turns of the soft material and held it up for inspection. It glowed softly.

"We will make you a dress for the dance," Crow Woman said. She cut off a length of material and wrapped it toga-style around the young girl. Crow Woman stood back and admired her creation. She smiled and nodded her head. The rest of the afternoon was spent in hand-stitching the dress. When they went to the bedroom for a final fitting, Crow Woman put her hand to her mouth and studied her. From a small trunk at the foot of the bed, she extracted a necklace with a large circular pendant and slipped it over Na-Ha-Ki's head. She pulled the girl's hair free and the necklace settled into place. The contrast of the blue-beaded necklace against the red velvet dress was striking. Next, Crow Woman fastened a belt of soft, white doeskin about the girl's waist and tied it at the front by heavy thongs that hung to her knees. Na-Ha-Ki's boots were charcoal colored, soft leather with a pattern of white beads running horizontally about the top of the foot. Beads in diamond-shaped patterns ran up the sides. Across the front were narrow bands of beads tying the designs together.

"Ah, you will be the most beautiful woman there tonight," Crow Woman said. "There is one more thing." She rummaged in the trunk and extracted a silver bracelet. Before putting it on the wondering girl's arm, she breathed on it and rubbed it vigorously against her dress. It gleamed softly. Na-Ha-Ki could hardly believe the image that she saw in the mirror. Crow Woman laughed. "You see, it is as I said, you will be the most beautiful one at the dance tonight. Charles will be pleased. Now, we must fix the food. You change clothes while I start the fire."

The older woman hugged her and left. Na-Ha-Ki stood before the mirror, turning in one direction, then another. She smiled at herself, rearranging her dark hair, first in front and to one side, then in two parts, one on each side. At last she removed the dress and laid it carefully on the bed. The sight of her nude body in the mirror fascinated her, and she cupped a hand under each fully rounded breast and watched as it swelled up and out. Suddenly she felt warm and happy. The young white trader was interested in her. Already he had taught her several words of English. And, tonight at the dance he would see her in the red dress. Hearing the rattle of stove grates, she took one last look at herself and put on her work clothes. Crow Woman would be expecting her.

She and Crow Woman had just completed arranging the room when the musicians from Keno Bill's arrived and began a quick tune to warm up. By now, several Indian women had arrived and stood in a group, chatting and laughing. They were impressed with the room and its decorations. Crow Woman nudged Na-Ha-Ki.

"You go change. I'll be there soon," she said.

Most of the fur traders wore fancy shirts with colorful neckerchiefs at their throats. Their pants were stuffed into boots shined to a soft glow.

The trappers wore buckskin clothing with boots or moccasins, Indian style. Most of the men were bearded and many slicked their hair down with bear grease. "Where's the liquor?" one shouted to Jack.

"Time enough for that later," he replied.

The men lined up along the wall opposite the women. One of them lifted his boot to knock his pipe against the heel and stole a glance at the women. "Some pickings," he said. "Jack and Charlie have a good eye for the ladies."

"You can bet it was Crow Woman's doings. She's a right smart looking lady herself. Don't know how she ever got hooked up with old ugly Jack," his companion said.

The women were, for the most part, attractive and graceful. They were self-possessed and aware that the men were conscious of them. Most wore calico dresses with large multi-colored shawls thrown over their shoulders. However, a few wore doeskin garments with intricate designs formed by colored beads or porcupine quills dyed yellow, blue and red. Occasionally a soft laugh or giggle arose from their midst.

Traders and trappers usually took Indian wives and many favorable arrangements came from occasions such as this one.

In her room, Na-Ha-Ki admired her reflection in the mirror. If Charles were pleased with her tonight he might ask her father for her. It would be nice to live as the Crow Woman did. Her white husband treated her well. The music for the first dance started and Crow Woman burst into the room. "Hurry, Charles is waiting for you."

Na-Ha-Ki tied the thongs of the belt and slipped the bracelet on her wrist. A quick glance in the mirror and she was ready. Crow Woman held the door open and she hesitantly stepped into the large room. The music slowed, then stopped as everyone watched Charles stride across the room to her. His long, blond hair glowed softly in the lantern light. Fringes hung from the sleeves and pant legs of his soft white doeskin clothing. A pair of beaded moccasins completed his outfit.

He took her arm. The music started again and they swung into the rhythm of the dance. It was as if they had danced together all of their lives. His movements were light and graceful and she easily followed his lead. And it wasn't until the music stopped and the other dancers had left the floor that they were aware they were alone. His arm

945-JEYS

dropped to her waist as they walked to where the dancers crowded about the counter. Jack joked and laughed with many of them. The food disappeared and Crow Woman with Na-Ha-Ki's help quickly replenished it. Charles poured drinks with a long handled dipper from a large kettle filled with watered down alcohol. Na-Ha-Ki tasted the bitter stuff and made a face. Charles smiled at her and slowly sipped his drink while he looked over the rim of the cup. His eyes swept her entire body. She was self-conscious, but pleased with his attention. He set his drink down and went to another kettle and brought her a cup of cold water. She noticed that most of the women were also drinking water.

Suddenly the room noise ceased. At the entrance to the trading post, three Piegan warriors studied the crowd silently, their eyes darting from one person to another. Their expressions did not change, but the hostility on their faces was evident. The tallest of the three stopped when his gaze reached Charles and Na-Ha-Ki. He stared sullenly at them. Their upper torsos were bare, with buckskin leggings covering the lower part of their bodies, their faces painted black. The trio were Takes-A-Gun and his companions.

Charles eyed the scalp that hung by a long hank of hair from Take-A-Gun's belt. When war parties were successful, they painted their faces black before they rode into camp. Na-Ha-Ki edged closer to Charles and pressed against him. Without taking his eyes from the man, Charles touched her hand.

Takes-A-Gun now glared across the room at the others gathering there. His gaze traveled slowly from one couple to the next. A woman cowered in a corner, partially obscured by the trapper in front of her.

Charles motioned for Na-Ha-Ki to move behind the counter, then started for the tall Piegan. Jack's hand checked Charles. "Best stay out of this, boy. No affair of ours. If I be right, he's looking for his woman." Jack said.

The tall Indian strode across the quiet room toward the trapper and the woman cowering behind him. She whimpered and scrunched herself into the corner and turned away from the bronzed man. Takes-

A-Gun stopped in front of the trapper, then pulled his knife from its sheath and slowly wiped it on his pants leg. He raised the knife to the trapper's eye level and snarled. "Move, white man."

As the trapper stepped aside, Takes-A-Gun seized the woman's hair and jerked her to her feet. His voice was loud. "There is a thing we do with women like you," he said. His lips were drawn together in a thin line. The woman sobbed and pleaded with him. Takes-A-Gun glanced at his companions at the door. Their faces were stern. Words came from the woman's mouth in a torrent. The man looked at her coldly, disdainfully. His knife was now on the bridge of her nose. There was a sharp intake of breath as his intentions became apparent. Suddenly he jerked the woman's head violently backward and her hands fell free of her face. The knife flashed in a quick arc.

Her hand clutched her face. Blood spurted from between her fingers. He loosened his grip and she slumped and fell into the corner like a bundle of rags, branded for life. A cut-nosed woman, her nose severed from its bridge to the upper lip. Her body heaved convulsively.

Takes-A-Gun towered over her and slowly wiped his knife on her hair and then swiped it against his pants leg before returning it to its sheath. The blood soaked piece of flesh that had been her nose lay at his feet.

Quickly, Crow Woman stepped in front of Takes-A-Gun and with a piece of wetted buckskin picked the bloody flesh from the floor. She said something in Piegan and pointed toward the door, then turned and hurried toward the rear of the room.

Charles moved closer toward Takes-A-Gun, rifle in hand. The two men's eyes engaged each other. Charles motioned with his rifle toward the door. Takes-A-Gun's hand rested on his knife handle. His fingers closed around it and Charles' finger coiled about the trigger of the gun. The only sounds were those of the sobbing woman. Suddenly she raised her head and glowered at the man in the doorway. She held one hand pressed to her face.

45-JEYS

Blood oozed between her fingers and dripped from her hand onto the sawdust-covered floor. She pointed to Takes-A-Gun and shouted incoherently, then fell to the floor again, in a heap. She lay moaning like an injured animal.

Takes-A-Gun, knife in hand, moved toward Charles. One more step, another, and suddenly Charles thrust the gun against the red man's chest. He lowered his head and stared at the gun. His fingers uncoiled from the knife handle and it dropped into its sheath. He snarled something in Piegan, signaled to his companions and stalked away.

Crow Woman and Na-Ha-Ki knelt beside the injured woman and attempted to comfort her. She calmed a little and Na-Ha-Ki pressed a wet cloth to her face. It showed red with bloodstains. They helped her to her feet and led her to a bedroom and placed her on the bed.

"You stay with her, I will see to the others. Then I will need your help." She patted the woman on the bed. Crow Woman touched Na-Ha-Ki and left.

Conversation in the big room was subdued. "Lucky you're still sporting a nose, John." A fellow trapper slapped the frightened man on the back. "Sure enough when that Piegan came across the room with blood in his eye, I figured you was a goner."

John grinned sheepishly. "Didn't know I was dancing with a married woman," he said. "Thought all the women folk were supposed to be available." He turned to Jack Taylor.

"Guess she came along with the others," he said.

John dipped into the kettle and poured himself a large drink. He gulped it down, in one long draught, and wiped his mouth with the back of his hand. "Easy to see why them Piegan women don't fool around much," he said. "What'll happen to her now?"

"Soon as she is well enough she'll go back to the tribe. From now on she'll be an outcast. Even the women will treat her poorly. They don't generally last long," Jack said.

The women were subdued as they prepared to leave. Jack placed his hand on Charles' shoulder. "I told you Takes-A-Gun would call your bluff. He's a mean one. Before it's all over, you and those Crazy Dogs with him are going to have it out."

"You hadn't stopped me, I'd run him out of here first thing," Charles said.

"Figured as much," Jack said. "You had, we'd probably been in worse trouble. Them Piegan give their available women a lot of freedom, but once one of them is married, she better toe the mark."

Charles stared thoughtfully at a bloodstained spot on the floor. "You're right, I'll be careful with Na-Ha-Ki. I don't want anything happening to her."

Jack surveyed the room. All of the women had left, but the men still hung around in small groups, talking. "Looks like the dance is over," he said dryly. "Wasn't much of a success."

Crow Woman was at his side now. "I will need help from both of you men." She gestured toward the bedroom. "We will sew the woman's nose on. It must be done quickly."

Jack looked at her wonderingly. "She's right, Jack. Saw it during the war."

"Worth a try. Anybody can do it, Crow Woman could. Tell us what you want, we'll do it." Jack turned to Crow Woman. "I'll run the rest of those varmints out of here."

"You and Charles will hold her down, but first you must have her drink fire water. It will help with the pain. Na-Ha-Ki will help me with the sewing and bring me things I will need. We will do the best we can. With Sun's help perhaps we will be successful. Now we must hurry."

Charles and Jack strapped the drunken woman's arms and legs to the bed then helped hold her head still while Crow Woman and Na-Ha-Ki worked on reattaching most of the soft nose tissue with small stitches. When the woman realized what was happening, she held as still as she could, and moaned as she bit down on the folded buckskin Na-Ha-Ki offered her. Crow Woman worked quickly but carefully. At last satisfied that she had done all she could, she wiped her hands on the warm wet rag that Na-Ha-Ki held out to her.

845-JEYS

CHAPTER 4
I HAVE MANY HORSES

*(Nor heed the rumble of a distant Drum!)*_{XIII}

During the next few days, Na-Ha-Ki and Crow Woman cleaned up after the dance and attended to the cut-nose woman. While there was much swelling where Crow Woman had stitched, the wound healed quickly. In a short time the cut-nose woman was able to move about on her own. She was much relieved when Crow Woman told her that she could live at the trading post and help on a steady basis.

Charles had managed on one pretext or another to find opportunities to talk to Na-Ha-Ki as often as possible. They conversed freely now and Na-Ha-Ki's laughter was heard more and more. "Do you have a white woman of your own, where you come from?"

"No, why?"

"Oh, I just wondered," she said. She glanced toward the kitchen where Crow Woman had gone. She was not in sight. "Crow Woman will take me to my parents' lodge soon."

His hand tightened on hers. "I will miss you," he said. "When will you come back?"

Her heart leapt. "I am kept busy helping my family, it will be very hard for me."

Charles studied her face seriously, then spoke abruptly. "There must be many Piegan warriors who would like you for their wife?"

She lowered her head, then answered softly. "Yes, but none have gone to my father yet." She was afraid to look at him. Her heart raced."

"How old are you?"

"That is not the problem," she said sharply. "I was old enough two years ago. I will soon be eighteen years old. It is that many of those who desire me are afraid of what my father will say."

"And what is that?"

"Besides wanting many horses and fine things for me, he also talks about them proving themselves worthy of his daughter. According to him, the man she will marry will also have to show her his love and respect."

"Well, I have many horses and I will also find a way to show him I am worthy of you. I will go to him if you like," he said.

Na-Ha-Ki nodded. "I will speak with my mother first. She will help by speaking to my father. I will send word when it is time for you to come to my parents' lodge."

She smiled at Charles, then quickly kissed him on the cheek and hurried toward the kitchen. She knew that Crow Woman would be pleased with the news. She stopped by the door, looked back at Charles and quickly crossed her arms above her heart. It was the Blackfeet sign of love.

"I will wait to hear from you," he said.

It was a clear day and the sun shone brightly. Birds sang, and Na-Ha-Ki hummed a soft tune as she urged her horse toward the Piegan encampment and her parents' lodge.

Na-Ha-Ki was surprised at her mother's reaction when she told her that she and Charles wished to marry. "I know this young white man is rich and will offer many fine things to show us of his love for you. But your place is here with your own people." She looked at her daughter knowingly. "He is a white man. If you marry him, you will be sorry. He will some day go back to his own people and leave you and your children alone."

45-JEYS

"No, he has no other. He has told me."

"Do not be foolish daughter. You are still young and should listen to your elders. They are much wiser in these things than you are." Sa-Ka-Ki's voice grew louder. "You should enter the lodge of an older man of our people. Many Hawks spoke to your father about you. He is a rich man and is not too old for you. He and your father have been friends for many years. He has made a fine offer for you." She patted her daughter and dismissed the subject as settled.

Na-Ha-Ki's mouth trembled and she hung her head. "I will marry the white trader, even if I have to run away." She raised her head and looked at her mother defiantly.

"You will do as we say! Now go and change your clothes. We have needed you around here and have much work for you. Do you hear me?" her mother asked.

Na-Ha-Ki nodded her head and remained silent. But she had not accepted her mother's advice. At first chance, she stole away and searched out Charles.

"We must go together and talk to your father," he said. "It will be all right," He gathered many trade items together into bundles and packed them on several horses. They rode directly to her parents' lodge. The entrance flap to the lodge was thrust aside and her father motioned for them to enter. Na-Ha-Ki knew that he would be angry with her for disobeying her mother. His mouth was drawn into a tight line that went down at each end. When he looked like that he could be difficult.

Charles' gifts were unpacked and laid out on several blankets. Bright yard goods, beads, brass buttons, twists of tobacco, mirrors, knives, guns, ammunition, heavy brass combs, pots, pans, axes, several mauls and numerous other items were laid out for display. After arranging all of the items before Na-Ha-Ki's parents, Charles showed Eagle Chief a small box. He opened it and a tinkling sound filled the lodge. He closed the lid, opened it, and the music began again. He closed the box and handed it to the wondering Eagle Chief who opened it and smiled when the music began. He quickly closed it and passed it back to Charles. To Eagle Chief's surprise, the younger man spoke in the Piegan tongue. "I wish for your daughter in marriage. I will be kind to her and provide well for her. I ask that you accept these gifts from me." Charles swept his arm in an arc over the gifts arrayed before them.

Eagle Chief unfolded his arms and gestured as he spoke. "It is not good for a Piegan to marry outside of the people. How do I know that you will treat my daughter well?"

"My love for her is great and my heart is filled with longing for her." Charles gestured toward the doorway of the lodge and the horses standing outside. "Please accept the horses that I have brought to your lodge as a part of that expression."

The elder man frowned as he studied the trader's face. "She will make a good Piegan wife, but you are a white man." He glanced at the blankets and array of gifts, then reached for the music box. He examined it, held it to his ear, and then opened it. He smiled delightedly when it played softly, then frowned when it stopped. He shook it, closed and opened the lid several times, then handed it back to Charles. The trader turned it over, rewound it, and the tinkling sounds of a Viennese waltz once again filled the lodge. Charles handed the box to Eagle Chief, abruptly turned and left.

As soon as Charles was out of hearing, Eagle Chief began to lecture his daughter. "When I gave you the name Child of Laughter, it was because you brought happiness into our lodge, but now you bring trouble. Perhaps we have been too easy with you. Must you always have your own way?" He gestured at her. "Do you realize what you have done? This white man is not a Piegan and you are not a white person. It can never work." Eagle Chief held the music box before him. "Perhaps now is the time I must tell you something important. The White Man does not understand us and we do not understand the White Man." He paused and looked intently at his daughter. His voice softened. "You are very wise for your years and I have many times wished that you were a man. That way, you might become an elder in the Piegan. But there is a secret way that your Grandmother and I

45-JEYS

have. When I have something very important to decide upon, I consult with your Grandmother. She is wiser than I am and has always provided me with good advice. I have long thought that you are much like your Grandmother. You must become as she is, wise in the ways of the People. "Many years ago, when I was young like you, several of the elders traveled for many weeks to meet with the Great White Father. They wished to learn how and where he got his power."

Na-Ha-Ki leaned forward listening intently.

"We asked for his secrets, his power, how we might understand so we too might know what we must do to gain this power for ourselves. This is what I mean when I said that the White Man does not understand us or we understand him." Eagle Chief gazed off as if he were seeing into the distance. "In answer to our request for knowledge, he sent us holy men with a Jesus Book. But what we wanted was his wonderful things, not his Jesus book." Her father opened the lid of the music box and they listened until it ran down and stopped. "Charles Tucker showed me what I must do to make it sound again." He turned the box over and re-wound it. "It does not take a Jesus Book to show me this. My daughter, you and your husband and children will have to change and understand such things if you are to survive."

Na-Ha-Ki slowly nodded, lifted her head and looked at her father. Her lip quivered and a tear began to roll down her cheek. Eagle Chief touched his daughter's face and wiped the tear away. "Do not cry. You are young now but someday you will see that I am right." In a gentle voice he added, "You must think of the children first. They will be neither Piegan nor white. What about them?" He was pensive for a moment. "And it is different with the white man. He only takes one wife. You will have to do all the work yourself."

"They will be fine children. It does not matter to Charles and me. That is what is important." She looked at him defiantly. "When a white stallion mates with a red mare and the colt turns out spotted, it does not matter to you. You only care that it is a good horse. Your best buffalo runner is red and white!"

Eagle Chief touched her cheek again. "I have always allowed you to have your opinions in our lodge. However, we are only one part of the People. We cannot allow you to do something like this without their approval." He smiled at her. "What you say about my buffalo runner is true, but remember, people are not horses."

Na-Ha-Ki pressed her point. "That is right, father, but it will be to the advantage of the People to have the white trader as part of the Piegan. He can help us to deal with the other white men. Has not Jack Taylor the other white trader, been such a man?" She paused and looked at her father defiantly. "You think it is important for me to learn the white man's language. Well, Charles has cared enough to learn our Piegan language."

Eagle Chief suddenly laughed. "If I listen to you long enough, you will convince me that you are right. How I wish you had been a man. Now, go help your mother and sister," he said, dismissing her. Na-Ha-Ki smiled as she walked away from the tipi listening to the sound of the music box. Na-Ha-Ki considered what her parents had said to her. Yes, she thought, they were likely to be right. Things wouldn't always go smoothly, but she knew in her heart that she had made the correct decision about Charles and that their love for each other would carry them through any difficulty. In time, her parents would see that she was right.

845-JEYS

CHAPTER 5
THE WIND CHANGES

*(Come fill the Cup, and in the fire of Spring...)*_{VII}

Na-Ha-Ki's mind churned as she went about the work her mother assigned her. At this moment she did not wish to talk to her sisters. She needed some time alone to sort out her thoughts. Despite the comforting words of her father, she knew her arguments hadn't changed his mind. Her fleshing knife made a steady thunking sound as she worked at the buffalo hide before her. It lay hair side to the ground, stretched out tightly so she could cut small pieces of flesh from it. She stopped momentarily and brushed her hair from her eyes and face. Then, with a stone hammer, she drove several more small pegs about the periphery of the hide to stretch it even tighter. It would make a good robe. Soft like silk, worth five dollars in trade. Eagle Chief would say something pleasant to her when he saw what a fine job she'd done. It was hard work, but she did not mind. A warm breeze kept the flies away.

A large yellowish-brown dog slunk past and sniffed at the robe. He stopped when she tossed him a bit of meat. He gulped it down, then sat on his haunches, mouth open, his red tongue lolling. He spread his forelegs, rested his head between them and watched the girl. She tossed another piece of meat his way. His right ear cocked and his tail thumped the ground vigorously.

"Look at you, you lazy thing," she said. "I work hard and you lay there resting in the sun like Old Many Hawks." She tossed another bit in front of the dog and he sniffed it, then turned his head away disdainfully. "You don't know how good you have it, dog. No one tells you who you can be with or what to do all the time. Besides, we Blackfeet don't eat dogs, like the Crow People." She emphasized her statement with a vicious swipe of her knife. He cocked his ear again and thumped the ground with his tail in obvious agreement. Na-Ha-Ki continued. "If you want to mate with a white, no one will tell you that it is a bad thing. I wish I were a dog like you. I'd do what I wanted and wouldn't have to marry old Many Hawks." She stopped and patted the dog's head. His tail thumped the ground furiously and he licked her hand. The dog suddenly jumped up at the sound of a voice behind her.

"Ha ya," it said. "So you do not wish to marry Many Hawks, even though you speak to his dog!"

She held one hand over her mouth and gaped at him. It was Many Hawks himself.

This was the first time Many Hawks had addressed her directly. Na-Ha-Ki wondered if he spoke to all of his wives in this manner. She dropped her knife in confusion and he picked it up by the blade and offered it to her. Na-Ha-Ki smiled and accepted it by its handle.

"My other wives will like you. Especially since you do such fine work."

She knelt on the robe, her knife busy. Although Many Hawks was an older man she noticed that he held himself erect. Most of the unwed women of the Piegan would be honored to be his wife.

"You are very good at this work," he said. "You will make a fine wife." Somehow his pleasant manner and smile put her at ease.

She was conscious of the older man's gaze. The dark work dress she wore was stained and worn, but it fit snugly and showed her full young figure to good advantage. Self-consciously she wiped a dirty hand on her thigh and noted his eyes looking at the outline of her body beneath the tightened buckskin. She wondered how much of her conversation with the dog he had heard. He must think her a young and foolish girl.

A laugh burst from him and he spoke to his dog, "Come, Tail Thumper, we go to find you a white mate." He turned and stalked away. The dog rolled his eyes toward Na-Ha-Ki as if to say, "Well, what can I do about it?" He trotted after his master.

Na-Ha-Ki picked up her fleshing knife, wiped it on the grass and looked about to see if anyone other than Many Hawks had observed her talking to the dog. She slipped the knife into its sheath at her belt.

A small curl of smoke rose from the smoke hole of her parents' lodge. Her younger brother, Au-Ti-Pus, passed dragging a piece of firewood. He had apparently been listening, for he asked, "So, you will not marry Many Hawks?"

"No, never."

"What will you do if you cannot marry the white trader?"

"I do not know."

"Will you run away? I will loan you my horse." His eyes glistened with excitement. "I will tie him to the lodge by where you sleep tonight and you can ride him to the white trader's home. He is my friend, too. I will come to live with you and him in your new lodge."

"Why do you think I can ride that horse of yours? He throws everyone from his back except you." She squeezed the young boy's arm. "That Lightning Horse is dangerous, just like the lightning he was named after. He may throw you too, someday."

"Not me. I have big medicine." He dropped his firewood and danced about in a small circle. "I have big medicine. Hi-ya, Hi-ya, and so does the white trader."

"You'd better get that firewood to mother or she will be out here showing you her big medicine," Na-Ha-Ki said with a laugh. Au-Ti-Pus had a way of making her feel good.

"No, I will not run away," she added. "Now take that wood to mother. Thank you for offering help. I guess you and Many Hawks' dog are my only friends."

Au-Ti-Pus trailed off, dragging the wood behind.

It was late afternoon now and smoke came from most of the lodges in camp. Suddenly her mother ran from the tipi, looked up at the sky and watched the smoke drifting off to the north. She loosened the heavy pole holding one of the smoke flaps and attempted to fasten it in a better position to deflect the wind. Na-Ha-Ki hurried to help, just as her sisters and younger brother swarmed out of the lodge coughing and wiping their eyes.

"The wind changes," Sa-Ka-Ki said, as they anchored the heavy pole. "That's better. The smoke will go out all right now. It will storm tonight. It always does when the wind changes like this. Come help with the food," she said.

With the entrance open and front sides of the tipi rolled up for ventilation, the smoke inside soon cleared. Na-Ha-Ki glanced up at the top where the lodge poles were lashed together with rawhide. Although smoke rose through the opening, a patch of blue sky beyond showed, and a fleecy white cloud scudded by on its way to gather with the others. Yes, she thought, mother is right, it will storm tonight.

Theirs was one of the largest tipis in the Piegan Blackfeet encampment. More than twenty buffalo hides had gone into the making of it. Only this spring Na-Ha-Ki, her sisters and younger brother had made a special trip westward to the mountains to find and cut new poles for it. When they arrived back in camp with the twenty-foot long poles tied travois style behind the horses, the old lodge was torn down and overhauled. Off came the smoke flaps and fresh new ones took their places. "We will use these for moccasin soles next winter," her mother said as she rolled the old ones up and secured them with a rawhide cord. Many worn places were replaced with new hides and new tie-down cords were laced into place. When the lodge was erected with its new flaps and poles, Na-Ha-Ki viewed it with quiet satisfaction. As the eldest daughter she had selected the poles and tanned the smoke flaps.

"My daughter, you have done well," Eagle Chief had said. "You will make a fine wife for a Piegan warrior."

At the time, the words of praise warmed her. But now she had no desire to be the wife of a Piegan, not even the mighty Many Hawks. Sa-Ha-Ki's actions interrupted her thoughts. She poked in the coals of the fire with a pointed stick and extracted one of the camus roots that had been baking there.

"The food is ready," she announced as she broke away the root's clay covering and nibbled at it. "Get a bowl for your father," she told Na-Ha-Ki.

She stirred the contents of a fire-blackened pot with a spoon made of buffalo horn, then filled a bowl with steaming stew. Na-Ha-Ki set it beside the backrest where Eagle Chief sat. He stabbed a piece of meat and inserted it into his mouth. Then, holding the other end, he cut it in two with a quick swipe of his knife. He leaned back, thoughtfully chewing. Wiping his hand on a piece of moist buckskin beside the backrest, he smiled at his wife, reached for the bowl and horn spoon and sipped the stew noisily.

"You see, I have taught you how to take care of a Piegan man, but if you were to marry the white trader, he would expect you to cook the white man's food. You would not be able to take care of him as a woman should take care of her man." Sa-Ka-Ki waved the spoon in her daughter's face. "A white man should have a white wife. If you are his only wife, think of all the work you must do by yourself."

The girl picked up a bowl and began to fill it with stew. "He has told me he will teach me the white man's ways to cook. Then I will know two ways."

"Men do not cook, that is for women. It is the man's job to hunt and bring the furs and meat to the lodge. It is a sign of weakness for a man to cook." Her mother poked at a Camus root viciously as if it were the white trader.

"This white man, he will clean the lodge and sew for you, too?"

Na-Ha-Ki did not answer. She speared one of the roots, broke it open and nibbled on it as she tried to compose her thoughts. The rest of the family sat on robes about the fire, listening to Na-Ha-Ki and her mother.

"He will show me the white man's ways. I can learn and then I will take care of him as a woman should."

"Ah-ya, so now it is decided." Eagle Chief leaned forward from his seat at the backrest.

"You say that you will marry the white trader." All eyes focused on Na-Ha-Ki and waited for her answer. She felt trapped. Why couldn't they see Charles as she did, not just as a white man, an outsider, the enemy?

As if reading her thoughts, Au-Ti-Pus spoke. "The white trader can do a thing that no warrior among the Piegan can."

"What is that, Little Brother, sew a dress?" Little Sister said with a laugh. The family rolled about on the robes and laughed at the joke.

Au-Ti-Pus was furious. "Stop it! Stop it! I tell you!"

Little Sister ignored him and pointed a finger at her brother as she chanted. "Big white man, big woman, big cook." Before the unsuspecting girl was aware of it, Eagle Chief arose and grasped the child by one of her long braids, jerked it and glared at her. "My son speaks and you will listen to him with dignity."

She stared at her father, eyes opened wide in astonishment. She nodded, mutely.

Na-Ha-Ki gaped at her father. Was this the gentle Eagle Chief? Never before had he touched one of his children to discipline them. A soft word, meaningful look, or upon occasion, a studied silence were the only discipline he meted out, or ever needed to. The lodge was quiet now and the sounds of the rest of the camp intruded upon them. A horse tethered to the tipi stamped its foot and snorted, breaking the silence.

"Go ahead, Au-Ti-Pus," his mother urged.

The boy stood up and with an awareness of his newfound status looked at each one in turn. When his eyes met those of Grandmother, she smiled and he was much encouraged. He took a deep breath and began.

"The white trader Charles Tucker can ride Lightning Horse."

"What! Do not say foolish things, my son. How do you know this?"

"It is so, I will tell you of it. He has strong medicine. Did you not tell me yourself that it was a great sign from Sun that only I could ride him?"

"Yes, that is so. But go on, what of the white man and Lightning Horse?"

"It happened just this afternoon, when I went to the trading post." He looked defiantly at Little Sister. She opened her mouth, but after a glance at her father, closed it. "The white trader was there and he wanted to ride Lightning Horse. I told him that he was big medicine and that no one except me could ride him." He paused and looked around the circle at his mother and sisters who waited in anticipation, then continued.

"Surely one of the great warriors among the Piegan can ride him," he said. "What about White Quiver? He is the greatest horse stealer of all of them! Is he not able to ride this horse of yours?"

"No, not even him," I answered.

"I can ride him," he said. "I will give you this knife if you let me try." The boy pulled a knife from his waistband and held it out for inspection.

"Ai-ie, it is a fine knife. Let me see it." Eagle Chief extended his hand and the boy handed him the knife. "And what happened when he tried?"

"Takes-A-Gun was there and he joked about it. 'Let the white eyes try, he will throw him like he did that mueno, White Quiver.'"

"That Takes-A-Gun is a poor loser. He has not forgotten that Lightning Horse threw him off too. Go on."

"Yes, that is so. But the white trader spoke words to Lightning Horse that I could not hear and then he was on his back. He rode like a Piegan warrior. The horse ran like the wind. Speak to White Quiver yourself. He was there watching with many other members of the Crazy Dog Society."

Au-Ti-Pus stopped and looked around the circle. "That is why I say the white trader can do a thing that no Piegan warrior can. He has strong medicine." The boy drew a deep breath, looked around the circle at his gaping sisters and smiled at Grandmother.

Eagle Chief studied the knife. He turned it over and over while his face grew more and more thoughtful. Na-Ha-Ki's heart leapt when she heard of the wondrous thing that Charles had done. It was obvious that her father had been impressed.

He handed the knife back to his son. "Yes, my son, this is surely a sign that must be pondered. I must smoke and think on this."

He lifted his ceremonial pipe from its place beside the backrest and stuffed it with tobacco, lighted it and puffed smoke to the four directions, to Sun, then to Earth. His face wore a frown as he contemplated this new change in events. The news put a different perspective on the white trader's position. He could not be so easily dismissed as just another white man could now. Perhaps it would be well to have such good medicine as a part of his family.

He watched Na-Ha-Ki as she helped her mother and sisters rearrange the robes for sleeping. The girl's movements were supple and quick as she pushed the various household goods toward the outside edges of the lodge and spread the sleeping robes out around the dying fire. Sa-Ka-Ki had once been such a girl.

"Our life together," he ruminated, "has been a good one and the old ways were best then. But things are changing. The white man is growing in numbers. Things are not the same for the Blackfeet." He wondered what the future held for his favorite daughter.

Chapter 6
His medicine is strong

*(Have drunk their Cup a Round or two before,…)*XXII

Until now, Grandmother had remained neutral about the matter of the white trader and her granddaughter. But since Au-Ti-Pus had taken sides, she decided that she too must consider how she felt about the marriage. After all, she reflected, the boy was young and she wanted to make sure he was making a wise choice by being on the side of the white trader.

In Piegan lodges, the youngest boy slept with his grandmother. Au-Ti-Pus and Grandmother lay together now, sharing the same robe. She was his confederate and ally. When no one else cared to listen or share an experience, he turned to Grandmother. She always sensed when he needed shielding and her comforting arms enclosed him now. He snuggled closer to her. The lodge was quiet and the other occupants slept.

She stroked his head and whispered, "You are restless, little one, what troubles you? The others sleep, so speak softly." Their heads were close and they conspired in whispers.

"I will be a man soon and we can no longer be together like this. The Lightning Horse and the white trader thing, did you not notice how my father spoke to me? He no longer treats me as a child." He stirred in her arms and touched her face. His hands traveled over the familiar wrinkled forehead, along her nose, across her mouth, then pulled away from her cheeks. They were wet with tears. "Do not cry, Grandmother, I will never forget how you have protected me."

"I do not cry tears of sorrow, my child, but tears of joy. My heart is filled with happiness that you have grown into the fine young man that I see." She raised herself onto an elbow and rearranged the robe. "You will someday be an important man among the Piegan. It was a great sign from Sun that you alone can ride Lightning Horse. But now this white trader has ridden him also. This white man, tell me of him."

"He does not cheat the Piegan like the other traders do. He refuses them the firewater. He says it makes our warriors behave poorly. White Quiver is his friend also. And Crow Woman says the white trader saved her husband's life. His medicine is strong."

"Shush, little one. Now we must sleep."

"What will happen to Na-Ha-Ki? She does not wish to marry Many Hawks."

"It will be decided soon. Your father will speak with the elders, perhaps after the hunt. They are wise and we must trust them. "Now sleep, child."

He nestled close to her and his soft even breathing told her that he slept. Sleep did not come to her, for she knew that her son, Eagle Chief, would come to her for advice before he went to see the elders. What should she tell him? She did not know. Perhaps the answer would come to her in a dream. She thrust her thoughts from her and soon she too was asleep.

845-JEYS

Chapter 7

Firewater is not
Good for the Piegan

*("Fools! your Reward is neither Here nor There.")*XXV

However, even while she slept, the triangle between Na-Ha-Ki, the white trader and Many Hawks generated much discussion throughout the camp. But the great fall buffalo hunt also held the band's attention. The camp stirred with excitement, for a white buffalo had been reported to be running with the herd. New heads were fitted on arrows, bows re-strung and re-wrapped, guns and ammunition checked out. Tales of great hunting exploits were related around the fires at night.

The camp crier rode through camp followed by a swarm of young boys riding stick horses. They wheeled and pranced, reared, then galloped off after him as he moved on to the next area for him to make his pronouncement. "The great hunt will take place in two days. All warriors will assemble at the lodge of Many Hawks to make plans."

The crier sometimes stopped, slid off his horse and allowed one of the boys to hold it while he went inside a lodge to gossip. "Old Bull sends his greetings," he called to Short Man. Short Man acknowledged the greeting with a grin. Two missing front teeth produced a good-natured look on his face. He waved the bow he was re-wrapping with strips of rawhide. "So that bony old man is still alive. He is so skinny, I thought by now a wind might have blown him away. Can he still mount his horse or does his woman have to help him on it?"

The crier responded to the banter. "Old Bull says he will ride on the hunt and show you how to kill a buffalo."

"Ha, that old man is crazy. One day a calf will turn on him and trample him to death. He should leave the hunting to someone who knows how." He scrambled to his feet. Short Man's upper torso was heavy and well formed, the body of a large man, but his legs were short and stubby, those of a dwarf. He struck his barrel chest with a resounding thud.

"Enough of this," the crier said, "I must go on. The men will meet at Many Hawks' lodge tonight to make plans."

"Before you go, what is this I hear about the daughter of Eagle Chief and the white trader? I thought Many Hawks had already spoken for her."

"It is so, but the white trader also made a fine offer for her."

"Aie, it will not be an easy thing for Eagle Chief to decide," Short Man said. "I expect Old Bull and I have different opinions on the subject."

"You haven't said what you think," the crier said, hoping to learn something he could pass on. Short Man obliged him.

"Many Hawks is an important man and was seen speaking to Na-Ha-Ki. I do not think Eagle Chief will be foolish enough to turn down his offer," Short Man said.

"But White Quiver of the Crazy Dogs says it will be a good thing for the tribe to have the white trader on our side. They say this young man with the blond hair is a mighty warrior and has strong medicine," Short Man added.

"You mean the way he rode Lightning Horse? Not even White Quiver can do that." The crier said. "They think Eagle Chief should give his daughter to the white trader."

"Ha, that is only because White Quiver is a friend of the white trader. Takes-A-Gun is against the marriage. He is a mueno."

The crier glanced about, leaned over and lowered his voice, "There will be trouble between Takes-A-Gun and the white trader."

The dwarf thumped his chest. "Aie, that Takes-A-Gun is a bad one. He treated that Cheyenne Woman at the dance badly. She was not his wife, but he cut her nose off anyhow."

Short Man thumped his chest again. It sounded like a drum. "If I had been at the dance I would never have allowed that to happen. What do you think Eagle Chief will decide?"

"It will be decided by the elders after the hunt," the crier said. "If it were a daughter of mine, there wouldn't be any question. She would marry Many Hawks without questioning my decision. Eagle Chief is too easy with his children."

"Yes, it is not like it was in the past." Short Man replied. "No daughter of mine ever questioned my decisions."

"Things are changing. The young people do not have any respect for their parents like we did," the crier said. "I liked it better in the old days." He straightened, then rode away shouting his message in a loud voice, "The women of the Goose Society will meet at the lodge of Red Bird tomorrow night to pray for success."

The boys following the crier usually played games while he gossiped. However, when the name of the young white trader or White Quiver was mentioned, the boys had quickly gathered around to listen to the two men.

White Quiver and Charles Tucker were the boys' favorites. On one single night raid White Quiver had stolen over fifty horses from the Crows, single-handedly. The boys never tired of listening to his stories of forays against the enemy. As for Charles Tucker, he often came to camp with a pocket full of candy to share with the youngsters. He spoke Piegan fluently and liked to spend time with them. He knew them by name and taught them several new games. He wrestled and raced with them as well.

When the camp chose sides on the issue of the pending marriage, the boys knew where they stood. They were on the side of the white trader.

Jack's friendship for his partner generated a concern that none of the others could know. They were two white men thrown together in a different culture. Jack's face registered his concern. His black eyes, wide set, deeply recessed with shaggy eyebrows protruding above, engaged whomever he was dealing with. His eyelashes were long and the lid of the left eye, drooped. His high broad forehead with three vertical furrows above the nose further accentuated his eyes. His nose seemed out of place. It should have been broad and spreading, but instead, it was aquiline and delicately sharp as if it were meant for the face of a French Courtier. The skin coloration was swarthy, that of an outdoors' man. A black curly beard covered his jaw. His mouth, full and wide was the most reliable indicator of his emotions.

The Piegan children, at first wary of him, soon found that behind his menacing looking continence lurked a warm, friendly personality. He joked with them and showed an interest in whatever they wanted to visit with him about. There were always children hanging around the Post and on occasion, Crow Woman had to intercede and send them home to their parents. She always mildly complained that Jack and Charles would never get anything done unless she got the children out of the way.

As Charles studied his friend's face he asked, "What's troubling you?"

"I haven't said anything was troubling me."

"Didn't have to. That ugly face of yours never could hide what you were thinking. It's got worry written all over it."

"Maybe you're right. I was just trying to figure how you got yourself in such a mess with the whole damn Piegan camp."

"First time I knew that I was in trouble. Figured I have friends there."

"Not all of them are your friends. They're choosing up sides over you and that Na-Ha-Ki girl. White Quiver and his bunch on one side and Takes-A-Gun and some of the older folks on the other." Jack placed both elbows on the table, cupped his chin in his hands and stared at Charles. "You best be thinking of what you ought to be doing, not what you'd like to be doing."

"What the hell does that mean?"

Jack rose and slapped the table with his open hand. He stared at his friend. "Well, I'll be damned, its worse than I thought. Na-Ha-Ki ain't no ordinary woman. An important man in the band has asked for her. And there's another thing, supposing that one of these days a white woman you're interested in comes along. There'll be a lot of them one of these days."

"What about you and Crow Woman?"

"Fair enough. When she was a young girl they captured her from the Crow. She was a slave until I married her."

"But I love Na-Ha-Ki. Montana is my home. We plan to have children."

"It won't be easy for you or the children, if you do. After a while, when there are more white people, your children will be called half breeds and you'll be called a Squaw Man."

"Look, I don't let what someone thinks keep me from doing what is right for me.

Na-Ha-Ki and I have discussed this and we can handle it."

"No use in arguing, you're listening, but not hearing. It's your life, not mine." Jack smiled at Charles. "You're like a cat, no matter what, you always land on your feet. Whatever you do, just remember when you need a friend, I'll be here. Let's change the subject," Jack said. "How were you to ride that Lightning Horse?"

"I tell you everything I know, you'll know as much as I do. But first off you have to know horse language and be smarter than the horse." Charles shrugged his jacket on as he passed Jack. "White Quiver asked me to join the hunt with him. You're invited too. Supposed to be a White Buffalo running with the herd. Au-Ti-Pus is going to let me ride Lightning Horse."

Jack snorted. "In a buffalo hunt? Now I know you're out of your mind."

"Just watch us." Charles flung the last back at Jack as an afterthought.

"Being young sure has its advantages," Jack muttered under his breath.

*   *   *

Eagle Chief knew that no matter what he decided, he couldn't satisfy everybody. Now there was the added element of The Crazy Dog Society and their stand on the issue of his daughter's marriage. Their spokesperson urged him to decide in favor of the young white trader. "He has big medicine," White Quiver said. "This man can help the Piegan. If you had seen him with Lightning Horse, you would know."

Eagle Chief placed a hand on the other's shoulder. "Not all of our women who have gone with the white men have been treated well. When they grow old and are of no use to them, no one among the Piegan wants them either."

"Have you seen this man with the Piegan children? He is strong with gentleness. He has the greatest strength of all—a gentleness that comes from knowing he is strong.

"You speak well. You are a brave and gentle man also. I have observed you with the children. It is easy to see how you are this man's friend."

Eagle Chief smiled. "So he rides Lightning Horse. How is it he does this?"

White Quiver lifted his hands, looked up and shrugged his shoulders. "It is the way of Sun. This man spoke words I could not hear and it was as if they had known each other from before. I have never known a man such as this. Look what he has sent to you." He unfolded a piece of buckskin covering a flat board painted in natural colors. A young Piegan woman stood in front of a tipi, in her hands held up toward Sun was a child in its cradleboard. "Charles Tucker

845-JEYS

says that although your daughter will leave you, this will remind you of her."

The older man folded the covering back over the picture and gently placed it on the pile of trade goods. "You have eased my mind about this man, but what about Many Hawks?"

"That is something you will have to decide for yourself. The Crazy Dogs and I will support your decision."

Eagle Chief pondered White Quiver's words as he prepared to go to the gathering at the lodge of Many Hawks. Old Bull and Short Man's voices intruded upon his thoughts. They were so busy joshing each other that they did not notice Eagle Chief. They were a study in contrasts. Short Man, broad shouldered and thick-bodied, Old Bull tall and skinny. "So, you're going to ride on the hunt," the dwarf said. His stubby legs quickened to a run as he hurried to keep up with Old Bull.

"Someone has to show the younger ones how to do it. There isn't any need for you to go though. I'll kill a fat cow for you and you can help the women skin it."

"You'd better look out, old man." Short Man said. "I'd think an old one like you would get fat, but you get skinnier and bonier every day. How do you expect to kill anything? That old horse of yours can't run fast enough to catch a small calf."

Old Bull grinned a toothless smile. "Ha, tomorrow we will see who is the big hunter. Who knows? If Sun is willing, the White Buffalo might be mine. It will be a great thing for the Piegan if I should kill him."

Already several Piegan warriors had gathered at Many Hawks' lodge. They gossiped and passed time while their friends arrived. "Aie, it is true then, the young trader will ride Lightning Horse? This will be a thing to see." Small Hawk said.

"Yes, White Quiver told me. The white buffalo runs like the wind. White Quiver has seen him at night already. Do you think Lightning Horse can catch him?"

Takes-A-Gun stared scornfully at them. "That white eyes should not be allowed to ride with the Piegan."

Small Hawk glanced at his fellow Crazy Dog Society member. "Come, the meeting will start soon," he said as Old Bull and Short Man entered the lodge, followed by Eagle Chief. It was apparent that when the rest of the warriors arrived, the lodge would not contain all of them. The sides of the tipi were rolled up and late comers stood outside and peered through the crowd of men inside to see and hear what was going on. The women passed among them with bowls of pemmican. The sun-dried meat had been pounded fine, mixed with melted fat, marrow, and a dry paste of crushed wild cherries. As each man arrived Many Hawks handed him a cup filled with diluted firewater. The cups were emptied, filled again and passed to those standing out side.

Old Bull and Short man were soon shouting at each other and were showing the effects of the strong drink. Many Hawks handed a cup of firewater to White Quiver, but he demurred, handing the cup back. "No! The firewater is not a good thing. See how foolish our people behave?" He pointed to Old Bull and Short man who rolled about on the ground.

"Aie, you have him now, Short Man. Wrap your legs around him," Someone shouted. "Look out for his sharp bones. That Old Bull will stab you with one of them." The assemblage roared with laughter. The dwarf sat astride Old Bull and the crowd urged them on.

"So you think I cannot ride on the hunt? Look at how I can ride you." He bounced violently up and down on Old Bull. "You are an old one. Hah! A bag of bones like you is no match for a man like me." He suddenly jumped free of Old Bull and turned to face the assembly. He struck his chest with a thud. Old Bull rolled over onto his knees, then before anyone could stop him, savagely struck the dwarf in the back with his knife.

The little man stood for an instant. A look of wonderment crossed his face. He crumpled and fell. The lodge was silent. Old Bull leaned over his friend and attempted to turn him over. The knife protruding from Short Man's back prevented it. Old Bull stood uncertainly for an instant. Pushing his way through the crowd, he stumbled away.

51

White Quiver shoved his way to Short Man. Gently he lifted the old man and carefully pulled the knife free. A spurt of blood gushed as the knife left the body, but the flow slowed and gradually stopped. One of the women handed him a piece of wet moss. He pressed it into the wound and tied it in place with a piece of buckskin.

Short Man still breathed. Many Hawks motioned silently for the rest of the men to leave. The lodge quickly emptied. A woman handed White Quiver a bowl of water and he wet the wounded man's lips and forehead with it. "We must not move him. He will have to stay here." Many Hawks nodded in mute consent. He did not feel well himself and his head spun from the firewater. He slumped against a backrest and was sick. White Quiver muttered, "Firewater is not good for the Piegan." He eased Short Man onto a robe and covered him. He looked disgustedly at Many Hawks and strode from the lodge into the darkness.

CHAPTER 8

SADDLE IN THE SKY

*(...till Heav'n To Earth invert you like an empty Cup.)*XL

It was a quiet and subdued camp that he left behind. He walked slowly as he considered the significance of what had happened. He had known Old Bull and Short man all of his life. They had taught him to ride and shoot with a bow and arrow. Short Man taught him the ways of horses and how to conceal himself from the enemy. He learned from the old man how to work his way close enough to the horses so he could steal them easily. Short Man had even given White Quiver his real name. When he presented the boy with a new bow and a quiver of white doeskin, White Quiver remembered how he had stroked the quiver. He liked the feel of its softness. The dwarf had sensed the importance of the moment. He smiled and said, "We will call you White Quiver. You have learned your lessons well. Old Bull and I agree you will someday become a mighty warrior among the Piegan."

Yes, he had become a mighty warrior. The old man had been right. He mentally thanked the dwarf. Then he remembered the sight of Short Man lying face down, knife protruding from his back with Old Bull leaning over him with a distraught look on his face.

He reached the edge of a stream now. He filled his cupped hands with its icy flow and splashed it on his face and across his bare chest. He wiped his hands across his body, shivered, then raised his face and surveyed the night sky. A wisp of a cloud glided across the face of the moon, then the pale crescent shone brightly again. The outline of the front-range of the mountains superimposed themselves on the horizon. The profile of one of the peaks plunged steeply down, smoothed out, rounded gently, and rose sharply again, not as high this time, then fell off abruptly. Etched against the sky, it looked like a huge saddle. A lone star shone in the gap. White Quiver studied the familiar scene.

When he returned from night forays against the Crow People, he often used the landmark and the familiar star to guide him toward his home. Before, it had always been a comforting sight, reassuring, never changing. A great sadness overcame him and he fingered the medicine bag at his neck. He chanted softly, first to the earth, then to each of the cardinal directions and lastly to the sky. His song, soft and sad, filled the night air. He improvised the words as he sang with an intensity of feeling that mirrored his emotions. It rose in volume, quivered, then stilled.

> Oh, hear me, my helper. I cry to you in the night.
> I cry to you for the Piegan this night.
> I am White Quiver, who will lead the Piegan.
> Oh, come to me. Show the way for our People.
> This night I cry to you for my People.
> Give me your sign, oh my helper.

It was still and only the usual night sounds were heard. The wind, soft and low, the rushing water, and in the distance a faint sound, no more. White Quiver swiftly dropped to the ground, placed his ear to it and listened intently. He peered through the darkness toward the East. A low rumbling sound that grew stronger and stronger rolled through the night air. He ran to the stream, sprinted along its bank and crossed over and crouched low beneath the roots of a large cottonwood tree.

Sound crashed around him. He chanced a look and saw a white form charge past. It was the White Buffalo! Behind surged an entire herd of the massive brown bodies that slammed and smashed into each other. The tree shook and pieces of the bank caved in and tumbled about him.

Several bellowing beasts shoved by the mass of the herd, vaulted over the bank, slammed into the tree and continued their mad stampede.

One smashed into the tree and entangled his legs in its roots. A hoof narrowly missed the man crouched beneath. The bison's momentum carried him on until it somersaulted and landed on its back. Its legs jerked about wildly. It staggered to its feet, then tore into the turf, throwing huge chunks of it about. It bellowed in pain and rage then sank to its knees. It ploughed a deep furrow with his massive shoulder, then rose again to repeat the hideous act over and over.

White Quiver crept from the tree roots with knife in hand, and carefully approached the dying animal. He quickly slit its throat. He knew that he must awaken some of the women so they could tend to the buffalo before the wolves got to it. Although they would grumble about being awakened so early in the morning they would secretly be pleased to feed the men fresh meat before they went on the hunt.

The remnants of the herd passed at last and White Quiver crept from his shelter onto the bank. Suddenly he felt the ground moving under him. He jumped backward and wonderingly watched as the tree slowly toppled and slid into the stream. Carefully, he edged toward the caved out portion of the bank. The thick trunk lay directly where he had crouched. He touched his medicine bag, extended an open hand to the sky and chanted once more.

> Oh my helper, you have sent me a sign.
> Your power is great.
> This night I will remember.

845-JEYS

For you have shown me the way.

My people will hear me.

Your power is great.

The moon was high and the lone star over the saddle of the mountains had climbed nearly overhead when White Quiver finally stole into the tipi of Many Hawks. Short Man breathed slowly, but regularly. He quietly left the lodge and went to awaken the women who would go to butcher the dead buffalo.

CHAPTER 9
THE WHITE BUFFALO

*(The Wine of Life keeps oozing drop by drop,...)*VIII

While the men gathered to discuss the hunt, the Goose Society women made plans for the ceremonial dance and prayer for a successful hunt. Na-Ha-Ki's mother and Red Bird, the oldest wife of Many Hawks, were both depended upon by the other women, to plan and lead the ceremonial dance.

Almost immediately after Many Hawk's offer for her daughter, Sa-Ka-Ki had visited Red Bird and discussed the proposal with her. She was pleased with her friend's response. "My friend," Red Bird said, "I will welcome your daughter into my lodge. Her laughter will be a welcome thing. You have taught her well. She will make a fine wife for a Piegan warrior. Red Bird placed her hand on her friend's shoulder. "Many Hawks tires of me. A younger woman in his robes will bring him happiness. She will wear him out soon enough. He will treat your daughter well, and so will I."

They both laughed. "Ha, we grow old, you and I. It is well that we Piegan women look out for each other. It makes me happy that my daughter comes to your lodge. She will work hard for you. I have taught her this. Maybe someday I will welcome a daughter of yours into my lodge."

Things went well, until Na-Ha-Ki had gone to the white trader, and he too had made an offer for her daughter. Since that time Sa-Ha-Ki had avoided Red Bird. She felt trapped. Sa-Ka-Ki saw no way to get out of her responsibility as leader of the ceremony. Well, it must be. She would do it. That was the way of the Piegan.

It was especially important for everything in the ceremony to be done exactly right this time. According to Tail Feathers Coming Over the Hill, the medicine chief, the White Buffalo was a sign from Sun to the Piegan. "This White Buffalo is a sacred animal and its power is great. If the Piegan are to kill it, we will need the help of Sun to make sure everything is as it should be. In my dream, my helper has told me that on the hunt there will be a great danger for one of the men. If any of the women have bad thoughts in their hearts it will displease Sun. The men will have Sun's protection only if the ceremony pleases him." The old man drew himself up a tall as possible and added, "You must tell The Goose Society members this. I have spoken." With that, Tail Feathers swept his robe about him and left.

Now she wondered, was her own heart right? Her thoughts about Red Bird disturbed her. Should she speak to her friend before the ceremony? Perhaps she could excuse herself from leadership. But that wouldn't be fair to Red Bird. Still, what Tail Feathers said about special danger could not be taken lightly. His was the Buffalo Pipe Medicine and the messages he received in his dreams were seldom wrong.

"Is something wrong?" Na-Ha-Ki said interrupting her mother's thoughts.

"Yes, daughter, there is something wrong. When Many Hawks asked for you, your father and I were pleased for your sake." Sa-Ki-Ka continued. "After Many Hawks left, I spoke to Red Bird about you. Ha, she and I thought that it was all settled. But, then you went to the young white trader and he also came to see your father about you." The older woman placed her arm about her daughter, then pulled her close. "You always were the strong minded one, but that is not bad. It is as your father has always said, if only you had been a warrior."

The daughter laughed, and the tension between mother and daughter was broken. Her mother laughed too. "We will find a way that is best for you, my daughter."

"But Mother, why do you worry about Red Bird? It is not your fault that I went to Charles. If you tell her what happened, I am sure that she will understand."

Sa-Ka-Ki smiled. "Perhaps you are right. I will go to see Red Bird now."

Red Bird welcomed her into the lodge. They exchanged small talk and then Sa-Ka-Ki came to point of her visit. "I must tell you that I am worried about what you must think of me."

"What do you mean?"

"When you and I talked two days ago about Na-Ha-Ki coming into your lodge, everything was settled. Now the young white trader has made an offer for her, as well."

Red Bird smiled. "My children do not always do as I like, either. Are we not foolish to worry about such things? Perhaps Sun will give Eagle Chief a sign."

"You are a true friend. Now we can make plans for the hunt ceremony. Tail Feathers says it must be done just so."

"Oh, he always says that. Don't let him bother you."

"No, it is different this time. He had a vision, and his helper told him that during the hunt, one of the men will be in great danger. We must do every thing just so."

Red Bird placed her hand to her mouth. "Oh, we must be very careful. I am pleased that you have come to me for this talk. Shall we practice for tonight?"

"Yes, that is good, I will go to my lodge for the ceremonial things." She smiled happily, then hurried through the camp toward her lodge. Yes, she reflected, to have a friend like Red Bird was a good thing. She was fortunate to have such a wise daughter, too. The ceremony would go well tonight. Suddenly she looked forward to it.

45-JEYS

The Piegan camp pulsated with activity. The night horseherd watch had returned to their lodges. Smoke drifted from them. Dogs barked and yelped as Sun threw its first light over the camp. Snow covered peaks to the west glistened. A mountain stream full to its banks rumbled and roared down a narrow gorge below the camp. Men and boys dropped their robes and immersed themselves in its icy flow.

They shouted as they gamboled about in the frigid water. "Hi-Ya, this water is too hot. I will burn myself," Grey Dog, a Contrary, yelled as he drew back in mock fear. Another Contrary chided him. "Look, you woman, see how I am taking myself out of this hot water." He immersed himself completely. "See how I am staying in here," he called as he left the stream and ran to his robe. "I will take off my robe now," he shouted. He put the robe around his body. "This robe makes me cold," he shivered in mock chill. "Come let us walk to the camp," he yelled gleefully. The entire Contrary Society left at a dead run.

Au-Ti-Pus enjoyed the morning bath. He and the other boys usually counted on the Contraries to say or do something humorous. But not every morning was like this one. In winter, the wind blew harshly and Sun often hid behind the clouds and the stream was frozen. Then father commanded, "Come," and they dropped their robes and rolled in the snow. "This is how a Piegan warrior prepares for cold weather," Eagle Chief said. "We must stand the cold if we wish to hunt and keep from freezing." But this fall day was warm and the icy bath was enjoyable.

Au-Ti-Pus rubbed his body to remove as much water as possible, and ran to get his clothes. They were dry and felt warm. His skin tingled and he shouted to Spotted Horse, "Those Contraries are crazy. Did you see them? They say everything backward from what they do."

"Ah, it is so. They ran when they said they were walking, too," Spotted Horse answered. "Yesterday I saw one of them riding on his horse backwards. He said he came from his lodge, while his horse was going to his lodge."

Both boys laughed at the thought of a grown man sitting on his horse backward. "Maybe when I become a warrior I will be a Contrary."

"Aie, you must practice being crazy first," Spotted Horse answered. "Today I will ride on the hunt," he announced.

Au-Ti-Pus was quiet. His friend sensed what he was thinking. "When you are older, like me, Eagle Chief will let you go on the hunt," he said.

"I don't know why he won't let me go now. I can ride as well as any man of the Piegan and my Lightning Horse can outrun all the others."

"Is it true that you have told the young white trader he can ride Lightning Horse on the hunt?"

"Yes, and he will marry my sister. My friend White Quiver tells me that almost all of the Crazy Dogs are on his side. If anyone is to catch the White Buffalo it will be my friend, Charles Tucker and Lightning Horse."

Au-Ti-Pus noticed his father coming toward them. "Come," he said "We have much to do before the hunt. Your mother will have real food for us this morning."

"Why do we call the buffalo meat real food?"

"It is like this. Sun put the many different kinds of food on this earth for the other people. But when he made the Blackfeet, he said, this is a people worthy of real food and he made the buffalo for them."

"But what of the Assiniboines and Crow People?"

"They too, eat the real food that was given to us. But Sun gave it to the Blackfeet first. The other people have copied us.

He laughed and held both arms toward Sun. "Sun has given all this to the Blackfeet." His arms moved in a sweeping motion that encompassed the wide plain to the south. "You will learn when you take the warpath, that the Blackfeet is the greatest among all the people."

Au-Ti-Pus was quick to grasp his chance. "I am a Blackfeet and I can ride on the hunt. I will get the real food for our people." He looked at his father, hopefully.

"No, it is not your time yet. You must help your mother and sisters with the skinning and loading meat on the travois. Perhaps, next year. There is much to do and you can be helpful."

The boy's mouth trembled, but he ducked his head and held back the tears. His dog, Laughter, ran around the lodge and jumped against him. He wagged his tail furiously. The boy threw his arms about Laughter and hugged him. "Now I must eat," he said. "You stay and I will save some real food for you."

After eating, Au-Ti-Pus was dispatched to bring his father's fastest buffalo runner to the lodge. A born horseman, he had an uncanny way with the high spirited horses. He untied Lightning Horse's tether and the three of them, dog, horse and boy left the camp at a furious clip.

"Hi Ya," he called, as they cleared the camp. Now he was on the warpath and he leaned far to one side of Lightning Horse. Only a heel hooked over the horse's back and one hand were visible to the imaginary enemy on the far side of the horse. He peered from beneath the horse's neck, then dispatched a torrent of imaginary arrows. At a slight signal from the boy's hand, the horse skidded to an abrupt stop, wheeled about and galloped back in the opposite direction. This time he concealed himself on the opposite side of the horse and once more, as they raced past the enemy, another burst of imaginary arrows found their marks. Laughter raced along behind, barking furiously. This time, the horse wheeled abruptly. He was now a Piegan warrior on the hunt.

Boy, horse, and dog sped into an imaginary herd. Huge beasts crowded in from every side. The warrior fitted an arrow into his bow and rode alongside the buffalo and pulled the arrow back to its fullest. Shaft after shaft went into the imaginary beasts. At last he clenched an arrow in his mouth and when he was close enough extracted it, placed it in his bowstring, pulled the bow to its extreme and let fly. It sank into the White Buffalo, just behind the left shoulder. A heart and lung shot. The beast ran a few yards, stumbled, then fell forward onto its front legs and tumbled to the ground, dead. Au-Ti-Pus pulled his horse to a halt.

The red and white spotted horse was wet with sweat and its sides heaved. He slipped from its back, and with handfuls of sweet grass he rubbed him dry. The horse gratefully nuzzled his master and snorted. It was a game the three of them had often played.

Now Laughter crowded up for his share of attention. The boy scratched him behind the ears and spoke to him softly. "See over there. Get him." The dog barked sharply and darted forward toward a spotted horse grazing in the distance. The horse perked its ears and watched the dog suspiciously. Laughter darted forward nipped at the horse's heels and it trotted toward Au-Ti-Pus. When he had traveled but a short distance, he turned and started to rejoin the herd of horses on his right. The dog expertly cut him off and barked excitedly. The buffalo runner turned and headed toward the boy again, only to veer to his left and head back toward the herd again.

The dog anticipated his move and was already there in front of him, barking as if to say, "You can't fool me, horse. Now turn around and go where I'm taking you." The horse reluctantly turned, then suddenly lashed out with his rear hooves, narrowly missing the dog's head. The dog snarled, dashed in and bit the horse on its leg. The horse lowered its head and ran toward the waiting boy.

Au-Ti-Pus was astride Lightning Horse now and as the spotted horse ran by they fell in behind. Once more the horse half-heartedly attempted to turn back, but a quick maneuver by Lightning Horse cut him off. At last he gave up and trotted easily toward the camp. When they neared the lodge, Au-Ti-Pus rode alongside, grasped the buffalo runner's halter and attached a lead rope to it.

He slipped to the ground and swiftly walked inside to help with preparations for the hunt.

Eagle Chief looked up as his son entered. "Ah, you have come back. I go now to join the others." He slung a quiver filled with arrows across his shoulder and with a motion of his head acknowledged Sa-Ka-Ki.

"I pray that Sun looks upon your hunt with favor," she said. "May you kill many buffalo and perhaps the White One will be yours."

Au-Ti-Pus handed his father a short, heavy bow. "My friend, Spotted Horse will ride on the hunt. He is no older than I," he said.

"It is a mistake for one so young to ride on the hunt. It is more dangerous than you think. We will not discuss this again." Eagle Chief thrust the tipi flap aside, strode to his buffalo runner and swung onto its back. He pressed his knee to the horse, wheeled, and man and horse joined the growing band of warriors that gathered at the far end of the camp.

Au-Ti-Pus glanced at his busy mother and slipped under the rear side of the lodge. He untied Lightning Horse and raced toward the trading post. He knew the high spirited animal sensed this was a special day. The horse was a picture of beauty, fluid grace. Boy and horse moved as one.

The white mane and tail of the spotted horse whipped in the breeze. The legs of the horse were white, but large areas of his breast, thighs and face were reddish brown, with a jagged slash of white across its forehead. For all of its beauty, the animal was rugged, a true horse of the plains, tough and durable. As a colt it had showed no signs that it would be any more difficult to train than any other of the colts that frisked about trying out their new legs. However, Lightning Horse always had to be in the lead. Many Piegan warriors followed his progress with interest, especially White Quiver. When the horse was still a colt, he offered Eagle Chief, many fine horses and robes for him, but Eagle Chief demurred. "Lightning Horse is for my only son, Au-Ti-Pus," he said.

When the horse was old enough to train and ride, it turned, twisted, and bucked so furiously, that not one of the Piegan warriors could stay on its back. He was truly a one-man horse and allowed only the young boy Au-Ti-Pus on his back. It was truly a sign from Sun. Everyone knew that Au-Ti-Pus would be a great Piegan warrior when he was a man.

But one day, White Quiver announced that he would ride Lightning Horse. All of the Piegan gathered for the show. The Crazy Dog Society members were covering all bets. They were sure that White Quiver would ride the horse. No horse had ever thrown him. The other societies, Raven, Kit Fox, Little Dogs, Bull and Lumpwood, lined up to place bets against the Crazy Dogs. Even the Contraries got into the act, protesting that they would not bet, while offering robes, knives and other security to cover the bets the Crazy Dogs offered. If White Quiver were successful, the Crazy Dogs would be rich, for they were wagering everything of value they owned on the outcome. White Quiver showed his confidence in himself by betting his entire herd of horses. He knew his horse medicine was powerful and would not fail him.

Of all the warriors making bets, Takes-A-Gun was the most obnoxious. He was a Crazy Dog member and he and his friends raced their horses up to the crowd and pulled them to a sliding stop in front of the crowd. "Hi-Ya," he shouted. He waved his rifle wildly over his head taunting the other societies. "White Quiver will ride Lightning Horse, my helper has told me. Which of you will bet his gun and horse against me?" He slid from his horse, and walked rapidly back and forth in front of them. He stank of the white man's firewater. "Yellow Dog, you will bet with me?"

Yellow Dog nodded his head. "Ha, you are a fool, I will own your horse and gun. Look, look, at the fool who bets with me," he yelled.

Suddenly it was quiet. White Quiver slowly walked to Lightning Horse and stood near its head. The warrior was bare to the waist, his hair combed into tight braids tied together in the back. A loincloth and moccasins were the only clothing he wore. The horse stood quietly, only a slight twitching of one of his front legs indicated that he was concerned about the lithe man who stood at his side stroking him.

The warrior gathered the reins into his left hand and sprang lightly onto the animal's back. The horse stood still, apparently surprised, then exploded. He turned, leapt, pulled his feet together and came down with a jolt. Over and over Lightning Horse threw himself into the air and executed a series of twisting, turning maneuvers that brought cheers from the crowd. Surely no man could stay on this wild beast! But each time he came down, the man was still there, sitting tightly as a burr on his back. Suddenly, the horse stopped, trembled and stood motionless.

The man on his back relaxed and suddenly realized his mistake. He was lost. The animal sensed his opportunity, reared, twisted sideways and started to fall over backwards. White Quiver slipped off and watched mutely as the horse regained its balance and stood, riderless.

Takes-A-Gun was angry. He strode to White Quiver, looked him up and down, then spat at his feet. He turned and walked away. Yellow Dog stood by Takes-A-Gun's horse, reins in hand. "So I was a fool to bet with you?"

Takes-A-Gun glared at him. His hand went to his knife handle and his fingers played with it. Yellow Dog drew back. White Quiver grasped Takes-A-Gun's arm. "Yellow Dog has won. Pay him. You are the fool."

Takes-A-Gun tore his arm free and turned to White Quiver, "mueno!" he snarled. He dropped his rifle at Yellow Dog's feet and strode off.

White Quiver clapped Yellow Dog's shoulder. "It will be all right, it is the firewater that makes him act that way. The members of the other societies crowded around the Crazy Dogs collecting their bets and talking excitedly about the way the horse had bested its rider. In an instant, Lightning Horse had made paupers of the Crazy Dogs.

"Aie," moaned White Quiver, "that horse has strong medicine." He watched silently as Au-Ti-Pus ran to the horse, examined him carefully, then satisfied that nothing was wrong, swung onto its back and galloped off. White Quiver turned to Eagle Chief, "It is a great sign from Sun that your child alone rides that horse. He will be a mighty warrior among the Piegan."

Eagle Chief smiled and watched as the boy and horse rode out of sight. He turned to White Quiver. "That Takes-A-Gun must be watched. He is now your enemy."

*   *   *

Now, a year later, as the boy and horse raced towards the trading post, Au-Ti-Pus reflected on the way that Charles Tucker, the white trader had ridden the horse. The boy leaned forward and spoke into the horse's ear. "You will carry the white trader well this day. If Sun wills it, the White Buffalo will come to you." The horse flicked his ear as if in acknowledgment.

As they neared the post he pulled the horse to a halt and wiped him down with grass. The animal nuzzled him gratefully, and the boy rubbed him until he shone, sleek and glossy. He combed the white mane and tail free of snarls and tangles, then walking with the horse trailing docilely behind, they proceeded to the trading post.

Charles Tucker and Jack awaited them. Charles waved. "What brings you here?"

"I bring Lightning Horse for you to ride on the hunt. He has never done this before, but he is swift, and perhaps the White Buffalo will be yours."

"Well, I'll be dogged. You took me seriously when I asked if I could use him." He placed an arm around the boy's shoulder. "When a man offers you his best horse to ride, it is a great honor. But what will you ride, if I ride your horse?"

"My father will not let me ride on the hunt, yet. I must help my sisters and mother with the skinning and butchering."

"I bet you are good at it, too. Your father is thinking that you will be a big man among the Piegan some day and he wants to make sure you are ready for it first."

Au-Ti-Pus silently nodded in assent.

"Run in and see Crow Woman." He yelled into the trading post. "Crow Woman give my friend that bag with the round rocks in it. It is in my room."

The boy didn't know what to expect, but nearly every time he came to the trading post, the man had something new for him. He hurried into the building expectantly.

67

"What you got cooked up for that youngster now?" Jack asked.

"Oh, some marbles. Been meaning to show him how to play with them for some time now. Charles rubbed Lightning Horse behind his ears and rearranged his bridle."

"Sometimes I think you aren't quite grown up yet yourself, the way you play with the kids around here." Jack's tone showed a secret approval of his friend's nature. "You really going to try to ride that horse on the hunt?"

"Can't hardly get out of it now, can I?" Charles checked the load in his rifle. "Haven't ever killed a buffalo with a Spencer before. Might be sort of light, so Lightning Horse and I will have to get up close."

"Twenty-one shots ought to be enough for anyone, even a lousy shot like you. '

"You going to the big show?"

"Wouldn't miss it for all the tea in China," Jack said. He picked up his rifle and went to his horse.

"Au-Ti-Pus, you take my horse back to camp. I'll pick him up after the hunt," Charles said. They rode toward the Piegan encampment as Crow Woman and the boy watched. Jack's horse kicked up his heels, then pranced about champing on his bit. Jack reined him in. "Monte knows we're going hunting. Way he acts, you'd think he was a youngster."

"You two are a good match. Show that old fool a gun or a filly and he thinks he's a kid again. Neither one of you are as young as you think you are. Chase gets too much for you, leave it up to Lightning Horse and me. We've got all the big medicine we need."

"I was hunting buffalo when you were just a gleam in your daddy's eye. Old Monte and me has forgot more about hunting than you'll ever know. Just don't get no dust in your eyes from us."

"You just watch us. Only thing, don't let that horse of yours fall over any buffalo I shoot. This horse and repeating rifle are going to give those Piegan something to talk about."

"Just remember, that horse might be Big Medicine to the Piegan, but he's never been on a real hunt before. If I don't miss my guess, first crack out of the box, he'll get all stirred up and start pitching and tossing about. You aren't careful, you'll find yourself eating dust."

"We'll see. Come on, let's get limbered up. Looks like the action is about to start."

He touched his mount with his heels and Lightning Horse responded by breaking into a swift run toward the lower end of the Piegan camp and the large group of assembled warriors.

*   *   *

Bare-chested warriors astride their buffalo runners milled about restlessly, awaiting instructions from Many Hawks. Charles and Jack rode to the edge of the massed warriors and waited. Suddenly a horse tore past Charles and Lightning Horse. As it swept by, its rider struck Charles a sharp blow. Lightning Horse reared and nearly unhorsed the trader. He regained his balance and readied himself as man and horse charged at him again.

It was Takes-A-Gun. The side of Charles' head smarted where the man had struck him with a short heavy bow. He swung it once more and it whistled as it swept past Charles' averted head. His hand clutched Takes-A-Gun's arm, tightened and jerked him free of his horse. They slammed into each other and now they were both on the ground. Takes-A-Gun jerked his knife free and swiped at Charles. The red man lunged forward and stabbed at him. Charles stepped aside, grabbed the crazed man's wrist and twisted it inward toward his body. Charles swung his other arm around Takes-A-Gun's neck and jerked him forward into the knife. The breath whooshed out of the tall man and he clutched his middle. Charles relaxed his grip and Takes-A-Gun staggered away and fell in a heap.

Many Hawks dismounted and knelt by the man on the ground. He gestured at Charles. "He is dead." He rolled the limp body over onto its back and extracted the knife. He held it point down and a small trickle of blood dripped from the point. Many Hawks wiped the blade against his leg and handed the knife, handle first, to Charles.

Their eyes met for an instant. Many Hawks shifted his gaze to the dead man, then back to the trader. Charles dropped the knife beside Takes-A-Gun. He slowly looked at each of the Piegan warriors. They were silent, waiting.

Many Hawks, without looking at the dead man said, "Come, the White One awaits us. We will talk about this later." He mounted his horse and began to organize the warriors for the hunt.

Charles watched as Many Hawks rode away, seemingly oblivious to the violence which had just occurred. Now that it was over, the enormity of what he had just done hit Charles. During the war, he had engaged in hand-to-hand combat, but this was different. When he first came to Montana he had pushed the senseless slaughter of the war behind him, into some inner recess. But now incongruous scenes of soldiers, dying, and dead, their bodies torn and bleeding, horses thrashing about, blood pumping out of their gut-shot bellies and their high-pitched screams mingling with the sounds of battle, came flooding out from within him.

He shook his head and wiped his hands against his pants legs. He leaned against the Lightning Horse, light-headed, and slightly sick.

"You all right, boy?" Jack's voice seemed far away and faint, then all at once loud, insistent. He felt better now. "It was so sudden. Didn't figure it would happen quite like this."

"Well it's all over for him. Doesn't look like anyone cares much either," Jack said.

The scene at the trading post with Takes-A-Gun's woman holding her face, blood spurting between her fingers, imposed itself on Charles. He shook his head as if to clear it and prepared to mount Lightning Horse.

"At least the cut-nosed woman won't have to be afraid any more," he said.

"You still want to go on the hunt?"

"Let's go. I need to get away from this." Charles gestured at the still body. He quickly mounted and they rode towards Many Hawks and the assembled warriors. When he looked back, he saw several women gathered around the dead man. As he watched, they moved him to a robe and several of them dragged it behind a rock, out of the way.

Many Hawks had kept the party together until they arrived. Now he explained his plan. He divided the bands into three groups, Eagle Chief's Band, Rising Wolf's Band, and his own. They would surround the herd and at a signal from Eagle Chief ride into it and slaughter as many of the animals as possible.

The buffalo runners were the strongest and swiftest horses of the Piegan, but none of them could outrun a buffalo. The elusive White Buffalo had been seen at the head of the herd many times already. From this vantagepoint, he had easily eluded the swiftest riders of the Piegan. But this time, if Many Hawks' plan worked, the beast's swiftness would lead him into the Piegan's hands. To escape, the herd would need to pass through a narrow neck in a valley surrounded by hills on three sides.

The herd grazed calmly, unaware of the hunters above them, for the wind blew directly from the beasts toward the hill. It was a good sign for the Piegan. The White One grazed alone, at the far end of the valley near the edge of the hills. Occasionally, he lifted his head, pawed the ground and looked about suspiciously. Satisfied, he lowered his head to graze again A low range of hills rose sharply in front of him with the valley opening like a funnel at its far end.

Many Hawks smiled with satisfaction. He reigned in his prancing horse and rode to the front of the hunters, raised his gun and pointed to the herd. "Sun is good to us, and our hunt will be successful. My medicine is strong. Here is my plan. Eagle Chief and his band will ride quietly behind the hills over there." He motioned toward the hill that rose behind the White Buffalo. "Rising Wolf's and my band will come in from the other side, there." He gestured toward the open mouth of the valley. "When we ride into the herd, the White One will not escape." He motioned for Charles and Jack to join Eagle Chief and Rising Wolf's band.

45-JEYS

"Aie, it is a good plan," said Eagle Chief. "Sun has led the White One to us." He motioned to his band. "Come," he said. They followed him as he swung in a wide circle to the north and out of sight and sound of the herd.

The herd still grazed peacefully, but began to drift toward the north and the place where the White One stood. They were bunched together now. Many Hawks' and Rising Wolf's bands slowly closed the escape route by stringing out in a long line across the mouth of the valley. Eagle Chief had deployed his forces behind the hills, and they, too, were spread out in a long thin line that encircled the herd from that end.

Eagle Chief signaled the men to stop just below the summit of the hills. He crawled to the crown of the hill and peered down at them The buffalo grazed quietly, unsuspecting. The White One raised its head, scented the air and looked in Eagle Chief's direction. The man slowly withdrew and signaled to his band. The line moved forward.

Suddenly Eagle Chief rose and waved to Many Hawks at the far end of the valley mouth. Eagle Chief and his men charged down the hill, yelling. Simultaneously, Many Hawks and his forces charged into the now frightened herd. At once the startled animals ran wildly toward each other. The mass of bellowing beasts collided and shoved each other out of the way. In their midst the men rode, fitting arrow after arrow into their bows and sinking them deep into the fat cows.

When the killing began, man and horse entered into it with complete concentration. All was fury, frenzy. Lightning Horse was as eager for the kill as was the man on his back. After the initial charge into the herd and upon the killing of the first buffalo, the horse seemed possessed. It was as if he had at last found a challenge up to his capabilities.

Charles had no need to guide him. It was charge alongside a fat cow, fire into it and the horse sensing the kill, automatically turned to another, always placing the man on its back in the best position to shoot again. One animal after another dropped when Charles realized that they had neared the center of the herd.

He attempted to slow the excited horse. The animals crowded and slammed into each other as man and horse were carried along by the flow. A beast at his side veered off and made a charge that opened a small path toward the edge of the herd. Charles urged his horse into it. They were safer now. Buffalo streamed around them as they ran wildly toward the valley mouth and escape.

The White Buffalo had been the first to react to the Blackfeet's charge and was now at the center of the massed herd. His white form loomed over the brown backs of the other beasts. Many Hawks, like Charles, had also been carried along toward the center of the herd. Unlike Charles, he was unable to escape and now he and his horse were trapped with the massive beasts slamming into his horse from every side.

Charles reined in Lightning Horse and watched the huge animals surge and rear. Many Hawks was alongside of the White One now. The frenzied bull jerked his head around and his horn hooked Many Hawks' horse. It screamed with pain and terror and fell beneath the surging mass. The man on his back disappeared.

Dust and the seething mass of brown bodies obscured Charles' vision. He peered into the swirling herd. Lightning Horse suddenly shifted about and attempted to follow the buffalo as they streamed from the valley. Charles swung him around and held him in check. The massive form of the White Bull, swung from side to side violently and, as it did, the other buffalo grudgingly moved aside to allow it access toward the edge of the herd and freedom. The crazed animal plowed through the brown mass straight toward Charles.

A pair of bronze-skinned hands appeared over the animal's neck— it was Many Hawks! He watched in fascination as the White Buffalo turned his head and attempted to hit the man with his horns. Many Hawks' body flopped about like a rag doll, but his grip on the buffalo's mane held. Suddenly, he leapt. A moccasined foot appeared over the back and he sat astride the White One. He clung to it with both hands as it bucked, reared and spun about, trying to dismount its rider.

45-JEYS

The other buffalo surged past Charles in a steady stream toward the open end of the valley. Suddenly a path to the White One opened and Charles and Lightning Horse streaked toward the desperate man on the raging beast's back. They gained the side of the White One and Charles reached out for Many Hawks. Just then, the White One reared and Many Hawks slipped. Charles' hand grasped the man's arm and held. He urged the horse closer. With one last effort, Many Hawks pushed himself free and swung onto Lightning Horse behind Charles.

The bronze-skinned man grasped Charles about the waist. The horse sensed Charles' next intention and raced along side the White One so Charles could get a shot at it. He raised his rifle and placed a bullet just behind the front shoulder. The animal raced onward. Again Charles fired and once more the animal surged on. They were in the open now and still the huge white beast raced on. Charles raised his gun to fire again. Suddenly the bison faltered, and shook its head back and forth. Blood spewed from its nostrils in huge red and purple gobs. He swayed from side to side, slowly sank to the ground and plunged forward. His head plowed a furrow into the turf as he crashed to the ground, dead. He had run until the blood in his body had pumped itself into his lungs. Now a steady stream of the red fluid gushed from his mouth.

Many Hawks slid from Lightning Horse and motioned for Charles to dismount. Jack had already dismounted and was examining the White Buffalo.

"Where's White Quiver?" Charles asked.

"Think he went back to help Spotted Horse. He got pitched off his horse. He's a friend of Au-Ti-Pus." Jack smiled. "His daddy let him go on the hunt."

"Did he get hurt?"

"Nothing serious. He was limping along behind us. His horse took off following the herd. I expect his dignity was hurt more than anything else." Jack laughed. "White Quiver will know how to make him feel better. Soon as I saw him going back for him I went on.

Figured I better stay out of it. Boy had his dignity wounded enough without me adding to it."

"You're right, Jack. When Au-Ti-Pus finds out about it, he'll josh him some. Anyhow maybe he'll understand why Eagle Chief didn't let him go on the hunt." Charles patted the Lightning Horse. "He can brag on Lightning Horse plenty enough to make up for it."

Remnants of the scattered herd dashed past and the swiftly moving buffalo thundered across the plain, soon outdistancing even the fastest horses. Lather dripped from the tired Lightning Horse and Charles was concerned for the laboring animal. Its chest heaved in and out as it struggled to breathe. Horses had been known to run themselves to death. Charles shucked out of his shirt and wiped the horse with it. Now all at once his hands shook and his legs trembled.

Man and horse calmed now and both breathed easier. Suddenly Charles' emotions welled up within him and he yelled over and over, "Ya-hah ,Ya-hah, Ya-hahaaaaa."

Jack's face broke into a wide grin. "Looks like you did it. You and that Lightning Horse are powerful medicine."

"Whoo-ee, Jack, never saw the likes of this horse before. Took to hunting buffalo like a duck to water." A gust of wind blew the blond man's hair into his face and he brushed it aside. His face was still flushed with excitement and his eyes sparkled. "Wonder what happens next?"

"Don't know boy, but whatever it is, sure as hell you're going to be a big man among the Piegan. You best be getting over there to palaver with Many Hawks. He's over there prancing around that White Buffalo along with the rest of creation."

Yelling and singing warriors danced around the huge form and the women and children arrived and joined in the wild celebration. Many Hawks danced with the others. Charles quickly dismounted and he too pranced and yelled along with the rest. One by one they left the circle of prancing people to run forward and touch the animal, then return to the circle of dancers.

Now the packhorses and travois arrived to carry the meat and hides back to the village. The prairie seethed with humanity as the milling crowd chanted and danced wildly. Charles caught a glimpse of Au-Ti-Pus and Na-Ha-Ki across the circle. The boy grabbed the buffalo's tail, tugged it, then hurriedly dropped it as if the beast had shown signs of life.

Now, Charles left his place, ran to the white carcass and placed his foot on the beast's head. He waited. The ring of people slowed their dancing and quieted. A cloud of dust hung over them. They waited expectantly. Many Hawks was at the side of the trader. The bronzed man turned his face to Sun, extended both arms and chanted.

> To you, Sun, I give thanks.
> Your power is great.
> This day I will remember.
> Your sign has come to me."
> This man will be my friend
> My life is in his hands.

He motioned to Charles. "Come, we must smoke and talk. We will go to my lodge." The people moved aside as they passed. Jack Taylor was still mounted. He peered down at Charles.

"The way you prance and howl, seems to me like you're a regular Blackfeet"

Charles smiled at his friend. He had calmed somewhat now and felt a bit self-conscious about his actions in joining the dance.

"You go ahead, I'll see to the skinning of the buffalo. No way we can use all the meat from the ones we killed. It be all right with you, I'll give it to the old people and widows."

"Whatever you want to do." Charles motioned toward the White Buffalo. "What are they going to do with that one?"

"Looks like Many Hawk's woman is preparing to skin it."

Several men had turned the huge beast over onto his belly and spread its legs out.

Red Bird, as the oldest wife, was in charge of the skinning. She had already slashed the bull across the brisket and neck and folded back the hide. Sunlight sparkled from her long knife as she worked. Her movements were quick and sure as she carefully slit the hide down the middle of the spine.

"How come no one is helping her?"

"White Buffalo is a mighty powerful medicine and if she needs help, she'll ask for it. Only the wife of the fellow who killed it can skin it."

"Hell, I shot him."

"Yeah, but I guess old Many Hawks thinks he was the one who caught him first. I ain't never seen a buffalo rode before. Was sort of funny watching that big fellow buck and pitch about and Many Hawks hanging on for dear life."

"I thought he was a goner for a while."

"Tell Many Hawks to take my horse." Jack said. "You can bring him back later. Now git! If I be any judge, old Many Hawks has got some things on his mind, and you and Na-Ha-Ki girl are at the top of his list."

45-JEYS

Chapter 10

The willow couch

and a talk

*(Like foolish Prophets forth;…)*XXVII

The willow couch, covered with soft robes, was comfortable. Charles leaned back, letting the tension and excitement of the hunt drain from him. It was quiet and the drone of a fly flitting about the dim interior seemed loud. Many Hawks handed him a bowl of cool water. He drank deeply and wiped his mouth with the back of his hand, then handed the bowl back to his host. Many Hawks filled it again and drank.

From under a robe beside the couch he extracted his medicine bundle. As he unwrapped it, Charles saw a beaver skin, some weasel tails, several bear teeth wrapped in an elaborately beaded piece of buckskin and a long stemmed pipe. Many Hawks filled the pipe bowl with tobacco from the bundle. A bit of sweet grass tossed on the coals of the fire burst into flame and its pungent odor permeated the lodge. The motions of Many Hawks as he carefully refolded the medicine bundle were pleasant and restful to Charles.

Many Hawks chanted softly, almost inaudibly. It reminded Charles of the time during the war when he had listened as a priest intoned his incantations over the body of the dead. The red man rose and Charles aroused himself from his dreamy state. Many Hawks puffed a bit of smoke to the East, West, North, South, Sun and lastly, Earth. He handed the pipe to Charles. He held it at arm's length and studied it. Its stem wrapped in rawhide was long. Ermine and weasel tail tufts and an eagle feather hung from it. The feather undulated slowly, twisting and untwisting on its buckskin tether. The red stone pipe bowl was square with engravings on each side. Jack said they got the pipestones from a place far to the east. No wonder Many Hawks had handled it so carefully. Charles wondered how he had come to get it.

Charles turned the stem to his mouth and puffed on it. The smoke tasted strong, but not bitter. Its odor was pungent. Medicine bundle pipes were smoked only on special occasions and then in an exact way according to how the caretaker of the bundle had been instructed. Charles wondered had he done anything wrong in the way he had handled or smoked the pipe.

He handed the pipe back to the older man. Many Hawks now engaged in a ritual. He acted three times as if he were going to put it down on a dried buffalo tongue. Then, on the fourth time, he actually placed it on the tongue. Jack was right, these Blackfeet could sure get fussy about doing things exactly right when it came to ritual. Four was their lucky number and he guessed Many Hawks wasn't taking any more chances with his luck after today's events.

Now Charles' thoughts drifted. He wasn't sure that he could get used to all the fuss associated with the ritual Many Hawks had just engaged in. He remembered how a fellow soldier, during the war always crossed himself every time he thought he was in danger. Jack's comment was, "Superstitious bastard will be so busy crossing himself, that he'll forget to duck sometime and get his ass shot off." Jack was right. A Rebel sharpshooter's bullet felled the man. The Lord apparently had been taking sides that day.

Now the trader's thoughts took a different tack. Wonder why Jack wasn't bothered to see the Blackfeet indulging in ritual and superstition? Sometimes Jack was a mystery all right. He wiped his arm across his eyes and shook his head. His thoughts returned to the present.

His host spoke. "It is good that you speak our tongue. We have some important things to discuss." He waited for Many Hawks to continue.

"My life is now in your hands."

"It was nothing. A brave man like you would have done the same."

"It was you who saved my life. The White One would have surely killed me if it had not been for you." Many Hawks looked at his pipe and then back to Charles. "Your power is great. Sun smiles on you. You and that horse have great medicine. When the white robe is tanned, I will bring it to you."

"No, it is my wish that you have it. It should stay in your lodge."

Many Hawks smiled and Charles saw that he was pleased. Maybe this was his chance. He'd see, anyhow.

"The girl, Na-Ha-Ki, daughter of Eagle Chief," Charles paused when the man nodded at him. "I wish to marry her."

Many Hawks did not immediately answer. Instead he picked up the pipe and puffed it meditatively then returned it to its resting-place. He gazed at Charles, and smiled. "She is a good worker, that girl. Why do you want her?"

"Of all the Piegan women who would make a fine wife for me, she is the one I desire."

He studied Many Hawks' amused face. Was the old goat laughing at him? A disturbing thought came to his mind—if he hadn't saved him from the white buffalo, he wouldn't be a rival for Na-Ha-Ki.

Suddenly Many Hawks smiled. "Perhaps you will do me a favor. A new younger woman in the lodge can cause many problems. Red Bird says she will tire me out in a short time. She says I am not as young as I think I am." He paused and rubbed his arm and the calves of his legs. "After what happened today, I am not sure I can deal with a young woman under my robe. She will make you a fine wife, if you teach her well."

"Thank you," Charles said. He wondered at the ease with which the man had acquiesced. The older man smiled. "I will go to speak to my friend, Eagle Chief, now." He rose and held the tipi flap open for Charles.

Even though Many Hawks had withdrawn himself from the competition Charles had no idea whether Eagle Chief would allow his daughter to marry a white man. Furthermore, Charles himself was beginning to get some second thoughts about things. Many Hawks had called her strong-minded. That was all right. She was smart and would soon learn about the advantages of being a white man's wife. She was beautiful enough to be seen anywhere, even back east. Wouldn't they all stare when he pranced down the street with her and their children?

Of course there would be narrow-minded people who would make problems for anyone who thought or acted differently than others. Hadn't he put up with that being a minister's child himself? But he'd see to it that his children were treated fairly. Na-Ha-Ki and he had already discussed this and he was sure they could handle it.

It had been a long time since he'd thought about having been the only child of a minister. Father's liberal Unitarian religion had caused a lot of trouble for him. Well, he'd see to it that his children didn't experience that kind of interference with their lives.

He'd seen Na-Ha-Ki only once since the hunt, and then only briefly. Just long enough for her to show him her crossed arms pressed over her heart. She'd smiled and looked happy.

Jack said when Eagle Chief made up his mind, they'd let him know. Meantime he might as well not worry about it. Easy enough for Jack to say, he already had his woman. Sometimes, Jack could be downright exasperating. Like the times during the war when it seemed as if all they were going to do is sit around and wait for the generals to make up their minds. "Let them Rebs run their tails off," Jack said. "Time is what we got most of. They'll run out of steam one of these days and then you'll see. Fly buzzes all around, but a spider just

445-JEYS

keeps spinning its web, quiet like. Sooner or later the fly gets caught. Patience is golden, my boy."

Charles had come to respect Jack's wisdom, but still it seemed as if a man ought to take some action if he could. Just sitting waiting for things to happen wasn't his way. Things were slow at the trading post now, but he expected they'd pick up as soon as the Blackfeet women got all that buffalo meat cut up and dried and were busy tanning hides. Smoke from the fires under the drying racks trailed across the Piegan camp and even from the trading post Charles noticed there was plenty of activity down there.

As he often did when he had some time on his hands, he got out his paints and started a picture on a piece of buffalo hide. Once engaged in painting, he soon forgot about time.

"Looks like you got Old Many Hawks just like it was there on the hunt." Jack eyed the painting critically. "Don't know how you do it, Charlie. Believe you me, if I could paint like you, I'd be selling my paintings to a Maharaja somewhere and living a life of ease. Old Many Hawks looks like he knows what he's doing up there on that White Buffalo." Jack changed the subject. "How come you never tried to sell your paintings? Always giving them away. Seems to me an awful waste. Man with a talent like yours should sell his work, not give it to any jack-leg-no-account who admired it."

Charles laughed. "You keep talking like that, and I'll take your advice instead of giving this to you like I intended. Seriously, we've been all through this before. No fun in it if I think I'm working at it. Besides, there's plenty of others around that can paint for the rich." Charles paused and looked off to the East. "Those kind wear thin with me in a hurry. Saw too many of them when I was growing up in New Jersey. Montana's my home now. Just give me room to stretch out. Too many people here already, far as I'm concerned."

"Well it looks to me as if a new chapter in your life is about to begin. Eagle Chief is coming to palaver with you," Jack said.

Charles had just completed putting his painting equipment away when Eagle Chief arrived at the post. "You talk to him, Jack. He wants to see me, tell him I'm busy and will be out in a few minutes." Charles gathered his things and went toward the rear of the post. He'd been kept waiting long enough himself, wouldn't hurt to keep Eagle Chief waiting for a change. He put his paints away and waited. After a short while, Jack came to the door. "You best be getting out here. Looks like you and Eagle Chief have some dealing to finish."

Eagle Chief, his wife, and daughter waited. Na-Ha-Ki wore a buckskin dress of soft white doeskin. Fringes hung from its arms and the hem of the skirt. About her waist she wore a brightly colored beaded belt. On her feet were the most elaborately decorated and beautiful boots Charles had ever seen. They looked soft and comfortable on her small feet. Porcupine quills dyed red, yellow and blue arranged in geometric patterns decorated them. The tops were trimmed with ermine fur. Her hair, shiny and black, was carefully combed into two long braids tied at the tips with strips of red cloth. On her head was a white beaded headband decorated with geometric designs made of blue beads. About her neck, falling between the soft swell of her breasts hung a necklace with a single pendant made of a large blue stone.

She smiled at Charles, then looked quickly away. Her father spoke. "I bring my daughter to you. She does not come empty handed. Come, I will show you." He walked to the door and pointed to three loaded horses.

"Well, I'll be jiggered." Jack clapped his young partner on the shoulder. "You and Na-Ha-Ki are all fixed up to set up housekeeping, brand new lodge and all. Crow Woman told me Eagle Chief and his woman were planning a surprise for you. You've got a right fine set of in-laws. You're being treated to a new house with all its fixings, by your new family."

Eagle Chief studied his daughter then looked at Charles. "I will go now," he said.

"Wait!" Charles hurried into the post and from behind the counter pulled out a new Spencer Repeating rifle, placed several rounds of ammunition beside it and motioned for Eagle Chief to take them. He gathered the gun and ammunition together, strode towards his horse and his wife trailed along behind.

Na-Ha-Ki stood quietly waiting. "You two have just time enough to make it down along the stream to set up your lodge before dark. Now scat. I'll send Crow Woman along to help Na-Ha-Ki with the lodge. We can take care of things around here by ourselves for a while. You two go on about your business." Charles looked at Na-Ha-Ki. She waited expectantly. "Thanks, Jack," he said. "We'll camp down by those cottonwood breaks." He pointed to a secluded spot along the river. "Tomorrow we'll probably move to a more private place. We'll see you in a week or so. No need to send Crow Woman down, I'll help Na-Ha-Ki set up the lodge."

"Big mistake already. You help a Blackfeet woman with her chores, she thinks you don't trust her to do it right. Indian women aren't like white women. She'll get her feelings hurt if you try to help her. If she needs your help, she'll ask you." Jack placed his arm around Crow Woman's waist. "I learned the hard way myself. First time I carried some water into the lodge for Crow Woman, she wouldn't talk to me for a week. Took me another week to get out of her what was wrong."

"Well, send her down if you think you should." Charles stuffed some clothes in his pack and picked up his rifle. He looked at his bride. She smiled and crossed her arms above her heart.

CHAPTER 11
WIND FROM THE
MOUNTAIN

(A Jug of Wine a Loaf of Bread—and Thou)[XII]

They had pitched their tipi among a small clump of trees beside a clear sparkling stream where the water rippled and sparkled in the bright sunlight. Charles stretched lazily and listened to the restful sound. He reached to where Na-Ha-Ki lay. The spot was empty, but still warm. He smiled and started pulling on his clothes. Na-Ha-Ki had already started a fire. No need for her to do that. A good woman, that one. They'd been man and wife for only a week now and he'd already grown accustomed to her soft, warm body pressed tightly against his at night. They would have to be getting back to the trading post. Jack and Crow Woman would be needing help.

Na-Ha-Ki carried a pot of water into the tipi, placed it over the fire to heat, then gracefully rose and placed her arms about him. "I am so happy to be with you." Her hair smelled clean and fresh as it brushed across his face.

Charles gently pulled her to him. "Jack and Crow Woman will need our help."

Her mouth turned down at each corner. "Do we have to go today? Am I not pleasing you?" She pulled away and straightened her dress primly.

"No, no, that's not it. It's just that we've been here for a week now and we must get back. I told Jack we'd be back in a week or so."

"I go to fix you something to eat." Na-Ha-Ki walked stiffly away as if she had not heard Charles. She silently handed him his coffee and some small fried corn cakes. When he caught her hand and held it an instant, she pulled it away, looked at him solemnly, and turned from him.

"I will get things ready," she said in a toneless voice.

"Aren't you going to eat anything?"

"I'm not hungry. You eat. You will need your strength to travel to see your friends." She hurried outside to the stream and began to scour the pans.

Charles glumly chewed his food and studied her silently. He put down his plate and strode to her. She rose and scurried past him, head averted and body held rigid. Charles grasped her arm, swung her around and spoke sharply. "What's eating you? We can't stay here forever. Come on, where's the laughing girl I married?"

He suddenly pulled her to him and buried his face in her hair. He nibbled at her ear lobe and her rigid body relaxed. The pot she had held thunked as it fell to the ground. She nestled her face on his chest and softly sobbed. Charles slowly stroked her head and then gently worked his hand under the long black mass of hair and rubbed her neck. She leaned back and smiled at him.

They kissed and all was lost in their passion. The sounds of the wind through the cottonwoods, the music of the stream, birds chirping, and the sighing of the long grass as it swayed in the wind blended together against the eastern side of the tipi and its opened flap. It warmed the robes within.

Charles lifted her and they lay down gently. All sense of external stimuli faded as they lost themselves in each other. Their passion spent at last, they lay back. Na-Ha-Ki nestled her head on Charles' shoulder and idly played with the hair on his chest. One of his hands cupped her breast as he gently ran his fingers about its pink nipple. She rose to her knees and lightly kissed him on the mouth, laughed, swept up her clothes and ran to the stream.

In an instant she was in the icy flow and just as quickly had run her hands over her wet glistening body to dry herself. Charles shook his head slowly as he watched. Her moodiness was gone now and she busied herself preparing to break camp.

Chapter 12
High and dry

(Ah, take the Cash, and let the Credit go,...)[XIII]

Crow Woman and Jack were pleased to see them. Jack playfully slapped Charles' back. "Looks like you're in a weakened condition, son. Na-Ha-Ki looks frisky though. Sure you can deal with married life?"

"Listen you old goat, I can out-drink, out fight, and out work the likes of you, even in my weakened condition." Charles placed his rifle against the wall. "Decided that we'd better get back here to help you two, what with the trade being so heavy and all."

"Glad you're back old hoss." Jack said. "Got things to talk about, us two. Now that you're an old married man, maybe you'll be ready to settle down and attend to business."

"I always took care of business. What are you driving at Jack?" Charles stopped removing his capote. One arm was still in the hooded coat.

"Well, old John Stott was by while you were gone. He says he's got a proposition for us to consider."

"I'm not one to pass up a deal, but you know that old fake. He'd sell his grandmother if he could make a nickel."

"Sure enough, but we can't get hurt by just listening. I've been waiting for you to get back so we can talk to him together He's got a smooth tongue. Signal me if you think he trying to pull a fast one."

"Soon as Crow Woman fixes something to eat, we'll go over and see him if it's all right with you," Jack said.

"Fine with me."

John Stott was a big man, but his movements were graceful. His hair fell to his shoulders in a soft wave and its iron gray color went well with his faded blue eyes. His hands moved expressively as he talked, but his seeming sincerity was deceptive. Charles reminded himself that he'd been taken in before by the old fraud.

"What we need is some one to teach them heathens Christianity." John fondled a silver cross that hung from his neck.

"John, why don't you teach them? You're the one who is always spouting Bible talk. A fine Christian like you ought to be able to convert a passel of them"

"You know me, Brother Jack. I can preach with the best of them, but the Blackfeet tongue is just a little too much for me. My words get all tangled up and them heathen wind up making fun of me." John smiled at Jack. "Take them Flatheads over west of here. Now there is a bunch of good Indians. Most of them Christians, living peaceful-like, not stirring up trouble like the Blackfeet."

"Why, I haven't had any fuss with the Blackfeet, John. Some of them giving you trouble?" Jack winked at Charles.

"Why, not exactly, but you know how it is. Them Piegan, especially, is an independent lot. Like as not they decide they don't want to trade with you, they just up and leave a man high and dry, after he's gone to the trouble and expense of shipping trade goods all the way out from St. Louis."

Charles knew Old John was getting around to something, all right, but what?

They'd have to wait and find out. "Trade poor, John?"

"Well, passable, but you know how it is. With The Hudson Bay over Canada way and Astor and The American Fur, there ain't no way a little fellow is going to make it unless he deals with whiskey."

"I hear there's been plenty of firewater around lately. You been dealing with it in the trade?" Jack said.

"Sure enough. So's everyone else. How's a man to stay in business unless he does? That's what I wanted to talk to you fellows about."

Charles leaned forward and studied the big man's face. It was amazing. In one breath he could talk about converting the Indians and in the next breath justify trading alcohol to them. It was enough to turn a man's stomach. Charles started to speak, but he caught a warning glance from his partner.

Now Jack leaned forward, interested. "Sounds like you got something in mind for us. What makes you think we'd be interested? You know we don't deal in the firewater hardly at all."

"It's bad stuff all right. Don't know how you fellows can stay in business without using it in your trade."

The big man's face was serious and the look in his watery blue eyes intent. Charles sensed that John would soon tip his hand. But not all of it. Just enough to keep them interested. One had to hand it to the old goat; he had a way of dealing that you had to admire. Jack was right. They'd do well to listen and learn all they could before committing themselves to anything.

"Sometimes it ain't easy, John. Seems like those Piegan have a taste for the firewater that just has to be satisfied. Guess if you didn't sell it to them, somebody else would," Jack said, leading him on.

"That's right Jack. Since you can see my point, I'm going to put my cards right on the table. I always liked you two. That's why I come to you with my offer first."

Charles glanced at Jack. His forehead was furrowed and his left eyelid drooped. Wonder what was going through his mind. When Old John told you he liked you, you'd better look out. He was about ready to give it to you.

"Done took you long enough to get around to it, John. What kind of favor you going to do for us now?" If John heard the cynicism in Jack's voice, he ignored it. Charles knew from the looks of Jack's face that he had his belly full of John. Wouldn't be long before Jack blew up.

"Well, I am dealing with the Bloods and Northern Blackfeet some and they're going to winter up along the Titty River. Going to deal with just me."

"Now what kind of favor is that?" Jack had his emotions in check now, and he winked at Charles. "Doesn't seem like you're doing anything for us. You must have promised them something special to get them to trade just with you. Hope you can deliver when it comes time to settle up. When those Bloods get liquored up they can get mighty wild."

Old John had played his cards well, both Charles and Jack were listening intently.

"If we joined forces, what with you two being in so good with the Piegan, we could just about sew up the trade all for ourselves. Once we crowd those other traders out, those Indians have to take what we offer. Couple of good years, we get out, rich men, all of us. Go back east and live like real Na-bobs the rest of our natural lives." He leaned back with a big smile. "Well, what do you think?"

Charles shoved his chair back. "Can't speak for Jack, but this is a little too quick for me. Like to have time to think it over. How about you, Jack?"

"John, you've thought it out real well. What happens if we decide not to throw in with you?" Jack asked.

"Well, there's others. But like I said, I always liked you and wanted to give you first chance. Think it over and let me know." The big man rose and shook the two partners' hands warmly. "Sure I can't fix you up with a drink before you leave? Got some real good stuff I save for my friends."

"No thanks, some other time. Have to be going. Charlie here left his new bride to come over to see you. He's chomping at the bit to get back to her."

"Heard about that. So, you got yourself a Piegan squaw now. Ought to help with the trade. No harm having your woman be an Indian." John put his arm about Charles' shoulder. "You think about converting her to Christianity. Children come along, you'll be glad you did. God bless you. Hope to see you again soon."

They were hardly out of sight of John's place when Jack burst out laughing. "You hear that hypocritical old fart?" Jack cleared his throat. "Makes me want to spit. Doesn't bother his Christian morals at all to take advantage of the Indians. Guess he thinks if they're not Christians they aren't real people." Jack furrowed his brow and spat.

"How come you went along with him when he was giving you all that stuff about joining up with him?"

The temperature had dropped several degrees in the past hour and they were glad when the lights of their own place appeared. They were soon taking care of the horses. "Oh, he always says that. Don't let him bother you."

Jack dragged his saddle from Monte's back. He grunted. "I figured I'd play along with him and see what he was up to. Was tough listening to all that bullshit without showing how I felt. What's it sound like to you?"

Charles rubbed his horse with a piece of burlap. His motions stopped and the horse shifted about. "Looks as if he isn't getting all the cooperation he'd like us to think he is, among the Bloods and Northern Blackfeet especially. No way he is going to get all of those people to trade with just him. There's too many other traders around." Charles slapped his horse on the rump and he moved aside. "Besides, he hasn't got enough trade goods to deal with that many of them all by himself. Won't all of them just deal in firewater. Charles finished rubbing his horse. "Wonder where he's getting the firewater anyhow?"

Jack had completed taking care of Monte. "I hear there is a new still over Fort Union way. Knowing Old John, he's got some deal cooked up. You can bet your boots he's not going to tell us of his source if he can help it." The partners headed for the inside of the post. It was dark and the yellow lantern light in the window welcomed them.

"You ever see anyone make firewater? Looks pretty vile to me."

"Don't know how Old John fixes his, but an old hoss, name of Slatterly, gave me his recipe. Was powerful stuff, time he got done with it. Can't remember exactly what he put in it, but seems like it was a quart of pure alcohol, pound of old black tobacco, some red chili peppers all ground up, some ginger, quart or so of black molasses and four or five times as much water right from the old muddy." Jack motioned in the direction of the Missouri River flowing not far from the post. "Cooked her all up till the tobacco and chili peppers had all the strength pulled out of them. Drain her off and water her down some more. Indians went wild for it."

Charles made a face. "Ugh, no wonder the Indians are having stomach problems. Wonder if that was some of the 'good stuff' Old John saves for his friends?"

"Wouldn't be surprised, probably figures as long as they're heathen, it won't do them any harm," Jack laughed shortly. "I hear that some even put a little gunpowder in it to spice it up. Long as it gives the old belly a bite, the Indians think it's the real stuff. Sad part is they don't seem to realize what it is doing to them."

Charles gazed at his partner thoughtfully. "Na-Ha-Ki and I have talked about it just a little. She tells me that even some of the women and children drink the stuff when they get a chance." Charles paused before going on. "There isn't enough of them like White Quiver around. He tells me he'd like to talk the Piegan into giving it up altogether."

Jack shrugged off his capote and hung the hooded coat on a peg by the door. "Let's sit a while. There's something important here and we best get it settled as soon as we can." The older man's face reflected his concern. Crow Woman and Na-Ha-Ki had come to greet them, but retired to the rear of the post when the men indicated that they wanted to talk.

Jack produced a bottle of Bourbon. "Now, this is a real man's drink." He poured drinks for himself and Charles. It was late when they finished their talking, but their plans were laid. Old John Stott had forced their hand by asking them to join forces with him. But they had decided just the opposite. They would go it alone and try to talk the Piegan into making a dry camp for the winter. They would reward the Piegan for their cooperation by offering them bargains on the trade goods. They would be cutting it thin, but if the first steamboat from St. Louis arrived as expected they could fill the post with a new supply of trade goods.

White Quiver would be enlisted to try to convince the Piegan of the wisdom of the plan. Charles also agreed to use his influence with Many Hawks as well. After a long evening of planning, Jack spoke seriously to his young friend. "Charlie, we are seeing a proud people go down hill. I don't know where it will all end. There's times when I see what is going around that it makes me ashamed. Especially when I think of Short Man and Old Bull. Then again I see people like you and White Quiver that want the best for everyone and I hope that you might prevail." Jack placed his arm around Charles' shoulder. "I'm proud to be your partner, son. This old hoss better get to bed before I get downright maudlin. See you in the morning."

Na-Ha-Ki was curled up under a robe, asleep, when Charles finally went to their bed. He held the lantern and studied her peaceful face. She breathed softly and evenly. He blew the lantern flame out and carefully eased into the bed, so as not to disturb her. She snuggled against him and moaned softly, then stilled. Her breathing was regular and quiet again. Her presence in his bed was comforting and Charles slept.

White Quiver was pleased with the proposal that the Piegan winter along the Marias and have no alcohol in camp. "The firewater is not good for my people. I have talked with The Crazy Dogs," he said. "Since the time when Old Bull nearly killed Short Man at the lodge of Many Hawks, many of them have stopped drinking it."

"How is Short Man?"

"He will recover, but he is old. His wives were pleased with the meat you gave them from the hunt."

"We couldn't use it all—glad to help out. You think the rest of the Piegan will go along with you and the Crazy Dogs?" Charles asked.

"I believe so. It will be a bad winter for the Bloods and Northern Blackfeet if the firewater is in their camp. The big Trader John is a bad man. They will find this out."

"I hope it isn't too late." Charles muttered. "There is feed for the horses up there and they say the buffalo are thick, too. Looks like it might be a good winter for the Piegan."

"Yes, it is as you say. The others will agree." White Quiver rose.

On his way back to the post, an uneasy feeling was upon Charles. It was like a nagging thing he ought to take care of, but had neglected to do.

He wondered when things would burst loose. When things looked too smooth and quiet, trouble was often in store. Like the time he and Jack had been out hunting. The air was warm, the sky blue, and everything seemed peaceful. Jack had reined in Monte, looked around and headed at a trot toward some cottonwood breaks along the stream. Charles followed, puzzled about Jack's intent. Jack dismounted. "Let's make camp here," he said.

"Early to make camp, isn't it? Two or three hours of daylight left."

Jack dragged his saddle from Monte. "Charlie, time you been around Montana awhile, you'll learn what to watch for. It gets quiet, everything comfortable, look out, something's brewing. You watch, in about an hour all hell will bust loose but we'll be fixed high and dry."

"Doesn't look like anything to me Jack, just a cloud or two over there by the mountains." He pointed to a couple of small clouds moving rapidly across the tip of a snowy peak.

"Just wait. If I don't miss my guess, those little clouds are fixing to be big ones. See those cottonwood leaves turned over, showing their white sides to the sky? Sure sign of rain. Always does. No birds singing either."

As usual, Jack had been right, and they were high and dry when a heavy wind and rain started a short time later.

*   *   *

Now his thoughts returned to Na-Ha-Ki. Most every time he went somewhere with Jack or off to see his other friends at the Piegan camp, she moped around for two or three days. Maybe he'd talk to Jack and see if Crow Woman acted the same way. As far as he could tell, Crow Woman always seemed to be the same.

Charles looked at the sky. Wouldn't be long before winter set in. His thoughts returned to Na-Ha-Ki and her family. Could it be that Na-Ha-Ki's family was causing trouble for her?

Seemed like every time she visited them or one of them came to see her, she'd be in a bad mood afterwards. Maybe it would be a good thing for them to spend the winter camped with the Piegan up on the Marias with her family close by. She might realize family could wear thin.

The business of his mother-in-law was a problem though. Seemed foolish to be married to a woman and not be able to look at or talk to her mother. He didn't think he'd ever get used to that. Na-Ha-Ki had not liked it when he'd complained to her about it. Sometimes she could be downright miserable when it came to her family and their ways. Didn't she know she'd married a white man and it was time for her to learn the white man's ways?

Maybe Au-Ti-Pus would come to live with them. He'd already talked about it to Na-Ha-Ki. The boy was bright. Ought to be getting a white man's education. Things were changing fast and the way it looked, the future might be difficult for the boy, especially if he decided to live as the Piegan always had. Eagle Chief was a good father but there were a lot of things Charles and Na-Ha-Ki could do for Au-Ti-Pus to help him.

Maybe their own family would get started one of these days. No sign as yet, but like Jack said, "It'll happen before you know it and you and Na-Ha-Ki will have a passel of youngsters running around underfoot." That was it. She was moody about not being pregnant yet. He'd talk to her about it.

Anyhow things weren't anywhere near as bad as Jack had made out they might be, with him and Na-Ha-Ki.

All that talk about the two of them missing their own people and not being able to share things had been a lot of bunk. Of course, he couldn't really make her understand how it had been back in New Jersey when he was growing up, but it wasn't all that important.

New Jersey. It had been a long time since he had thought of home. Images of his parents' red brick house next door to the McIntyres came to him. His had been a happy childhood playing with Robbie McIntyre and his kid sister, Ruby. Those had been fun times for the three of them together. Even though he and Robbie had been 3 or 4 years older than Ruby. He remembered how she always tagged along and wanted to join them in their fun. She had been such a gawky kid with her long pigtails, missing front teeth and knobby knees. But she'd grown up to be a beauty. If only they'd had the good sense to work things out before he'd enlisted.

Now his thoughts drifted back to the last time he'd seen Ruby. She was only 16 but she was no longer the tag-along little sister. He'd dropped out of college against his parents' wishes to enlist in the army. He'd been busy visiting friends, attending parties and he hadn't seen Ruby until they met in church. When she came in with her family, she smiled and nodded at him, and instantly, he knew he was in love. The McIntyres sat across the aisle and all through the long service he and Ruby exchanged knowing looks.

Things moved rapidly after that and when the two found a way to meet privately, they soon told each other of their love. Charles would leave for the army in two days. When they talked about making plans for the future, Ruby wanted to marry as soon as possible, but Charles was opposed to marrying until the conflict was over. Ruby was adamant in her desire to marry immediately and Charles left for his post with the issue unsettled. They had kept up communication, but it wasn't long until he heard that Ruby was to be married. Two years later, he found out her husband James Kohl was killed at Cold Harbor, just before the war ended. Fortunately there were no children. Well, he'd been daydreaming long enough. He'd better be heading back to the trading post. However, he couldn't dismiss the thoughts of Ruby and his life in Morristown. Life had a way about it. He thought, perhaps he'd been wrong about not following up about Ruby. But that was all in the past and he'd started his new life in Montana. Likely he'd never see her again.

CHAPTER 13
NOTHING BUT THE
WIND

(And those who husbanded the Golden grain,
*And those who flung it to the winds like Rain,)*_{XV}

Winter on the Marias, a good trade, 2,000 prime buffalo robes, and a time to remember. But the vague uneasiness that lay at the back of his mind, like an itch that couldn't be reached, had not gone away.

One night when the wind moaned and groaned down the valley and the trees rubbed their limbs against each other with a rasping thunking sound, Charles lay awake and listened. Na-Ha-Ki slept, her warm soft body pressed close to him for warmth. Outside a horse stamped. The fire in the tipi center still glowed softly. Charles snuggled deeper into the robes and listened. Sometimes the wind got inside a man. In this country it always seemed to be blowing. You got used to it after a while, but it was always there, twisting, turning, moaning, groaning, growling and whining like some hurt animal. If a body listened close on a dark cold night like this one, he could hear voices. The Piegan said it was the night people talking to each other.

The wind sounds rose a bit now and Charles turned over, pulled the robe tighter and tried to push the sounds from his mind. Na-Ha-Ki muttered softly and stirred against him. He rolled over onto his back and again he heard the muttering, moaning, whispering voices. A low moan, a soft step, a sorrowful groan.

His memory went back to Gettysburg. He could see it in his mind's eye again. Culp's Hill, the long day, the thirst, the smell of spent gunpowder that hung like a fog over the low spots. The clank of canteens, soft moans from the wounded men. In his mind he had returned to Gettysburg, the second day, and now another long night. How long would it go on? Culp's Hill this place was called. Strange the way things had worked out. Coincidences sometimes made a body wonder just how much of life's doings were by accident. Who'd ever thought that when Wesley Culp had grown up in this very place and played on this hill as a child, that he would be engaged in a desperate battle here? That he'd lay dead, victim of a rebel bullet, on his parent's own farm? Maybe it was meant to be that way. Charles hunkered down in the hollow he'd carved out for himself and peered through the thick underbrush and down the heavily wooded slope. The brief spurt of firing had spent itself now, and only an occasional sharpshooter's bullet whined past to thud against a tree. The still figure of a Confederate lay in the brush where he'd dragged himself to die. Charles was thirsty, his mouth dry. He held a piece of hard tack in his mouth trying to soften it. No fires tonight, maybe no water either. Just before he'd been killed, Wesley Culp had told them that there was a spring at the bottom of the hill behind them. Spangler's Spring it was called. The thought of cool spring water made Charles thirstier. He licked his lips and with his eyes opened as wide as possible stared into the darkness. "Jack, think those Rebs will ever stop coming up that hill?"

"Don't know, boy. They are a persistent lot."

"Think we can find that spring down at the bottom of the hill— the one Wesley was talking about?"

"Might be worth a try, kinda quiet now. You slip on back and see what you can do. Drink of water seems mighty fine to me right now. Here, take my canteen." The container made a thunk as Jack tossed it toward where Charles lay. "I'll keep a look out while you're gone."

The spring was there all right, just like Wesley Culp had said. Its water was cool and refreshing. Charles drank long, then filled both canteens. "Hey Yank, mind if we share some of that water?" A voice whispered out of the dark. Charles flattened himself to the ground. "Ain't no need fer that. I had a bead on you the last 10 minutes. Could a killed you a long time ago if I'd been a mind to. We got some wounded need tending. Need some water, too."

"Thanks Reb, guess there's plenty for everybody." Charles raised to his knees and gave his unseen observer a mock salute. "I'll be going on up the hill now. Hope we meet again under more favorable circumstances. Name is Charles Tucker, Morristown, New Jersey."

"Deiber, Fred Deiber, Louisville, Kentucky. Good luck, Yank."

Charles hurried up the hill. The moon had risen now and he saw the form of Jack stretched out, resting. "Found her, huh? Tastes might good. Thanks, Bub. Any trouble?"

"No, only a Reb down there wanting the same thing we did. Plenty for both of us. Nice fella. Said his name was Deiber."

"War is hell. Don't hardly seem right for us ordinary folks to be fighting each other, trying to save some jackass general's honor. I suppose it'll always be that way, till man comes to his senses. Sometimes I'd like to just light out for Montana where a man can be alone. Peace and quiet. After this war, that's where I'm going if I'm still in one piece. Gonna marry me an Indian gal, settle down and live off the land."

"Hold it, Jack. Listen! Hear that?"

Charles grabbed Jack's arm. A low moan came from the clump of brush where the wounded Confederate soldier lay. "Mother, oh mother." The voice was weak, but clear.

"I'm going over there," Charles said.

"Careful, boy. I'm thinking that's the one you shot. Same one that was sneaking up on us. Watch yourself."

The moaning voice came again, with the call for his mother at the end. Charles closed his eyes and saw a mental picture of his own mother. Canteen in one hand, rifle in the other, he snaked his way toward the moaning sounds. The man still called out and Charles crawled to his side. With wetted fingers he touched the man's lips. The light was dim, but he saw him clearly now. He was just a boy, 13 or 14 years old. His gray cap had fallen off, and in the patch of moonlight that fell into the clearing, Charles saw a pale white face and bright red hair. "Oh Mother," he groaned, "it hurts, it hurts. I want to go home. Take me home."

Charles pillowed the boy's head in his lap and continued to moisten his feverish face. He quieted now and relaxed a bit, but his hand grasped that of Charles' convulsively. Blood oozed from the boy's side and the ground was wet with it. Suddenly the hand tightened on Charles. The figure stiffened, but the man held the boy in his arms and rocked back and forth. Huge rasping sobs tore from Charles.

"Why, why? What sense did it make?" The sky paled, as dawn neared. Someone shook him.

"Come on, boy, nothing we can do here. Got to get back to our positions." It was Jack.

Charles awakened with a start. He was in the tipi on the Marias. He sat up and shivered with the cold. Na-Ha-Ki stirred beside him, reached up and grasped his arm. "What is it, Charles?"

"Nothing, it's all right. Thought I heard a sound. Nothing but the wind." He burrowed under the robe, and she wrapped her arms about him. Her body pressed close to him and warmed him. The wind howled and whined again. The sounds blurred and faded as he slept.

*   *   *

Another winter on the Marias, then spring, the arrival of the river boats up from St. Louis, summer, fall and winter again. Two years passed and it was spring again. But the uneasiness Charles harbored still lurked in the back of his mind. Na-Ha-Ki was a worry, too. Things had gone fairly well the first two years of their marriage. Trade at the post was brisk. But Charles was often restless. When no children came to them, Na-Ha-Ki began to worry.

One night she snuggled close to him and asked, "Do I make you happy?"

"Of course. Why do you ask?"

"A woman should have children for her man. Have you grown tired of me? Perhaps my sister, White Grass, pleases you?"

"What are you talking about? I don't need another wife. You are all the woman I need around here. If the work is too much, I'll get someone to come and help you."

"But a man must have children. My mother thinks there is something wrong in our lodge. She says perhaps my sister will bring you children."

"It's none of your mother's damn business! I don't want you seeing her so much. You hear me? What we do in our home is none of her business!"

His face filled with rage. "Tell her to keep her nose out of our business."

Then more softly as he put his arm about the confused girl he said, "It's all right, but I don't want your sister for a wife. You're the only wife I'll ever need. Don't worry, a child will come along one of these days."

He pulled Na-Ha-Ki toward him and kissed her gently. "I'm sorry I spoke harshly to you. Do you think our first child will be a red-headed boy?"

She smiled and kissed him as she extracted herself from his embrace. "I must fix us something to eat," she said. Charles watched her as she made her way toward the rear of the post and the living quarters. Things seemed to be better for a while after their discussion, but the restlessness that Na-Ha-Ki had sensed in Charles still seemed to be with him.

45-JEYS

But it was not until the message arrived from the East that she really let it worry her. Charles seemed different and thoughtful after he had received the letter. She wanted to ask him what had been in the message, but she was afraid of what he might tell her. Perhaps it was as her mother had predicted. He might have another woman where he came from. He had tried to tell her about his life before in the East, but she couldn't always understand. And now, since the paper had arrived, he was more restless than ever.

Suddenly he pulled the letter from his pocket and looked at it. "I'm sorry," he said.

"This is not an easy thing for me to say to you, but I guess you have to know sooner or later. I've got to go away for a while. There are things I must do. I'll be back as soon as I can take care of everything."

"Mother was right. She told me before we were married that you would go back to your own people. I will never see you again, I know. My people have a way of knowing such things."

"Oh, don't be foolish. I would never leave you and not come back. It's only that I have to take care of the house my father left me and some of his things. You do not understand the ways of my people. I would take you with me but it would be very hard for you away from here and your own people." Charles lowered his voice. "Jack Taylor and Crow Woman will take care of you while I'm gone." He put his arms around her and kissed her. "No need for tears. When you see the nice presents I will bring you, you'll be sending me back for more." She smiled at him, blinked back her tears and attempted to thrust her fears away.

Once the decision was made, Charles was anxious to be on his way. She cooperated in getting his things ready for the trip, fixed his meals and did her daily work flawlessly, but she refused to talk to him. Finally Charles lost his patience, grabbed her, and scolded, "You think all I want for a wife is someone to wait on me, fix my meals and lie in bed with me? What the hell is this silent treatment anyhow? Here I am almost ready to leave and you mope around, acting like I'm doing something terrible to you. Don't you understand—I've got to go and that's all there is to it."

Na-Ha-Ki stared at him and he continued, furiously. Her silence goaded him on. "Say something, dammit. I'm not doing anything so terrible as you make it out to be. A man's got responsibilities he's got to take care of and I've got to go and take care of mine!"

She lowered her head, tightened her lips, but still said nothing. Anger washed through him, a tension built within and then burst. Suddenly he furiously shook her.

"I'm sorry, I'm sorry." He pulled her to him and kissed her passionately.

"Please don't go—I will never see you again." Over and over she pleaded with him. He led her into the bedroom and motioned for her to lie down. She smiled, unfastened the top of her dress, took his hand and guided inside the opening and over her soft breasts. He kissed her full on the mouth and suddenly they were swept into an overwhelming mutual emotional response.

The violence of their emotions was spent in the sexual frenzy that followed. They lay easily together touching, talking softly and looking into each other's eyes. Shadows moved across their bodies, forming a mirage that engulfed them . . . warm then cool, smooth, rough, firm, soft, hard, fast, slow, wild, gentle . . . all . . . then, at last, quiet.

Charles moved sleepily, she positioned her head against his chest, and they slept.

CHAPTER 14
STRAINING AGAINST
THE TRACES

*(. . . Summer dresses in new bloom)*XXIII

Late spring, the first of the steamboats was about to arrive. The River Queen had battled the twisting, tortuous Missouri, 2600 miles from St. Louis to Fort Benton. More boats would soon follow as the yearly cycle of trade goods flowing to the trappers began. Each boat's decks and holds were gorged with pots, pans, calico prints, blankets and bolts of silk for the trappers'and traders' wives. For the men, guns ammunition, axes, tobacco, and alcohol smuggled past the government officials along the way. For those who could read, packets of mail, newspapers and books. Fort Benton's occupants and the Blackfeet Indians in the many lodges below and beyond the traders' camp milled around in excited anticipation.

Charles, Jack, Na-Ha-Ki, and Crow Woman shouted with the rest as the River Queen whistled, then gently nosed to a stop at the landing point on the levee. Her captain waved jovially to the noisy crowd, then ordered the gangplank lowered.

Charles and his party were among the first allowed on board. They were anxious to restock their post and wanted to assure themselves that their orders had been filled. Many of the bales of furs and hides at the landing were theirs.

Captain Shelton handed Charles a package of letters and a bundle of newspapers. "Got most of the stuff you and Jack ordered," he said. He turned to watch as an Indian charged by, firing his gun wildly into the air. Two of his companions followed behind him, the hooves of their horses spraying mud as they tore past the crowd. People scattered, a child fell and one of the horsemen brought his horse up short, slid off and helped the frightened child to its feet. He laughed, leapt onto his horse, shouted, and rode after his companions.

"Liquered up already!" Shelton turned back to Charles. "Some crowd."

"Be wilder once the firewater is unloaded," Charles said. Our hides are over there, almost all prime." He motioned toward several bales of hides piled at the levee. "When do you want us to load?"

"Just got here, Charlie, let me catch my breath first."

"Not trying to crowd you, Sam." Charles placed his hand on the Captain's shoulder. But I know how you operate. First one up the river, first one back. Might get in an extra trip this year if you're lucky."

Sam grinned. "Early bird gets the worm, I always say." He leaned over the rail and spit a long stream of brown juice into the muddy river. He swiped his hand across his mouth and laughed. "Day after tomorrow soon enough for you?"

Charles nodded. "I'll get out of your hair. Know you're sort of busy right now."

Jack Taylor stepped forward. "My partner sort of forgot his manners, Sam. Soon as you're free, come on over to the post. Crow Woman and Na-Ha-Ki are mighty fine cooks. Maybe we can talk a spell then."

"Sounds fine to me. We can swap lies about the war. Tonight too soon?'

"Wouldn't have asked you if we didn't want you. Be expecting you." Jack smiled and he and Charles walked over to inspect the crates marked for Charles and him.

In the short time it took to unload the River Queen and reload it with hides and furs, another boat had arrived. Now that his boat was loaded, Sam was anxious to leave. He informed them he would leave in the morning. "A bit soon for me," Charles said, glancing at Jack. "Was thinking I might ride along. Have to go back to Morristown to settle some things. Sort of hate leaving Jack with all the work on such short notice though."

"No skin off me. Think I can't manage without you?" Jack peered across the table at his blond friend. "You don't fool me, you don't want to leave Na-Ha-Ki that long. We'll manage. Do you some good." He jerked his head toward the rear of the post and the living quarters. "Go on, get your things ready. She'll be all right."

Charles studied his friend's face momentarily. "I'll get back as soon as I can, fall at the latest." He hesitated, placed both hands on the table and stood up. "Guess you're right. Sooner the better. No matter what, she isn't going to like it." He shrugged and went toward the rear of the store.

It had been a short night, what with the hurried last minute preparations, and excitement boiled within him as Charles strode toward the River Queen. Na-Ha-Ki hurrying along beside him, sensed his mood, and her pace slowed. Apprehension swept through her. The valise in Charles' hand swung in a quick rhythm. Suddenly he was aware that Na-Ha-Ki was no longer at his side, he turned, concerned. Her troubled face mirrored her inner emotions and guilt washed over him, chilling his excitement.

She smiled faintly and hurried to catch up. His outstretched hand grasped hers' and tightened on it. He quickly embraced her and kissed her upturned face. "It'll be all right. I'll be back before you know it, with lots of nice things for you. She nodded mutely. The corners of her lips quivered and she managed a small smile. "That's my girl," he said. He picked up his valise, and walked across the gangplank to the boat, eager to leave, but feeling the tug of her emotions at his back.

She stood apart from the others, alone, serious, a striking figure in her long black velvet skirt trimmed with ermine. The gold locket Charles had given her glowed softly against a simple white silk blouse. Moccasins with cut beads in geometric patterns complemented her dress.

Charles waved and she lifted her arm as if to respond, but partway through the gesture, turned and quickly walked away.

The River Queen pulled into the swift stream and the people on the levee faded into the distance, then disappeared as the river curved. Charles flexed his hands as he released his tight grip on the rail. He wiped his wet palms on his pants leg and moved to the forward deck.

Staring into the river as the prow of the steamer ploughed through the muddy water, suddenly Charles was anxious to see his old home and friends in Morristown.

*   *   *

Things had changed little in New Jersey and Charles was relieved to find that the settlement of his parent's estate was relatively simple. "I believe everything is in order, Charlie." Marty Colberg, his attorney assured him. "We'll see that the property is well maintained and the money from the rental goes into the Iron Bank in your account." Marty pushed the papers across the desk for Charles to sign. "I'll send a full accounting every six months. It would provide you with a tidy sum in a few years, in case you want to move back here among us more civilized folks."

"Not much chance of that, but it's good to have friends who look out for you."

"Anything for an old friend," Marty said. "How about lunch?" Charles nodded and Marty went on. "You can tell me about the Wild West, Indians and all that. I remember when we used to talk about what we were going to do when we grew up and you always said you wanted to go west." Marty stuffed the papers into a file and locked the door behind them. "Any place you'd like to go in particular?"

"I'm with you. Since you're picking up the bill, you name the place." Charles grinned at his friend.

"Sam Wilson's place is still here, remember it?"

"I sure do. What I remember best, is that big hunk of cheese they put out for the customers to cut for themselves. Sounds fine to me. Oh, by the way, maybe you can answer a question for me, Marty. When I was a kid, I always wondered who Sam Wilson was. Do you know?"

"Sure. I thought everybody knew. He was the quartermaster for the Revolutionary Army. Was a war hero. Way my dad told me the story, Sam Wilson didn't collect the money the Army owed him until many years after the war. Anyhow, there are several Sam Wilson places in New Jersey, and all of them seem to be making money."

"Interesting. I wonder if his son was a quartermaster in the Civil war?" Charles said.

"That'd be a coincidence, wouldn't it? Let's ask someone when we get there." Marty responded.

Marty pushed back from the lunch table and looked inquisitively at Charles. "What finally made you to decide to pull up stakes and go west?"

"Well, I suppose in rebellion against my father as much as anything. You know he was a Harvard graduate and with me being an only child, he had big plans for me. Wanted me to be a Unitarian minister like he was. Can you imagine me in a pulpit sermonizing?"

"Well, you raised enough hell when we were kids. You might be an expert on that." Marty laughed. "Remember that time my mother caught you and me in the barn behind the house having a pissing match?"

"Yeah, I don't know who was embarrassed most, her or us," Charles said. "But you know even then I was straining against the traces." Charles pushed his chair away from the table and stretched his legs. "No, Harvard wasn't for me, but I didn't go uneducated. Time I was 14 or so, I'd read a lot of the books in Father's library. Still carry one of them with me—The *Rubaiyat* of Omar Khayyam. Had it with me all through the War."

Marty interrupted. "Wasn't your father an abolitionist?"

"That's right, and so were a lot of his friends."

"I know your father was a smart man, and my folks respected him greatly."

It had been a long time since he'd thought about his father with respect to his intellect.

Somehow, now that Marty had brought up the subject, Charles wanted to talk about him.

"Marty, did you know that one of Abe Lincoln's best friends, Theodore Parker, was a fellow Unitarian minister and a close friend of my father? Lots of times I was allowed to stay up late just to listen in on their conversations. I'll bet you didn't know that our house was one of the stops on the Underground Railroad."

"Really?"

"Didn't know it myself until I was about 15 years old. One night I stole down to the kitchen to grab a snack to eat. I'd been lectured about raiding the pantry so when I heard voices, I hid behind the pantry door. One of the voices was my father's but the others were unfamiliar to me. Suddenly the door flew open and my father was there holding a lantern up high so the glare in my face blinded me. 'So, it's you,' he said. 'Well, you might as well know what's going on. But, keep your mouth shut. People's lives are at stake here.' A large black man and a woman stood behind Father. 'These people are slaves who are running away. We are providing them shelter until they can move on to the next stop,' he said. It was long before Lincoln's emancipation proclamation that freed the slaves. My parents risked imprisonment by helping the slaves to escape."

"No wonder folks admired your father. He practiced what he preached."

"I guess you're right, Marty." Somehow Charles hadn't thought of his father in that way very much, but it made him proud to hear Marty praise him so warmly. He went on, "It was quite a while until we could talk about it openly. Father died the year Lincoln freed the slaves and Mother was left alone. The news of Father's death reached me at the Army hospital where I was recovering from a case of typhoid. Nearly died of it. Did lose my hair but it grew back. Remember how red it used to be? Been almost white like this ever since."

Marty looked sharply at Charles' light blond hair. He smiled. "At least you've got yours."

Charles went on. "Soon as I got better, I got leave to come home to take care of Mother. She only lasted about six months. Guess she lost the will to live without Father. Anyhow, there wasn't anything to keep me here, so I packed Father's books, rented the house out, sold everything else except a couple of keepsakes, put the money in the bank and went back to my outfit and finished fighting the war. Guess you got into the act when the troubles with my parents' estate cropped up and I turned it over to your Dad's firm."

"And then my father died," Marty said simply.

"Sorry to hear about his death, but it looks like you're doing all right."

"I'm trying," Marty said, "but sometimes I get restless and wish I'd kicked over the traces like you did. But, never mind me. Go on, tell me the rest. How did you finally decide to go west, and why Montana?"

"One of my war buddies, Jack Taylor, had lived among the Blackfeet Indians a while. His stories got me all fired up. I was sick of the war, the senseless killing and all, and I just wanted to get away to a more simple kind of life."

Marty leaned forward, his look intent. "Did you find what you were looking for?"

"Well it certainly was different, and I learn new things every day. About the time I think I understand the culture, something happens and my understanding has to start all over. Makes life interesting anyhow. But to be honest, I'm afraid our government is buying into the destruction of the Indian culture."

"I thought you liked it out there?"

"I do. The land is beautiful and the native people can be wonderful, but greed, graft, alcohol, and the government's ignorance, is destroying the Indian culture before we even understand it."

Marty was still leaning forward, staring at Charles. "You know, Charlie, for a while there, you sounded just like your father. I suspect you're more like him than you'd ever admit."

"I expect you may be right, Marty. I'll take that as a high compliment. Seems like some lessons in life come too late, don't they?" Charles leaned back and studied Marty, before going on. "But let's talk about the more pleasant things about the west. My friend Jack used to keep us entertained for hours talking about the Blackfeet women. I can just hear him now. I used to jibe him to get him started. Jack, I'd say, I've heard Kimberly talk about those Indian women. He says they all have hour glass figures, only problem is the sand has all run to the bottom. Down in New Mexico, they climb a hill to get water, and dig for firewood. Hot as hell in the summer, and cold as a well digger's ass in January. That always got Jack going. 'Charlie,' he'd say, 'let someone who's seen more than a bunch of half starved Indians living on a chunk of sand, eating snakes, lizards and cactus, tell you about the real west. Let's talk about the important things first,' he'd say, 'like women, food and fun. You ever lay eyes on one of them Blackfeet maidens, you'd throw rocks at any white gal you ever saw. Most of them ladies run tall and slender. They know what it takes to make you feel like a real man. None of that prissy high faluting society stuff.'

'You likely heard that the Indians are dirty. Don't you believe it. One of them Blackfeet women catch you bringing dirt into her lodge, she'd skin you alive. She owns the lodge, lock, stock and barrel. Camp is always set up by water where they can clean up.' Jack would pause for breath and let things set in for a moment or two before going on. 'What about in the winter?' someone would always ask. 'They break the ice and wade right in to wash up. You better do the same or you'll find yourself out in the cold.' He'd be just getting wound up by now. 'Mountains reach the sky, snow on their peaks the year around. Buffalo thicker than hair on a dog's back. Them Indians come from a different stock than most. Mormons say they are the lost tribe of Israel. Some say they came from Wales. Don't know myself, but I do know them women is mighty fine. Ever tell you about the time we come on the Blackfeet gals swimming?'"

"He told me this story at least ten times, but he'd change the lie every time. He'd go ahead anyway, couldn't stop him if I wanted to."

"Jack would go on. 'Well, it was back in about '52 when Bill Jamie and I were out scouting and we came upon a little bunch of cottonwoods down by the mouth of a creek that flowed into the Judith river. Looked like a good place to hole up for the winter, and get acquainted with the local Indians and start our business.'

'We'd just started down off the bluff above it a ways, when we heard all this giggling and laughing. We got off our horses and snuck up through the grass and there in the stream behind a beaver dam, were six Blackfeet maidens, not one stitch of clothes on, just racing and tearing around, splashing water on each other, having the time of their lives. Bud, we thought we'd fallen into seventh heaven. Every one of those gals had long black hair hanging clear down to their, you know what. They couldn't have been more than fifteen or sixteen years old. Real beauties, every one of them. Man! Titties every shape, and size. And that wasn't all you could see either. They weren't ashamed of their bodies. You know the Blackfeet worship the sun. Well, those gals were sure sun worshippers, all right, because they were soaking up all the sun they could get.'"

"About this time, Jack would pause, knowing he had us all set up. He'd refill his pipe, light it and take a few puffs, all the time while we waited with our tongues hanging out, waiting for him to go on. He wouldn't do it either until someone would beg him a little. Sometimes I think it was lucky Jack didn't get killed by one of us. But eventually he'd go on. 'Them maidens had wet the clay bank along the creek and were getting in and out and sliding on their bare asses right into the water with a big splash. Don't know how long we lay there watching the fun. I could tell Bill Jamie couldn't take too much more of this watching 'cause he wanted to get out of there before we got noticed and got our scalps lifted.'

'I nodded and reluctant-like we retreated through the grass back toward where our horses were tied up in a clump of trees. All at once Bill pointed to a passel of young bucks sitting on their horses up on the bank opposite us, just watching the fun. With a whoop, they charged right down into the stream, each of them grabbed a gal, pulled her up onto the horses and took off on a gallop across that prairie. Them gals screamed and yelled and kicked, but it wasn't no use. Wasn't long before a couple of braves came back and picked up them gal's clothes. Bill and I snuck over, grabbed our horses and hightailed it out of there before someone came looking for the gals. Never forgot that day. Someday I'm going back and find an Indian gal of my own.'"

"That's the way he'd always end that story, except for one thing. After the war, we both went to Montana, started our fur business and married Blackfeet women."

Marty edged his chair closer to the table. "Sometimes I envy you," he said. "I've always seemed to get caught up in what I have to do, rather than what I wanted to do. Take the law business, for instance. I'd rather be a boat builder. I made my first big mistake when I let father talk me into going to law school. Should have done what you did, just refused to go."

"Ever read Omar Khayyam's, *Rubaiyat*, Marty?"

"Not really, 'A jug of wine, loaf of bread and Thou,' is about it."

"Well, that's the main idea. Old Omar knew what he was talking about. He believed in living first and then getting around to the more mundane things later."

"You always were a Hedonist, Charlie."

"Speaking of living first, I'm going to get the hell out of this overgrown jungle and head for God's country where a man can stretch his arms without hitting something."

Marty eyed his friend enviously wishing he could go with him. But there was Louise and the children. Three already and another on the way. "If you don't mind a personal question, what ever happened between you and Ruby McIntyre? Almost all of us thought the two of you would marry."

"Can't really say. I went back to the war, thinking we'd wait until it was over to get married, but she felt differently. One day I got a letter from Mother telling me of Ruby's marriage. Hit me hard, but I got over it. Was a lot of the reason I went west after the war. My Blackfeet woman is enough of a wife for me."

Suddenly Marty stood up. "Married to an Indian?"

"Sure thing. And she's everything old Jack Taylor said the Blackfeet women were."

"Like what?" Marty said

"Most of them are hard workers and they are usually smart, good looking, and feisty."

Marty extended his hand. "Sounds like a good combination to me. It's been great to visit with you. Would ask you over for dinner, but Louise isn't feeling too well these days. The kids get her down and she's expecting again."

"That's all right, Marty. Tell her I said hello. Squaw man isn't always welcome at a lot of places. I understand." Suddenly Charles was homesick for the shining mountains, the broad plains, the wide Missouri and most of all Na-Ha-Ki. His whole being ached for his wife and the familiar things in Montana.

"Which way you going back?" Marty said, self consciously, aware of the remark Charles had made about being a Squaw Man. Marty realized that Charles was probably correct, Louise might be uncomfortable with Charles at her table.

"Shortest route is through Denver, then head overland on horseback. Be traveling the last six hundred miles or so by myself. Long way and I'm hoping to get there before snow flies."

"Just thought you might be interested. Ruby McIntyre and her folks live in Denver now. Run a big hotel. Here I'll give you their address." Marty wrote out the information on the back of his business card and handed it to Charles. Be sure you stop if you can. I'm sure they will be glad to see you again."

"I'll try. Depends on the weather. I want to get home before winter sets in.

The friends parted. Marty went back to his office and Charles to the train station to make arrangements for travel to Denver, Colorado and points west.

Chapter 15
Wayfarer's dilemma

*(Beside me singing in the Wilderness.)*_{XII}

The rail trip to Denver was long and tiresome and he decided to stay over before going on. A hot bath and a comfortable bed were an inducement. He pulled out the card Marty had provided him. WAYFARER'S INN, DENVER, COLORADO. Robert McIntyre, Prop.

He remembered the McIntyre family as pleasant people who had lived next door to them in Morristown. Mrs. McIntyre had served homemade cookies and milk for the children. Her son, Robbie, and Charles had always greedily gobbled them up after their play. Robbie had joined the Union Army but was killed in battle of Gettysburg and the couple was left with their only other child, Ruby. It would be good to see them again and he wondered if Mrs. McIntyre still baked those good cookies.

The Wayfarer's Inn stood in the heart of Denver. It was a large two-story white frame building. Charles checked in, soaked himself in a tub of hot water, changed into his finest fringed buckskins, combed his hair, and presented himself at the desk to inquire of the clerk behind the counter about Mr. and Mrs. McIntyre.

The clerk gazed at him intently for a moment. Her hazel-colored eyes looked directly into his and he was momentarily confused. He felt a constriction in his throat and caught his breath. The clerk was Ruby!

"And who is inquiring about the McIntyres, may I ask?" she said softly.

"Come on Ruby, you know me. Charles Tucker," he answered.

"Yes, I know. I wondered if you remembered me," she said. "I'm Ruby, the tagalong kid sister you and Robbie used to ignore or tease. It's nice to see you again, Charles." She impulsively reached out and covered his hand with hers. "I may sound like a silly school girl but when we moved to Denver, I somehow felt I would see you again. Does that seem silly to you?"

He looked into her eyes again and they held his, steady and sure. The warm pressure of his hand under hers registered and when she made no move to take her hand away he was pleased. "Mother and father will be ecstatic about you stopping by," she said as she self-consciously released his hand. "Can you stay a while?" She blushed at her sudden impulsiveness and looked down. "I'm sorry I wasn't at the desk when you checked in."

"Well," he explained, "I'm on my way back to Fort Benton, Montana and sort of in a hurry, but I guess I can spare a day or so before I head out."

"I'll get father." She walked around the counter and toward the dining room. He watched her movements as she glided gracefully across the lobby. In a few minutes she returned with Mr. McIntyre.

"Ruby is so excited about your showing up here," he said as he shook hands. "This calls for a special party to celebrate. Ruth will be delighted. She speaks of you and Robbie sometimes and how much fun you three used to have playing together as children." Mr. McIntyre paused as his gaze went to Charles. He cleared his throat, then went on, "She is lonely for home, back in New Jersey. I'd better warn you, Charles, if these two women have their way they'll hog-tie you and keep you right here." He gave his daughter an affectionate hug. "Ruth will be here shortly."

Charles smiled at the father and daughter. His throat constricted again and he breathed deeply, looked away, muttering an inanity.

Mrs. McIntyre's reaction to his visit was just as her husband had predicted. "Charles, Charles," she said again and again. There were questions about Morristown and about other parts of New Jersey.

"And do you still paint those lovely pictures—scenes and animals—with all the beautiful colors you used so well?"

Charles nodded. "Sometimes, sometimes," he said wistfully. "I haven't as much time for it as I'd like, but I carry my easel with me wherever I go. I have it set up in my room here already. I bought a lot of new supplies when I was back east and I'm anxious to try them out."

It was late when Charles retired to his room but his meeting with Ruby was still uppermost in his mind. He was certain that he loved Na-Ha-Ki, but this sudden surge of emotions with Ruby was different. Like the silent thing that passed between them and the way they were content to look into each other's eyes for long periods of time, with no need to say anything. Now he knew, what the love Omar Khayyam spoke of in the *Rubaiyat* meant: '*A jug of wine, a loaf of bread and thou.*'

Charles Tucker and Ruby McIntyre were once again wildly in love. He could hardly wait until morning when they would meet for breakfast. At her door, she had touched his hand, looked directly at him with her steady hazel eyes, and the strange something passed between them. "Till morning, Charles. Pleasant dreams," she said. Her lips brushed his cheek and her door closed behind her.

Charles stood uncertainly for short time and quietly walked away. As he readied himself for bed, he looked at his hand where she had touched it. He raised it to his lips and gently kissed it, imagining the pressure of her hand on his. He breathed deeply, sighed and lay back against the pillow, locked his fingers behind his head and smiled. As he reflected upon the events of the evening, waves of warmth and well being swept over him. What did it all mean, and what was next for them? It seemed as if fate had thrust them together and he decided that he would not question it. Tomorrow would be soon enough to worry about the practical aspect of things. He turned onto his side, touched the hand she had squeezed, smiled, and slept.

The following week was filled with a constant round of activities, providing Ruby and Charles few private moments. Ruby's mother was especially pleased with Charles' visit and as they discussed it, Mr. McIntyre said, "Charles disturbs me, Ruth."

"Why, in what way, Robert?"

"I can't say exactly, but there is something he isn't telling us. He seldom talks about Montana territory and the life he lives there. And I wonder what ever motivated him to go there in the first place."

"Oh Robert, you're just worried about your daughter. She's a mature woman who has even been widowed. Don't forget you and I had been married four years already when I was her age. Every father thinks the young man his daughter picks out isn't quite good enough for her. Don't forget, Charles is from a good family." She grasped her husband's hand. "Robert, in case you haven't noticed, your daughter is in love. Ruby isn't likely to meet anyone half as well educated or mannerly out here. I don't know why I let you drag me out here to this God-forsaken country anyhow!"

"Ruth, if you think about it, it was your idea in the first place," Robert said. "We came here for your asthma, remember?" She smiled at her husband and squeezed his hand.

"Really, Robert, I do appreciate every thing you do for us, but I do get so lonesome for New Jersey. It's so, so much more—," she placed her hand to her mouth as if to stifle her next words, "so much more civilized, and I want so much for everything to go right for Ruby."

Robert nestled her hand in his. "I know honey. It's hard, but Ruby's had more than her share of misfortune as it is. Maybe I was wrong about Charles, but he quit Harvard to go to war against his parents' wishes. And Ruby never told us what actually happened between her and Charles. Why she ever married James Kohl, I'll never know," Robert said. He shook his head.

"Plain and simple a childish mistake." Ruth said. "As much as I wanted grandchildren, I'm glad there were no children in their marriage. Especially since James was killed at Gettysburg."

Robert nodded. "We may never know about Ruby and James, but I can tell you I smell trouble. But you do have to admit, your asthma has been much better in Denver than it was in Jersey."

"Yes, that's so. But I do get lonely for home and so does Ruby. But since Charles has shown up. I've never seen her so happy. Maybe we ought to give them a little more time to themselves. You remember how difficult it was for us to be alone when you were courting me?"

"Of course. You're right dear. She's all we've got now that Robbie is gone and I suspect I am just a jealous father."

He patted his wife's hand affectionately, gazed into her hazel eyes, then sighed. "Ruth, you're still the most beautiful girl in my world," he said.

Denver, in the year 1869, was a bustling 'cow-town' perched at the eastern foot of the Rocky Mountains. Its fame as a haven for asthmatic sufferers was still growing. Except for the wives and daughters of the local businessmen, its inhabitants were mostly cowboys and miners.

In woman-starved Denver, Ruby's full figure, long blond hair, graceful movements and self-possession caused passing males to stand taller, smile broader and tip their hats as she passed. With classic male conceit, each assured himself that he had made a favorable impression on her. On a morning walk with Charles, Ruby suddenly stopped and looked at the mountain range to the west.

"Isn't it beautiful?" she asked. She grasped Charles hand and looked at him seriously, "Will you take me with you when you go to Montana?" she asked. "I'll be lost without you near me, Charles."

Visions of Na-Ha-Ki, their life together and his home in Fort Benton raced through his mind. This was something he had not anticipated. Charles had been so involved with Ruby that until now his obligations to his wife had been pushed to the back of his mind. He clenched and unclenched his hands, then wiped them on his pants' leg before answering. "It's a long and dangerous trip and there really isn't much of a place for you to stay when you get there. It'll be best if you stay here with your folks until I can come back in the spring."

"But, I'm not a child, Charles. I'm twenty years old and have been married before. I can pull my own weight. I can ride a horse as well as most men. When we were kids in New Jersey, I was the biggest tomboy around? I love you and want to be with you for good or bad wherever you are."

Charles wanted to sweep her into his arms, to tell her that he would take her with him, that life without her would be impossible, but right now he needed time to figure things out. He looked up at the towering Mt. Evans and tried to compose himself. The peak's snow cover had increased during the night. "Look, Ruby," he said, pointing toward the massive slope. "That's fresh snow on Mt. Evans— it's already snowing in the high passes and unless I start soon and travel fast, I'll be caught by early snows. I'll come back for you in the spring when we can take our time going to Montana. I might even decide to move back here and live in Denver."

Ruby smiled. "Oh Charles, I'm so happy. Forgive me. I know it's impractical for me to think I might go along with you right now, but you remember how impulsive I can be." Ruby paused and looked into his eyes. "I've never completely out grown it," she said.

"Another reason I love you," Charles said. "But between us we'll manage just fine. Who knows, by next spring you might feel very differently about me."

"No, Charles. I've been in love with you all of my life."

"But you married Jim Kohl, didn't you?"

"Yes, but that was an impulsive thing, and I have always regretted it. Let's not discuss that now. Some day I'll explain what happened, but right now, let's not waste time on that."

Charles' mind whirled. Should he tell her about Na-Ha-Ki? He wished he had time to do some serious thinking. He turned from Ruby and studied the snow-covered mountains to the west. "Look, honey," he said. "You are right. It is impulsive of you to think you could go with me now. But I am going to start back as soon as I can. Do

45-JEYS

you want me to speak to your father now or when I come back in the spring?"

Ruby shook her head. "No," she said. By next spring mother and I will have him thinking it was all his idea." She paused and looked at the snow-covered mountain. "Let's not talk any more about your going. You just make your arrangements and we'll spend as much time together as we can before you go."

"I'll go to the stage office now, you go back to your parents. They're probably wondering what's happened to us."

Now that his obligations to Na-Ha-Ki had forced themselves into his consciousness, Charles was confused. The previous week, that scintillating emotionally charged interval in time, had streaked past with barely a conscious thought on his part, except for what was occurring between Ruby and himself.

He wished for someone like Jack Taylor to talk to. He mulled the problem over and over on his way to the stage office. Only non-acceptable solutions filled with all sorts of impossibilities came to mind. For example, what if Na-Ha-Ki was pregnant? Or would she be treated well if she went back to her people. And Ruby, he was sure she would be appalled to know that he had deceived her. The thought that at this moment, Na-Ha-Ki might be bearing the seed of his child pressed upon him. Perhaps that might explain her erratic behavior just before he left for the east. He knew intuitively that she would be a good mother and he realized with a shock that he had been denying his own feelings about their childless marriage.

What if he didn't go back to Montana? After all Blackfeet women were taught to expect such things if they married a white man. Hadn't Na-Ha-Ki already accused him of having someone back east? Maybe she had prepared herself better than he thought. Maybe it would be best to do nothing for the moment, other than to go back to Montana. Once there, things would sort themselves out and a solution would present itself.

The stage office attendant cleared his throat. "Sir, may I help you?

"Oh, guess I was day dreaming. Sorry."

"Ain't no trouble for me, just figured you was thinking of something important. Didn't want to interrupt your thoughts. What can I do for you?"

"Need to get to Fort Benton, Montana. Have you any advice on the quickest way?"

"Fort Benton, huh? Looks like you best be hightailing it out of here before bad weather sets in. There's a stage leaving for Cheyenne first thing in the morning—five o'clock. Most everybody going North or West is already gone. Sure you have to go this year? Be a lot safer if you wait till next spring."

The man studied Charles quizzically before going on. "If you're bound and determined to head out right away, you might find some company to travel with in Cheyenne. Redskins on west and north are mighty hostile right now." He spat toward a cuspidor and looked inquisitively at Charles. "Know anything about the lay of the land or dealing with Redskins?"

Charles nodded. "Lived among the Blackfeet and traded with them for some time now. Wife is a Blackfeet."

The stage agent shook his head. "Squaw-Man," he said abruptly. "Might have known." Charles paid for his ticket and pocketed it.

"Thank you," he said.

"Best I could do for you," the agent said. "Watch your topknot"

At the Wayfarer Hotel, Charles quickly packed his belongings, then turned to his easel and the partially finished picture on it. It was late afternoon when he had it finished. As often happened when he painted, time slipped by unnoticed. Ruby would be expecting him and he must inform her of his decision to leave in the morning.

When Charles announced his plans, the McIntyres glanced at each other. Ruby looked down at her plate, in silence. Charles raised his glass. "Until I come back to Denver," he said.

Ruby's mother studied Charles' face. "When do you expect that to be?"

"Just as soon as I can. It depends on things there of course. I've got a partner and you know how it is with business. Jack's been running things by himself while I've been gone," he added lamely. He looked at Ruby as she picked at her dinner. He turned to Mr. McIntyre. "Sir, I'm very grateful for your hospitality and want you and Mrs. McIntyre to know that this has been very pleasant week I've spent with you."

"We were glad to see you again, Charles. My wife and daughter have been happier since you've been here than any time since we left New Jersey." He paused and looked seriously at his daughter and then to the young man beside him. "I should tell you that Ruth and I have been discussing, or should I say speculating, about you and Ruby, and I will be frank with you. We're not so old that we can't remember what it was like for us at your ages. We'll just run along to our suite and leave you to yourselves tonight." He shook Charles hand and Ruby's mother kissed him soundly.

"We'll miss you, be sure to come back soon."

"Yes Ma'am. Thank you for everything."

Her parents gone, Ruby studied him carefully. He shifted about uncomfortably and picked up his drink and sipped it without meeting her eyes.

"Charles, put that down and look at me. Now, tell me what's bothering you."

Charles set the drink down and looked at Ruby. Her eyes looked directly into his, searching, questioning "Is there something about your life in Montana you haven't told me?" Ruby said.

"What makes you ask?" He sipped his drink, wondering what he could safely tell her.

"You're acting strange and I just don't feel right about us tonight. You haven't told me much about your life there, really. When I ask you about it, you get evasive. If you really loved me, you'd tell me everything about yourself."

Charles drained his glass. He poured some wine into her glass and smiled at her. "You're just worried because I have to leave in the morning. Don't worry, I'll be back in the spring for you. I'm just preoccupied with having to leave. You'll wait for me, won't you?"

"Of course, there's never been anyone but you. Even when I was a little girl back in Morristown and you hardly knew I existed." She smiled, then tears formed in her eyes. He moved to her side and dabbed at her eyes with a napkin.

"Come on, I've got something special to show you." He grasped her arm and guided her toward the stairs.

"Where are we going?" she asked.

"My room. It'll be all right, I've got a present for you there."

She slid a secret glance at him and noted the expectant look on his face. "Charles, what are you telling me?" Ruby stopped at the foot of the stairs. "If you are taking me to your room to seduce me, I'll make it easy for you. Let's go."

Charles followed her lead as she quickly went up the stairs. He opened the door and as soon as they were inside the room, she fell into his arms. They embraced and after a long kiss, Ruby extracted herself and loosened her clothing. Her aggressive behavior had surprised him and he pulled away trying to control the sexual emotions surging within him. Ruby now sensed his confusion and laughed self-consciously.

"It's just that it's been so long." She moved easily into his arms and soon they were lost in the wild, wonderful, raging, experience of sex. Now their physical actions slowed and their lovemaking was gentler, slower and shared with each other, lingering over each new exploration of their bodies. At last their breathing stilled and Ruby lay her head nestled on Charles shoulder. She nibbled at his earlobe and ran her fingers through the hair on his chest. Ruby traced her finger around one of his nipples and re-positioned herself so she could touch it with her tongue.

Charles was aroused again and they languidly made love once again, neither of them knowing when they fell asleep.

Charles was the first to awake. He gently shook Ruby and she drowsily awoke. "It's very late," he said.

Ruby was awake now and rubbed her eyes. "Tonight was so wonderful, Charles. I can't wait until we can be together for the rest of our lives."

Charles was fully dressed now and self-consciously turned away as Ruby dressed. "I've got something for you," he said.

Ruby smiled. "What you already gave me was wonderful. Oh, I love you so much. Please hurry back."

Charles kissed her cheek and went to his easel. "Now close your eyes, and don't open them until I tell you."

"Can I open them yet?"

"No, just a moment."

"Charles, don't keep me waiting, the suspense is killing me."

"All right, now," he said.

Ruby opened her eyes. Her hands went to her mouth and tears gathered in her eyes. "Oh Charles, I never would have guessed. It—it's beautiful."

"Of course it is. It has to be, it's of you." Charles stood by the painting and smiled at her. In the painting, a young girl, Ruby, stood by a large silver beech tree. In the background was a brick house. It was her home in Morristown and the big old tree they had played in as children.

She was in his arms now, laughing and crying. Her face rose to his and their lips met. "Charles, Charles, oh I love you so." Her lips covered his face with little quick kisses.

He pulled her to him. "Ruby, Ruby," he murmured. The light dimmed, time faded, and the two were as one. Their lovemaking was wild, soft, tender, joyous and beautiful.

"Oh Charles, I never thought it would be like this." Ruby nestled against his shoulder. She kissed his cheek and rose to her knees on the bed, peering into his face. "Do you still love me?" Her expression was serious, questioning.

He ran his fingers along her bare back and slowly stroked her. He kissed her carefully, thoroughly, "Yes, yes," he answered. "I love you, my dearest." He pulled her to him. "Yes, yes, my darling." A vision of Na-Ha-Ki shattered the moment. Now an emotional letdown smashed into him as he realized the reality of his position between Na-Ha-Ki and Ruby.

"Is there something wrong?" she asked.

"No, nothing," he murmured.

Chapter 16
A not quite stranger

*(Ah, make the most of what we yet may spend.)*_{XXIV}

It was early morning before she left his room. "Till spring, dearest." One last kiss, a smile and goodnight. There wasn't much time before the stage left. He'd just have time to pack his gear, grab a quick breakfast and get to the stage office.

Denver to Cheyenne was only the first leg of the long journey to Fort Benton and Montana Territory. The tough part would be from Cheyenne on. Charles mentally ticked off his options. He doubted if any organized parties would be setting off this late. In a couple of days it would be October. Even if he found one, they'd probably travel too slowly for him. Perhaps he might find someone like himself, just waiting around for a partner before heading out. He could chance it alone. With an extra horse and one pack animal, he could travel light and fast to avoid trouble with hostile Indians. He'd have to cross Northern Cheyenne and Crow territory before he hit Blackfeet country. Risky, at best.

He'd see what turned up at Cheyenne. Never paid to borrow trouble. Something usually happened that changed the best-laid plans anyhow. For better or for worse, he thought wryly. Look at the mess he'd made for himself with the two most important women in his life. It was usually a waste of time, worrying about future events, but he knew that letting himself get involved with Ruby wasn't fair to her or himself, and least of all Na-Ha-Ki. He knew what Jack would say.

"You'd had sense enough to keep your pecker in your pants, you wouldn't be in trouble." He'd grin in that maddening way of his and add, "Stiff pecker hasn't any conscience, you ought to be old enough to know that by now without asking my advice."

The stage driver blew his horn and whipped the eight-horse rig into a run and they wheeled into Cheyenne in front of the Wells Fargo office. Cheyenne was much as he expected, dusty, dirty and full of cowboys, Indians and soldiers. He checked in at the only hotel, a two-story frame building that advertised hot baths. The bath was hot, if you didn't mind waiting until a sleepy looking attendant carried the water to your room in a bucket and poured it into a small metal tub housed in a corner behind a curtain. By the time Charles was ready to bathe, the water was lukewarm, but it felt good to wash the dust and grime away. He changed into fresh clothing and headed for the nearest saloon.

Buckhorn Bar, the sign over its door proclaimed. It was early evening and the only occupant sat at a table, feet propped upon it, resting. He lifted his eyebrows at Charles. "Howdy stranger, can I help y'all?" He said. The man had not stirred from his chair that leaned against the wall. Charles noted the gun strapped to his waist. The man laconically drew his coat open and exposed a silver badge. "You be looking for someone in particular?"

"No, but maybe you can be of some help. Name is Charles Tucker. I'm heading for Fort Benton, Montana. Know of anybody going that way that I might join up with?"

The tall man pushed his broad brimmed hat back on his head and studied Charles carefully. "Seems as if I ought to know you. Been in this country long?" His gaze traveled up and down the tall frame of the blond young man before him.

"No, been back east on a visit, going back to Fort Benton. Got a partner out there in the Indian trade."

"Back east, where'd you say you were from?"

The man's sudden interest in his business set Charles on edge. He might be a sheriff, but he didn't have to know everything. Besides that, it didn't pay to tell a stranger too much about yourself. You never could tell what they had in mind. He studied the man's face carefully. There was something oddly familiar about the lawman that Charles couldn't quite place.

"Didn't say where I came from. You talk like you might have been a Reb?"

"That's right. Name's Fred Deiber." The man slid his feet off the table and onto the floor and rose from the chair in one fluid motion. "Looks like we've met under more favorable conditions than the last time, Yank." He stuck his hand out at Charles. "Culps' Hill, Gettysburg, 'member?" His black eyes crinkled with amusement. "Life's sort of hard to figure sometimes. Never figured to meet up with you again. Same fellow, ain't you, Morristown, New Jersey?"

Charles smiled as he grasped the man's hand. "Sure enough! It's a pleasure. You're from Louisville, Kentucky if I remember correctly. I've thought about meeting you at that spring many times. You sure scared me, talking out of the dark like you did. What brings you into Yankee territory?"

"Can't rightly say, just seemed to fit in out here. Was handy with the gun here." He patted his hip. "People decided they needed a sheriff and it looked like I could do the job. Nothing too tough about it, mostly handling drunken cowboys and Indians. Lock them up till they sober up. Haven't had to use my hog-leg more than once or twice, then it was only for tapping an uncooperative puncher on the noggin. Been sheriff for the last couple of years now." The man stroked his black beard and studied Charles. "Big chore ahead of you if you plan to get to Montana afore cold weather. Looks of things, it's going to be an early winter. Snowing in the high passes already. Can't you wait till spring?"

Charles shook his head. "No, I have to get back for the winter trade. Been gone too long already. Any ideas?"

Deiber stroked his beard again and looked thoughtful. "Might," he said. He studied Charles face intently before going on. "How'd you feel about traveling with me as your partner?"

"Depends, I've been figuring on traveling light and fast, avoiding the hostiles as much as I could. What do you have in mind?"

"Don't rightly know, just wondering. Let me buy you a drink. Last time we met you were mighty dry." His face split into a beautiful smile.

"Thanks, don't mind if you do. Never expected to have the chance. Funny how things work out isn't it?" He walked to the bar, where Deiber pulled his gun from its holster and banged the bar.

"Hey, Humphrey, get the hell out here and serve us a drink."

A stocky man in a white apron scurried out of the back room. He wiped his hands on his front. "Keep your pants on, man can't get anything done around here for all the commotion. Who's the friend, sheriff?"

Deiber nudged Charles in the ribs. "Old army buddy," he said with a broad wink. "Ain't seen each other since Gettysburg. Give me a whiskey. Kentucky Bourbon, not that rotgut you gave me last time I was in here. Same all right for you, Charlie?"

"Sure, sure enough Kentucky whiskey is the best." They touched glasses and downed the drinks

"Leave the bottle, Hump." Deiber grasped the bottle by its neck and stalked to the table. He turned his chair around, the back facing Charles, straddled it and studied the blond man.

Deiber's friendly manner dispelled any misgivings he had held about him earlier.

"Been thinking of going out that way myself," Deiber said. "I expect we can make it before snow flies if we push ourselves. Can you use an extra hand in your business out there?"

Charles stared at the man. "Thought you were sheriff here?" The blond man poured himself another drink from the half-empty bottle.

"Wasn't meaning to be too pushy, Yank. You were the one asking for company on your trip. Far as I'm concerned, you want to go off on your own, makes no never mind to me. Crazy damn fool idea anyhow, two men taking off across those plains this time of year. Like as not Sioux don't get us, we'd get caught by the weather." The bearded man sipped his drink. His black eyes didn't shift as they studied the man opposite him.

Charles lowered his drink. "Didn't mean to offend you, Fred. Just figured it might be a problem for you to get away on such short notice."

Fred smiled. "Guess I was a bit tetchy. Can't blame a man for wanting to know about his traveling partner. I got a deputy just itching for my job. He can do it, too. Won't be leaving things in no trouble here. Free as a bird, I am. Be glad to shed this here badge. Ain't been nothing but a lot of trouble, no how."

"I'm going to need horses and gear, how you fixed?"

"No problem there, Charlie. Got my riding horse and another for a spare. Old Muley over at the livery stable will fix you up. He's got a good string right now. I can be ready to go any time you are."

"Right away is not too soon." Charles answered. "Let's go see him. I'd like to be on the way in the morning. All right with you?"

"Right as rain. One more thing, Yank, I got me a kind of wander-foot, don't like to stay in one place too long."

"Figured as much already. All right with me. My partner and I can use you in the trade as long as you want to stick around. Won't pay too much, but better than some. Place to stay and eat and $30 a month to start. More later if it works out."

"Fine with me. You got any kind of family out there?"

Charles hesitated, "Yes, I'm married. Indian girl. Blackfeet."

Deiber stood up. "Come on boy, we best be getting at it. Probably getting anxious to see your woman. Any young ones?"

"No." Charles grinned self-consciously. "Could be though, one of these days." He was relieved that the decision was made. Deiber looked like a good man to have around in case of trouble, and there would surely be trouble before they reached Fort Benton, unless he missed his guess.

The first three days out of Cheyenne were uneventful. Deiber was an excellent traveling companion and the horses Charles bought were good ones. Charles shifted about in his saddle, and reflected on things. Three days of hard riding sunup to sundown, stopping just long enough to eat at noon were beginning to tell on men and horses alike. Deiber sat easy on his buckskin. Charles and Deiber both favored buckskins. They were tough, held up on the long rides and had even dispositions. Deiber and the horse he rode seemed to be a good match.

"Best be stopping pretty soon. Probably water and feed over there." Deiber pointed to a clump of trees ahead and to the right. "Rest and water the horses a bit, then push on a ways after the moon comes up. Horses could stand some grain. Can't push them too much on just grass."

"Can't make as good a time by dark, Fred. Why not get up early and start off fresh in the morning? We been pushing pretty hard for the last three days. Must have covered close to hundred fifty miles already."

"Sure enough, Charlie. Done real good, but right now we be on the edge of Sioux country. Safer, moving at night. We can rest till the moon comes up, move on until early morning, then bed down and rest in some safe place during the day." Deiber looked ahead of them toward a dense thicket by a small stream. "This will suit us fine. We get across this strip of territory, we'll be all right. Cold supper. Fire might give us away."

Charles looked at the bearded man quizzically. "You seem to know a lot about this part of the country. Been across here before?"

"Can't say I have, but I know some that has. Big herd of cattle trailed up from Texas just last year. We'd do well to follow that trail all the way to Bozeman, then north up along the Missouri to Fort Benton."

"Shorter, going north soon as we hit the Big Horn Mountains. We can cut across the Yellowstone and Musselshell rivers and be in

Blackfeet country a lot sooner. I speak the tongue, and most of them know Jack Taylor, my partner, and me."

"Sounds fine to me, Charlie. Friends is friends wherever you find them in this country." Deiber's horse perked its ears forward and quickened its pace. "Dusty smells that water." Deiber patted his horse on its neck as they moved toward the stream. "We can stop here and rest a while if it's all right with you, Charlie. Makes no never mind to me which way we go. Shorter, the better. Only thing, the next couple of days we have to go careful, no matter what. The Sioux and Northern Cheyenne are almighty stirred up, what with the way their territory's being swarmed over with whites."

They were among the trees now and had stopped to let the horses drink at a small stream. They washed off and refilled their canteens. "You figure we'll have trouble going north through Sioux territory, Fred?"

"Can't tell. If it weren't for the military keeping people out of there, the Black Hills would be full of gold seekers. There's going to be trouble with all the Indians sooner or later. The Black Hills are sacred country to Indians and they won't take it lying down, people crowding in and acting like Indians got no right to be there."

Charles wiped his lips and munched on a biscuit and dried meat. "You think they'll bother us?"

"Not if we don't give them a chance. We ride hard at night, hole up during the day, and keep a sharp eye out, we'll be all right. "Let's rest a while now and push on when the moon comes up."

"It's a good plan, Fred. I was a lucky man to have met up with you," Charles said. He pulled his bedroll from his horse and spread it out. It felt good to lie down and stretch out.

Fred eyed his young partner and grunted. "You never know about a man until you see him under fire. I expect you know all about that. I'll accept your compliment, son." The bearded man rolled over and was soon asleep.

It was slower, traveling at night and resting during the daytime. Although the air was cold and small fringes of ice gathered at the edges of the streams during the night, the days were warm and dry. The horses showed signs of weariness and both he and Deiber could stand a good rest. They knew that they would likely be on safer ground as soon as they crossed the Yellowstone. They decided it would be a good idea to hole up for a while before pushing on.

It had just turned daybreak, and Charles studied the country ahead. "Think that's the river up there ahead," he said.

"Sure hope so. Could use a good rest and bath."

"Buffalo seem to be moving that way. Maybe we're in luck. We'll cross on to the other side and spend a couple of days resting up. Horses can use it."

"Reckon it'll be all right if we be careful. Crow country, though, liable to be some of them around the river." Deiber peered toward the fringe of trees along the river's banks.

"Unless I miss my guess, they're east of here, getting ready for winter. We'll look around first," Charles said.

They forded the river and splashed out onto the other side. Charles scouted up and down the stream for some distance. "Plenty of grass for the horses and a good spot where we can watch in case we get company," he said.

"Reckon we can build a fire and heat up some grub," Deiber said. He pulled his saddle from his riding horse, Dusty, who promptly rolled in the grass, then got up and began to graze.

"Keep the fire small and use dry tinder, we don't want to signal our presence with smoke." Charles said. "If I thought we could risk a shot, I'd get us some fresh buffalo meat. Some boss ribs would taste mighty good right now."

"Don't know as we ought to push our luck, Charlie. Sound of a shot is liable to carry a long way. Might bring some unwanted guests."

"Guess you're right, Fred. I can wait. Beans and bacon will have to do for now. At least they'll be warm for a change."

Two days rest along the Yellowstone and they pushed on. Another night's ride and they'd be on the other side of the Musselshell. A couple more days of hard riding and they'd be to the Missouri River and Blackfeet territory. They'd been lucky so far and the worry Charles had harbored began to lessen. Even the weather cooperated. Fort McGinnis and the South Judith Mountains couldn't be over a couple of days away. Once across the Musselshell, they could ride during daylight hours. They'd make better time. Only one more night in the saddle. Charles reflected that his buckskin had held up well. He patted the animal on its neck and it responded by flicking its ear and picking up its pace. The gait of the big horse was smooth and even after a long day of riding, it responded immediately to its riders urging. He hadn't named him yet, but now, he thought wryly, he'd pull a trick on Deiber.

"What was the name Bobby Lee called his horse?" he asked innocently.

"Traveler, why?"

"Oh, just wondering. Haven't named this buckskin yet. He doesn't move the fastest or look the most handsome, but he's there at the end, asking for more. Been thinking of naming him U.S. Grant."

Deiber turned in his saddle, and grinned at Charles. "Now, Charlie, iffin I was you, I would do the same thing. Ain't no way the Yanks would ever won that war without old Useless Grant. Always admired him, myself." He urged his horse ahead of Charles and saluted. Charles studied the square set of Deiber's shoulders and decided once more that it was a good day when the two of them met up with each other.

The last stretch had been rough going and the horses were having trouble picking their way through the rugged country. The moon had set and it was too dark to see well. Charles checked the stars. The Big Dipper hung low in the northern sky. "We better hole up until daybreak," he said.

"Sure got dark once the moon went down, didn't it? Looks like a good spot to stop." Fred swung from his horse and leaned back against a rock. He pulled his jacket around him for warmth. "Be daybreak soon and we can move on."

45-JEYS

"Hold it, Fred." Charles' voice was low, tightly controlled. A coyote yipped, then another. The sound seemed closer. Charles cocked his rifle and hunkered down between some rocks. He stared into the dark. One of the horses snorted. He crept to it and waited. The coyote yipped again. It was quiet out there. Too quiet. Deiber crouched beside him now, holding the horses on a short rein.

Off to the east, the sky paled. Charles' eyes hurt from looking into the darkness. The horse stirred and snorted again, restless. It grew lighter now. A shadowy form moved behind a bush. Charles aimed and fired. A yell and then an arrow bounced off a rock beside him. Deiber snaked along the ground to a more advantageous position. Charles pulled his horse closer to him, calmed it and crouched behind the animal.

Deiber was flat on his belly behind a rock. He leveled his gun and studied the terrain. In the growing light, Charles saw the figure of an Indian lying face down beside a bush. "Must be on foot," he muttered. "Keep down. Is your horse alright?"

"Yep, Charlie, how about you?"

Charles studied the area in front of them. He was thankful for the rocks at their backs. "Think we scared them off, Fred. Let's make a run for it. They're on foot, or they'd be riding back and forth out there. Probably a Crow war party starting out for Blackfeet country and just run into us by accident. Aimed to steal our horses and got more than they bargained for."

A coyote yipped, this time further away. "I'm thinking you're probably right, Charlie. Let's get out of here."

Charles fired several shots in the general direction of the yipping coyote before they mounted and hurried off. It was full daylight now, and in the distance they saw the Musselshell River. He reined in his horse and yelled to Deiber, "Look." Five Indians were gathered around the fallen figure on the ground. They yipped and waved their bows at the men on horseback.

"Like you said, was a war party on foot. Closer than I like for comfort. We best be getting as much distance between us and them as possible. How far you figure to Fort McGinnis?"

"At least a couple of days," Charles said. "We'll be all right from there on in."

Deiber grinned and stroked his beard. "Begin to wonder if we was going to keep our topknots back there. "You be a right cool customer in a tight spot."

"Didn't see you having any problems, Fred. Looks like we're going to have to ride all day, though." He patted U.S. Grant and he moved out.

"Sure like your choice in horseflesh," Deiber said. "Closer we get to the Fort, the better it'll suit me." They urged their horses toward the Musselshell.

They crossed the Musselshell River near a bend where it flowed from nearly east to straight north. The going was easier now. The trail paralleled the river and their route followed it until it reached the mouth of Box Elder Creek. The horses were tired and Charles ached all over. They had been in the saddle for a night and most of the day. It was late afternoon and when Box Elder Creek came into sight, he relaxed. "There's a good spot to camp a mile or so up the creek. Fort McGinnis is about a day's ride from here."

There had been no sun all day long and it was chilly and oppressive looking. They were still a long way from Fort Benton, but with luck they should make it all right. He studied the angry looking sky. A sharp wind blew from the northwest and clouds had gathered together into one leaden colored mass. He hunched his shoulders forward and pulled the hood of his capote over his head. U.S. Grant's body radiated heat and he was thankful his legs and lower torso were kept warm by it. Snowflakes swirled about them now and the ground was quickly covered with white. The wind rose in intensity and the figure of Deiber blurred in the white mist.

Charles pulled up in the shelter of a cut-bank out of the direct path of the blizzard. Out of the wind it seemed suddenly warm. Steam rose from the horse's bodies. Already snow begun to drift in and around the cut-bank. "Better make camp right here. Looks like we might have to wait this one out."

Deiber nodded. He had already pulled the saddle from his horse and was busy rubbing the steaming animal down. Charles unlashed the packs from the horses and stacked them into a makeshift shelter to break the wind that swirled around the cut-bank. Snow immediately started to drift around them.

"Reckon we can find some fire wood over there?" Deiber pointed in the general direction of some trees that grew along the creek. The wind blew steadily now. It was turning dark and the trees were barely visible. Charles moved closer to Fred. "I'm afraid you might not find your way back. Here, hang on to the rope. I'll tie it to a pack."

Deiber pulled a tarp from a pack and motioned to Charles. "Rig us a shelter, be back soon's I find some wood." He grabbed the rope and tied it around his waist. In a few steps his figure blurred and disappeared. Charles busied himself with the tarp and soon constructed a shelter of sorts by using the packs and rocks. Wind whipped one corner of the tarp and it rattled and popped. He held the flapping canvas while he knotted a rope to it and then secured it to a saddle. There would be barely enough room for two men to squeeze under the rude shelter, but it served to block the wind. Snow drifted high around the packs now and Charles packed it more firmly around the cracks and crevices. He felt a tug on the rope tied to one of the packs. Deiber must be coming back. The tall form of the bearded man swam into sight through the white haze, his arms filled with firewood. "More over there. You get this started, I'll go for more," he shouted above the roar of the wind. "Got some more rope? This isn't hardly long enough." He banged his arms against his sides and stomped his feet. "Getting colder than a witches' tit."

Charles handed him some more rope. "We'll need all the wood we can get. It's going to hang on for a while."

The wood was dry and brittle. Charles quickly scraped an area clear of snow and piled some of the smaller pieces into a tipi shape.

He split several pieces with his sheath knife and then from the dry insides of the wood, whittled several shavings. The match flared yellow in the darkness and flickered. He hunched over the tiny framework of wood to protect it from the wind and carefully fed small slivers of shavings to the yellow flame. It grew, wavered as the wind whipped against it, then rose and licked against the pieces of wood forming the tipi. Charles carefully piled some larger pieces of wood on top of the fire. The flames rose higher and shadows danced and cavorted against the sides of the shelter.

Deiber was back. He dropped a large arm-full of wood down and untied the rope from his waist. "Fire looks good. Reckon we can weather it now. Come daylight, we can get plenty of wood over across the creek."

"Maybe we should have made camp over by the creek" Charles said.

"Not too sure about that, cut-bank provides a good windbreak and will help shelter the horses. They're all bunched up over there, together. If it doesn't turn off too cold they'll be all right. Snow drifting in will protect them some. Bunched up like that they keep each other warm," Deiber said.

Charles spread the saddle pads and blankets on the ground under the tarp. He and Deiber crawled under, lay back and watched the fire. Its heat radiated into the shelter and they soon shed their capotes. Deiber dragged his pipe from his coat pocket and stuffed it with tobacco. "Good idea, Fred," Charles leaned forward, pulled a glowing stick from the fire and held it to Deiber's pipe, then lighted his own. "I'll fix some grub in a bit," Charles said. "Think we got enough wood for the night?"

"If we Joe Hall that big log I dragged over, it'll last until morning."

"Joe Hall, what's that?"

Fred puffed his pipe and his eyes crinkled with amusement. "Guess you Yanks never heard of old Joe Hall. My pappy told me about him when I was just a pup. Figured everybody knew about Old Joe Hall. Seems like there was an old fellow, Joe Hall by name, built this cabin

141

with a big fireplace in it. Used lots of wood. Old Joe got tired of carrying wood to it, so he got this idea for feeding that fire all winter long with the same log." Deiber knocked the ashes from his pipe and stuffed it back in his pocket.

"Don't suppose I ought to ask, but how did he aim to do that?"

"Well, he just built a trap door in the side of his cabin and then he cut down a big tree close by and shoved some rollers under it. Shoved one end right through the trap door across the cabin and into the fireplace. Pap claimed Old Joe Hall never stirred out of his cabin for firewood all winter long. When the end of that log burned down, he just shoved it a little further into the fire. Best way I know of feeding a fire all night. I figure we can Joe Hall that log all night and keep nice and cozy."

"Fred, it was a lucky day for me when I met you. Don't know what I'd do without you. How'd some hot coffee and some grub taste."

"Would hit the spot. Belly's been rubbing against my backbone some time now. You don't mind, I'm going to slip out of these boots and dry my feet while I watch you."

"Go ahead. Won't take me long. Joe Hall, huh. I can see you and Jack Taylor are going to like each other."

Charles packed snow into the pot and began to melt water for coffee. It acted as if it would snow forever. It came in spells. All through the first night the wind whipped and blew fine powder snow through the cracks in the shelter and drifted against and around the cut-bank. By morning the wind dropped, but the snow continued to fall. When Charles ploughed through it to check on the horses, he had to lift his feet high and the path soon drifted over. They went to the stand of trees by the creek and with the help of the horses pulled several dead trees down and dragged them to the camp area. From a distance, the camp looked like a hole with smoke coming out of it.

Charles began to peel the bark from the cottonwood branches and feed it to the horses. "I hope this lets up soon, it'll take a lot of bark to feed those horses."

"Not too much for us to do, anyway. Give us something to keep busy." Deiber skinned his knife along a branch and a long sliver of bark curled free. He cut it crosswise and threw it in on a pile in front of him. The wind picked up now and the snow came at them at an angle nearly horizontal with the ground. The horses huddled together near the shelter and ate the bark as fast as Charles and Deiber threw it in front of them.

"Might as well hole up again, looks like it might be getting worse." Charles tossed another branch of wood on the fire. He crawled under the tarp and lay back to dry his feet. Steam rose from his boots as the heat from the fire warmed them. "You got any kind of family, Fred?" he asked.

The bearded man combed his beard with his fingers. It was wet where the snow had melted and his fingers caught in the tangled curly mass. He pulled them free. "Used to. Wife and my two young ones, boy and a girl, died of smallpox six weeks before I got home from the war. I picked up and left. Had a case of the wanderfoot ever since." Deiber pulled out his pipe and prepared it for smoking.

"Didn't mean to pry into your private affairs. Sorry about your family."

"It's all right. I can talk about it now. Wasn't always that way, but time sort of eases things a mite." Fred shifted into a more comfortable position. "You aiming to live among the Indians all your life?"

Charles pulled one of his boots off and propped it up where it could dry off. "No, but right now I don't know what I'm going to do. Mind if I ask you a personal question?"

"Shoot, I'll let you know if it's too personal."

"Well, you see I'm married to this Blackfeet woman, Na-Ha-Ki. Been a good wife to me for two years now. But when I was in Denver, I met this woman I used to know in New Jersey. Grew up with her, played together as kids and all that." Charles paused and shifted his boot away from the fire some. "Her folks run a hotel in Denver now."

Fred began to run his fingers through his beard again. "Sounds like you got one too many women, Charlie. This woman in Denver, what's she like?"

"She's different than any girl I ever knew. We're just made for each other. I know I shouldn't, but I'd like to find some way I can go back to Denver in the spring and marry her."

"She know about the Indian girl?"

"No, I couldn't tell her, least not yet. She wouldn't understand. I just don't know what to do for sure."

Fred shoved his pipe into his pocket. "Can't be too much help to you. Maybe you just better let time help you work things out. Back there in Cheyenne you told me it could be that you might have a young one on the way. What are you going to do if you get back to your little woman and find she's got something cooking in the oven for you?"

"Don't know, but I don't suppose there would be anything for me to do, but to forget about Ruby. Fate takes some strange twists," Charles said. "Like you and me meeting for the first time at Gettysburg, then meeting again at Cheyenne four or five years later."

"Don't think I'm being too much help to you, Charlie. Things have a way of working out. Give it a little time, something will turn up."

"I guess I can't complain. If I had a problem like yours, losing my whole family and all, I'd have something to complain about." He leaned forward and peered into the leaden sky. Snow still fell in huge slanting sheets. The trampled down area around the fire was rapidly drifting over. He shoved a log into the fire. The snow on it hissed and bubbled into water, then steam as the fire dried it out. It emitted a soft sigh and a hiss, then fell into the flames.

"Looks like there's no end to it, Fred." He pulled a branch into the shelter and began to strip the bark from it.

Another night and day of the ugly weather. The drifts around the cut-bank were waist high now. The horses were continually hungry, crowding around the men expectantly, waiting to be fed. Charles studied the sky hopefully. It was still filled with leaden clouds to the east, but towards the west, the layered clouds glowed a dull red. The afternoon sun broke through at the horizon, an angry orange globe that quickly fell behind the mountain range. The snow had stopped and the temperature was skidding downward. Another cold night, but the drifted snow and cut-bank protected them from the wind. The wood supply was low and they would need to replenish it in the morning.

Fred joined Charles. He rubbed one of the horses. "Hungry, old boy." The horse nuzzled Deiber. "Hope we can bust out of here soon, for the horses sake. What's it look like to you?"

"Red sky at night usually means a clear day in the morning. If those clouds move east like I think they will, it's going to get plenty cold tonight."

"How far did you say it is to Fort McGinnis?" Fred asked.

"No more than a long day's ride along box Elder Creek. Of course, that's without snow on the ground."

"Any shelter along the way?" Fred asked.

"Sure, all along the creek. It gets as cold as I think it will tonight and tomorrow is clear, we can travel right along on top of the snow. Have to go easy on the horses though. They're mighty hungry and we will need to find food for them soon as we can."

"I'll take your word for it, but walking a horse on top of the snow I never seen before."

"Well, we'll have to see, but there's a crust there hard enough to hold a man already. I've seen it hard enough to hold a horse lots of times in this country. If the wind doesn't blow, it won't be too bad traveling."

Deiber whacked the snow with his hand. "Guess you're right Charlie, never would a thought it. Maybe we got a chance of getting out of here after all."

It was nearly dark and there was no wind. Only an occasional pop of the fire or a horse moving about broke the quiet. "Be good to get out from under that tarp. Not that I'm complaining, but it sure is getting to smell like something up and died in there."

"Hell, Charlie, I figured it was just me. Them beans you cooked for us ain't helped much. Never blown so much gas out of me in all my born days." Fred laughed. "You ever hear tell about that fella who was courtin' this gal? Just got up from a supper of beans and by the time he'd gotten over to his girl friend's house they was working on him pretty good."

Fred grinned at Charles. Small bits of ice clung to his beard and his breath formed a cloud of steam as he talked.

"What happened, Fred?"

"Well, the girl's father asked him in and they proceeded to sit around the fire and visit a while. Fellow felt the pressure building up inside of him so he sorts of eases a fart out of him, nice and quiet like. Kept on talking and he notices the girl wrinkling up her nose. Figures he'd better do something, so he looks down at the dog, laying there and says sort of accusing like, 'Shep!' Some time passes and he eases out another, and blames it on the dog again. Well, he finally feels a big one coming on. He moves over closer to Shep and eases another one out, nice and quiet like. This one was a real smeller. 'Shep,' he says again, looking at the dog. Shep stands up and walked over to the girl's old man and gives a whine."

"'Can't say as I blame you, Shep,' he sez, 'come on let's get out of here before that fellow up and shits all over you.'"

"Fred, you and Jack Taylor will get along. Jack's full of stories."

"Doesn't hurt to laugh once in a while. Does your liver good. Don't know about you, but I'm a getting all mighty cold standing out here. The stink of that shelter is better than freezing to death."

Once inside the shelter, they lay back, nursed their pipes and stared at the fire. "Talking about freezing to death reminds me of something that happened last winter up on the Marias where we camped with the Blackfeet," Charles said. "One of the men was out on a hunt all by himself and got caught in a bad storm like this one. When he didn't show up back at the camp, we figured he was a goner for sure." Charles shoved a branch into the fire and sparks flew into the black sky. He looked out and saw a star, then another. "Clearing up, sky is showing stars, bound to get cold, with no cloud cover."

"What happened to the fellow that got caught out in the storm?"

"Soon as it broke up, we went looking for him. His woman was crazy to go along. Thought for sure she was a widow. Anyhow, we'd gone only a short distance and we sighted him, walking in. Looked fit as a fiddle except for blood and slime all over him. Turned out he'd killed a buffalo just before the storm hit. He just slit it open, pulled the innards out and crawled inside. Stayed in there three days and nights. Claimed he was warm as toast."

"Well, you know what the sailor said, any old port in a storm. Sounds like one smart Indian to me."

"He is, you'll meet him, once we get to Fort Benton. White Quiver is his name."

Deiber knocked the ashes from his pipe. "I'll bank the fire before I turn in. I can feel the cold creeping in already. Wish we had a buffalo robe or two to crawl under tonight." He rose, went to the fire and began to arrange it for the night.

Charles arranged his bedding around him and closed his eyes. Thoughts tumbled through his mind. He pictured Na-Ha-Ki as she had been on the day he had left to go east. Suddenly he was anxious to see her. He asked himself, could a man love two women at the same time? He pulled his blanket about him and settled down and was soon asleep.

Morning arrived, clear, bright and bitter cold. Frost hung in the air and formed small rainbows where the sun glistened from it. Already the men's eyes hurt from the glare. Men and horses moved about slowly in the chill. Charles pulled one of the reluctant animals onto the snow and tested the icy surface. "We take it easy, we can manage. Ready to try it, Fred?"

"Sure enough. Anything to get out of this hole." The horses hung back, reluctant to leave the sheltered area, but once on top of the snow, they moved along willingly enough. The route beside the creek was slow going but they traveled steadily until midday. They protected

845-JEYS

their eyes from the glare by wrapping cloths about their faces, leaving only a slit to see through. It didn't warm up enough to melt the icy crust, and except for a horse's hoof occasionally breaking through, the crust held them with little trouble.

Light reflected from the frost in the air and formed a halo around the sun. On each side of it were miniature suns. 'Sun Dogs', they were called by the Indians. In extremely cold weather this was a common occurrence. The air was still and the horses' hooves crunched on the snow crust and the creaking of the saddles was loud and distinct. The creek was frozen solid. The trees were so thick in spots that they had kept the snow from drifting too deeply and they were able to scrape the snow away to the grass beneath. The horses ate greedily.

Charles pointed ahead. "Been a buffalo through here, not too long ago."

"Wonder what one buffalo is doing all by his lonesome?"

"Probably an old bull, chased off from the herd and wandering about by himself. Usually the wolves get them"

"Even tough old bull meat would taste good right now, Charlie. He ain't too far away, if I don't miss my guess."

Deiber was right. The lone buffalo was only a short distance up the creek. A couple of shots from Fred's rifle brought the beast down and they quickly cut the choicer parts from the dead bison.

"At least the tongue will be tender," Charles said. He piled the cuts of meat onto part of the hide and they headed back to the clearing where they had left the horses to graze. "Might as well make camp right here. Plenty of firewood and shelter. Horses can feed themselves and some fresh meat will sure taste good."

"You bet, things are looking up. Couple more days we can make it to Fort McGinnis. Reckon the weather will break long enough for us to make Fort Benton?"

"Sure, this is just an early storm, Fred. It's bound to clear up for a while before winter sets in for good. Maybe we'll even get a Chinook wind and the snow will all melt away."

"Chinook? Never heard of such an animal."

"That's right, Fred, Chinook. A warm wind coming right down the face of the mountains, and in no time, the snow will all be gone."

Fred shook his head. "Storm comes up out of nowhere and it snows for three or four day's straight. Now you telling me it will soon all be gone if this Chinook wind comes up?"

"Seen it before. You never know when it's going to happen. Every year we get a couple of them. Wind comes in from the west, warm and gentle-like, blows for two or three days straight. Temperature goes up and all the ice and snow melts."

"Charlie, you don't strike me as one to tell tall tales, but I'll just wait and see on that one. No way I'll be convinced unless I see it with my own eyes."

"It happens now and then. Sometimes it's mighty sudden. Jack Taylor told me about a Chinook blowing in so fast it gave him a lot of trouble."

Fred looked suspiciously at Charles. "Sounds like Jack's got lots of stories?"

"Sure does. I didn't say I believed it, but he told it for the truth. Said he was out with a team of horses pulling a bobsled. Snow was two or three feet deep. Had gone a couple of miles from home and this Chinook wind hit him in the face. Turned the rig around and headed for home on the dead run. By the time he got to the trading post the horses and front runners were still on the snow, but the rear runners were dragging behind in the mud and the dog was running along choking to death from the dust."

Deiber laughed heartily. "Some story. I believe that Jack and I'll get along even if I do come from the South."

"I don't hear much out of you about the war, but if I'm not getting too personal, it strikes me as a bit strange that a fellow like you would want to get tied up with a couple of Yankee traders like Jack and me."

"Thought about that, some. Way I see it there ain't too much difference between a bunch of darkies and the Indians. They're both pretty ignorant of the white man's ways."

Charles swung from his horse and began to make camp. Deiber's response had surprised him. He sensed he'd need to be careful with how he responded to Fred's last statement. "You ever own slaves?"

"No, my kin were all hill people. Couldn't do much more than scratch out a living. But from what I seen though, most of the niggers needed a white man to look out for them or they'd starve to death."

"Well, you're right about one thing. The Indians are ignorant about the ways of the white men, just like a lot of Negroes. But there is one big difference as far I can tell."

Fred looked at Charles quizzically. "How's that?"

"The Indians I know have never been enslaved and are used to freedom. They may not understand the white man, but the white man doesn't understand them either."

"Well, I always figure I was a fair man, and I'm willing to make up my own mind about things from what I learned." Fred grinned at Charles.

His personable manner had a way of winning a person over. "You'll do well if you take that approach. Come on, let's fix some of this buffalo. I'm hungry as a bear."

The fresh meat revitalized their spirits. The horses grazed contentedly and Fred and Charles relaxed. In the morning they struck out for Fort McGinnis. The cold weather held and they made good time.

They arrived at the fort in the late afternoon. It held a small contingent of cavalry in command of a Captain Keener. Charles had met the man a year before in Fort Benton. He provided them with quarters and invited Fred and Charles to eat dinner with him and his wife.

"Not sure that Yank would have been so quick to invite us to eat with him if he'd knowed I fought with the South. He 'peers like a right feisty sort to me."

"Blackfeet don't much like him," Charles said. "I expect we can manage with him for a night or two though."

"What's the Blackfeet's beef about him?"

"His men caught a group of them with some horses they'd stolen from the Crows. Now the Blackfeet and the Crow have stolen each others horses as long as anybody knows." Charles pulled on a boot. "Crows probably stole most of the same horses from the Blackfeet at one time or another. Blackfeet figured they were just getting back what rightfully belonged to them. They didn't take too kindly to Keener taking their horses and giving them back to the Crows."

"Seems like a stupid thing for Keener to do. Sort of like getting between a married couple when they are scrapping. You don't look out they'll both turn on you."

"Was stupid. But Keener doesn't strike me as being too bright."

"We had our share of them kind on our side too."

"Bout a week later, the Blackfeet stole their horses right back."

"What happened when Keener found out about that?"

"He came up to Fort Benton looking for White Quiver and the horses. White Quiver was way ahead of him. He'd already gone to Canada with the entire herd."

"Sounds like one smart Indian. Looking forward to meeting with that one." Deiber tucked his pants legs into his boot tops and stood up. "How come you took a squaw for a wife anyhow?"

Charles studied his friend before answering. "When you meet Na-Ha-Ki you'll understand. She takes good care of me. She's beautiful, and I love her. I just wish I knew what to do about her and Ruby. I don't suppose it makes much sense to you, but I wish there was a way I could keep them both."

"I hear that some of the Indians have more than one wife. You ever think about becoming a Mormon? They can have as many wives as they like."

"As much as I love those two women, I don't think it'd work with either one of them. They are strong minded, and if one finds out about the other one, they'll both split the blanket with me." He added as an afterthought. "I didn't know how much I missed my own people though, until I was with Ruby for a while."

151

"Just give things some time. It'll work out someway. Always does, you know."

"Easy for you to say, it isn't your problem. Ruby expects me back in the spring. If I left Na-Ha-Ki, she could always find a good Piegan man. There's more than one who'd like to have her. I wouldn't leave her poor."

"So, your mind's made up, you're going back to Ruby in the spring?"

"Not for sure. But if there aren't any children for us to worry about, Na-Ha-Ki will forget about me after a while."

"I've seen lots of people marry away from their own kind and it always seems to bring some sort of problem down on them."

"I'm not sure how Ruby will take it when I tell her I had an Indian wife."

"Don't buy trouble. I suspect you'll work it out some way." Deiber laughed and slapped Charles' back.

Charles placed his hand on Fred's shoulder. "You've been a lot of help. I hope you and Jack hit it off. If I have to leave to go back for Ruby next spring, he'll need all the help he can get." He paused. "Other thing, Jack and I don't call our wives 'squaws'."

"How come? I thought that was what all Indian women were called."

"Not around us. Squaw is a white man's term and it is usually degrading. Just thought I'd let you know, so you won't be ignorant."

Deiber grinned at his young friend. "I knowed right off there was something I liked about you, Charlie, now I know what it is. You can cut a man down to size the prettiest I ever seen without even raising your voice. I done stand corrected. Won't happen again."

Charles straightened his clothing. "We better get to cracking or we'll be late for that meal Keener said his wife was going to cook for us. Someone else's cooking will taste good."

"Why, you done hurt my feelings. From now on, you do all the cooking."

"No, Fred, you fix things just the way I like them. I always did like my meat raw. You cook just the way I like it."

"Too late my boy, you tipped your hand. You're the cook now. Them that complains about the food and cooking in my camp does the cooking."

Charles grinned at Deiber. The man was easy to take. It seemed as if he could turn almost any situation into humor. Maybe the man would stick around for a while and help with the trade.

"Penny for your thoughts, Charlie."

"Just thinking about what was going on at Fort Benton. Nearer we get to it, the more I wonder how I'm going to deal with Na-Ha-Ki."

"Won't be more than two or three days now, isn't that right?"

"That's right, and I sure have some mingled emotions."

"Let her ride, there's not much you can do worrying about it anyhow." Deiber abruptly changed the subject. "Wonder if Keener's wife is the only woman on the post?"

"Guess we'll find out soon enough. Why do you ask?"

"I sort of like the idea of having women around, not that I mind your company, of course. Was plenty of male company during the war. I told myself if I ever got out of it alive, I'd never get caught where there weren't at least one or two women around."

"Didn't think people bothered you that much, Fred."

"They don't usually, but that Keener fellow rubs me the wrong way. Maybe it's just because he's an officer and a Yank, but I can smell arrogance a mile away."

"You're probably right Fred, but try to keep it from showing. He's in a position of power and could cause problems for us. He is already playing the Blackfeet and Crows against each other. He's hired a bunch of Crows as Scouts and Guides. Doesn't set too well with the Blackfeet, especially when the Crow scouts are guiding Keener through Blackfeet territory."

"I'll try to keep my lips tight. When we supposed to go to dinner anyhow?"

"Keener said he'd send an orderly over to tell us, soon. Maybe that's him now." Charles opened the door.

45-JEYS

"Private Smith, sir. Captain Keener requests the honor of your presence for dinner in ten minutes."

"Thank you, we'll be right there," Charles said to the short, dumpy private.

The food was delicious, and Mrs. Keener was delighted to display her culinary skills to her appreciative guests. She was a slim woman who carried herself well. When she found that Charles had originally come from New Jersey, she was ecstatic. "You don't know how much pleasure it brings me to talk to someone with a little bit of culture." She glanced quickly at her husband. "My home is Philadelphia. We were almost neighbors."

Captain Keener leaned back and puffed on a cigar. "Donald, must you smoke that horrid thing in here?" She wrinkled her nose in distaste.

Keener refilled the wineglasses and winked at Deiber. "Woman talk, thinks she has to say that. Don't pay any attention to her." He blew a puff of smoke at the ceiling. "So you're heading up to Fort Benton. I'm sending a patrol up there soon as the weather breaks. Be glad to accommodate you until then."

"Thanks, we'll be heading out as soon as we can," Charles said. He stole a glance at Deiber. The bearded man appeared relaxed. He sipped his wine and watched Mrs. Keener take the dishes from the table.

Keener ground his cigar into his cup." You know a trader at Fort Benton named John Stott? Big sort of man."

"Yes, I know John." Keener had Charles' attention. Old John must be up to usual trouble-making behavior. Maybe if he drew Keener out, he could learn something useful. Mrs. Keener was at her husband's side now.

"Wasn't Mr. Stott that wonderful man who was talking to us about starting a Christian mission for those poor heathen Indians?"

"Yes, dear." Keener turned away from his wife and addressed Charles. "John has been a big help to me in dealing with the Indian problem up there at Fort Benton." I didn't get a chance to talk with your partner. What did you say his name was?"

"Jack Taylor" Charles said. So old John had wormed his way into a position of confidence with Keener. Mealy mouthed old hypocrite. He wondered how old John could have helped Keener. "You been having Indian trouble up there?" He tried to keep the concern from his voice.

"Not lately, but there's some of them bears watching. Fellow named White Quiver. Stole some horses some time back. He went to Canada with them. John just sent word that he's back. I'm sending a patrol to apprehend him before he gets away."

Keener's grating voice played on Charles' nerves. "You gentlemen cooperate with me and I can guarantee that we'll get along fine." Keener arose and went to the kitchen. "Mildred, let's have our dessert and then we can sit and talk a while before these gentlemen have to retire."

"Yes Donald, I'm getting it ready now." As she came in from the kitchen with a hot apple pie, Deiber smiled. "Ma'am, your cooking sure does beat it all." Keener looked at him sharply.

"Why Mr. Deiber, it's not often I receive such a nice compliment." Keener grunted, and mumbled with his mouth filled with pie, "very good, Mildred."

"Do you have a wife, Mr. Tucker?" She asked.

"Yes ma'am."

"You must be anxious to get back to her. What part of the East did she come from, New Jersey?"

Deiber's eyes showed amusement at Charles' discomfort. He stroked his beard and looked away from Mrs. Keener.

"No, ma'am, she's from Montana. She's a Blackfeet Indian," Charles said quietly.

"My lands, did you hear that, Donald? A Blackfeet Indian." Her hand went to her mouth in confusion. "Are you Christians?"

"My father was a minister."

"Still doesn't keep you from being a squaw man." Keener said abruptly.

155

Charles stared at Keener and his wife. Being a Christian obviously meant a great deal to Mrs. Keener, and her husband's disdain for squaw men was obvious. It was a time for a distraction. He surreptitiously slid his pie plate to the edge of the table and with a quick movement, knocked it to the floor. "Oh, I'm terribly sorry, let me help you with that." He knelt and started to pick up the broken pieces of the plate. "I hope this wasn't your good china."

"It's all right, Mr. Tucker. I know how it is with you men. Donald is always dropping things, aren't you?"

"Yes, dear." She gathered the broken pieces and left to dispose of them.

Charles quickly engaged Captain Keener in conversation. "How long have you been in the army, sir?"

"Enlisted when the war started in 1860. Let's see, about eight years now." Charles was on safer ground now. Maybe the woman would forget what they had been talking about before he broke her dish.

"Were you at Gettysburg?"

"Sure was. We handed Lee a real thrashing. My outfit was under General Custer. He got his commission as General there, for handing Jeb Stewart and his boys a real whipping. Man's going to go a long way before he's through."

Deiber stiffened and turned toward Keener. His eyes narrowed and he was about to speak when Charles shook his head. Deiber caught the signal and picked up his glass and gulped down the remainder of the wine.

As Charles spoke, he moved his body slightly between Deiber and Keener. "I was there at Culps' Hill, mostly. You must have been off to our right a ways. Sometime I'd like to go back and see that place again."

Keener turned toward Fred. "You fight in the war, Fred?"

Deiber slowly approached Keener. They were face to face. His eyes glared at the younger man and his mouth worked back and forth. "Yep, Yank, I sure was. I was one of those Rebs you said you whipped. Let me tell you something, there ain't no way two Yanks could whip one of Jeb Stuart's boys in a fair fight. Old Jeb had just rid plum around the whole Union army afore that fight with Custer. His men had been in the saddle three days and nights and were half dead from lack of sleep." Fred's voice was soft, but dangerous sounding. "Way I see it, Captain, you Yanks were lucky Jeb and his boys weren't rested. Been a different fight then."

Keener grinned. "You Johnny Rebs never could admit it when you were whipped. Come on Fred, it's all over now. Let's let bygones be bygones." Keener slapped Fred on the back. Fred stiffened, then moved away from him.

"Charlie, I think I'd best be going to bed. You can stay and chew the fat if you like, but I'm tired." He bowed at Mrs. Keener.

Her hands clasped and unclasped as she glanced first at her husband, then at Fred. "I was about to pop some corn. Sure you don't want to stay just a while longer?"

"No thank you Ma'am. Thank you again for your hospitality."

"Just a moment, Fred. I'll be right with you." Charles said a few words of appreciation to their hosts. He touched Fred on the shoulder and they left.

"Don't think we left a friend back there, Charlie. Sorry if I caused you any problem. I couldn't take that jackass any longer."

"I don't think it made a bit of difference, Fred. I had all I could handle with his wife. Soon as she got on that business of Christianity, I knew we were in trouble."

"You got out of it pretty slick, even if you did break one of her dishes. She like to had a fit when you told her you were married to an Indian. Don't know how you kept from reacting when he called you a Squaw Man. Was right proud of you son." Deiber pushed the door open. "Suppose we can get out of here first thing in the morning?"

Charles pulled his boots off and rolled onto the bed. "I'd sure like to get to Fort Benton ahead of that patrol. Keener can cause a lot of trouble for the Blackfeet."

"Think the captain will lock White Quiver up?"

"Have to catch him first. More than likely he'll be gone time the patrol gets there. All the same, Old John is a troublemaker, Christian or not."

"We ought to pull out of here first chance we have. I don't cotton to traveling with Yanks, present company excepted."

Charles' eyes lifted. "Thanks, Fred. For a Reb you aren't half bad." Charles ducked the boot Fred tossed at him.

"What you going to tell Keener? Nosey bastard will want to know why you can't wait for his patrol."

"I'll tell him my wife is pregnant, expecting any time, and I'm anxious to get home. Might be the truth anyhow."

"Sounds like a good plan, Charlie. If he decides to send somebody along with us, we'll just have to figure things out as we go along."

Deiber patted the bed. "Feels pretty good after sleeping on the ground. Bet you'll be glad to cozy up next to that Na-Ha-Ki woman of yours."

"Sure will, Fred. Can hardly wait. Maybe we ought to get out of here in the morning instead of waiting another day. Horses can make it all right if we don't push them too hard."

"Suits me just fine. Sooner the better. I'm not sure I can take too much more of this Yankee hospitality."

It was easier to get away than they had expected. Captain Keener was busy the next morning and Charles sent word to him they regretted having to leave so soon. If they ran into trouble with the weather they would hole up and wait for his patrol to come along to help them.

They made good time and by mid afternoon they reached the Judith River and made camp. During wintertime the Blackfeet usually broke up into small bands and spread out along convenient streams where food and water for the horses were available. He scanned the horizon, looking west toward Fort Benton, looking for signs of them. There was another stream between them and the fort and since they had not seen anyone along the Judith, he was sure there would be a camp somewhere in the vicinity. Some of the Blackfeet always wintered in that area. The smoke from their campfires ought to be visible. The sky was clear, but still no signs of smoke.

"What you looking for, Charlie?"

"Signs of a Piegan camp. Ought to be seeing smoke up ahead. We'll likely run into some Blackfeet tomorrow." He dragged the saddle from his horse and started to make camp. Toward evening when the Piegan started the cooking fires there would be some smoke visible. Maybe they'd see some sign then. He looked again, shading his eyes against the western sun. Still no smoke. No need to worry, but it was strange. Ought to have seen somebody by now. Plenty of buffalo around. He watched as a herd trailed along the Judith River. "Missouri is only twenty miles north of here, Fred. Judith runs right into her. Look up there." He pointed at the shaggy animals, bunched together in the failing light.

"How many of them critters you figure are on these plains, Charlie?"

"Don't know, Fred. There must be millions of them. One time Jack and I tried to count a herd. We were on top of a bluff along the Missouri and they were crossing on the ice right below us. Wasn't long, we quit counting and just estimated. Must have been 25,000 in that herd alone."

Deiber looked thoughtful. "Down South, Kansas and Oklahoma country, they're hunting them just for the hides. Shipping them back east for the leather."

"Well, there's plenty of them. Probably won't hurt to thin the herds some."

"They're doing a lot more than thinning. The hunters have a gun, Sharps 50 caliber, which can kill three or four hundred yards away. They set up a stand just over a hill from the herd and pick them off one at a time. Sometimes they pick off fifteen or twenty before the herd spooks and runs off. A good marksman can kill 50 or 75 in a day, easy." He observed the buffalo trailing along the Judith in front of them before going on. "Skinners come along and skin them out, just leave the meat lay there for the wolves, or to rot." Deiber had a strange look on his face.

"Something wrong, Fred?"

"Yes, but it's not something I can do anything about. I keep thinking of the stink of those rotting animals lying all over the landscape."

"Don't the Indians kick up a storm, Fred? They're dependent on the buffalo."

"Did for a while, but you know how it is. The Indians just don't stand a chance. After a while they just moved off following the herd that was left."

"There's a lot of buffalo. Hard to believe they could kill enough to make a difference."

"Don't know, Charlie, I hear tell there used to be a lot more beaver a few years back. Old trapper I met in Cheyenne told me when he first went into the mountains every stream was full of them. He didn't think they'd run out either."

"That's what Jack said, too."

Deiber stared at the brown stream of shaggy beasts. "All them skinned animals a lying around on the prairie just rotting away, makes a man think."

"Hunters like that come into this country, there's going to be a lot of trouble with the Indians. The Cheyenne, Sioux and Blackfeet won't take it laying down."

"Don't know, Charlie, but it seems to me what with the likes of that Keener fellow and with his kind running things, the Indian don't stand much chance." The bearded man shook his head slowly. "Don't mean to sound pessimistic, but if I don't miss my guess, you're seeing the end for the buffalo and Indian both."

"Maybe so, Fred, but I don't believe it. Wait until you meet the Blackfeet. They're a different kind of Indian than you're used to seeing."

"Been looking forward to it, especially that wife of yours. Must be some pickings to latch onto the likes of you." Fred slapped his young friend on the back. "We been standing here jawing at each other and it's mostly dark. We best fix something to eat. You're the cook now."

*   *   *

They took a last look at the buffalo heading toward the Missouri. The scene etched itself on Charles' mind and he muttered, *"A blind understanding, heaven replied."*

A still night. A wolf howled, then another and soon the lonesome sounds filled the air. Charles sat up as the sound jarred him awake. One of the beasts, silhouetted by a full moon, sat on a butte across the river, nose pointed to the sky. Over and over it flung its mournful call toward the moon. The wolf finally tired of his serenade and trotted off, bushy tail arched over his back like a giant feather. Charles studied the scene with a painter's eye, fully awake now. Might as well check the horses. They would be restless. Funny, how the wolves howled like that in the dead of winter. Their mating call was so different. You couldn't miss it.

He was restless himself, maybe because he was getting closer to home. His thoughts turned to Na-Ha-Ki as she had looked on the levee the day the steamboat headed out toward Saint Louis last spring. It had been a long time. Wolves weren't the only ones who mated in the winter. She would be glad to see him. He'd deal with the Ruby thing later, but right now he'd try to keep things on an even keel for a while.

In the moonlight, shadows stood out distinctly. He watched his own, a ghost against the snow. A feeling of unreality came over him, as if only he existed in all of this vast expanse. Snow crunched beneath his feet and the sound was loud. The horses, alerted to his presence, snorted and pawed. He checked their tethers, then relieved himself. His warm urine arched and fell in a yellow stream, drumming loudly against the frozen snow. Steam rose into the still air. He shivered and tugged his capote closer about him. After a last look at the horses he started for the shelter.

Suddenly the sky filled with color. Long ribbons of light rippled and danced across the broad expanse, a huge drape that hung high in the sky and fell to the horizon in the north. Over and over the yellow, orange, blue and purple sheets of lights undulated. The snow reflected the colors. To the north across the Missouri River, the Bear Paw Mountains etched themselves against the wavering curtain. The aurora borealis it was called, or northern lights. There were so many things that were beyond understanding. It was enough to make a body wonder about the why of things. Perhaps the creator had his easel and pallet out himself.

The lights' intensity slowly diminished and faded into a few feeble flickers that glowed against the backdrop of the Bear Paws.

And now as Charles stood under the great inverted bowl of the night sky and marveled at the interplay of raw natural forces, he felt an inner ache to articulate his emotions. He sensed a slight tremor of the earth, or was it just his imagination. He wondered if the sage, Omar Khayyam, had felt like this when he created those beautiful verses that comprised the *Rubaiyat*.

A new understanding of the meaning of Omar's words infused Charles now. Was there no end to the depths of the *Rubaiyat*? He searched his mind until he recalled the verses that fit his mood. Now he had them.

> *There was a Door to which I found no Key:*
> *There was a Veil past which I could not see:*
> *Some little Talk awhile of ME and THEE*
> *There seem'd—and then no more of THEE and ME.*
>
> FIRST ED., XXXII
>
> *Then to the rolling Heav'n itself I cried,*
> *Asking__ "What Lamp had Destiny to guide*
> *"Her little Children stumbling in the Dark?"*
> *And__ "A blind Understanding!" Heaven replied.*
>
> FIRST ED., XXXIII

Charles was suddenly aware that he was cold. He swung his arms about to start his circulation going and headed for the shelter. Fred snored softly, oblivious to the light show he'd missed. Charles fed the fire, then crawled under the tarp, pulled his blankets about him and was soon asleep.

*   *   *

He awoke to the sound of dripping water, that and Fred Deiber cursing. "Damnedest country I was ever in. Freeze the balls off a brass-monkey one day and it's hotter than hell the next. Charlie, you'd better get your ass out of there before you drown. Biggest mess I ever saw."

Fred squatted on one of the saddles and surveyed a gradually widening pool of water that edged its way toward Charles. Deiber rolled his bedroll into a soggy bundle and tossed it on top of a tarp.

Charles sat up and rubbed his eyes and quickly rescued his bedding before the pool of water reached it. He pulled on his boots. "What are you doing Fred? You look like a rooster."

"Trying to get dried out. Last thing I knew before I went to sleep, it was cold as hell. Woke up this morning and everything is melting. Water hit me, was still asleep. Figured I'd pissed the bed."

Charles roared and Fred threw a wet sock. He caught it, wrung it out and tossed it back. "Didn't believe me about the Chinook wind. What do you think now?"

Fred hopped over to the dry spot where Charles' bedroll had been. "Sure is warm. This rate, most of the snow will be gone before the day is out."

"Yeah. I'm glad now we got a head start on Keener's boys. We ought to break camp soon as we can if we're going to get there ahead of them."

"Sure enough Charlie. I'll take care of the horses and start packing while you fix breakfast. You sure cook the way I like it. Glad I turned the job over to you."

"All right Fred, I can take a hint." Charles threw some tinder on the fire and started to cook breakfast. As he cooked, he studied the western sky. Still no sign of smoke. Strange. Should be some Piegans camping nearby. Well, they'd find out soon.

845-JEYS

The horses perked up with the change in temperature. By midmorning patches of grass poked through the rapidly melting snow and they stopped to let the horses browse on it. There was still no sign of The Piegans. Square Butte loomed in the distance. Charles was in familiar territory now. Just ahead, the trail would take a sharp turn around it. Four lodges were pitched in a broad meadow at its base, but there was no evidence of life except for several magpies. They squawked and flapped about, then settled down when the men on horseback stopped.

The breeze brought the stink of death with it. It had been the same at Gettysburg. Bloated bodies that quickly rotted in the sun and putrid odors that permeated everything. Charles spat. The taste of death was everywhere. He breathed small shallow breaths. Deiber looked sick. "Whew. It looks bad."

"No need for you going over there, Fred, I'll take a look." Charles dismounted and flung a rock at the magpies. They scattered and screamed their protests at him. He held his nose and thrust the flap of the first lodge aside, dropped the flap and pulled back, then looked again. The interior was dark, but enough light came through the opening so he could make out the figures inside. They lay on robes, three of them. A man, woman and young child, their bodies swollen and black. Magpies had pecked away the eyes and maggots crawled from the empty eye sockets and rotting flesh from parts of the bodies. Charles backed away, then in a daze, inspected the bodies more closely. Dizzy and sick, he staggered to his horse and leaned against it. His stomach contracted and knotted. He retched again and again until he ached with pain. At last the heaving stopped and Deiber silently handed him a canteen of water. Charles rinsed his mouth and spat. "Smallpox, must have been at least six-eight weeks ago. Dead. Everybody. You had it?"

Fred nodded. "Any of them people you know?" Deiber's voice was gentle, quiet. His arm rested on the younger man's shoulder.

"So far gone, I couldn't tell, except for one. He was a dwarf called Short Man." Everything about the camp was in disarray. Now nausea assailed Charles again and he momentarily was disoriented. Waves of color swept across his tightly closed eyelids. His lungs burned and he cautiously released his fingers from his nose and a putrid stench from the rotting corpses surged into his lungs. He knew he had to escape. Spittle issued from his mouth and his eyes burned, and a faint ringing sounded inside of his head. The odor of human excrement mingled with an overpowering sweet sickening putrid scent that permeated everything. He retched again and puked once more, then gagged on the vomit that burned in his throat. Over and over he heaved and puked until his stomach ached from the violent reactions.

Charles' legs trembled and suddenly his body sagged and sunk to the ground. He began to vomit once more, but nothing came out except a burning bit of acid that burned his throat and mouth. He spit it out.

Deiber helped Charles move upwind from the Indian encampment. "We best be going on, son. Ain't nothing we can do here."

The magpies were back. They milled around, squawking, arrogant and obscene. Charles picked up a large tree branch and flung it at them and they scattered, circled and lighted again.

"Come on son, let's get out of here." Deiber led Charles' horse to him and they made a wide sweep around the camp. Some distance upstream, they stopped. Charles and Fred dismounted and washed themselves all over, then burned their clothing and put on fresh. The icy water was refreshing, and although they rinsed their mouths with it again and again, the taste of death remained. Fred extracted a bottle from his pack. "Take a swig, Charlie."

Charles tilted his head and drank several long gulps. He wiped his mouth with the back of his hand. "Thanks Fred. Mighty good whiskey."

"Medicine, boy, Medicine. What do you say we make camp right here?" Fred took a long pull on the bottle and handed it back to Charles.

845-JEYS

Charles held it up and eyed what was left in the bottle, then quickly took a swig and handed it back to Fred.

"Feel better, boy?"

"Sure enough, Fred. Jack Taylor once came upon camp like that. Back in 1837 when the smallpox first hit the Blackfeet, it nearly wiped them out. Jack says they lost almost half the tribe that year."

Charles felt light-headed now. Fred's voice seemed far away and faint. "You just set there, Charlie. I'll fix up camp and take care of the horses."

"Thanks, Fred, you're a real pal. Don't know what I'd do without you. Best damn Reb I ever knew." Charles smiled at Fred. "You know, Fred, after we met that night there at Culps Hill at Gettysburg, I went back up the hill and told Jack Taylor I met a nice fellow down there, even if he was a Reb. I was right, too. Nicest fellow in the world."

"You were mighty thirsty that night Charlie. Here, have another swig of this." Fred handed the bottle back to Charles. He tilted it up and emptied it. "Fred, I drank all of your whiskey. You aren't mad at me, are you?"

"Naw, Charlie, that's what it's for. You just stretch out there and rest a bit while I take care of the horses."

The bearded man pulled a blanket from one of the bedrolls and tossed it over the sprawled out figure of his friend. Charles leaned back and closed his eyes. When he awoke, it was morning. The sun shone brightly, warm on his stretched out body. He sat up quickly, then held his head. Deiber squatted by the fire and filled a cup with coffee. "Couple of cups of this will help" Deiber said smiling.

"Thanks Fred." Charles took the tin cup from Deiber. He brought it to his lips, then drew back from the hot metal. He blew on it, then sipped it while he eyed the bearded man.

"Hungry?"

"You bet! I'll fix it, Fred."

"No need, almost done. Last of the buffalo. Ain't nothing like buffalo meat first thing in the morning."

Charles took the plate of food Deiber offered and began to eat. "Wonder if any more of the Piegan had trouble with the smallpox?" He looked in the direction of Fort Benton, concerned for Na-Ha-Ki and his friends.

"We'll find out soon enough. We best be getting." Deiber said, not answering Charles' question. He rose and started to pack. The warm weather held, and nearly all of the snow had melted. By mid-afternoon, Fort Benton came into view and their horses' pace increased. They sensed the end of the journey. Smoke spiraled from the chimney of the trading post.

"Well, Fred, here she is. Reckon we ought to go in?"

"You go ahead, boy, you might have somebody to talk to before you want to bother with me. Just show me where you keep your horses and I'll take care of them for you."

Charles pointed to a lean-to stable at the back of the post and Fred moved off with the horses. Na-Ha-Ki was at the rear of the post when Charles entered. She looked up, squealed, and dropped the pot she held. It clanked against the wooden floor and rolled back and forth with a thunking sound. She stood, arms opened and smiled. "My man has come back. You did not forget me!"

Charles swept her into his arms and brushed her cheek. It was wet with tears. "You have been gone so long." She pulled herself free and examined him. "Are you all right?" she asked.

Charles studied her. She was no longer the young girl he had left six months before. The dress she wore was bulky and full. He pulled her to him again and gently felt her soft, swelling body. He looked into her eyes. They were soft, brown, like those of a doe.

"My man will have a son."

Charles kissed her. She snuggled close and laid her head on his shoulder. Her soft body merged with his and he felt a warm stirring within him. So, he was to be a father. His hands sought her body again and the wonder of it began to penetrate. Na-Ha-Ki sensed his mood and snuggled happily against her man. She murmured unintelligible words to him, soft, meaningless, happy words as her emotions bubbled over at the joy of her man's return.

Charles' mouth found hers and they kissed once more. His lips stole to her ear and he softly whispered to her, "Our son, our very own son." His arm tightened about her. The door to the post opened and they pulled quickly apart. It was Jack Taylor.

"Wagh! This here chile turns his back and you come traipsin' in here without warning." His hand sought Charles'. "How be you hoss?"

"Fine, fine, Jack. Looks like I got back just in time." He glanced at Na-Ha-Ki. "You meet Fred Deiber yet?"

"Sure did, where'd you latch onto him?"

"It's a long story and I'll tell you later. Where is he?"

"Unpacking the horses. Wanted to wait till you were ready for him."

"How have you been?"

"Tolerable, tolerable," Jack said, eyeing his partner for a moment. "Have you heard about small pox south of here?"

"We came across some, but made a wide birth around it soon as we recognized what had gone on. Was Short Man's bunch. Only four tipis. Everyone dead for some time." Charles shook his head. "We burned our clothes and washed up and got out of there soon as we could."

"Bout all you could do. We ain't seen nothing around here, but you never know." Jack said. "Don't mention about the small pox to the women, only upset them about something they can't do anything about."

Charles nodded, wondering what Na-Ha-Ki might say if he told her about the camp he and Fred had seen.

"We best be fixing you fellows up with something to eat. Expect you're hungry."

"Where's Crow Woman?"

"Over to the Piegan camp. Expect her back shortly." Jack placed his arm around Charles' shoulder. "Sure good to have you back," he said.

Na-Ha-Ki took Charles' hand. "I will go fix some food. Tell your friend to come in." She squeezed his hand and hurried toward the kitchen. Charles noticed that she had filled out in the hips also. The young girl he had left six months ago was now a woman.

"Looks like you brung some plunder back with you."

"Something for everybody, but especially the ladies," Charles said.

He went to the door and called Fred to come in to be introduced.

When Charles informed Deiber about Keener and the patrol he was sending up to check on White Quiver, they decided that it could wait, at least until after supper. In the meantime they needed to get Deiber fixed up with a place to stay.

"Fred, I want you to meet my wife. This is Na-Ha-Ki," Charles said.

Deiber smiled at her and slowly stroked his beard. "Charlie, you've been holding out on me. You never told me you married such a pretty gal." Na-Ha-Ki shyly smiled, not sure of everything Fred had said, but it was obvious that he approved of her. His friendly smile was disarming. She intuitively sensed that the man would be her friend.

"The food is ready. You men sit down and I will bring it," she said. Crow Woman had arrived and expressed her pleasure with Charles' return, then helped Na-Ha-Ki with serving supper. The meal over, Charles showed Deiber a room he could use for the evening. Jack glanced at the kitchen where the women were washing the dishes. His voice lowered. "Don't want them to hear this, but there's a heap of trouble brewing among the Piegan."

Charles leaned forward resting his elbow on the table and his chin in his cupped hand.

"Anything to do with John Stott?"

Deiber shoved his chair back and stood up. "Listen, you fellows want to talk private like, I'll give the women a hand with the dishes."

Jack leaned back in his chair and laughed. The deep furrows above his nose smoothed out and his eyes twinkled. "Fred, you best let this chile learn you something right away about those ladies. You go out there and offer to help them and one of two things is going to happen and both of them is bad. If they don't ask you to mind your own business,

I'll be surprised. That will be the nicest thing they'll do. Otherwise they might threaten you with your life."

Deiber stared at Jack. "It appears as if I need a little education. I thought I'd strike up an acquaintance with them. Maybe you best educate me. Don't want to offend any lady. Especially one of your wives."

Charles reached into his pocket for his pipe. "Don't underestimate this guy, Jack. You notice the way Na-Ha-Ki warmed up to him? Smooth talker, he is. He's liable to go out there and sweet talk those two into most anything."

"Come on Charlie you'll be giving Jack the wrong idea about me. I just wanted to bow out in case you two wanted to talk private like."

Jack motioned Deiber to sit down. "Fred, if you going to help us, you need to know what's going on. Charlie tells me you're all right and that's good enough for me. Now let me warn you about those ladies. They're Blackfeet and proud people. If a Blackfeet woman needs help, she'll ask for it and not before. Ain't that right Charlie?"

"You're damn right," Charles said. "I learned the hard way. Killed a big grizzly, see his hide?" He pointed to a rug spread on the floor. "Na-Ha-Ki was picking berries while I was chopping some wood nearby. It seems like the bear was picking on the opposite side of the thicket. When they met at the end, I'm not too sure who was the most surprised, she or the bear."

"What happened?" Fred said.

"Na-Ha-Ki screamed and ran toward me. The bear just stood there surprised and I grabbed my gun and shot him. Got him right in the mouth. Took three more shots before he fell dead, almost at our feet."

"Holy Jumping Moses, Charlie, get to it and tell Fred what happened to you when Na-Ha-Ki caught you trying to help her flesh the skin?" Jack slammed his fist against the table. "Hell, I'll tell him. You'll probably get it all messed up anyhow. You won't believe it to see that sweet, innocent looking girl of his, but she picked up that fleshing hoe and ran Charlie around the lodge two or three times, threatening to beat the hell out of him if she ever caught him interfering with her work again."

"Like to have seen that. What did she say to you?" Deiber grinned at Charles' discomfort.

"The Blackfeet haven't any swear words, but if they had, she'd been using them. Worst thing she could think of was to call me was a Dog Face. That's pretty bad language for a Blackfeet. She's got a temper, but most of the time, she's easy to get along with. You just don't want to try to push her around, that's all," Charles said proudly.

"Thanks for stopping me from offering to help, Jack. Looks like you saved me from getting scalped or some such thing." Deiber fished in his pocket for his pipe. "If you don't mind, I'll just set here and listen. Maybe I'll learn something else I need to know. Seems like I've got a lot to learn about this country and the people in it."

"Charlie, I think you picked a good one. We are going to get along fine, Fred. You got an opinion, let her fly. Never can tell, you might know just the way the stick floats about something we don't."

Jack lighted a lantern and they all leaned over the table and talked. The women watched from the doorway of the bedroom. Na-Ha-Ki went to the kitchen and brought them some coffee. "Hits the spot." Charles put his arm around her as she stood by his chair, her full body pressed against his arm. There was a sudden movement within her. He squeezed her waist. "We'd better be fixing Fred up with a place to sleep. We'll have to bunk you in the store room tonight, Fred, but tomorrow we'll get a place fixed up proper for you." Charles said.

"Any place is alright. Don't go to any trouble. You know me, I can sleep anywhere, anyplace, anytime."

"That room don't shine, but we'll get you fixed up better tomorrow," Jack said. "We'll see you in the morning, Fred."

"You folks make me feel right at home," Fred said. He smiled and closed the door.

"Maybe you can go over and see White Quiver first thing in the morning," Jack said to Charles. "Tell him about that patrol." Charles nodded.

Charles' arm tightened about his wife as they moved toward their room. It would be nice to have her curled up next to him under a warm robe. He suddenly stopped and they pressed close to each other and kissed. His hands slipped to her body and ran cautiously over it.

"Come," she said. She took his hand and led him to their room.

CHAPTER 17
ENOUGH ROPE

*(But not the Master-knot of Human Fate.)*xxxi

Two days after Charles and Fred arrived, Keener's patrol showed up at Fort Benton. White Quiver had frustrated them by taking his horses and crossing into Canada before they arrived. Sergeant Hannigan was disgusted and worried. He jerked his broad brimmed hat free and mopped his bald head with his bandana. "Keener's going to be madder than hell. Mark my words, someone is going to pay for this. He's a hard man."

"Bob," Jack Taylor said, "you and your boys can stay long enough for a drink and something to eat. Horses could stand some food and water, anyhow." He motioned toward the water trough. Come on in and sit a spell."

Hannigan licked his lips. "Keener wouldn't like us doing that." He looked at his horse. "Guess it won't hurt to stop for a little while. Horses could stand a rest." He dismounted and followed Jack into the trading post.

"Sure you won't have a drink, Bob?"

"Well, maybe just one."

Jack poured out two cups of whiskey. They sipped from them. "So White Quiver gave you the slip again?"

"No more than I expected. Can't tell that Goddamned Keener nothing. He don't know nothing about Indians."

Jack refilled the Sergeant's cup. "No fault of yours, Bob. You did the best job you could. He didn't really expect White Quiver to not know you were coming did he?"

"Damned if I know. The simple-minded bastard still thinks he's at West Point, I guess. Them Indians will make an ass of him before it's all over."

Hannigan's face was red and beads of sweat stood out on his forehead. He mopped them off, and drained his cup. "Have to go, Jack. Keener will be madder than hell if I go back empty-handed. Got any idea where that red skunk White Quiver went?"

Jack refilled the Sergeant's cup. "Stick around a while, Bob. Crow Woman's got the fixings almost ready. Fat cow for everybody. Tell your men to wash up and come on in."

"Don't know." Hannigan eyed the cup of whiskey. "Food sure smells good."

"You just set there and finish your drink. I'll go tell your men for you."

Hannigan smiled and waved his arm lazily at Jack. "Sure it ain't too much trouble?"

"No, when I first saw you, I told Crow Woman to fix enough for everybody." Jack put an arm about Bob. "Nothing is too good for my friends." Hannigan lifted his cup and saluted Jack with it. "Mighty good whiskey, Jack." He licked his lips and his face took on a conspiratorial look. "You and them Piegan is thicker than thieves. Sure you can't tell me something about that thieving White Quiver? I got to get Keener off my back someway."

The deep furrows over Jack's nose knit together, as if he were in deep thought. "Now this is just between us coons. Friends have to scratch each other's back."

The Sergeant placed his cup down quickly and whiskey slopped from it onto the table. He mopped at it with his coat sleeve, then leaned forward and stared at Jack intently. His body swayed back and forth as he strove to focus on the trader's face. "You know me, Jack, you say it's between us and that's where she'll be. It's just that damned Keener. I only got eighteen months to go till retirement."

Bob mopped his brow again. "Don't know why I had to get stuck with that double barreled prick anyhow. He's out to get me."

"Bob, I can tell you something if you don't tell Keener where you got it. You ever meet old John Stott?"

"Yeah, big fellow. Him and Keener are close."

"Well, old John is putting it to Keener right along with White Quiver. I can't tell you how, but old John is arranging for White Quiver to deliver horses in Canada. He's probably the one who tipped off White Quiver about you fellows coming after him."

Hannigan leaned back in his chair and smiled. "Always figured that old coot for a swindler. Him and his fine talk. Don't know if Keener will believe me though."

"That's all right Bob. Even if he doesn't, it'll give you something to tell him to get him off your back for a while." Jack put his arm over Hannigan's shoulder. "There has been small pox down south of here where White Quiver hangs out. He might even be dead by now. That ought to satisfy Keener."

The Sergeant smiled to himself and emptied the cup as Jack went to the door and spoke to the soldiers. Hannigan thought as he watched Jack, 'friends like Jack are hard to find.'

It had been more than two months now since Charles and Deiber had arrived. For the most part the Piegans were along the Marias. To their knowledge, only the band that Charles and Fred had encountered had suffered from the smallpox. Jack had not been able to talk them into a dry camp this year and John Stott traded whiskey freely with them. Rumors of trouble in the camps came into the post from time to time and Jack was concerned.

175

"Jack, you worry too much. If you give old John enough rope, he'll hang himself," Charles said.

"Maybe you're right, but he's sure stirred up a heap of trouble. Crow Woman says there was another killing last week."

"I know it isn't good, Jack, but the Piegan have to learn about the evils of whiskey just like the white man did. Take White Quiver, he wouldn't touch the stuff with a ten-foot pole.

"Where you find one of him, you'll find a hundred more, crazy for the stuff." Jack said. "Even some of the children are drinking it. Lots of gambling going on up there too. Mix that with the drinking and sometimes tempers flare. Been some people killed and hurt on account of the stuff."

Deiber had sat silently throughout the discussion. He stroked his beard slowly, then spoke in his soft southern drawl. "Wal it 'peers to me that Charles got a point. Them Indians is growed up boys, Jack. Ain't no way we can keep them from buying the stuff. If old John don't sell it to them, somebody else will. Hudson Bay up in Canada uses it all the time."

"That's right Fred, but damn it!" Jack was on his feet now and his black eyes snapped. The table thumped as his fist hit it. "Stuff is illegal as hell and any damned fool can see the way the stick floats. Blackfeet is already pushed up here in the corner of Montana. White man is running cattle on the land south of here." Jack stopped and caught his breath. "You think a fool like that Keener is going to do anything to stop the trade with the Indians?"

"Now, Jack, it's not all that bad. There's plenty of buffalo left and nobody is going hungry." Charles smiled at his partner.

Deiber's face grew thoughtful as he listened to the partners arguing. "Might not be a bad idea for someone to take a little trip up there. Find out for ourselves what is going on," Fred said.

"What do you think you can do about it anyhow?" Charles asked.

"Don't rightly know, just thought maybe it'd make more sense than sitting here arguing about it. Least we could see for ourselves what the situation is."

"Fred, you sure hit on a good idea. How about you and me going tomorrow?"

Charles rose to his feet. "You two think you're going off and leaving me here, you got another think coming. You better figure on me going along too."

Jack smiled. His white teeth stood out in contrast to his black beard. "Son, Na-Ha-Ki is about to pop with that child. You best stay with her. Woman needs a man at a time like that."

"How the hell would you know. You haven't ever had any kids."

"Wal, maybe he has and maybe he ain't. But I have, and Jack knows what he's talking about, Charlie. Your woman needs you. Your place is here, son." Fred's arm was about the younger man's shoulder, his voice gentle.

"Thanks Fred, I guess you're right. Forgot for a while there. Somebody's got to take care of the post anyhow," Charles said.

CHAPTER 18
TROUBLE ON THE
MARIAS

*(And this was all the Harvest that I reap'd—)*_{XXVIII}

Fred and Jack left early the next morning for the Marias River camp. It was January, the month of the moon when the snow blows into the tipis. The day was cold and raw. They pulled the hoods of their capotes over their heads and hunched on their horses, faces down, out of the biting wind.

Fred followed Jack. His horse needed no guidance and his body moved to the rhythm of his horse. The steady movement was soothing, hypnotic and before he realized it, the mental guard that he unconsciously kept in place lowered. In his mind's eye he was back in Louisville.

It was spring, the dogwoods were in bloom and in the midst of the death and destruction of the war, new life sprang anew everywhere around him. He stood by a bedside with a sprig of dogwood in his hand. "Thought you might like this." He bent and kissed her lips and placed his face against that of the child who nursed at her breast. The infant was momentarily distracted, and lost the nipple. He gently guided the child's mouth back to the nipple and it sucked contentedly again.

"He's just like his daddy," she said. She smiled at him and ran her hands through his beard. The horse stumbled on a rock hidden beneath the snow. The break in the rhythm roused Fred from his thoughts. He shook his head and urged his horse to the side of Jack Taylor. "There's a spot up ahead there, let's pull in and make a pot of coffee," he said. The coffee warmed them and in the shelter of the thick brush, the air was still. "You figure Keener will stir up any trouble with the Blackfeet this winter, Jack"

"Naw, he probably thinks Old John Stott has done him in. By now, Sergeant Hannigan has told him that cock and bull story I gave him about White Quiver and John Stott. He'll probably be stirring the pot trying to get the goods on old John. Serves them right, they deserve each other."

"You sure fixed old John up, if it works."

"Yeah, it ought to keep both of them out of our hair for awhile."

"How far we have to go before we get to the camp?"

"Not far, another eight or ten miles. Several bands spread out up and down the river. Charlie's in-laws are in one of the first camps. Charlie and Na-Ha-Ki have spent a couple of winters up here."

Jack glanced at the sky. "It's beginning to ugly up. We best be moving out." He kicked the fire apart and covered the smoking embers with snow. The snow hissed as it hit the still burning wood. The wind swirled about them in gusts and the forms of Jack and his horse, Monte, were dim blurs in a white mist.

Suddenly Jack stopped, held up a hand and indicated for Deiber to wait. He cupped his hand to an ear and listened intently. "Thought I heard shots . . . . there they are again. Come on." He kicked Monte and galloped in the direction of the sounds. Suddenly two figures on foot emerged out of the storm. When they saw Jack and Monte, they scurried into the thick brush. Jack dismounted. "There's something strange going on," he muttered. "Best go careful, Fred."

Jack stood next to Monte and stroked the horse's head. Another figure staggered down the trail toward them. It was an old man. Jack recognized him now. It was Old Bull. He would recognize that skinny figure anywhere. The old man stopped, then dived into the brush by the trail. Jack ran after him. Old Bull had fallen and lay huddled on the ground, his arms wrapped over and around his head. He cringed and looked up at Jack, then began to chant a mournful song.

"I'm not going to kill you," Jack shouted. Then, when he realized he was speaking English, he repeated himself in the Piegan tongue. Old Bull stopped his chant and for the first time recognized Jack. "Tell me what happened."

The old man spoke rapidly and at times incoherently. Jack motioned to Deiber. "Best get off the trail and out of sight. This be a Piegan, Old Bull by name." He jerked a thumb in the direction of the old man. Old Bull was on his feet now and had pulled the blanket Jack handed him about his body for warmth. "We done rode into a mess. He says the Blue Coats attacked their camp without warning. Killed most everybody, women, children, anybody they could find. Several lodges of people killed."

Jack glanced up the trail and put his finger to his lips as they withdrew into the thick brush. The trail was suddenly filled with blue-coated soldiers riding two abreast and in their lead rode Captain Keener. He sat rigid on his horse, his face stern and inflexible. The creaking of leather saddles, an occasional clank of metal and their horses' hooves were the only sounds. The old Indian crouched in terror and began to chant. Jack grabbed him and held his hand over his mouth. A Blue Coat stared at the bushes, raised his gun, then lowered it and went on. The long column filed past. They waited for a while, and then leaving Old Bull behind, Deiber and Jack mounted and hurried toward the camp.

It was worse than they expected. The Blue Coats had fired the camp. Women, children and old people lay where they had been killed. Blood and gore smeared their still bodies. The Blue Coats had gutted them all. Deiber tried to turn away from the carnage, but was unable. The camp was quiet, except for the hissing sounds of the tipis burning into the snow. A child whimpered. Deiber dismounted and searched about. He heard the sound again, this time nearer. He shoved some brush aside and under a pile of tree branches where its mother had hidden it, lay a child. The bearded man picked it up, opened his coat and warmed it with his body. It cried softly in low tones, then nuzzled him and sucked at his wool shirt. He pulled his capote tighter about him and looked about the camp. Suddenly he was sick. Sick of killing, sick of life, sick of being a human being. The child under his coat stirred and he opened the coat a bit and studied it. His hand crept to the child's and he cupped it in his. He pulled the tiny body closer to him and leaned against his horse. Huge, rasping sobs broke from him. His frame shook with the violence of them. At last the sobs slowed and stopped. He was washed out, exhausted.

Jack was at his side. The man's usually dark face was white. "Fred, we got to get back. I saw Na-Ha-Ki's family over there. All of them dead."

"All of them?"

Jack spoke slowly, his voice tight and low. "Her brother was lying in front of the tipi. Looks like he tried to protect his family the best he could." Jack's mouth worked back and forth as he chewed his lips. "Sons a bitches ripped him wide open, let him lay there with his guts hanging out," he paused. "Died while I was looking at him." Jack's mouth worked back and forth again. He glanced at Fred. "What you got?" Fred carefully opened his coat and revealed the baby. "I'll be damned, ain't over two or three days old. Maybe Crow Woman can take care of it. Let's go, can't do no good here." Jack shook his fist at the sky. "God damn! God damn you! If ye be a loving God, you got a hell of a way of showing it. God damn Keener, rotten sons a bitches."

Deiber gently guided the trader toward Monte. Fred mounted, looked around, then pointed his horse toward Fort Benton. A gust of wind blew a piece of burned tipi past. It lodged against a snow bank. Deiber stared at it, then opened his coat and peeked at the sleeping baby. It stirred and he closed the coat and held the child closer to him. It cried lustily and waved its fists until one found his mouth. He sucked greedily. "It's all right, baby, you got a daddy. Old Fred's gonna take care of you." The crying stilled and the bearded man smiled.

Suddenly Jack reined Monte in and eased him off the trail. At a motion from him, Deiber waited. In a short time Jack pulled his horse back on the trail beside Deiber. "No sign of Old Bull. Must have found some shelter." He glanced down at the bundle in the bearded man's arms. "Best keep moving." He kicked Monte and they moved off in the direction of the trading post.

*   *   *

The wind was still. The storm eased and leaden clouds lay like an oppressive sheet ahead of them. The sun that hung low over the mountains at their backs broke through to cast orange and charcoal streamers across the gray mass. Deiber glanced at the scene to the east. Over and over a rhyme ran through his mind...Red sky at morning, sailors take warning, red sky at night, sailor's delight. Tomorrow would be a clear day. He was tired and he gave his horse its head. It knew its way home. He cradled the child inside his coat carefully. Now his thoughts were again on his former home, back in Louisville Kentucky. He saw himself walking to and fro, slowly, gently, and humming a tune to the child in his arms. The baby awoke and stirred. Its eyes opened and studied the man who held it. A bubbling laugh and a tiny fist tightly clenched about the bearded man's finger. Man and child, lost in each other. A moment of contentment. Feelings swelled inside the man. It was as if he would burst with them. They started somewhere deep within and expanded and grew outward until his throat restricted the emotion. He sighed, breathed deeply, then relaxed. He smiled, contented. A child. His son, his own son. A tiny fist clamped about his finger tightened and jerked.

Fred was awake. The reins wrapped about his hands had tightened when the horse turned his head. Deiber shook his head and he was abruptly back in the present moment. He studied the figures of Jack

Taylor and Monte ahead of him. In the distance a yellow patch of light spilled from the trading post onto the snow. The baby stirred restlessly and whimpered. It must be hungry. Suddenly a surge of emotion welled within him. This child must survive. It was the only thing that made sense to Deiber now. He rocked the infant back and forth and its crying stilled.

Jack spoke. "I'll go ahead and tell Crow woman about the child. We have to think up something to tell Na-Ha-Ki."

"She may know already, Jack. Those Blue Coats were heading this way."

"She doesn't have to know about her parents and family."

"Ain't no way to keep it from her. She's going to find out sooner or later. Maybe Crow woman can think of something to tell her, least until she has her own child." Jack pulled a rectangular box from his pocket. One corner of it was burned partially away. He opened it and the tinkling sounds of a waltz floated incongruously through the air. He quickly closed it and stuffed it inside his coat. "Was a present Charlie gave his daddy-in-law," he said.

A figure in the doorway awaited them. Deiber grasped his burden and slid carefully to the ground. "Charlie, go get Crow woman if you can. I got something to tell her, I don't want Na-Ha-Ki to hear," Jack said softly.

"Can't, Jack, she's with Na-Ha-Ki. Taking care of the baby." Deiber and Jack looked at each other. Charles smiled, and his eyes sparkled. "What's the matter with you two, ain't you seen a real live daddy before?" He laughed at the shocked look on their faces. "Happened less than an hour ago. Na-Ha-Ki and I have a son."

Jack grasped Charles' hand. The older mans' forehead was furrowed. "Congratulations, son."

"Put your horses away and come on in and see him." The blond man stared at Jack's face. "What's the problem, Jack?"

Jack slowly withdrew his hand from within his coat and handed Charles the music box. "Dead, all of them. Na-Ha-Ki's whole family and the rest. Keener and his boys attacked the camp. Killed most everybody. I'm sorry, boy." His arm went around Charles' shoulder. Jack gently squeezed his friend.

Charles stared at the box. "You sure, Jack? Doesn't make sense. What about Au-Ti-Pus? Was he killed too?"

Jack mutely nodded his head.

Charles shifted the music box to his other hand. He opened it and it started to tinkle. He stared at it with a disbelieving look. He slammed the box shut and the tinkling sounds stopped. Charles stuffed it into his pocket. "Lousy bastards. No good, stupid, ignorant sons of bitches!"

The child in Deiber's arms cried. Charles stared at Fred. "That's right Charlie. You ain't the only one who become a daddy today." Fred opened his coat. "Found him in the camp, hidden under a pile of wood. Only living thing there." Deiber studied Charles' face. "Hate to ask you, but as soon as Na-Ha-Ki's milk comes in, well, you know, this baby needs a mother's feeding. It's the only chance it's got." Fred stroked his beard.

Charles pulled Fred's coat open and looked at the baby again. His lips tightened. "Rotten bastards would have killed him, too, if they'd found him."

Deiber nodded. Jack Taylor's arm tightened around Charles' shoulder. He glanced at the baby in Fred's arms. "I'll talk to Crow Woman now, she'll know what to do till Na-Ha-Ki can nurse him." He stepped around Charles and went into the post.

Charles voice was tense. "I better talk to Na-Ha-Ki. Don't know what to tell her about her family."

Fred studied Charles. "Best tell her the truth, son. Most women are stronger than a man thinks. With you there to back her up, she'll manage. Maybe the baby will help things a bit."

Charles nodded and walked into the trading post. When Charles looked at Na-Ha-Ki, and their newly born child, it was as if he was facing a new reality. They were his responsibility. Her family was dead, killed by the Blue Coats. He and their baby were all the family she had now. How could he tell her what had happened. As he mulled over what he would say to Na-Ha-Ki, he made a mental note that he would have to let Ruby know the truth, that he had in a moment of passion, taken advantage of her. He didn't expect her to forgive him, but it was the only honorable thing he could do. He would send her a letter as soon as he could. Any lingering thoughts about Ruby had to be dismissed.

Charles went to his wife and haltingly and gently informed her of what had happened to her family. Fred was right. Na-Ha-Ki was emotionally strong. After a brief period of sobbing, she kissed Charles and held their son out to him. "Hold your son, we will go on. There are three of us now," she said. She smiled as Charles took their son and held him tenderly.

45-JEYS

CHAPTER 19
TWISTS AND TURNS OF FATE

*(I came like Water, and like Wind I go.)*XXVIII

Six months had passed since Charles left Denver, but Ruby thought about him every day. It was spring and he would be coming for her soon. As she daydreamed over her job of cleaning the hotel room window, she gazed westward toward the front-range of the Rockies. To the south were Pike's Peak and Colorado Springs, sixty-five miles away. Directly in front of her, the 14,000 foot Mount Evans towered over the city of Denver. Seventy miles north along the rugged barrier, Longs Peak loomed, a huge shadow on the horizon. Water from the melting snows that covered the high peaks already surged down Cherry Creek toward the Platte River. If the mild weather held, the high passes would soon be open to travel.

She shoved up the window, letting in the thin dry fresh air. A slight breeze, with a hint of pine odor in it, ruffled her hair. She brushed a wisp of it from her face and looked north and westward. Etched against an azure sky in a rough vee shape, a flock of Canadian geese winged north. As she watched, they veered, swung in a sweeping circle and flew directly overhead heading due north again.

Ruby pressed her fingers to her lips and blew a kiss toward them. Perhaps they would fly over Charles. He may have started on his way to Denver already. In her mind's eye she saw him. He sat easily upon his horse. His tall rugged body was clothed in soft buckskin, fringed at the sleeves and along the legs. His reddish blond hair flowed over his collar. Glints of sunlight reflected from it. His blue eyes sparkled and a smile played about his lips. Charles Tucker, her beloved, coming to claim her! The sound of the geese honking came faintly to her ears. She smiled a secret smile, then kissed her palm and blew another kiss in their direction.

The stage from Cheyenne was due at any time. Perhaps the letter she had been expecting from Charles would come today. A gust of wind swept through the open window and the door slammed shut with a bang. Ruby started, then pulled the window closed. She had work to complete before she could go to check on the mail. Her fingers trailed along the frame of the picture that Charles had left with her. She paused and studied the painting. Charles had captured the rugged grace of the old silver beech tree perfectly. The tree house that Charles and her brother Robbie had constructed nestled in its limbs. A crude ladder wound its way up the massive trunk. Pleasant memories of warm summer days spent building the cozy hide-away returned to her. The boys had magnanimously allowed her to have an occasional peek into their 'secret club house,' All this for her untiring help of finding and carrying building materials to them, and making innumerable trips for cold drinks and lunches packed by their mothers.

How she savored that day when the boys agreed to let her actually climb onto the wooden platform! She tumbled her feelings about it over and over in her mind, for it was the day she had fallen in love with Charles. The boys had climbed the ladder ahead of her. They perched on the platform and peered over the edge at her while she climbed towards them. "Come on Sis," Robbie said impatiently. "Me and Chuck got important things to do."

Ruby's mouth turned down and her eyes filled with tears. Charles extended his hand and smiled at her. "Don't pay attention to him, Ruby, he's always in a hurry." He made room for her beside him on the platform. His arm encircled her and held her securely.

Ruby smiled. "Thank you, Charles," she said pointedly looking at her brother. "At least someone appreciates all the work I did for you in building this place."

"We couldn't have built it without your help, Ruby," Charles said. He turned to Robbie. "I vote we let Ruby into our club."

Ruby's brother looked disdainfully at his sister. "This is a Bachelor's Club and girls can't belong."

"Well I've changed my mind," Charles said, "We'll call it The Three Musketeers Club and Ruby can be a member."

Ruby quickly kissed Charles on the cheek.

"Geez, Sis, you don't have to act like that," Robbie said. "If Chuck wants you to be in the club, I guess it'll be all right with me. Just don't bring any of your friends around and no more of that hugging and kissing. This is our secret hiding place now, just us three." Robbie grinned at them."

"The Three Musketeers, that's a good name. Where'd you get it?" Ruby asked.

"You know, from the book by Alexander Dumas. He wrote the Count of Monte Cristo, too."

"Aw, I never read it." Robbie said. "Seems like you've read everything, Chuck."

Ruby had looked admiringly at Charles. "Well, I guess I have read a lot of the books in father's library, anyhow," Charles said.

A sharp knock on the hotel room door jolted Ruby back into reality. "You there?" called her mother. "There's a letter for you. I think it may be from Charles."

Ruby jerked the door open and grasped the brown envelope in her mother's hand.

"Hold on, not so fast, you'll tear it."

"I'm sorry, it's just that it has been so long in coming."

"I understand," her mother said. "I'll leave you alone so you can read it. I was just teasing you.

"Thank you," Ruby said wishing her mother would leave. She pressed the letter to her, and closed the door. She took a deep breath and raised the letter to her lips, tentatively ran a finger along the edge of it, then carefully cut one end of it open and slid two sheets of paper from it. Charles' neat handwriting covered both pages. Over and over she read the letter and at last lay down on the bed and sobbed.

What did Charles mean when he said he had been unavoidably detained and wouldn't be able to get back to Denver as soon as he expected? Was something wrong with him? What was he hiding from her? Had something gone wrong in the business? Maybe he had been hurt and didn't want to worry her about it. But then he had assured her that he was all right and in good health. She had hoped he would be on his way to her already. There was a soft knock on the door.

"Ruby, are you all right?" Her mother's voice sounded anxious. Ruby sat up and wiped her tears, then opened the door. Her mother appeared worried. "You want to tell me what Charles said?" she asked. A hesitant smile crossed her face.

"Oh, mother," Ruby burst into tears and buried her face in her mother's shoulder. "Charles can't make it this summer and I was so sure he'd be back. He told me he would." Her words were muffled and choked. The older woman patted her on the back and helped her to the bed. "I know he truly loves me," Ruby sobbed.

"Now Ruby, baby, you just lie there awhile I get some cold cloths for your face. You'll be all right." She patted her daughter again and hurried to fetch a pitcher of water. She poured some of it into a china wash basin, wet a cloth and pressed it to the distraught girl's eyes and forehead. "There, there," she murmured over and over. Ruby lay back and smiled gratefully at her mother as she held the cloth to her daughter's tear stained cheek.

45-JEYS

"Thanks mother. I'll be all right now. I'll be down to help you with dinner in a few minutes." Her mother leaned over the girl and brushed her lips to her cheek.

"You just lay here and rest, honey. I'm sure Charles will come as soon as he can." She squeezed Ruby's hand." When a man is getting started in business, sometimes it is very difficult for him." Ruby's face brightened. "He probably didn't want to worry you. Men are always like that. They think we women don't have much sense for business."

Ruby felt better now. Her mother's explanation seemed reasonable. After all, Charles had said that he had been unavoidably detained. That was it! He was having trouble with the business.

Ruby's mother patted her daughter's hand. "Your father thinks he runs this hotel all by himself and I let him think he does," she said. She laughed lightly. "I guess you know by now that most of the major decisions are made by me." Ruby nodded and wiped her eyes with the cloth.

"I've suspected as much,"she said. "How do you manage it?"

"It isn't always easy," her mother said. "Your father can be headstrong at times, but usually if I wait until the time is right and drop a suggestion or idea, he'll pick it up and later decide that it was his own."

Ruby smiled and swung her legs over the edge of the bed and sat up. "I'm all right now." She stood and straightened her dress. "You've been really helpful, Mother," she said. Her heart raced within her. She knew now what she must do. Charles needed her. A woman's place was beside her man. If Charles couldn't come to her, she'd go to him. She would manage it some way. "I'll be right down, Mother. You can go ahead."

"Good girl." Her mother patted Ruby and left.

The letter lay where Ruby had dropped it on the bed. She carefully smoothed it out and studied it once again. The last words were clear to her now. How could she have missed their meaning before? She read the closing sentences again. "When I left Denver last fall, my intention was to return for you this spring. However, I have been unavoidably detained by a serious problem that I hope to have resolved by this fall. Please forgive me." Ruby lowered the letter and sighed as she read the last line, "I love you, I love you, I love you, always. Charles."

Yes, that had to be it. Charles had a problem and needed her by his side. Like Mother said, Charles didn't want to worry her about it. Ruby's emotions swirled within her and she pressed the pages to her lips. Charles had always been so thoughtful of her. Well she would show him that she could help him. She pictured herself at the trading post in Montana. Charles stood beside her, tall and strong. His arm would be around her. Together they could overcome anything. Wherever he was, that was where she should be. Her parents would understand.

There would be parties going through Denver and on west to Montana. Father could help her arrange to join one of them. Of course, he would refuse to hear of it at first, but her mother wasn't the only one who knew how to handle him. Ruby smiled to herself, folded the letter and stuffed it into her bosom. It nestled between her breasts and she imagined that it was Charles' lips kissing her. Suddenly she felt warm all over.

She glanced at her image in the mirror and made a face. If Charles saw her now, he'd laugh at her. She grabbed her comb and pulled it through her hair, then dabbed some powder on her cheeks and under her reddened eyes. She bit on her lips to redden them. The face that looked back at her from the mirror was a merry one now. The eyes were bright with excitement and the mouth smiled at her.

On impulse, she swept her long skirt high and admired her trim legs and figure. If things worked as she had planned, she'd be doing that for Charles before the summer was over. She dropped her skirt, stuck her tongue out and grinned at herself. Her feet moved in quick light steps as she hurried down the hall to the stairs.

Ruby had been right about her father's reaction to her going to Montana by herself. It took a week for him to come around to seeing her way. At first he was dumbfounded, then outraged. When he finally realized that his strong-willed daughter was not going to give up until he agreed, his attitude softened. At last he smiled, put his arms about her and said, "Ruby, we've raised you to think for yourself. I guess we haven't anybody to blame but ourselves if you do what you've been taught." He held her at arm's length and looked her up and down. "My baby has turned into a woman, and a fine looking one at that," he said. He brushed his eyes with the back of his hand and pulled out a handkerchief and blew his nose loudly. "If it was anybody but Charles Tucker, I'd never consent to it. But sending you to Charles is almost like sending you to your brother. Remember how you three used to call yourselves 'The Three Musketeers?' You and your mother will have to get cracking to get your things ready." He smiled a crooked smile at her. "I can't say I'm not jealous of losing you to another man again, but you'll still keep a place in your heart for me, won't you?"

Ruby's eyes filled with tears and she hugged her father. She raised her face to him and smiled. "I've got the best father and mother in the entire world." She squeezed her mother's hand, "Thank you, thank you. Charles and I will come back as soon as we can, you'll see."

As Ruby left, Robert's arm slipped around his wife's waist and held her close. "What do you think is going to happen for our little girl?"

"Only time will tell. But in the meantime, we need to get practical and make sure she is protected as far as money goes," Ruth insisted.

"Of course, of course," Robert agreed. "Her inheritance from her Aunt Laura will help with that. I will go to the bank in the morning to make arrangements for her."

"It's like you said, Robert, she's a woman now and it's time for her to make her own home. All we can do is support her all we can and hope for the best. At least we know Charles comes from a fine family. If he is half the man his father was, he'll be all right for Ruby." She paused and sighed, "I just wish Montana wasn't so far away."

"It won't be forever, Mother, she'll probably be back next spring and who knows, maybe one of these days we'll be grandparents."

"Oh you men are all alike." She smiled and kissed him. "It would be nice to hold a baby again. It's been so long, I've probably forgotten how."

"It'll come back to you." Robert McIntyre smiled and shook his head. To think, Ruby, his little girl, a mother. "Do you suppose they might call him Robert?"

"What are you talking about? Ruby hasn't even left for Montana yet and you've got her naming a baby after you! Besides it might be a girl. I wonder how Ruth Tucker will sound?" She nudged her husband. "Come on, let's figure out how we can help Ruby to find a way to get to Fort Benton. We can't let her go unless it is with someone who can see that she is safe. What about that Major Ozman you were talking to yesterday?"

"Say, you might have something there. I've got an idea. He told me that his wife and a couple of the other officers' wives are going along with them to Fort Ellis. That isn't too far from Fort Benton. Perhaps he could provide her with an escort from there on. Surely she would be safe with them."

"That's a wonderful idea. You always think of something, for even the most difficult problems." She kissed him again. "I'll go help Ruby plan. Maybe you can find the Major this evening. I don't think they plan to stay too much longer, so the sooner you speak with him the better."

She left his side and hurried toward the stairs. He watched her admiringly. He wondered what she would have thought if she knew that he had already made arrangements for Ruby to accompany Major Ozman and his party to Montana. Well, he'd let Ruth think she made all the decisions. She liked to think she did anyhow.

It would be nice to have a son around again. They had been terribly lonely since Robbie had been killed during the war. Ruby could do a lot worse than Charles Tucker. A stiff drink was what he needed. After all, a man didn't lose a daughter and gain a son every day. Ruby's father threw his shoulders back and whistled a tune as he strode briskly toward the barroom.

Three weeks after Ruby left with Major Ozman for Montana, a letter from Charles arrived in Denver. Shortly after the birth of his son and the massacre of Na-Ha-Ki's family, Charles had written a second letter to Ruby, disclosing to her that he was married and that he had a child.

*   *   *

The year was 1870 and an uneasy peace existed between the hostile Cheyenne, Sioux and the White Man. The U.S. Army prowled the plains, harassing the Indians. They, in return, responded by attacking small parties of whites who crossed their territories. It was these same territories of the Cheyenne, Sioux and Crow, which would have to be crossed before Ruby and her party could reach Blackfeet country and Charles Tucker. Only the Crow Indians were friendly to the whites.

Major Ozman had signed on several of the Crows as scouts. They would travel with the party until they reached Fort Ellis. The Major had assured Ruby's parents that their daughter would be safe in his care. After all, he'd reminded them, he wouldn't have considered allowing his own wife to make the trip otherwise. They were accompanied by a small contingent of U.S. Cavalry, about twenty men in all.

He had requisitioned a renovated ambulance so the women would travel in style. It was pulled by a four-horse team driven by Corporal McFarling, a born-again Christian. At any opportunity, he would engage whoever would listen, in a discussion about his religious beliefs. After a few rather spirited arguments with the Corporal, Ruby decided he was a lost cause. There was no place in his previous religious experience to allow for some of the liberal religious views that Ruby held.

However, when she become bored with the endless chatter of the Officer's wives she occasionally baited the Corporal into a discussion. He was actually a kindly soul and took his duty of looking after his charges seriously. He carried his well-read Bible with him everywhere he went. Ruby came to like him and admired his dedication to his beliefs. In time, she came to feel somewhat ashamed that she had, in their discussions, taken advantage of his mental limitations.

There were four women, Major Ozman's wife and the wives of Captain Baines and Lucas, as well as Ruby. All of the women were older than Ruby and had traveled with their husbands before. They were congenial and regaled Ruby with stories about their experiences as Army wives. Ruby especially liked Mrs. Ozman because, in many ways, she reminded her of her own mother.

A Lieutenant Hawkins was assigned to stay close to the ambulance at all times. Every morning the serious looking young man stood by their vehicle to assist the ladies if they needed help. When he offered his assistance and Ruby thanked him, his face brightened and he replied, "My pleasure, Miss McIntyre. If I can be of service to you at any time, please feel free to call on me."

Ruby smiled and settled herself in her seat.

Major Ozman raised his hand, signaled, and the party moved out. The day was warm without being hot. The soft breeze was refreshing and Ruby soon loosened her hair and let it down. She felt happy and content. The road toward Cheyenne paralleled the front range of the Rockies. Mt. Evans towered above them and sixty miles to the north along the southern Wyoming border, sunlight glistened from the ice and snow covered slopes of Longs Peak. In the distance, its lower slopes loomed like a huge shadow. The scenery fascinated Ruby. As the sun rose higher and the distance between them and Longs Peak closed, the angular interplay between sunlight and shadows constantly changed. The peak sparkled and glistened like a many-faceted jewel.

Ruby had never felt so free, happy, and overwhelmed by absolute beauty. She breathed deeply and smiled to herself. Charles was out there. In his short stay in Denver last fall, he had attempted to communicate his feelings to her about the mountains. More than once they had looked at them while he spoke of their grandeur and beauty. She felt that now she understood more clearly how he felt. To think, in a few short weeks they would stand hand in hand and share such beauty together.

45-JEYS

Her thoughts were interrupted by a clatter of hooves. Lieutenant Hawkins touched his hat and smiled as he passed. His face was friendly and pleasant looking. She smiled and waved at him. He saluted and galloped toward the front of the line.

"Looks like you have an admirer," Mrs. Ozman's voice sounded a little wistful.

Ruby smiled, "He is just being friendly."

Mrs. Ozman nodded, then laughed, "I noticed that he's friendlier to you than to us old biddies."

The other women laughed and nodded in agreement. "He does cut a fine figure," one of them said.

Ruby settled back in her seat and closed her eyes, trying to visualize Charles.

However, Ruby's free spirits and youth did not go without notice. As Mrs. Baines remarked, "a widowed woman without a wedding ring and who chooses to be addressed as 'Miss Ruby', was likely to bring trouble down on herself if she wasn't more prudent."

But Ruby's pleasant manner and her willingness to help in any way she could, soon won the women over. Mrs. Ozman's approval of Ruby helped. Most of all, the women all liked the fact that Ruby was a good listener. The first week of the trip passed swiftly. They were now two days out of Cheyenne heading northwest along the Bozeman Trail. On Sunday, they had drawn up among a small grove of trees along a creek in buffalo country at the edge of the Cheyenne and Sioux territories.

Lieutenant Hawkins proved to be good company. He was knowledgeable about the country and kept Ruby informed as to what to expect next. When she discovered that he was from Trenton, New Jersey, they had a bond in common.

Although the other women were pleasant enough company, their constant chatter about children, families and seemingly insignificant matters, bored Ruby. The companionship of someone more her own age was welcome. It was Sunday, a day of rest. The young officer and

Ruby strolled away from the camp to observe a herd of buffalo some distance away.

"Be seeing Indians soon," Lieutenant Hawkins said.

"Really, what makes you think that?"

He watched the brown bodies of the buffalo herd as it slowly flowed in a steady stream toward the north, then pointed to a cloud of dust. "Where there's buffalo, there's generally Indians. Usually follow the herds this time of year."

"You think that cloud of dust is made by Indians?"

"Could be. Might also be hide hunters." He pointed to the west. "Something's stirring the herd. Look over there."

The steady brown stream was separating like a river parting, one branch moving leisurely northward. However, the other branch flowed directly at them in a rapidly increasing pace. A huge cloud of dust rose above the herd obscuring from vision what might be behind it. A rumbling, roaring sound came to their ears. The herd was in full stampede now, headed directly toward the small rise where the two of them stood. Lieutenant Hawkins glanced at Ruby, and then back at the camp. They were on foot and there was no way to reach it before the wildly charging animals reached them. The first of the beasts had reached the foot of the slope already and would be upon them soon.

"Get behind me," the Lieutenant said. "Can you shoot?"

Ruby nodded. He handed her his cocked pistol. "We drop one or two, maybe the rest will go around. Don't fire till I do." He knelt and aimed at the first of the charging herd. The noise was deafening. The buffalo were a brown wall that moved rapidly toward them. Ruby held her breath and clenched the heavy Colt revolver in both hands and pointed it in front of her. Her heart thumped wildly. She felt dizzy. Kenneth reached back with his free hand and pressed her close to him. "Stay next to me," he shouted.

She took a deep breath and her aim steadied. His rifle cracked once, twice, three times. The brown wall was upon them. The bison's shaggy heads were low to the ground and froth dripped from the crazed beasts' mouths. Their black pointed horns glistened and their eyes rolled wildly in their heads.

The rifle spoke again. The gun in Ruby's hands bucked over and over. A buffalo stumbled, fell to its knees and skidded to a stop directly in front of them. Ruby pulled the gun down and dropped behind the fallen animal. Kenneth pulled her closer under the still quivering beast. He raised up and fired into the mass of buffalo again. The wall of flesh parted and passed on either side of them. Dust rose about them thickly. Through the dim haze, a massive form charged directly toward them. It smashed into the still body of the dead buffalo and veered off. Kenneth rose and fired again. Three quick shots in succession, and another charging bison ploughed into the ground, stumbled and slammed into their barricade. It rolled forward and stopped, its massive head and shoulders resting atop the pile of dead buffalo. Blood rushed from its nostrils and open mouth. It kicked spasmodically, gasped, then fell limp, dead.

The barrier of flesh protected them more adequately now and the herd passed on either side of it. On and on it thundered. Ruby buried her head against the soldier's body and pressed closer to him. The animals screamed and bellowed in terror. Hooves pounded the earth. The beasts' labored breathing rasped like the sounds of a steam locomotive. Urine odor mingled with that of gunpowder, and Ruby, pressed against the young officer's back, was suddenly aware of his sweaty man-smell.

Would it never stop? She opened her eyes and attempted to see through the cloud of dust about them. Brown bodies still rushed past on either side, but now they were mostly older buffalo and young calves, attempting to catch up to the rest of the herd. At last it ended and the dust settled. The sounds diminished as the herd rushed on.

Kenneth looked at Ruby. His cap had fallen off and a lock of dark hair fell over his forehead. His torn blue uniform was dust covered. The heavy Colt revolver shook as she handed it to him. He laughed and placed it in his holster, smiled and held Ruby at arm's length. "You all right?"

Ruby opened her mouth but no words came out. Suddenly she pressed to him, head against his shoulder and sobbed convulsively. Now that it was over, she was frightened. She trembled and was cold. Kenneth's arms tightened about her and she felt better, secure, and safe. She pulled away and looked into his face.

"Thank you, thank you," she said breathlessly, and pressed against his chest again. He tightened his embrace and slowly stroked her. The touch motion relaxed her and her sobbing stilled. "I'll never be able to repay you for this," Ruby said.

"Never mind that," he said, as his arms tightened around her.

She pulled away and attempted to smooth her hair. It was matted and tangled and she realized for the first time that blood from the buffalo had splattered over both of them.

He retrieved his rifle and cap. He set the cap on his head, adjusted it and brushed himself off. "We'd better be getting back to camp. They'll be wondering about us," he said calmly.

Ruby smiled at him. "You are a brave man, Kenneth. There are not many that could have done what you just did. I'll be forever indebted to you."

"You did all right yourself, Miss McIntyre. I heard the sound of that Colt firing several times. You didn't lose your nerve and shoot too soon, either."

Ruby grasped his hand. "After what we went through, Kenneth, please call me Ruby. It's all right if I call you Kenneth, isn't it?"

He smiled his crooked smile at her and solemnly winked. "Sure enough, Ruby. However my friends usually call me Ken. For a while there, I even thought you liked me more than just as a friend."

She laughed and patted his hand. "You remind me of my father. His smile is like yours, and he winks at me too. I do like you more than a little bit, Kenneth," she said softly. "It isn't every day a handsome knight rescues me from a herd of dragons."

Ruby was the center of attention. The other women marveled over her narrow escape. The buffalo had by-passed the camp but until Ruby and Lieutenant Hawkins showed up, almost everyone had assumed they had been trampled underfoot by the herd. The women quickly heated water and filled a tub for Ruby. She sank into it gratefully and soaked the dried blood and dirt from herself. In its warm depths she felt languid and listless. After she dried off and dressed, Mrs. Ozman offered her a glass of whiskey and water. It tasted strong, but she dutifully drank all of it.

"Do you good besides helping you rest," Mrs. Ozman said in a motherly tone of voice. "Maybe just a wee bit more wouldn't hurt." She handed Ruby another glassful.

"Thank you," Ruby said. She tipped the glass and drank again. "This is good medicine," she said. Her own voice sounded strange to her, as if it belonged to someone else far away. She felt lightheaded and dizzy, but happy, uncaring.

"Kenneth is a nice boy. I like him a lot." She giggled. "He rescued me from the dragons. He's a brave man and he saved my life." Ruby looked at Mrs. Ozman questioningly. Her face blurred and Ruby had a hard time focusing on it. It seemed to move around. The girl passed her hand over her eyes and peeked out between her fingers at Mrs. Ozman. Her mouth quivered and she looked like she might cry.

"Honey, now don't you fret about anything." Mrs. Ozman put her arm about Ruby's shoulder and gently guided the girl toward her cot. "Just lie down and rest, honey, right here." She fluffed the bedding.

"You're so nice to me. Just like mother. Thank you," Ruby lay back, stretched out and the relaxing effects of the strong drink took over. Her breathing slowed and the exhausted girl was soon asleep. Her blond hair framed her face. She looked peaceful and content and the older woman carefully arranged the blanket and sat beside the bed. Mrs. Ozman intercepted Lieutenant Hawkins as he poked his head through the tent flap. Her finger went to her lips. He nodded his head and studied the sleeping girl, then whispered. "Is she all right?"

"She will be when she wakes up. I fixed her a stiff drink of whiskey and it sort of went to her head." She stepped outside the tent where they could talk. She studied the young officer. "She's probably dreaming of being rescued from dragons by her white knight right now. That was a brave thing you did, young man. I will speak to my husband about it."

The soldier held up a hand. "Ruby did her share of the shooting." His voice was intent, serious. "I envy the man she is going to in Montana. He's getting one heck of a woman." He squared his shoulders and strode off. She stared after him.

She never failed to marvel at the twists and turns of life. Sometimes, she thought, it was strange the way fate threw people together. Who knew? There might be more than one twist of fate for Ruby and this young Lieutenant before they reached Montana. She secretly wished she could trade places with Ruby. That young officer was so nice and handsome, too. His kind was few and far between nowadays.

*   *   *

At this point, the Bozeman Trail and The Big Horn Mountains paralleled each other. Fort Reno was not far ahead. This was the Powder River country, the favorite hunting grounds of the Southern Cheyenne and Sioux. Wild game abounded here. There were elk, bear, mule deer, wild turkey, antelope, Big Horn Rocky Mountain sheep, and of course, the buffalo herds. Kenneth had been correct about something stirring up the buffalo. When the bedraggled pair arrived back at the camp and told their story to Major Ozman, he immediately dispatched his Crow scouts to investigate. They soon rode back to report that a party of hide hunters had been sighted to the west, near the foot of the mountains. It was midmorning the next day when Major Ozman's contingent reached their camp.

A heavyset man in blood stained buckskin clothing stepped from behind a tent as they approached. His beard was matted and tangled and his long unkempt hair hung in gray snarls over his ears and across his shoulders. With one hand, he held a Sharps Buffalo Rifle by its barrel, while he shielded his eyes against the sun with the other. He peered from under his hand at the men in blue.

The coach with the women in it was close enough so Ruby saw the man plainly. His hands were filthy and three fingers were missing from the one that shaded his eyes. Tobacco juice stains ran out of each corner of his mouth and down his beard. "What kin I do fer you, Generil?" he asked in a garrulous voice. He wiped his mouth with the back of his hand and shifted his cud of tobacco to the other side of his cheek.

Major Ozman looked disdainfully at him. Then without answering, dismounted. He drew to his utmost height and glared at the man who slouched before him. The Major was tall, square shouldered and his presence usually commanded attention. "I wish to speak to the man in charge of this camp," he said, formally.

The bearded man lowered his hand and scratched his behind, then stuck a finger in his right ear and dug into it, meanwhile looking the Major up and down. He removed his finger from his ear, examined it minutely, then cocked his head and squinted at Major Ozman quizzically. His mouth worked back and forth and suddenly spat out a messy brown tobacco cud at the Major's feet. Splatters of the brown spittle stained the officer's boots and blue pants.

"Sorry' bout that, General. Ain't used to havin' such important people call on us." He shoved the wad of tobacco cud out of the way with the toe of his boot. It rolled in the dust kicking up a stream of fine powder. Major Ozman had not moved, but his mouth drew into a thin tight line and his eyes narrowed. One hand went to his belt and loosened the white gloves that hung there. His lips barely moved as he snarled.

"Mister, I asked for the man in charge of this camp. I want a civil answer, now." He emphasized his words with a sharp slap of the gloves against his opened palm.

The heavy man scratched his head and grinned. "Don't get your balls in no uproar, Generil. Was gitting around to that." He fidgeted and scratched himself under one arm. "Goddamn fleas get bad this time of year. Damn near eat a man alive." He scratched his crotch, and dropped his bomb. "Frank Ozman, ain't ya?"

The Major's gloves stopped their slapping motion. His mouth flopped open. He stared at the man.

"Hell, Generil, ain't you never seen a real live buffler hunter afore?" He swung about and bowed to the women. "Go ahead 'n look all yer a mind to. Move on over here, upwind where the stink ain't so bad."

"Who are you?' growled the Major. "I want an answer right now, or I'm placing you under military arrest." He was in command again. He resumed his military posture.

"Hell, Generil, ain't no use getting riled. Name's Betters. Greasy Betters. You want the man in charge? You're lookin' at him. Me!" Greasy pointed to himself with the remaining two fingers of his right hand. "Greasy Betters, that's me!"

The Major stared at him. "Corporal Stanley Betters, bounty jumper, Company C 80th Indiana Volunteers, court-martialed, drummed out of the Corps, 1864." The Major's gloves slapped his hand violently.

"Same one, Generil. Took you long enough. Now what's on yer mind?" Greasy leaned against a pile of green hides and pulled a twist of black tobacco from his pocket. He worried a chunk of it loose with one corner of his mouth. He held the tobacco twist out at the Major. Want a chaw Generil?" His eye caught Ruby's, and his mouth parted in a leering grin. "Howdy, Miss, pleased to meet you."

Ruby averted her head, then looked again as the Major spoke. "I've heard enough of your foul tongue, you insolent whelp," the Major began. "I drummed you out of the corps before and I'm about to run you out of this country right now."

"Think so, pretty boy? I'm within my rights as a genuine U.S. citizen and I intend to stay right here and hunt them buffler jes' as long as I please." He emphasized his point by poking at Major Ozman with the twist of tobacco. "Now jes' lissen to me, Mr. Big, your job is to protect us upstanding citizens from them hostiles. You and your bullyboys just go ahead and do your job keeping them thieving Redskins off our backs and we'll help you by thinning out the buffalo. We done wiped out most of the herd over Kansas way already. Ain't no quicker way of bringing them Indians to their knees than killing off their food."

Ruby was appalled at the man's appearance and behavior. At the hotel in Denver, she had come in contact with all sorts of people, but this man's unkempt appearance and the absolute filth and odor of the camp was overwhelming. Uncured hides were spread out everywhere and the stench of rotten flesh hung in the air. She pressed her kerchief to her nose and mouth and breathed small, short breaths. Her insides were queasy and she looked away and fought down her urge to vomit. Swarms of bluebottle flies buzzed about the hides and the droning sounds of their wings were loud in her ears. One of them landed on her arm and she brushed it off.

Mrs. Ozman spoke to the driver and he pulled the stage away, upwind from the smell. The air was better there and they breathed deeply of it. Mrs. Baines suddenly leaned out of the window and was ill. She raised herself and touched her mouth with her kerchief. Her face was pale and drawn and she gratefully took the canteen of water Ruby handed her and rinsed her mouth.

The Major remounted and rode alongside. "Sorry for the inconvenience, ladies. I had no idea we would be running into anything so unpleasant." He glanced up as one of the Crow scouts rode up beside him. "Looks like Charging Bear has something to report." He touched his hat and trotted off to confer with his waiting officers and the Crow scout.

Charging Bear, the Crow Scout, pointed in a northeasterly direction. Three wagons pulled by mules raced wildly toward the hide camp pursued by several Indians on horseback. Each wagon contained three men, a driver frantically urging the mules and two others who rode facing the rear, shooting at the Indians. It was the rest of Greasy Betters' hide hunters. The soldiers arrayed themselves in front of the supply wagons and Lieutenant Hawkins was dispatched to see that the women were safe. He directed the driver to pull their converted ambulance at right angles to one of the wagons. The women got out and crouched under the ambulance and watched the running fight.

A bugle blasted, and several blue coated soldiers charged across the plain. At the sound of the bugle, the Indians discontinued their pursuit and gathered some distance away. Shot after shot came from the camp as Greasy Betters fired at the Indians with his heavy long-range buffalo gun. The hide hunters stopped their wagons near the camp, jumped down and began to shoot at the Indians in earnest. A horse fell and an Indian dropped to the ground. He was quickly helped up behind another mounted warrior. The Indians brandished their weapons at the soldiers then turned and rode away. The Blue Coats stopped their charge and rode back toward the camp.

Greasy Betters shook his fist and yelled at the retreating Indians. "Come back and fight, you sons-a-bitches." He ran to the first of the hide wagons. A man lay on his back, his mouth open, an arm hanging loosely down. Greasy lifted the arm and let it fall. It flopped and dangled over a pile of bloody hides. "Dead," Greasy announced to no one in particular. The butt of his heavy rifle kicked up a trail of dust behind him as he ran to Major Ozman's horse.

"Look here Generil, you kin see how them thieving Injuns is acting. Done kilt one of my boys already." His mouth worked his tobacco vigorously. He spat in front of the Majors' horse. "Ain't no call for them varmints acting like that. You and your bully boys do your job like you should and we wouldn't be bothered by them."

He stood near the supply wagon and the foul stench of his body odor floated past Ruby's nose. She turned away and caught her breath.

"Betters, your kind are the scum of the earth. I had my way I'd let those Indians rub you out." Major Ozman pulled his pistol free of its holster and pointed it at Greasy. "Now get your stinking hide away from my wagons. You'll hear from me later."

Greasy glowered at the Colt revolver pointed between his eyes. He shuffled his feet and muttered. "You got the drop on me, Generil, but I got my rights as a U.S. citizen. I'm a businessman, and we got our rights. You check in Fort Reno and see."

Greasy shambled back toward his hide wagons. He grabbed the dead man by an arm and leg and jerked him free. The body rolled from the pile of hides and hit the ground with a muffled thud. A puff of dust rose and one arm jerked spasmodically then fell. "Jesus Christ, he warn't dead yet." Greasy touched the man with his foot. "He's a goner now, though." He turned to the other hide hunters and snarled. "What the hell's the matter with you? Get your asses moving and bury him."

Several of the men hurriedly grabbed shovels from the sides of the wagons and began to dig a grave. The Major reassembled his troop and in a short time they were headed for their camp. He had decided to camp there another night until he decided what to do about Greasy Betters.

Greasy stood in front of his camp and watched them as they rode off. The dead man had already been wrapped in a blanket, tumbled into the ground and buried. As far as Ruby could tell, no one had said anything over the grave. At lunch time the food was unappetizing to her and her insides still felt queasy. Even though they were some distance from the hide hunter's camp, Ruby couldn't dismiss the odor of it from her mind.

Greasy's disposition turned from foul to ugly. The soldiers were hardly out of ear shot before he loosed a fluent stream of abuse at his hide skinners. "You bunch of yellow livered cowards," he ranted. "You let them Redskins run you off like that, and we'll never see the last of them."

He paused just long enough to spit, then put his finger to one side of his nose and blew. Yellow mucus and brown stains of tobacco juice mingled together in his beard. He jerked the cork from a bottle of whiskey with his yellow teeth, gulped several swallows of it, then wiped his mouth with the back of his hand. He swung around and shouted at the skinners. "How many hides did you leave out there for them Indians to steal? Ain't no more than a handful in them wagons."

A tall dark-faced man with a long scar running diagonally across his face muttered something under his breath. Greasy sidled up to him. "You got something to say, Sneed?"

"Ain't no call for you to talk that way Greasy," Sneed whined. He glanced quickly at the men bunched together behind him. Their faces were surly looking. "Way you let that Blue Coat back you down, don't look to me like you got too much room to talk none." Sneed's voice turned cynical and insulting as his courage grew. "I always figured all that talk about you being a hero during the war was a lot of bullshit."

Greasy's heavy fist buried itself in the tall man's middle. Sneed bent double, then his body slammed backward as Greasy hit him with a violent uppercut. He flopped on his back. His legs twitched, convulsively. Greasy kicked him in the ribs. Sneed moaned.

"Any more of you got something to say?" Greasy glared at them. "That Blue Coat ain't seen the last of Greasy Betters yet." His face was livid and his eyes rolled wildly. Spittle ran from one corner of his mouth. He licked his lips and the men watched him warily. His words came out rapidly, disconnected, at times incoherent. He swung his arms wildly and paced back and forth, raging. "You see them whores? Was always that way with the officers." He spat.

"Enlisted men got our asses shot off while them yellow livered bastards lived like kings."

He stopped in front of them. "That snooty whore in that ambulance? Turned her head and wouldn't even look at me." Greasy mimicked Ruby's motions of placing her kerchief to her nose and turning away. "I got me a notion to mosey on down to that camp and help myself to a piece of the Major's personal merchandise." Greasy licked his lips and pulled at the bottle again. The men broke up and scattered about the camp. From time to time Greasy shouted unintelligibly. Toward late afternoon, he emerged from his tent with a blanket over one arm. He saddled his horse and rode off in the general direction of Major Ozman's camp. Several men watched as he rode away.

"Hey Murphy, wonder what he's gonna do?" one of the men asked.

"Don't know. I hope they shoot his ass off. Right liable to if he goes messing around down there in after dark," Murphy answered.

CHAPTER 20
ANOTHER TWIST

*(And many a Knot unravel'd by the Road;…)*_{XXXI}

The troop lay over for another day while Ruby recovered from her scare with the buffalo. As she walked along the stream by the camp, it looked so appealing that Ruby took her shoes off so she could wade. A school of fish darted in front of her. She became so intrigued with them that she waded after them upstream some distance from the camp. Scrub oak thickets, willows and cottonwood trees lined the banks. Out of sight and sound of the camp, the grassy bank looked so inviting that Ruby lay back and rested. The afternoon sun warmed her and she dozed. A faint rustling noise roused her and she looked about, fearfully. She was farther from camp than she had realized.

She'd better be getting back. In the early twilight things looked different. Shadows lurked along the creek and the air was damp and chilly. She scrambled to her feet, slipped her shoes on and started in the direction of the camp. Faint sounds of voices came to her ears and she headed for them, then stopped.

Someone was behind her! She screamed, but her voice was muffled by something heavy thrown over her head. She tried to run, but was held firmly. She couldn't move. She flailed out with her feet, but to no avail. Her attacker's hands covered her mouth and nose. Pinpoints of light appeared before her eyes. She gasped for air, then relaxed as she fainted.

She awoke to the motion of a horse. The cover was still over her head, but her captor had loosened it slightly. Smells assailed her nose and sickened her. She sucked in short breaths and fought down her nausea as she realized that she was draped like a sack of potatoes over the horse's back. The horse stopped and she slid down to the ground. The covering was torn loose. She sat up and attempted to see. "Ain't no use for you to holler, bitch, they can't hear you." It was Greasy Betters!

Light headed and dizzy, Ruby trembled all over. The stench of the man made her ill and the taste of vomit came to her throat. She buried her face in her hands and sobbed. Greasy grabbed the front of her dress and jerked.

"Stand up, you whore. Let me get a look at you," he gloated. "You and me are going to have some fun before this night's over." Ruby turned her head away. Greasy entwined his hand in her hair and jerked her about to face him. She sucked in her breath with the pain that tore like fire at the roots of her hair. "I'll teach you to turn away from me, you little whore. Think you're too good for Greasy, huh? Time I'm through with you, you'll know better," he raged.

His fingers wound tighter in Ruby's hair. He tilted her head backward and suddenly Greasy's face pressed to hers. She reacted instantly to the odor of his breath and the slimy feel of his beard. Her fingernails raked his cheeks. One finger hooked his eye and tore at it. Greasy twisted and swore. "You feisty little bitch."

Ruby tore loose and ran wildly. She had no thought of direction, only escape. Greasy's feet thudded heavily behind her. He was gaining. Her body stopped with a jerk as the hide hunter grabbed her dress. Ruby twisted, the dress ripped and she was free again. She dodged off into the dark and tumbled forward into a buffalo wallow. She rolled sidewise just as Greasy landed heavily beside her. He swore and then snarled, "You little bitch, you'll pay for this."

Ruby held her breath and slithered away into a shadow. He pulled himself erect and climbed out of the wallow. Ruby lay still and watched the outline of his body against the night sky as Greasy limped away from her. He was hurt. Maybe this was her chance. She scrambled from the wallow and ran. "Come back here, you whore," he shouted.

Ruby's breath rasped as she ran. Her legs felt wooden, but she pressed on, mechanically. Her lungs burned with each breath, but she no longer heard the sounds of Greasy's voice behind her. She finally sank to the ground exhausted.

Her dress was completely ripped down the back. She pulled it loose and wrapped it around her. Now that she had stopped running, she was conscious of the chill night breeze. Her body trembled. Ruby's teeth chattered loudly and she feared the sound would be heard by Greasy. She scrunched into a hollow and pressed against the earth, pulling the dress closer about her and clenching her teeth to keep them from rattling. The landscape brightened as the moon rose. Ruby stiffened. A long howl, then another, and soon the night air reverberated with the terrifying sounds. Her trembling froze into a paralysis of fear. Wolves! How long would it take for them to find her? The howls changed in tempo, closer now. Ruby huddled in the hollow and pressed both hands to her ears. It was no use. The wolves were nearby. The baying sounds stopped. She held her breath and strained to hear. The clattering sound of a horse's hooves!

Maybe it was someone from the soldiers' camp looking for her. She stared across the plain toward the sounds. A horse and its rider were outlined against the sky. There were other riders. It had to be Kenneth and the other soldiers looking for her. Ruby called out, then suddenly realized her mistake.

"Over here, Greasy," called a voice. The horse and rider rode to where Ruby crouched. She collapsed and sobbed helplessly.

*   *   *

Major Ozman stared across the dark plain toward the Big Horns and Greasy Betters' camp. It seemed unlikely to him that the hide hunters would have kidnapped Ruby. More likely Indians. He mentally kicked himself for having taken on the responsibility of the young woman.

He'd been a fool to listen to his wife. Her and her romantic notions. Damn! The girl had already been nearly killed by buffalo. What's more, his best officer Hawkins was acting moon-eyed over her. He had to admit that Ruby was an eyeful. Now she was missing, last seen down by the stream in the late afternoon. Ought to know better, wandering off alone. Well, he had to do something or his wife would jaw at him all night. Didn't make sense to go prowling around in the dark, though. His force was too small to split up. Maybe he ought to call a staff meeting. Someone might have an idea.

"Sir." A man stood at the tent flap. It was Hawkins.

"Come in, Hawkins. Anything new?"

"Yes sir." Hawkin's face was intent.

"Sit down, son." Major Ozman's voice was gentle. The boy reminded him of his own son, Frank, Jr. They were always so young, most of these soldiers, boys really. But they grew up fast out here. "What did you find out?"

"Sir, one of the Crow scouts found signs of a struggle up the stream a ways. He says she was grabbed and taken off on a horse. Tracks lead west toward the hide hunters' camp." He paused, his hands twisting the brim of his hat as he turned it around and around. "There were boot prints. I'd be much obliged if you would let me check it out, sir."

Major Ozman studied Hawkin's face. "It's against my better judgement, son, but we ought to be doing something. Take Charging Bear with you and be careful." The Major placed his arm about the younger man's shoulder. "Be cautious, son. Don't go charging in and get hurt. That Betters is crazy and dangerous."

"What do you want me to do if they have her?" Kenneth asked.

"Use your own judgement. I trust you. Report back as soon as you can."

"Thank you, thank you, Sir." Lieutenant Hawkins snapped a salute and rushed from the tent. The Major watched silently as Charging Bear and the young officer rode from the camp. He studied the heavens. The stars hung bright and steady in the dark sky. The silhouette of the Big Horns spread out along the western horizon. With moon-rise, the light would be better. Major Ozman shook his head slowly. Wonder what had happened to the girl already? Hide hunters might do her more harm than Indians. The night was chilly and he shivered.

*   *   *

Ruby roused to the sound of voices. A fire burned brightly and the warmth of its glow felt good. She sat up and tried to move her legs. They were tied together at the ankles. She looked around the fire and recoiled. Ranged in a semi-circle were the hide-hunters. Their eyes glittered in the firelight. The man directly across from her grinned and licked his lips. Greasy swaggered to her and grabbed her hair. Ruby sensed his next move and attempted to scramble to her feet. The binding about her ankles prevented it. She fell heavily and moaned from the searing pain that tore at her scalp. Greasy slashed at the bindings at her ankles. Scratch marks down his cheeks and a trickle of blood at the corner of one eye marked his first encounter with Ruby. He watched her warily. "Get up you little slut," he said. He jerked her hair and Ruby lurched to her feet. She swayed back and forth but the man's fingers entwined in her hair held her upright. She bit her lip and tasted blood. It distracted her from the searing pain at her scalp. Greasy's other hand flashed out and grabbed the front of her petticoat, ripping it open. Ruby wrapped her arms about her exposed body. Greasy motioned to one of the men. "Hold her arms." Murphy seized Ruby roughly and bent her arms behind her. She sucked in her breath and groaned. Greasy towered over her and gloated. His dirty yellow teeth gleamed in the firelight as he stared at her. "Some punkin'? Ain't right for them bullyboys to keep something this good all to themselves." His hands moved to Ruby's breasts. She screamed as he twisted one of her nipples.

"Hey Greasy you ain't screwing a nut on a wagon wheel," someone shouted. The rest of the men laughed raucously. They crowded close to Ruby and their lust-filled faces leered over hers. Greasy swung around and knocked one of them flat. Another reached out to grab her breast. Greasy cursed and violently knocked him aside. "Keep your fucking hands off. Give me some room," he snarled. "I'm taking firsts and you can fight over what's left."

Ruby's body tensed as she recoiled. The men drew back a step, still looking at her greedily. "Hell, I can't tell where your legs end with all them clothes on," Greasy said. He laughed harshly and ripped the rest of her clothes from her. He ran his hands over her thighs and rubbed between her legs.

"Jesus H. Christ, Greasy, hurry up and get on with it," one of the men shouted. "I'm as horny as a three peckered billygoat."

The rest of the men roared with laughter. Greasy fumbled with his britches and Ruby saw her chance. She kicked him squarely in the crotch He held himself between the legs and grunted. "You bitch," he snarled. He scrambled to his feet and shouted, "stake her out!" His fist lashed out and Ruby fell in a heap.

Ruby sputtered and choked as cold water hit her. She attempted to sit up, but couldn't move. Her legs and arms were spread apart and lashed to stakes driven into the ground. Greasy Betters stood over her, his trousers open, his face red. "Now you fucking whore, before I'm through with you, you're gonna' pay for that kick. He lowered himself over Ruby. She felt an explosion in her head, shuddered, then fainted.

Ruby awoke, aware that her limbs were free. Kenneth was kneeling beside her, his coat covering her. She opened her eyes, remembered and then sobbed. Kenneth's arms went gently around her, pulling her to him.

45-JEYS

"It's all right, Ruby, no one will hurt you now."

Finally her sobs subsided and she looked around. Charging Bear stood with his rifle pointed at the hide hunters. A still form lay beside him. The face had a hole in it, right between the eyes. Greasy Betters' ugly yellow teeth were bared in a frozen leer. Ruby pressed her face into Kenneth's coat and shook convulsively.

*   *   *

Ruby's feverish mind was filled with dream-like scenes mixed with periods of wakefulness in which she was conscious of Mrs. Ozman. The woman was holding a glass in her hand. "Drink it down, Ruby, it'll relax you."

She remembered the sharp taste of the whiskey—Charles leaned over her, "You'll be all right now," he said. They sat together in the tree house in the limbs of the old silver beech tree. She snuggled closer in his protective arms and looked into his face. Now he wore a blue coat and looked different. It was Kenneth. His face lowered to hers and the slimy foul beard of Greasy Betters pressed to her face. She struggled to escape. It was no use. She couldn't move her arms or legs. She twisted her body about as the heavy man lowered himself onto her.

Cool hands soothed her forehead. It felt wonderful to lie still and feel their tender touch. Ruby stretched and relaxed. She didn't want to wake up. She turned her face to the pillow and the cool freshness of it against her cheek was comforting. Her mother's voice sounded in the distance. "You just sleep now, Ruby honey. You'll be alright," she said.

Now there was motion. She was on a horse, not riding it, but lying over its back like a sack of flour. She couldn't breathe. It was hot, stifling. Ruby thrashed about, unable to escape. She was loose, free. She ran. Her legs moved mechanically, back and forth. Someone behind reached for her. Her step quickened but she was still in the same place. She screamed over and over. Reality leaped out at her.

Mrs. Ozman cradled Ruby's head in her lap and stroked her hair. She smiled weakly. Her fingers went to her face. It was sore and swollen. Then she remembered Greasy Betters had hit her.

"Feeling better?" Mrs. Ozman's voice was gentle, soft. A tear worked its way down Ruby's cheek. She pressed close to Mrs. Ozman. "Feel like something to eat?"

Ruby managed a weak, "No."

"Just a bit of soup. Will strengthen you."

Ruby just wanted to lay back. It was so comforting and peaceful. Maybe if she went to sleep, she wouldn't ever have to get up again. But first there was something she had to do. What was it? A nagging thought crossed her mind, she couldn't catch hold of it long enough to examine it. What was it she had to do? She wanted to just go to sleep and never wake up, but the nagging thought kept interjecting itself on her consciousness. She stirred and attempted to sit up. "Honey, you just lie still now." Mrs. Ozman eased Ruby back onto the bed.

Ruby pushed herself up again. "Charles, Charles," she said over and over.

"You go to sleep now," Mrs. Ozman's fingers brushed Ruby's forehead.

Ruby lay back and placed her head against the soft pillow and closed her eyes. A face smiled at her. It was Charles. Blue eyes, blond hair and a tall body clothed in buckskin. That was it. She must go to him. She smiled and sank into a peaceful sleep. Her breathing came slowly and regularly and Ruby's face was serene, her face cool. She slept. Mrs. Ozman bent and kissed the troubled girl and quietly went to the door.

It had been several hours since she herself had slept. Throughout the long night while Ruby was missing, Mrs. Ozman had tossed and turned, wide awake, worrying. When they brought Ruby to the camp, Mrs. Ozman had urged her husband to order the troop to head for Fort Reno as fast as possible. The girl needed rest in a real bed.

Ruby had been delirious all through the day's trip to Fort Reno. Mrs. Ozman had held her in her arms the whole time. At the fort,

45-JEYS

Ruby was put to bed and Mrs. Ozman stayed with her throughout the next night. It was morning of the second day now.

"She is sleeping soundly," she said in answer to the questioning look of Mrs. Baines.

"I'll watch her. You get some sleep," Mrs. Baines said.

"Thank you." She was suddenly very tired. She felt old. She didn't remember going to her room and to bed.

* * *

Fort Reno was one of a series of forts established along the Bozeman trail for the protection of travelers. The trail crossed the Powder River at that point.

When Major Ozman and his party splashed across the river and entered the fort, Major Eno, the fort's commander welcomed them. His wife was especially pleased to see the women who accompanied the party. The Ozmans and Enos, old friends, greeted each other enthusiastically. As soon as possible the men went into conference. "So, what can I do for you?" Major Eno asked.

Major Ozman placed his glass on the table. "By damn, Al, I want you to give me a hand running those hide hunters out of this country."

"Something's got you fired up, Frank. Only hide hunters I know of is a fellow named Greasy Betters and his bunch."

"That's the man. Full name is Stanley Betters, Company C, 80th Indiana Volunteers. I drummed him out of the corps in '63' for bounty jumping. Worst kind of louse you could imagine. Picked up his bounty for enlisting three or four different times. Would hang back when the fighting started, desert first chance he got, then sign up and collect his bounty all over again." Frank stopped then went on. "I should have had him shot then, would have done the rest of the world a favor."

Major Eno raised his glass to his lips and sipped slowly. "Never knew you to hold a personal grudge, Frank. Far as I know, Betters is within his rights."

"Within his rights? No way. Anyhow, he's dead now."

Major Eno stopped his glass part way to his mouth. He carefully sat it down on the table. "What happened?"

"One of my men shot him. Good job if I ever saw one." Frank emphasized his point by slapping his open palm against the table.

"How did it happen."

"Well, after they nearly stampeded the buffalo herd over us, I went to their camp to investigate. Biggest mess I ever saw."

Al grinned. "You didn't shoot him just because his camp stank, did you?"

"Should have," Frank said dryly. "Would have saved a lot of trouble later." He slapped his palm against the table again. "I listened to a lot of insolent talk from him about his rights as a U.S. citizen and so on."

Al interrupted. "You do know that he was within his rights to be there, Frank. We just got word this spring to allow the hide hunters to come as far north as Fort Reno."

"I thought the Treaty of 1868 guaranteed the Indians that we would keep people other than travelers out of this territory?"

Major Eno studied the remaining drops of liquid in his glass before answering. "You know how I always try to stay out of politics, but as far as I can tell there's a lot of people making money off the hide trade. The pressure must be on in Washington to open up more and more of the Indian lands to the hide hunters." He paused. "Sorry to interrupt you. Finish what you were telling me about Betters. Why'd your man shoot him?"

Major Ozman drained his glass. "Betters must have gone nuts. After I left his camp, he came down to where we were camped and kidnapped one of the women. That's the girl the other women are looking after."

Major Eno leaned forward. "He must have been crazy. How'd he do it?"

"Caught her alone down by the creek. She had no business going off alone like that, but you know how it is with young people. They think nothing is going to happen to them. Anyhow, my man and an

217

Indian scout found them, just as Betters and his men were about to rape her. Had her stripped bare, all staked out. The Lieutenant shot him right between the eyes."

"Girl all right?"

"Don't know yet. Margaret is with her now. She raved out of her mind most of the way in. Betters had beaten her pretty badly."

"Guess you'll be staying a while till you see how she's doing?"

Major Ozman held out his glass while Al refilled it. Guess we can spare a few days, Al. Think we got enough on those hunters to run them out?"

Eno grinned. "You know me, Frank. It'll be a pleasure. I'm a soldier just like you. I do my job as I'm ordered to do. My orders are to keep the hostiles north of here, and to protect any U.S. citizen who comes legally into this territory." He paused and looked quietly at his friend for a moment.

"People who stampede buffalo, kidnap and rape aren't legal as far as I'm concerned." Al coughed lightly. I'm no Indian lover, Frank, but personally if I had my way, I'd run all those kind of whites right out of the country. But we don't make the laws, just try to enforce them." He put his hand on his friend's shoulder. "Let's talk about more pleasant things. How's that family of yours?"

* * *

Ruby awoke ravenously hungry. Before long she was up and about. Kenneth visited her several times but seemed embarrassed when he talked to her. She was uncomfortable having him see her bruised face, but after three or four days and with the help of some powder, there was little visible evidence of the dreadful things she had experienced. "You have saved my life twice." Ruby said. "Thank you."

Kenneth shifted from one foot to the other. He started to say something, then stopped and started again. "You can count on me any time, Ruby," he said. He smiled his crooked smile. "Just call me 'Sir Galahad.'"

Ruby took his hand in hers. "Kenneth, you mean so very much to me. If it weren't for Charles....," she paused, then let go of his hand.

"A day late and a dollar short," Kenneth said. "I'll see you tomorrow." He hesitated then turned abruptly and left.

Ruby welcomed the change in routine that the few days at Fort Reno afforded. It was good to sleep in a regular bed rather than on an army cot. She had no idea before this that three meals a day sitting at a table was such a luxury. But the opportunity to wash clothes and bathe regularly was what she appreciated most. It was only her urgency to see Charles that caused her to be pleased when they left for Fort Ellis.

On the first evening, as she studied the scenery to the west, the sun dropped, an orange-red globe on the ridge of the Big Horns. White clouds towered high in fluffy piles like sacks of feather ticks, their undersides reflected hues from charcoal to orange-red. Long gray fingers of rain filtered downward in curtains against the western horizon. The sun rapidly sank beneath the rim of the mountains, but its rays spread across the underside of the clouds. The reflection cast an eerie light. Objects about her took on a special presence. Shadows blurred and merged with the fading light.

Ruby caught her breath. The beauty and massive grandeur of this country sometimes seemed too much for her to bear. She felt as if she would burst from the feelings inside of her.

A footfall sounded behind her. She was not alone. Startled, she turned and saw Kenneth, mouth partially open, eyes fixed on the sky and hills. His face had a look of rapture not unlike that of a person in the midst of a religious experience. It was a side of him she hadn't seen before. Ruby looked at the sky again, pleased to be sharing it with another who enjoyed nature. It was darker now, and chilly.

"We never had anything like this in New Jersey." Kenneth said.

"Do you miss New Jersey?"

"At times, but I don't want to ever live anywhere but here, near the mountains. How about you, Ruby?"

"Sometimes I miss some of my friends, but I've come to love this country. What were you thinking about just now when you were looking at the sunset?"

He lifted his cap and ran his fingers through his hair. His mouth arranged itself in his crooked smile and Ruby thought of her father. Kenneth's facial expression was pensive. "Sometimes I think a sunset is so beautiful it can't ever be surpassed, then along comes another one that makes me think the same thing all over again." He laughed embarrassed. "I was thinking something like that, mixed up with a lot of other things, I guess," he said. His voice trailed off as if the thought were unfinished.

"Sorry if I intruded on your private thoughts. I feel like you do, about the beauty, I mean," Ruby paused. She was suddenly ill at ease, uncomfortable. She wanted to go on and tell him more about her feelings, but something stopped her. She was impatient with herself for having lost her composure. "Well, I must go see if Mrs. Ozman needs help. Thank you, again, Kenneth," she said.

"For what?"

"Well, . . . well, I don't know. I just felt better knowing someone feels like I do. I guess it is almost too much for one person alone." She touched his sleeve as she quickly passed him.

As Kenneth slowly walked off, Ruby suddenly felt uneasy. She explored her feelings for him. She realized that her life would never be the same without Kenneth in it. In a deeper sense she knew that perhaps he was the finest man she had ever known. Now she reasoned, with a twinge of remorse that perhaps the very idea of her going to Montana to find out what had happened to Charles was childish and impulsive. She hurried to catch up with him to explain her feelings to him, but he had already stopped and was busily engaged in conversation with Major Ozman. As she passed them, she had her emotions under control.

CHAPTER 21
THE CHANGEABLE
WINDS

*(Beset the Road I was to wander in,...)*LXXX

Approximately 150 miles north of Fort Reno along the Big Horns, at the northwestern end of the range, their party crossed the Little Big Horn river, or the Greasy Grass river as the Indians called it. At this place where the Bozeman trail makes its turn from north to due west, General George Armstrong Custer and his ill fated Seventh Cavalry would make its last stand. This would be six years in the future, in 1876.

Here the plains spread north, east and west as far as the eye could see. This was buffalo country, jointly claimed by Sioux, Cheyenne and Crow Indians. The rolling hills were cut through with small streams lined with cottonwood and willow. Chokecherries grew in profusion. Wild berries, onion, turnips, camus, and other edible root plants provided the Indian women with a variety of foods to supplement their larders. Flowers carpeted the hills and every coulee and low place where water stood, spouted cattails and tall reeds. One had to climb the higher hills or ridges to gain a view of the country to the north. An outstanding feature of the landscape was named Pomp's Tower. The huge rock some fifty miles to the north was named after Pomp, the son of Sacajawea, the woman guide of the Lewis and Clark expedition.

Soft warm winds brushed across the buffalo grass in undulating waves. The animals that grazed in this gigantic park were more than adequate to provide for the needs of the bronze-skinned people who populated its vast expanses.

But not everything in this land was idyllic. Survival of the fittest, the basic law of nature, prevailed. The wolves would often cut out a pregnant buffalo cow from the herd. They were fond of eating unborn calves and would sometimes tear open the living cow's belly to get at them. And of course the worst predator, man, slaughtered the buffalo for their hides, leaving the bodies for the wolves. When there was too much meat for them to eat, it was left to rot.

But for the present, Ruby was oblivious to this vast interplay of nature. She only knew that as each day ended she was several miles closer to her beloved, Charles Tucker.

Charles and Ruby Tucker, she said the words over and over to herself. Would they have children? Of course. A blond, blue eyed boy, like Charles. He would soon have a sister and then, who knew? They would go to Denver to see her parents and maybe even journey to the east so the children could see where their parents had grown up. Would the tree house in the silver beech tree still be there?

A stick snapped and she turned to see Kenneth with the broken ends of a dry cedar twig in either hand. "Thought I'd let you know I was around," he said. "You seemed to be deep in your own thoughts."

"Thank you for being so thoughtful." Ruby smiled.

"Won't be long before we reach Fort Ellis," he said

His statement about Fort Ellis excited her and Ruby's thoughts focused on Charles Tucker again. Fort Ellis was only a week's travel from Fort Benton. Charles would be surprised to see her. She was aware of Kenneth's voice but his words did not penetrate her consciousness. She turned to face him.

"I'm sorry, Kenneth, I missed what you said."

He laughed, nervously. "Maybe it's for the best."

"Go ahead, tell me what you said. I really do want to know."

He grasped Ruby's hand. "Look," he said. "I know that you are going to a man in Fort Benton to become his wife." He paused and lowered his voice. "This may be the last time we will be able to talk privately, and well, I just want to let you know how I feel about you."

Ruby bit her lip. "You needn't say anything," she said. She pressed his hand. He swallowed painfully, his Adam's apple bobbing above his shirt collar.

"I can't let you go without telling you," he said doggedly. "Ruby, I love you." He took a deep breath, squared his shoulders and looked directly into her eyes.

Ruby was confused. What could she say? Things had taken an unexpected turn. "I'll always remember you fondly," Ruby said. "You've been like a big brother to me." She smiled at him. "When I tell Charles how you saved my life, I'm sure he'll want to meet you and thank you personally." She was surprised to find she was still holding his hand and quickly let it go. She was on easier ground now and went on without noticing the sag in Kenneth's body. "You're a lot like Charles. Maybe that's why I was drawn to you from the first."

Kenneth shifted awkwardly from one foot to the other, fighting a sudden distaste for Charles. "I'm sorry if I said something wrong, Ruby."

"No, it's all right," Ruby's face brightened. "Maybe the Major will let you accompany me to Fort Benton, then you'll get a chance to meet Charles. You'll like him, I'm sure."

Lieutenant Hawkins smiled sardonically. "Don't expect that would work out," he said. "But remember if you ever need help, I can always be counted upon. Just in case things aren't what you expected at Fort Benton." He studied her quietly then abruptly strode away.

Ruby watched as he mounted his horse and galloped off. Impulsively she kissed her palm and blew a kiss in the direction of the soldier.

*   *   *

Their passage through friendly Crow country was without incident, except for daily encounters with bands of Crow Indians. They were congenial and rode away, pleased when the Major presented them with gifts of coffee or tobacco. Interested in the converted ambulance and its occupants, they usually rode up to it and examined it carefully. They reminded Ruby of curious children.

Fort Ellis was situated on the Bozeman Trail, about ten miles east of the Gallatin river. Ruby's route from there to Fort Benton would take her north, where the trail roughly paralleled the Missouri River. Three days after reaching Fort Ellis, Ruby was on her way to Fort Benton and Charles.

A contingent of replacement soldiers was going from Fort Ellis to Fort Shaw on the Sun River. Ruby would accompany them and go on to Fort Benton, only a short distance from there.

Ruby and Lieutenant Hawkins had not talked privately since he had declared his love for her. On the day she left Fort Ellis, Ruby inquired about the young officer and was dismayed to find that he had left the day before with a patrol. Ruby's own emotions about Kenneth troubled her. She liked him and had planned to talk with him once more before he left. On the other hand, she was relieved that an awkward situation might have been avoided.

Late the first afternoon out of Fort Ellis, a lone rider galloped his lathered horse into their camp beside the Jefferson River. He swung down and hurried to the Sergeant in charge. They were only a few feet away from Ruby, but their voices were low. Occasionally they glanced in her direction. Their faces looked serious. At last the sergeant came to where Ruby stood. "I'm sorry, Miss Ruby," he said. He shifted from one foot to the other as he talked and avoided looking at her. At last he blurted out, "Lieutenant Hawkins was hurt this morning. Man rode in to tell us."

Ruby stared at him. It couldn't be. Not Kenneth. She felt faint and swayed back and forth. She closed her eyes, opened them and took a deep breath. "What happened?" she asked. Her voice sounded strange to her, faint and far away as if it belonged to someone else.

"Happened just this morning on the way back to Fort Ellis. Was bushwhacked by a hostile." His face was grim. "I'm sorry, Miss Ruby, knew you would want to know."

Ruby nodded her head. "Where was he hit?"

The sergeant turned his hat in his hand as he answered Ruby. He shuffled his feet and looked down. "Uh, well, like right here." He placed one hand on his buttocks.

"Sergeant, look at me," Ruby's voice was sharp. "I want to know how badly he was hurt. Don't be embarrassed."

"Well, he can't hardly move, bled a lot," the sergeant looked up at Ruby then grinned. "Doctor says it'll be a couple of months before he can sit comfortable again."

"Thank God," Ruby said. "You scared me to death! I thought he'd been killed." She smiled and then seeing the amusement in the Sergeant's eyes, laughed in nervous relief.

"He'll have to sleep on his stomach," the Sergeant added lamely. "Uh, I got to go now, Miss Ruby." He twisted his hat in his hands and looked down.

"Thank you Sergeant."

The relieved soldier quickly left her presence. She went to her tent, sat on her cot, slipped her shoes off, lay back and thought about Kenneth. He had been so kind and gentle to her. She remembered his crooked smile and the way he looked that evening while he watched the sunset with her. If only she could help tend to him as he had tended her when she was in trouble. She trembled and was cold. Mrs. Ozman had given her a bottle of whiskey before she left the Fort.

Ruby hadn't thought of the incident at Greasy Betters' camp for several days. But now, she was mentally reliving the scene. She sat up and shook her head. This wouldn't do. She poured some whiskey into a cup, diluted it with water, and drank it down. She made a face at the cup and put it down empty. A warm glow spread through Ruby and she relaxed. She pulled the blanket over her and was soon asleep.

225

*   *   *

Sergeant Burns reigned in his horse next to Ruby's. "Fort Benton ain't too far ahead Miss Ruby," he said. "What is the name of that fella you was wantin' to find?"

"Charles Tucker. He and a man named Taylor run a trading post," Ruby said.

The sergeant shaded his eyes against the mid-day sun and studied the trail ahead. A bearded man on a buckskin horse rode slowly toward them. His tall frame slouched and he appeared to be lost in his thoughts. "Maybe that man up ahead can direct us. Guess we might as well wait for him." The Sergeant signaled the patrol to hold up.

"Howdy, can I help y'all?" the tall man's voice was soft, friendly. He eyed the soldiers and tipped his hat to Ruby. "We don't get many ladies as pretty as y'all out here, mam," he smiled at Ruby. "Name's Deiber, Fred Deiber. If I can be of any help, just let me know."

Sergeant Burns spoke curtly. "We're looking for Charles Tucker. Runs a trading post at the fort." He jerked his thumb in the direction of Fort Benton.

"Well, ain't that a coincidence, Yank," the bearded man said. "I work for him. He's gone over to the fort for something, but I expect he'll be back soon. You can wait for him at the post if you like. Rest and freshen up a bit." Deiber's voice was friendly and his smile disarming. "Post's just around the next bend."

"Right nice of you, Reb. You are one, ain't you?" Sergeant Burns had warmed to Deiber's friendliness.

"Was, but that's all in the past." Deiber made a sweeping gesture toward the East and South. He studied Ruby intently. She wondered at his curiosity. Had Charles mentioned her to the man? She liked his friendly good manners.

Ruby spoke impulsively. "Mr. Deiber, I'm Ruby McIntyre. I'm the one who is looking for Mr. Tucker."

"Well, I'll be dogged, so you're Miss Ruby?" He placed his hat back upon his head. "Charlie told me you were a beauty, looks like he was right." He studied Ruby. "Charlie will be mighty surprised to see you."

"Is he all right?"

"Fit as a fiddle, Miss." Deiber shifted in his saddle and gazed toward Fort Benton.

His voice was nearly inaudible. "Charlie ought to be back in just a little while."

"Are you sure I won't be any trouble, Mr. Deiber?"

Deiber answered almost as if talking to himself. "It'll be all right, Miss Ruby. Like I said, Charlie's going to be surprised to see you though." His words tailed off as though he were asking a question.

"If it's inconvenient for you to have me at the post, I can go into Fort Benton and wait for Charles there," Ruby said.

"It's no problem for me, Miss Ruby," Deiber said with a slight smile. "I'll get you fixed up at the post, then I can ride in and tell Charlie you're waiting for him."

"That will be fine with me, Mr. Deiber," Ruby said.

The post appeared to be empty. Sergeant Burns spoke to Deiber. "I'll leave Miss McIntyre's horses and belongings with you. I'll send a man to pick them up later."

"Sure enough, Yank. You get into town this evening, maybe I can buy you a drink over at Keno Bill's. Sergeant Burns saluted Deiber and the patrol left at a trot for Fort Benton. As she watched the bluecoated soldiers ride away, a look of dismay crossed Ruby's face.

"Anything wrong Miss Ruby?"

"No, nothing, but in all the excitement, I'm afraid I've forgotten my manners. I didn't even thank those men for their assistance before they left."

"Well, come on inside out of the heat. Don't worry about them. They aren't thinking of much except getting to Keno Bill's so they can swill down some of his liquor, anyhow." He walked into the post ahead of Ruby. "Hey, Crow Woman," he shouted. "You got something cool for a lady to drink?"

An Indian woman appeared at the open door at the far end of the room. When she saw Ruby, she stopped and looked inquisitively at Fred. "Friend of Charlie's. Come all the way from Denver to see him," he said. "Crow Woman, this is Miss Ruby. I'll be right back, Miss Ruby. Think I heard someone outside. It might be Charlie."

Ruby's hands went to her hair. Maybe it had been a mistake to go directly to the trading post. She should have gone into Fort Benton first. That way she could have changed clothes and gotten herself ready to see Charles. But she was so anxious to see him. Her heart raced and she felt her face grow warm. She heard a sound behind her and she turned around, startled. The Indian woman held a tin cup filled with water and extended it toward Ruby. Ruby wished that Mr. Deiber would come back. Her hand shook and some of the contents of the cup spilled on the floor. Crow woman watched her drink, then took the empty cup and silently left.

Although the room was cool, its shadowy interior and unfamiliar odors were threatening to Ruby. She shifted her weight to her other foot and peered about the room's gloomy depths. Was this the place where Charles spent most of his time? She twisted the scarf she held between her hands, then wadded it into a sweaty ball. She was annoyed with herself for being so nervous. Ruby's palms were moist and her entire body felt hot, sticky and dirty. It had been a mistake to come here. What would Charles think of her, sweaty and disheveled? Ruby's mouth was dry and her tongue felt thick. The objects in the room seemed to close in on her.

Ruby glanced at the doorway to the room where Crow Woman had retreated. Where was Mr. Deiber? He had been gone a long time. A shadow fell across the entrance to the trading post and Ruby shrunk into the shadows to make herself as inconspicuous as possible. It was an Indian man and woman. Crow Woman appeared and silently passed Ruby on her way to the long counter. The Indians talked in their native tongue and from the occasional looks in her direction, Ruby knew she must be the subject of their conversation. Things weren't working out at all like she had planned.

The sound of Fred Deiber's voice came to her now. His words were indistinguishable, but she felt relieved. Maybe Charles was with him. She went to the doorway. The Indians at the counter stopped their conversation and silently watched as she passed. Fred and a swarthy-skinned man stood outside the door talking intently. Fred gestured toward the trading post and then noticed Ruby. He waved to her.

"Miss Ruby, this is Jack Taylor, Charlie's partner," he said.

"I'm pleased to meet you, Mr. Taylor," Ruby said. "Charles told me about you when he was in Denver last fall."

Jack's forehead wrinkled into three vertical furrows above his nose. "You should have let Charlie know you was a coming," he said abruptly. "Come on Jack, ain't no call for you make Miss Ruby feel unwanted," Fred interrupted. He touched Ruby's hand. "Don't pay no never mind to Jack, Miss," he said. "He's always looking out for Charlie."

Fred's words relieved Ruby. Jack's abrupt manner had disturbed her. "Maybe I ought to go into Fort Benton and find a place to stay," she said.

Ruby sensed that someone stood behind her. It Was Crow Woman. Her silent approach was disconcerting. At least she could make a sound to let a person know she was around. Crow Woman spoke to Jack in a language Ruby didn't understand. It sounded to Ruby as if she were asking a question. Jack answered her and then smiled.

"Didn't mean to be so abrupt with you, Miss Ruby," he said. "Was like Fred said, I was just thinking of Charlie being surprised." Jack motioned toward the woman. "This is my wife, Crow Woman. You're welcome to stay with us as long as you like."

Ruby turned to the woman. She nodded her head and without saying any thing went to the interior of the post. It was obvious to Ruby that the woman resented her presence. Ruby wished intensely that she had gone to the fort before coming here.

"Maybe you would like to freshen up a bit, Miss Ruby," Jack said. His voice was friendly now and Ruby began to feel more at ease with him.

"Thank you, I'd like that," Ruby said.

"Right in here." Jack showed her to a room and poured some water into a tin wash basin for her. Ruby looked at her reflection in the mirror above the dresser and set about straightening her hair and washing her face and hands. The cool water against her skin refreshed her. She breathed deeply, then smiled at her reflection. She stuck her tongue out and made a face at herself. She felt better. Charles might be here any time now. She bit on her lips to redden them. She was excited and pleased with herself. She was ready for Charles.

The rumble of male voices sounded through the door. One of them was Charles! Ruby's heart pounded furiously. She went uncertainly to the door, slowly opened it and there stood Charles. Ruby smiled at him, threw herself into his arms and rained quick little kisses on his face. "Kiss me," she said.

Charles placed his hands on her shoulders and pushed her away from him. His face was pale, serious, drawn with tension. Something was wrong. Ruby felt her body grow cold, rigid. When he spoke, his words sounded dull, wooden, mechanical. A slight ringing sound in her ears added to her confusion. Phrases came to her in snatches.

"This is Na-Ha-Ki. Meant to tell you. Didn't know how. My wife. Our child."

Ruby, for the first time, was aware of an Indian woman at his side. At last he stopped talking. Ruby heard her own voice as if it were someone else speaking. "I've been a fool. A damned fool. Oh Charles, how could you?" Suddenly she was pressed against him. Her body shook uncontrollably as she sobbed. Charles held her awkwardly, his own body rigid. He patted Ruby on the back several times. At last Ruby pulled away and daubed at her eyes. She was in control of herself now and managed a weak smile.

A baby's cry sounded and she watched dully as Charles lifted a red-headed child, cradle board and all, from the back of the young woman who stood at his side. Crow Woman crossed the room and took the child. She flung a look of hatred at Ruby and turned away.

Na-Ha-Ki's mouth was drawn into a thin line, turned down at the corners. She appeared as if she were about to cry herself. She stepped away from Charles and looked first at Ruby, then at her husband. She spoke rapidly to him and motioned toward the door. Charles looked confused and distraught.

"I don't know what to say," he began. "I wrote to you. Didn't you get my letter?" Ruby ignored Charles and looked directly into Na-Ha-Ki's face. She was so young. The expression in Na-Ha-Ki's eyes reminded Ruby of a wild rabbit that she and her brother had once trapped. Ruby had felt so sorry for the wild thing that she had forced her brother to let it go. Now, as she stared at the young woman, her own feelings of confusion and anger were replaced by a new, more powerful emotion.

An overwhelming feeling of sorrow, compassion and absolute depression combined within her. She continued to stare at the girl for a moment, then lifted a tear stained face to Charles. His face was white and his hands clenched and unclenched. His eyes met Ruby's, then turned away. The corners of his mouth twitched. He shook his head slowly and avoided her eyes.

"I hate you! Don't tell me to leave. I know when I'm not wanted." Ruby's voice rose in volume. "Don't worry, I won't cause you any trouble." She tried to slap him and he caught her arm and held it. Ruby yanked her arm from his grasp. She panted, then caught her breath. Ruby turned to Na-Ha-Ki. "You can have him. You have my sympathy! I'm sorry for you. I hope you are happy."

"Now Ruby" Charles said haltingly.

"Don't you 'now Ruby'me. I invest my whole future in you and you dismiss me with 'now Ruby.' Must be nice, living with you as a husband. I wash dishes, cook, scrub floors and you reward me by getting me pregnant. Is that the way he treated you?" Ruby turned to Na-Ha-Ki once more. "Maybe next time he goes through Denver he can bed me down again. To think I had hoped you might have got me pregnant. No such luck, Charlie."

Charles started to say something but Ruby cut him off. She spoke slowly, biting each word off as she uttered it. As she spoke, her anger rose again. She lost control again and her fury erupted once more in a fusillade of words. "Don't 'now' me! You don't have to make explanations Charlie Tucker." She looked directly at him, quieted somewhat then went on. He turned his head to avoid her stare. "I've always been a fool over you. Never, never again." She bit her lip and the salty taste of the blood in her mouth registered vaguely in her consciousness. Charles moved toward Ruby as if to place his arms about her. Ruby placed both hands against his chest and violently shoved him away. "Don't touch me, you fool. I don't ever want to see you again, Charlie Tucker."

"My name is Charles, Ruby"

Ruby smiled, "I'll call you anything I want, Charlie. I don't belong to you like she does." She pointed at Na-Ha-Ki.

"I tried to work things out so no one would get hurt," Charles said.

"Don't get self-righteous with me, you hypocrite, Charlie," Ruby said scathingly. To Ruby's surprise her voice was calm now, suddenly under control. "I told you before, you don't owe me anything. I'm just a girl you bedded down in Denver, that's all." She swept her things together and brushed past Charles and Na-Ha-Ki. Ruby stopped and glared at Charles one last time. "Goodbye Charlie Tucker." Charles clenched and unclenched his hands over and over.

Words tumbled from Ruby's mouth in a torrent. "I've traveled 2,000 miles, was kidnapped and nearly raped, then turned down the love of a man who saved my life, twice." She paused and motioned toward Charles, Na-Ha-Ki and then herself. "For what? For this?" Ruby pushed several trade items off the counter and onto the floor. "I'm the biggest fool that ever lived." She went to the door and through tear filled eyes looked at the adobe walls of Fort Benton. She lowered her head and started toward them. Fred Deiber hurried to her side and attempted to talk to her. Ruby stared blindly at him and strode swiftly on without answering.

He stopped for a moment and watched as she continued doggedly toward the fort, her shoulders hunched forward, head down staring at the road.

A hollow feeling inside of Ruby grew and grew until it seemed as if it would engulf her. The day was warm, and puffs of dust rose with every step. Tears and perspiration combined coursed down her face, leaving small dirty trails. Deiber was at her side again. This time he grasped her arm. She tore free and increased her pace. He watched her for a while.

"Oh shit," he said. He kicked the dirt and then ran back to the trading post, untied Ruby's pack horse, mounted his own horse and followed her. Jack Taylor and Crow Woman stood in the doorway and watched. Jack put his arm around Crow woman's waist. The woman's mouth tightened. She pulled free and went inside. Jack stared after her in surprise. What the hell did I do, he asked himself?

As Ruby entered the fort, people stared at her curiously. Her dress was wet with perspiration and her hair had fallen about her face. She brushed it back and as she did, stumbled and fell. Deiber was off his horse instantly and attempted to help her. Ruby struggled to her feet and brushed herself off. She ignored Fred and struck off again down the narrow rutted main street. Her foot caught in one of the ruts and she nearly fell again. She pulled herself upright and staggered to a wooden stoop in front of an adobe chinked-log building. Her body slumped as she sank down upon the step. Ruby buried her face in her hands, lowered her head and sobbed.

When Ruby's sobs stilled to an occasional soft moan, Fred leaned over and spoke softly to her. She was aware of his presence now and mutely nodded her head when he suggested that he find her a place to stay.

The room was stifling. Its only window, high and small, afforded little ventilation. Ruby sprawled on the bed and pressed a wet cloth to her forehead. She managed a smile. "Thank you, Mr. Deiber. You've been most kind. I'll be all right by myself now," she said.

Fred smiled at her. "All your things is brung in, Miss Ruby." He stroked his beard thoughtfully. "I'll check on you later."

Ruby raised her hand. "Don't fret about me. I'll manage."

He shifted from one foot to the other. "Well, I'll see you in the morning. Anything I can do for you before I leave?"

Ruby pushed the wetted cloth aside and sat up. "Yes. In my valise, there's a bottle of whiskey. Fix us a drink before you go." Fred stared at her. "That's right, Mr. Deiber. I carry it with me for medicinal purposes, and right now a stiff drink is the best medicine I can think of."

"I believe you're right, Miss Ruby." He extracted the bottle and poured some whiskey into a glass, adding water from the pail sitting on the stand. "Here," he said handing the glass to Ruby.

"Where's yours?" she asked.

"I'll just mix it in the dipper." Fred poured a bit of the whiskey into the half-filled dipper of water. They touched dipper and glass.

"To many more happy times in Montana," Ruby said. "For you, at least," she added. A tear rolled down her cheek and Fred gently brushed it away.

"Things will look better tomorrow," he said gently. "Now drink up." He tilted the dipper, then watched as she drank. She drained the last of it and held the glass out to him.

"Can I fix you another?" Deiber asked.

"No, I'll be just fine," she paused, then watched as he placed the glass on the stand, next to the water pail. Ruby's voice was hesitant, small. "If it wouldn't be too much trouble, Mr. Deiber, could you come back in the morning? I'll need to find out about arranging to go home."

"Sure enough, Miss Ruby, you can count on me."

She lay back on the bed and rested her head against the pillow. Her eyes closed and she appeared to be asleep. Deiber tiptoed to the door and quietly closed it behind him as he left the room. "Thank you, Fred," Ruby called. The bearded man stood outside the door and gazed thoughtfully at it then quickly strode away.

He did not go back to the post as he had originally had intended, but hung around Keno Bill's for a while. Sergeant Burns and his men were there and exchanged pleasantries with Deiber and bought each other drinks. It was nearly dark when Deiber left the bar.

Fred quietly went to Ruby's room, knocked on the door, listened, then when there was no answer, eased the door open and looked inside.

Ruby slept peacefully. An opened letter lay on the bed beside her, its pages stained with tears. The tall man stroked his beard thoughtfully as he recognized the hand writing as that of Charles Tucker.

Ruby's blond hair framed her face. She moaned softly, stirred, then lay still again. Emotions pressed in on Fred and visions from his past surged to the surface of his consciousness. He slowly shook his head and ruminated.

Life had strange ways sometimes. He wondered what was in store for Ruby and for that matter, Na-Ha-Ki and Charles. He silently closed the door behind him as he left.

* * *

A week had passed since the confrontation between Ruby and Charles. "Peers to me Charlie bit off more than he could chew with that Ruby girl," Jack Taylor said.

Fred tossed a pack to one side. "Sure enough looks like it. Was a mighty touchy situation there for a while."

"I always told Charlie he'd meet his match someday." Jack drew out his pipe and prepared it for smoking. "Wonder what is going to happen to that Ruby gal?"

"Well, she's got a lot of spunk. She'll get along all right after a while," Deiber said.

"Crow Woman tells me Na-Ha-Ki hasn't had anything to do with Charlie since Ruby got here," Jack said.

"Serves him right, can't say as I blame her none. Must have been as much of a shock for her to see that Ruby girl as it was to Charlie," Deiber said.

"Well, for that matter, Crow Woman hasn't been treating me none too good neither" Jack tossed a hide on top of a pile. "You'd think the way she's acting that it was me instead of Charlie that Ruby come to see."

"She'll get over it soon as things get better between Charlie and Na-Ha-Ki again," Deiber said. "Reckon by now, them women figure a man's skin is white, he just can't be trusted," Fred said. "I'm not too sure that things are going to get better between Na-Ha-Ki and Charlie," Jack said. "Those two are mighty strong willed people. If I don't miss my guess, Na-Ha-Ki isn't ever going to trust Charlie again."

"What else could she be expected to think? White man killed off her family, kin-folk and all. Only thing she's got left is Charlie. Wouldn't expect her to take too kindly to a white woman showing up out of the clear blue expecting to take her man away from her, too." Fred wiped his bandana across his brow. Jack knocked his pipe against his boot heel. "Charlie done the right thing by her, though. He could have left Na-Ha-Ki and the baby and gone off with Ruby. She's a right fine looking girl." Jack frowned, then added, "Reckon he just wanted to have his cake and eat it, too. Understand Ruby's leaving tomorrow."

"Sure enough. I made arrangements for her with the captain of the Montana Lady." Fred removed his hat and ran his fingers through his hair. "Was a tough predicament for Charlie. Once I saw that Ruby gal, I could see why he was in such a pickle. He grew up with her living right next door to him when he was a kid." He paused, then continued. "Wonder what it'd be like having two good looking women like that fighting over you?" A wistful look came into his eyes. "Always figured I was lucky to have jest one interested in me."

Jack snorted, then laughed. "Crow Woman suits me fine," he said. "One at a time is good enough for me." He slapped Fred on the shoulder. Deiber looked thoughtful. "Well now, you and Crow woman seem to be happy enough."

Jack grinned at Fred. "Way I figure the stick floats, a man can get mighty lonesome without a woman."

"Well, maybe, but I'll wait and see," Fred said thoughtfully.

Only Fred Deiber was on hand to say good bye to Ruby. He saw to it that her belongings were safely loaded aboard the river steamer for the return trip east. She thanked him, then quickly kissed him on the cheek. "I don't know what I'd have done without your assistance."

Deiber grasped Ruby's hand. "Now Miss Ruby, take care of yourself. Captain told me he'd look out for you." Fred looked at her thoughtfully before continuing. "I expect you ought to know that all of us wish the best for you."

Ruby cut him off before he could go on. "This might not sound like good sense to you, Fred, but I don't really blame Charles for what happened anymore than I blame myself. I was a fool. My good sense tells me that, but another part of me is angry at myself for being so naive." Ruby looked at Deiber, her lip quivering. "It's, it's just that I never thought Charles would do something like he did. If he'd just told me, I'd have understood."

Ruby daubed at her eyes with her kerchief and smiled bravely at the bearded man. "You ought to get back to shore, I think they are about to leave."

"Miss Ruby," he began as he squeezed her hand, "I just want you to know I'll be wanting the best for you back there in Denver." He hurried to the gangplank and waved to her as the Montana Lady pulled into the swift current of the Missouri River and headed East. He watched until the boat rounded a bend and passed from sight.

A warm steady breeze rippled the water that day, in July of 1870. It cooled off toward evening and the wind held a hint of dampness. Ruby still leaned against the rail and stared into the muddy waters of the Missouri. What would have happened, she wondered, if she had taken Kenneth more seriously? Where was he now and would he ever find out what had happened to her? Would he care? How was she going to explain things to her parents? Questions filled her mind, but the answers were slow in coming. The water swished past the boat, soothing her even as the damp breeze chilled her.

45-JEYS

CHAPTER 22
UNEXPECTED TURN

*(To Drug the Memory of that Insolence...)*xxx

Keno looked up at the sound of the batwing doors as they softly swung back and forth. The saloon was empty except for Keno and the sole occupant at the end of the bar. Keno slowly wiped the polished surface and eyed the slender blue-coated cavalry officer who stood in the doorway. He shaded his eyes until they adjusted to the gloomy interior of the room. Late afternoon sunlight penetrated the cracks in the shutters and cast bars of light across the floor.

"Come in and wet your whistle." Keno beckoned to the man in the doorway. "First drink is on me," he said.

The man smiled and walked with a pronounced limp toward the bar. "Something cold would hit the spot."

Keno placed both elbows on the bar and studied the man. "Not too much choice, but it's wet." He shoved a glass and a bottle of rye whiskey across the counter in front of the soldier. "I can put some ice in her if you want it."

The soldier nodded. Keno opened a door under the counter, carefully extracted a piece of ice and placed it in the glass. The man held up the glass and eyed the chunk of ice in it.

"Good clean Missouri River ice," Keno commented, answering the unasked question. "A little Missouri River mud never hurt nobody."

The soldier poured some whiskey over the ice, sloshed it around and sipped it. He made a face and put the glass down.

Keno's gaze had not left the man's face. "Seems like I ought to know you from some place."

"That so?"

"Yeah, I know I've seen you before." Keno's voice was curious, questioning.

"First time I've been to Fort Benton. Couldn't have been here." The Blue Coat sipped the whiskey and made another face. The ice had nearly melted and Keno dropped another chunk in his glass.

"This ain't the only place I've ever been. How about Fort Ellis? Fort Ellis that's it. You were shot and they brought you in to fix you up," Keno said.

Suddenly Keno grabbed the glass and emptied it into the sink. He slid a fresh glass with some clear sparkling ice in it in front of the astonished soldier. Then he reached under the counter and from a fresh bottle of liquor, poured some amber fluid into the glass. "Virginia Gentleman is what you deserve, my friend, we'll save the rot gut for less deserving people." He placed the bottle of rye whiskey back under the counter.

"I'm not sure what brought all of this on, but I'll share your Virginia Gentleman with you. To your health." The man at the counter lifted the glass to his lips and sipped. He held the glass up and eyed it as he savored the whiskey. "Now that's what I call real good bourbon." He placed the glass down, put both hands on the bar and looked Keno full in the face. "Now tell me, to what do I owe the great unexpected honor of being served your best whiskey?"

Keno slowly wiped a glass with a towel and set it on the shelf behind the bar.

He leaned across the bar and refilled the glass. "I knew Greasy Betters, and I got a look at that Ruby girl you saved from him." He swiped the bar and continued, "I heard how you saved her from being run over by a herd of buffalo, too." Keno swiped at a wet spot on the bar and continued. "Ken Hawkins. I even remember your name." His voice rose and the figure at the other end of the bar moved closer. Hawkins grinned and sipped his drink again. "Didn't do me much good," he said slowly. "She was going to marry a man here in Fort Benton. Charles Tucker is his name. You know him?" He swirled the ice in his drink around slowly as he talked. The only sound in the bar was the clink of ice against the glass.

Keno smiled, "It never happened, my friend. Charlie already had him an Indian wife."

Kenneth's glass thudded against the bar surface as he quickly placed it down. "What happened to Ruby?"

"Well, you might ask Charlie himself. He's right here," Keno gestured at the other occupant of the bar.

Kenneth quickly turned to Charles. "What did you do to her?" Without realizing it, he had moved uncomfortably close to Charles.

"Back off, friend, and I'll tell you." Charles' voice was tightly controlled. "I didn't do anything to her. She showed up unexpectedly and before I could make an explanation, she read me the riot act." He paused and slapped the bar with his open palm. "Let me finish before you say anything, if you will." He looked steadily at Kenneth. "I had it coming. I was a damned fool." He let his breath out slowly before going on. "Let's sit down and talk over here." He gestured toward a table away from the bar. "This is personal, Keno." Keno moved toward the other end of the bar, out of earshot. Charles waited until Kenneth was seated, then motioned toward the bottle between them. Kenneth shook his head. Charles placed his elbows on the table, cupped his chin in his hand and looked squarely at the soldier. "First off, I want you to know how much I appreciate what you've done for Ruby." Charles paused and held up a hand as Kenneth started to speak. "I know I've acted like an ass and deserve whatever you think of me, but hear me out, please." Kenneth's mouth tightened. He pulled away from the table and studied the man across from him, then nodded. Charles continued, "You know Ruby and I grew up together back in New Jersey?"

"Yes, she told me, Morristown."

"When I saw her in Denver after all those years, I lost my head." Charles clenched and unclenched his fist. "This is hard for me to say, but I owe both you and Ruby an explanation."

"You don't owe me anything. The sooner we can finish this conversation, the better." Kenneth pushed his chair back and attempted to stand up, faltered and grasped the chair back and managed to rise to his feet. "Any man that would treat a woman like Ruby the way you did ought to be horsewhipped," his voice rose.

"Don't push me!" Charles placed both hands on the table and pushed himself to his feet. His voice was low, carefully controlled. "I don't often eat crow. There's been enough damage done already without us doing more."

Kenneth stared at Charles, his face taut and his arms shaking. He pulled his gloves from his belt and slammed them against the table. The bottle tipped. He reached out automatically and set it upright. His grip loosened on the bottle as he slapped the table emphasizing each point. His voice came out between clenched teeth. "Where's Ruby now?" The gloves slapped the table and the glasses jumped.

"She started back to Denver last week on the Montana Lady," Charles reached out as if to touch Hawkins' hand. The gloves swung in a quick arc, slapping Charles' hand away. They glared at each other across the table. Only the droning of the ever-present flies disturbed the silence. Keno reached under the counter and slid an oaken club along the bar tapping it lightly against the shining surface, breaking the silence. "You fellows want to scrap, do it some place else, like outside." He paused. "Ain't none of my affair, but the harm's already done. Won't help for one of you to kill the other."

Charles dropped into his chair and pulled the bottle toward him, filled both glasses and raised his glass. His eyes were level as they sought Kenneth's. The soldier slowly sat down, raised his glass and with a slight gesture toward the man across the table drank. Charles did likewise. The glasses clinked softly as they were simultaneously placed on the table.

"Go on, then," Kenneth's voice was calm now, quiet.

"Not much to tell. When I met Ruby in Denver last fall, it was like my life out here was in another time and place."

"I can understand that. I've almost forgotten what it was like back East. But you had an Indian wife here, at the time, didn't you?"

Charles nodded at Kenneth. "That's right, but for a while it was as if she didn't exist." Charles paused, passing his hand over his face. "Looking back on it now I can't condone what happened." He stopped again and looked at his hand as it automatically clenched and unclenched. "I love Na-Ha-Ki, but with Ruby it was different."

The man in blue stared into his glass, then looked at Charles. "Why didn't you ever tell Ruby you were married?"

Charles turned the glass in front of him around two or three times before he answered. "Sounds crazy now, but somehow I thought I could work it out, so no one would get hurt." He shook his head slowly. "I'd planned to send Na-Ha-Ki back to her people. She'd have been rich." He paused again. "Happens out here." Charles coughed. "Our marriage hadn't been perfect. We didn't have any children and I guess I just wanted to believe everything would work out for the best. But she was pregnant when I got back and I just didn't know how to tell her. And there was Ruby to consider. I was a fool, a damned fool." He stopped and studied Kenneth's face and slowly went on. "Na-Ha-Ki's entire family were massacred the same day our son was born." Charles chin sunk to his chest. He blew his nose quietly, then went on. His voice was stronger now. "I couldn't leave her alone. But then I made the biggest fool mistake of my life. "

Kenneth leaned forward. "Mistake? It was the only honorable thing to do!"

"No, I don't mean staying with Na-Ha-Ki. You're right, I had no choice there. My mistake was that I didn't level with Ruby. I wrote and told her I couldn't come back right away as I was unavoidably detained.

I had no idea that she would come charging out here." His voice lowered. "I didn't have the guts to tell her what really happened."

Kenneth started to say something, then stopped as Charles raised his hand. "I did finally send a letter explaining it all to her, but she had started out for here before it arrived. Ruby was always impulsive and impatient. But I never dreamed she'd try to come out here." He raised his head and looked at Kenneth. "I know I can't undo the past. I'm truly sorry. Maybe you and Ruby…" His voice trailed off.

Kenneth stood up, placed both hands on the table and slowly shook his head. "Ruby was fortunate things worked out the way they did. She might have married you." Kenneth spoke more quietly now. "I'm sorry I can't be more charitable, but maybe under other circumstances…" He left the sentence unfinished. "At least you admitted your mistake."

Hawkins paused, "For you're information, I'm being discharged from the army. I'm heading for Denver. Wish me luck." He flung a mock salute at Charles.

Charles watched as Hawkins limped to the bar, flung some money on it and left. The batwing doors swung softly back and forth behind him. It was nearly dark now and Keno had lighted several lamps. After a long time Charles pushed away from the table and placed the half-empty bottle of Virginia Gentleman on the bar in front of Keno.

"What was that soldier's name, Keno?"

"Hawkins, Kenneth Hawkins."

Charles nodded. "Quite a man, Ruby deserves him."

"What did you say, Charlie?"

"Nothing. Thanks." Charles put some money on the bar. The saloon was filling with people and the batwing doors flopped softly behind him as he left.

45-JEYS

*　　*　　*

The hot winds of summer melded into the cooler changeable winds of fall. One morning the high peaks were covered with white. And still the wind. This time cold, biting, with promises of winter. The winds swooped down off the mountains and chilled the land. Small fingers of ice formed on the sloughs and ponds. Wild geese gathered in huge vees and winged south and eastward. And still the wind. It was winter now, cold, bitter and snow laden. A time for pulling in. A time to read, talk, think and to mend. A time to prepare for the advent of spring. And the wind, never relenting, continued.

It was spring again, and the first of the geese returned. The streams and ponds fill with snowmelt. A time for life to renew itself. And still the wind. A continuous circuit of seasons with the ever-present wind at its center. The year was 1876 and the seasons had made six circuits since Ruby left Montana.

*　　*　　*

Fred Deiber had taken an Indian wife, and his adopted son, with the unlikely name of Jefferson Davis Deiber, now had a younger sister. Fred had lost his wanderfoot and was a family man again.

Jack Taylor and Crow Woman had aged, but otherwise were very much the same. Chuck, the red-haired son of Na-Ha-Ki and Charles, born on the same day that his mother's family had been massacred, had grown into a precocious six-year-old.

Charles and Fred sat on the steps of the Trading Post and watched their sons play. Deiber stroked his beard, removed his pipe from his mouth, knocked the ashes from it and stuffed it into his pocket. "Boys are growing up fast, Charlie. Doesn't seem any time since I brought Jeff home under my coat. He was a mighty little fellow for such a big voice."

"Time gets away from you all right, Fred. I'll have been in Montana ten years this summer. Doesn't seem like it was that long."

"Things are a changing, Charlie. Things are different."

A marble rolled across the packed ground and thudded into Charles' boot. He stooped over, picked it up and rolled it back to his son. Chuck caught the agate, then smiled at his father. "Want to play, Pa?" he asked.

"No, you boys go ahead. Fred and I will watch. Maybe later."

Chuck studied his father's face for a moment, then turned to play with the bronze-skinned boy at his side.

"Those two are quite a pair, Charlie. Take that boy of yours, bright as a whip, but serious. He doesn't say too much, but he's always studying things out. Jeff, he doesn't care if school keeps or not. Some pair, all right."

"They might be different, but they sure get along well."

"If a person didn't know better, he'd never know little Charlie was half Blackfeet. Red hair, fair skin and all."

"He's got those big eyes of his mother and an Indian nose if I ever saw one,"

"Ain't no mistaking Jeff for anything but an Indian. I often wondered just who his folks were." Jeff looked up at Fred, then ran to him and stood at his side. Fred ran his fingers through Jeff's thick black hair.

"Come on, Dad, let's play. Me and Chuck will show you how."

"Well, I ain't too sure son, but if you'll show me how, I guess I can try to learn." He took Jeff's hand and they went over to where the boys had been playing marbles. "Come on, Charlie, these lads want us to play with them." Fred knelt and aimed a marble at a hole the boys had dug.

Jack Taylor and Crow Woman came to the doorway. The trader had his arm about his wife's waist. "I can't tell which of you fellows is the biggest kid," Jack said.

"Come on and join the fun, Jack, the boys are getting pretty good. Fred and I could use some help."

"I got work to do. Can't everybody play. Charlie, you remember how you taught Au-Ti-Pus to play marbles?" Jack asked.

Charles looked toward the stable and studied the blaze-faced horse that stood there. "Sure do, Jack. Been a while since I thought of that boy." Charles' redheaded son stood quietly at his father's side. "Who was Au-Ti-Pus, father?" Charles hesitated, then put his arm about his son.

"See that horse over there?" He pointed to Lightning Horse. "That horse belonged to the boy Mr. Taylor spoke of. When he wasn't too much older than you, he could ride that horse like a man. His name was Au-Ti-Pus." Charles studied his son's face. "He was your uncle, your mother's brother." Charles took his son by the hand and together they walked to the corral and Lightning Horse. He sat Chuck on the fence rail and the horse sniffed the boy.

"Go ahead and pet him, son, he just wants you to pay attention to him." Fred and Jeff were with them now and Jeff had climbed up beside Chuck.

Jeff stroked the horse and laughed when the horse snorted and stuck his nose against his body. "What ever happened to the boy?" Chuck's eyes were trained on his father's face.

"It's a sad story, but Au-Ti-Pus was killed. Some time when you're a little bit older, I'll tell you about it." Noticing the disappointed boy's face he slipped an arm about him and pulled him close. "Your uncle and I are the only ones to ever ride this horse, Chuck. We'll talk about it some other time. Remind me, will you?" Chuck nodded.

"I thought you guys wanted to play marbles," Fred said.

"You bet. We'll be over there in a moment or two," Charles said. Lightning Horse nosed Charles and snorted softly as Charles gently rubbed the horse's nose.

Charles swung his son off the rail, then reached over and patted the horse. He wondered if Lightning Horse ever thought of Au-Ti-Pus, too.

Spring slipped into summer, and it was already July. The day had been hot and the room was still uncomfortably warm. Charles turned over and moved away from Na-Ha-Ki. Her breathing was regular and she slept easily. He eased himself from the bed so as not to awaken her and pulled on his pants. Maybe a smoke would help. The air was a little cooler outside on the step. He puffed his pipe and leaned against the doorframe. A man could think at a time like this. He let his mind drift back to times that he'd nearly forgotten.

He remembered the red brick house in Morristown. He and his father were in the study. Against every wall were shelves lined with books. The white-haired man looked up from his writing. His blue eyes studied the young blond headed man who stood before him. "Charles, you look serious, something bothering you?"

Charles had unbuttoned his jacket and twisted one of its buttons back and forth as he studied a spot on the desk in front of his father. "Son, if you have something to say to me, look me in the eyes." His father's voice was firm, but gentle.

Charles lifted his head and looked at his father. The man no longer smiled. "I've decided not to go to school, father. Robert McIntyre and I are enlisting in the Union army."

His father's mouth opened, then closed. He picked up the open book before him and inserted a paper marker in it. The book made a soft whoosh as he closed it. Charles watched as his father went to the bookcase and shoved the book into its place. It made a dull thunk as it hit the back of the shelf. Without turning, the white-headed man spoke quietly.

"You're mind's made up then?"

"Yes, Sir."

"No use of me giving you advice, son. We've talked about it before and you know how I feel." Charles' father still faced the books and he fiddled with one of them. Suddenly he turned and went to his son. "You told your mother yet?" His arm was about his son's shoulder.

"No, I thought I'd better tell you first."

"It won't be easy for her. Maybe you can pick up your education later."

"Yes, sir."

Charles stirred on the step as long buried emotions surfaced within his consciousness. His remembered feelings were vivid. The obvious disappointment of his father, who had always expected that Charles would attend Harvard, as he, himself, had done.

His own excitement and anticipation of glorious adventure ahead was all that he had seemed to be able to think about. Sometimes he wondered how he could have been so self-centered and selfish. It all seemed so long ago and yet in many ways was like only yesterday. And now, Charles thought, my own son, will he disappoint me by going away some day?

A long mournful sound intruded upon his reflections. The wolves were singing to the moon. The man on the step shook his head. It was strange how a man's thoughts drifted sometimes. Here lately he'd been thinking about the past a lot. Maybe it was the boy that caused it. It was too bad that little Charles would never know his grandparents He knew that little Charlie would have brought much happiness to them. He could imagine them now, talking at great length to each other. The serious nature of the boy would have appealed to them. He'd have to see that before long the boy was able to visit the East. He was getting lonesome for it, himself.

An image of a blond girl with hazel eyes and a merry smile crossed his mind. Ruby. Wonder what had happened to her? Wouldn't do, to think too much like that. She was a part of his past. Wouldn't do either of them any good to try to go back to something that couldn't be. He stood up, stretched and stared eastward into the darkness.

He wondered how his parents would have reacted to Na-Ha-Ki and his son, little Charles.

He was sorry that neither of them had ever had a chance to know their Grandson. He smiled as he imagined how his very proper father and mother would have spoiled little Chuck. Now for the first time, Charles understood at an emotional level what it must have been like for them when he choose to enlist. Well, there wasn't anything he could do about it now.

It had cooled off. He yawned, stretched and headed back to his bed.

Chapter 23
A matter of time

*(There was a Veil thru which I could not see,...)*XXXII

"By God, he got what he had coming to him."

Fred shoved a pack of furs against the wall so hard, they fell over and scattered about the floor. "Nothing but a glory hound anyhow. Way he killed women and children, serves him right."

"I know how you feel, but you can bet your bottom dollar those Indians are going to pay dearly for it. I've seen it happen before," Charles said.

"What the hell you guys arguing about anyhow?" Jack stopped in the middle of rearranging a pile of yard goods.

"Guess you ain't heard yet. Bunch of Sioux and Cheyenne done in the whole of Custer's 7th over on the Little Big Horn. Must have killed a couple hundred of them. Captain Keener was among them." Fred tossed a bolt of cloth on the pile in front of him.

"Was bound to come sooner or later, I guess," Charles said. "Ought to make the Piegan happy to see Keener get his. Any of the Blackfeet involved?"

"Not that I know of. They have been staying out of trouble. But the way I figure it with the white man grabbing all the buffalo country for his own and crowding the Indians onto the reservations, there can't help but be trouble here before long. Only a matter of time."

Deiber stroked his beard. "Guess you're right, Jack. They got the excuse they need now. Won't no Indian be safe. Good excuse to take the Black Hills from the Sioux and Cheyenne. There is supposed to be gold and silver in there."

"Them bluecoats will be on the prowl," Jack said.

Charles glanced out of the door to where his son and Jeff were playing. "I've been thinking I'd like to take the boy and Na-Ha-Ki back East so they could see what it's like. Suppose you could do without us for a while. Things will blow over some after a while."

"I guess we could get along without you. But last time I let you go, you got a mess stirred up with that Ruby girl. I expect Na-Ha-Ki wouldn't let you go by yourself, anyhow. What do you think Fred?"

"I just work here. Don't know why you asked me. But since you asked, it seems like a good idea, especially if Charlie wants the boy to get an education some day." Fred paused and looked thoughtfully at his son and young Charles.

Jack nodded his head in agreement. "Deiber's right Charlie, you best be thinking of school for the boy some day when he gets older."

"My God, you two are showing your age. You talk like a couple of old men. Chuck is just a little boy. Besides he might not even want to go to school in the East when he grows up." He looked at Fred. "What about Jeff? You going to let him grow up without an education? I'm putting Chuck in school here next year."

"Wanted to talk to you about that. Suppose they'd let Jeff attend?"

"They damn well better," Jack growled. "I donated them plenty of money and helped build that schoolhouse with my own hands. I'll speak to them about it."

"Well, I don't want to cause no problem," Deiber said. "But if you can manage it, I'd sure appreciate it. Like for him to at least read and write."

"We'll see that those boys get educated, even if you and me do all the work and let Charlie do the teaching." Jack slapped the counter. He peered at Charles. "We best be having a palaver with the Piegan, before they get all excited about the big fight with Custer and do something foolish. Charlie and I ought to both go." The three furrows that always appeared when Jack was worried were on his forehead.

"Good idea, the sooner the better." Charles glanced at the boys playing in the doorway again. "Hate to go off and leave you with all the work, Fred, but we might be able to head off trouble. The Piegan are camped over along the Teton River. Two days' ride over there. Guess we'll be gone most of a week."

"Don't make no never mind to me. I get you two out of my hair, I can get some work done." He went to the door. "Hey you two," he called to Jeff and Chuck. "Come on in here a bit. We got some important business to attend to."

The boys jumped to their feet and ran to Deiber. Fred stooped and grabbed each of them under an arm, lifting them high to sit on the counter. Jeff laughed and clapped his hands. Chuck's face held a serious expression.

"Now listen you two, we got to run this here Trading Post all by our lonesome for a while. Them two is going off gallivantin' about and leaving everything for us to run while they're gone."

Jeff smiled, "I'll help you, Pa."

"Me, too," said Chuck"

You'll help Uncle Fred and your mother for me won't you?" Chuck nodded and ran to the rear of the trading post to tell his mother.

They left for the Piegan camp early. The day was bright, and the high peaks glistened as the sunlight reflected from their icy covering. This was the Teton River country. The camp was strung out along the river, with a large horse herd bunched together in the center of a large meadow whose edges touched the river on one side and the foot of the steep mountains on the other. It was a large encampment. Charles estimated it to contain thirty or forty lodges.

Jack reined in Monte. "Old boy is still a better horse than a lot of younger ones," he said. Jack patted Monte on his neck. The animal flicked an ear in acknowledgement.

"He sure is, sort of like his owner, sometimes. How old is he anyway?"

"Seventeen or eighteen years. That Lightning Horse ain't no spring chicken." The spotted horse shifted about nervously, as if he knew the men were taking about him.

Charles studied the pointed peaks behind the camp. "Easy to see how they got the name of Grand Tetons. Great titties they be, too. Look at that pair over there." Charles pointed to a pair of matching peaks that rose from the plain to points where snow formed gigantic white nipples. Charles pointed to a gray horse tied to a lodge. Several raid marks were painted on its neck. "White Quiver's horse. We're in luck. Last I knew he was in Canada." They rode to the lodge.

The entrance flap was thrust aside and White Quiver stepped out, smiling as he greeted his old friends. "So, you come to visit the Piegan. You are welcome to this lodge. Come in." He motioned and stepped aside. "Sit my friends," He gestured at some willow backrests toward the rear of the tipi. "We will smoke."

White Quiver lifted a long stemmed pipe from its place beside his rest, lighted it and puffed smoke to the four directions, and to Sun and earth, then handed the pipe to Charles. He puffed it once and passed it carefully to Jack. He puffed it, and then gave it back to their host. "My woman will be here soon. She will see to your horses and come soon with food."

"We have eaten a short time ago," Charles said. "We are here to talk to the Piegan. When did you get back from Canada?"

"Only last week. I will only visit for a short time. My woman gets lonesome for her people. That is where she is now."

"Have you heard of the fight at the Greasy Grass River?" Charles asked.

"Yes they killed many bluecoats. Even the one with the yellow hair was killed. What do you think will happen now?" White Quiver leaned forward in anticipation.

"That's what we wanted to talk to you about. Remember when the bluecoats surrounded Eagle Chief's band and killed everybody in camp?"

White Quiver closed his eyes and bowed his head. His head lifted and he looked at Charles. His eyes were soft and gentle, but they but contained a hurt. His mouth tightened.

"Yes, my friend, it is a time that I do not like to remember." He made a motion toward Charles. "What can the Piegan do? The bluecoats will kill our women and children if we fight them!" He spat at his feet. "They are dog faces."

"Do you know if there were any Blackfeet at the Greasy Grass fight?"

White Quiver shook his head. "No, we did not join with the Sioux. They have always been our enemies, but if they kill the bluecoats…" He left the sentence unfinished.

"Yes, the Indians must forget their old enemies now," Charles said. He touched White Quiver's arm. "The Sioux, Cheyenne and Crow are between you and the white man. If the Blackfeet were living where the Sioux are, it would be the Blackfeet against the white man."

White Quiver was silent for a moment or two. He picked up his pipe, held it in front of him and studied it thoughtfully. "What you say is true. It is difficult for the Sioux, especially when the Crows help the white man against the other Indians. The Crows are muenos. I have thought about this, but right now my medicine is weak. I do not know the way. Sitting Bull of the Sioux did send word to the Blackfeet that we should join him to drive the white man away."

Charles glanced at Jack. The vertical furrows above his nose were gathered together. "What did you tell him?" Jack asked.

White Quiver replaced the pipe before he answered. "The young men wanted to go. It is always that way with them. When the chiefs and older people reminded them of the bluecoats attacking our camps and killing our women and children, they laughed and made fun of us."

Charles studied White Quiver's face as he spoke. The man had matured in the last few years. The role of leadership had aged him. "The chiefs kept the young ones from doing anything foolish. We do not want to fight with the white man. We only want to live on our land and hunt the buffalo as we always have. Now the white man tells us we must stay in one place and tear up the ground to plant corn. This is not the way for a warrior to live" He spat on the ground and twisted his foot on the moisture.

"There are many more bluecoats in the Great Father's army," Charles said. "He will send them to destroy Sitting Bull and his people. If you join the against the white man, he will destroy the Blackfeet, too."

"But if we are to stay in one place we cannot hunt the buffalo. We will starve. It is better to die fighting than to die of starvation." White Quiver's voice rose in volume and intensity.

"It is your women and children and old people who will suffer most if you fight," Jack Taylor said. He rose from his sitting position and stretched. "What about moving to the North, Canada, where you have been living? The bluecoats won't bother you there."

"That is my plan, but most of the people will not listen. They think the bluecoats will go away after a while and leave us alone. They also say that this is where most of the buffalo are found."

The flap of the tipi opened and White Quiver's woman came in. She quickly began to prepare food for her guests.

It was late when the three friends ended their serious talking. White Quiver passed the pipe to Jack and Charles again. Charles carefully studied long stemmed pipe. Several tufts of weasel tails that hung from it swung slowly back and forth. The red bowl was different than any Charles had seen. "Where did the stone for this pipe come from?" he asked.

"From the East. Many moons' travel. My father got it from the Ojibway. His vision told him where to go. First he found the Black Panther and killed it. Then he traveled to a land of many lakes where he traded the panther's skin for it. It has always been good medicine for our lodge. But now...?"

Charles smoked and passed the pipe back to his friend. White Quiver set the pipe in its place again. He suddenly smiled. "I will think on your plan for us. I will call on my helper to guide me. Perhaps you are right, but it is hard for me to think that soon there will be no more buffalo." He grasped Charles by the arm. "Now tell me how you found Lightning Horse. When I saw you last, you did not know where it was."

"That's right. When the bluecoats attacked the camp on the Marias, they ran off the horses, and Lightning Horse was among them." Charles took the bowl of steaming meat that White Quiver's woman handed him. He ate some of it before answering. "No one saw the horse until a couple of years ago. Turned out that the Crow people had him. When we heard about it, Jack and I went over and traded for him."

"They must have asked many things for that horse," White Quiver said.

Jack grinned at Charles and White Quiver. "You should have seen how we fooled those Crows. You tell him, Charlie. I get all tangled up trying to talk that Piegan. I swear you were born half Indian, the way you talk their lingo."

"Well, when we heard they had him, we figured they might hold out for a high price if they knew we wanted him. So we acted like we wanted to buy robes instead of horses. I don't speak Crow too well so most of our talk was by sign language." Charles wiped his fingers on the moistened leather beside the backrest. "I pretended to just notice the horse by accident and asked if I could buy it. Was funny to watch them. They told me it was a strong medicine horse and was worth many blankets and guns."

"Didn't they tell you it couldn't be ridden?" White Quiver asked.

"No, that's where Jack tricked them."

"I sure did, Charlie, but you were the one who had to pull it off. I wasn't sure that horse would remember after all those years."

White Quiver leaned forward, listening intently. "What did you do?"

"Wasn't me, it was Jack. He told them that I was big medicine, too, and that I could ride any horse they had." Charles turned to Jack, "You ever think what might have happened if they had picked out another horse instead of Lightning Horse?"

"Sure, but I would have thought of something to get you off the hook. Besides that, I ain't too sure you couldn't do it. But go on and finish the story for White Quiver."

"They took the bait all right. You know how the Crows like to gamble. Before he was done, Jack had them betting twenty of their best buffalo runners against a pile of trade goods, that I couldn't ride Lightning Horse."

White Quiver's woman sat at his side now and her arm rested on his shoulder. A slight smile played around White Quiver's lips as he anticipated Charles' story.

"I wasn't too sure what would happen when I tried to get on Lightning Horse. It had been three or four years since I'd seen him. By now the entire Crow camp was gathered around to watch the show. Jack had bet everything we brought with us. There was a pile of robes as high as your head stacked up there." Charles paused and watched as the tipi flap moved in a gust of wind. He continued, "They roped the horse and led him up to where I could get on his back. He acted gentle, like he always does until someone tries to ride him."

Jack interrupted. "Charlie wasn't too sure of himself, about then. You should have seen him. He just walked around and around that horse letting him get use to him. I figured he'd worn a path clean up to his ankles. Talked in his ear a lot, too. Them Crows were all a'laughing and shouting to each other. Figured they was going to win an easy bet, and see a white man get bested, too."

White Quiver was excited. "What happened?"

"Not much, except for us leaving a bunch of disappointed Crows. As soon as Lightning Horse stopped laying his ears back and cocked them forward for a while, Charlie knew that this was a signal that the horse knew who he was. Charlie, sort of quick-like, slipped onto that horse's back and rode off as slick as you please. Charlie's big medicine to them Crows now."

"Did you collect your bets?" White Quiver asked.

"Sure enough, took twenty of their best buffalo runners back with us. Left them with their robes and some of the trade goods. Figured we better if we wanted to get back with our scalps."

White Quiver laughed. "You have brought joy into my lodge. Will you stay with us?" Jack and Charles agreed to stay and White Quiver's woman went to their horses to get their belongings.

"You are a true friend of the Piegan. That was a good trick you played on the Crows. Now it is time for sleeping. My woman will show you your robes."

CHAPTER 24
LOST IN A WHITE MIST

*(To-morrow!—Why, To-morrow I may be
Myself with Yesterday's Sev'n thousand Years.)*_{XXI}

It was cool there next to the Tetons and the pleasant sound of water rushing over the rocky streambed mingled with the rustling noises of the trees. Charles listened to the night sounds and gradually relaxed. He sensed there was something special about this visit with his friend. He locked his fingers together at the back of his head and stared at the opening at the top of the tipi. It was a clear, dark night and the smokehole framed the bright cluster of the Pleiades. The wind whispered down the slopes of the Tetons and through the trees that lined the river. A horse snorted, moved about on its tether, then quieted. A dog barked for a while, then stopped. The rush of water in the river muted the soft, regular breathing of the lodge occupants.

The thick pile of furs beneath his bare body was smooth and soft. He pulled a robe closer about his shoulders and scrunched down into the comfortable bed. The scent of pine carried by the damp night air permeated the lodge. Suddenly, he was thirsty. Quietly, carefully, Charles eased his canteen from his pack. The water tasted fresh and cool. He swished it around in his mouth, then swallowed. He lay back and was once more engulfed with a feeling of total peace and serenity. He breathed deeply. The night air was cool. Emotions surged from a place deep within him and it seemed as if he would burst. His throat felt constricted and tight. A man couldn't ask for more out of life than he had right now. When a person had friends, a warm snug bed, peace, a family to love and be loved by in return, he had everything that was important in life. Sometimes a person ought to just stop, and enjoy living.

His thoughts returned to the conversation of the evening. White Quiver and the Piegan would see hard times ahead. Maybe it made sense to enjoy things while a body could. What was it Omar had said? He turned the verse over and over in his mind:

> *"How sweet is mortal Sovranty!"—think some:*
> *Others— "How blest the Paradise to come!"*
> *Ah, take the Cash in hand and wave the Rest;*
> *Oh, the brave Music of a distant drum!"* FIRST ED., XII

Now Charles' thoughts turned to his son. Charles hoped that he would be as fortunate as he'd been. Young Charles showed a serious mindedness that indicated intelligence. It was time he learned to read. Maybe he could teach him. It was a good thing he'd had all those books shipped out from the East last year. Education was important all right.

Things were changing fast here in Montana. There would be plenty of opportunities for an educated man in the years to come. Maybe Jack and Fred were right. Na-Ha-Ki and he ought to be thinking of a more formal education for the boy when he grew up. Maybe a trip to the East would convince her of the advantages there for the boy. His mind was made up. He would arrange with Jack to take care of things while he took Na-Ha-Ki and Charles to visit the East.

Well, he couldn't lay here awake all night. Before long it would be dawn. He and Jack would talk to the other leaders of the Piegan tomorrow. His thoughts went back to the *Rubaiyat*.

> *Ah, my Beloved, fill the Cup that clears*
> *To-day of past Regret and future Fears:*
> *To-morrow!— why tomorrow I may be*
> *Myself with Yesterday's sev'n thousand Years.*_{XXI}

Tomorrow? His hands slipped from behind his head. He turned onto his side and slept.

*   *   *

Fall, Indian Summer, a moody time. A time of quick changes, warm during the day but with sudden hints of things to come. The wind, ever present. Birds gather in an endless blue sky and point south. Then one morning the peaks are white. A chill wind from the west. The circuitous path of the seasons has completed its journey and winter was upon the land again. And still the wind.

The trader listened as it howled and moaned about the adobe-chinked log structure like an animal in pain. Although the seasons had made twelve circuits since Charles Tucker first came to Montana in 1866, the wind sounded the same to him as it had then.

It got inside a man after a while and just when he'd begun to forget about it, there it was again, jarring, tearing, raging about, and making its presence known. In this country, one learned to live with it. It was always there.

The sounds changed and the door to the trading post grated open. A woman backed through and held it open while a tall man entered. She closed the door and watched as he staggered and fell on a pile of hides.

The odor of watered-down alcohol mixed with sweat carried over to Charles' nose. Small beads of perspiration glistened on the old

Blackfeet's wrinkled face and a rivulet trickled down one cheek. The old man jerked his head up and mopped the moisture away, pulled his blanket about him and stared fixedly at the trader. The man's eyes were glazed and he looked confused. His head dropped against his chest and his body slumped. Old Many Hawks was drunk again.

Charles turned to face Red Bird. She carried a heavy robe, skin side out, to the counter and laid it down. Charles carefully unfolded the heavy fur and cautiously ran his hands over it. It was the sacred white buffalo robe! He felt a tingling sensation on the backs of his hands as he stroked the soft white fur.

Suddenly, the entire situation seemed unreal to him, like it had been that day so long ago in Many Hawks' lodge when he and the old man had first talked about the white robe. Now the robe had turned up again. There was something mystical and strange about it. The trader lifted one corner and let it fall against the wooden counter. It whooshed softly. He studied the woman.

She shifted her position and clasped and unclasped her hands as she pulled a thin, worn blanket about her. Her eyes shifted away from his. She bit her lower lip and slowly raised her head, glancing at the white fur. The woman's face turned toward her husband then back to Charles. The sides of her mouth twitched several times before she spoke. Her voice was low. He leaned forward so that he could hear her.

"Will you trade for it?" she mumbled, her voice barely audible. She shuffled back and forth, waiting for his reply.

"What about Many Hawks?" He indicated the old man on the hides. His tall frame slouched and he appeared to sleep.

"It is his wish," she said. "It is a nothing life we live now. The white robe does not matter to him anymore, only the fire water." Her voice was stronger now, bitter. "It is all we have," she added lamely. Her hands fretted with the edges of her blanket. Her body sagged. The blanket fell away from her head and he was shocked to see that Red Bird's hair was completely white. She had aged drastically since he had last seen her. He ruffled the heavy fur again.

"All right," he said. His voice was gruff, resigned. "Help yourself, I'll tell you when to stop."

Red Bird's eyes glistened and she brushed her cheek with a corner of her blanket, then quickly looked away. She began to move about the post, piling items on the counter until the trader motioned her to stop. She looked at him obliquely, then shifted her eyes to some cans of molasses. Charles placed one of the cans on the counter. He studied her, hesitated, then with a swift motion, drew two brightly colored blankets from behind the counter and tossed them atop the pile of trade goods. The woman's face brightened. She smiled and nodded her head.

Many Hawks had remained motionless throughout the transaction, but now he stood and supported himself against a post. The old woman arranged one of the new blankets about herself then held the other one for her man. He staggered to it and clumsily wrapped it around his tall frame. They picked up their trade goods and moved toward the door. The old man stumbled and lurched into the trader. Charles steadied him until the man straightened up. He peered into Charles' face and mumbled, "friend," then walked past his woman into the storm.

The wind whined as it swooped around the corner of the trading post. Three horses waited, tails turned into blowing snow. Their heads hung listlessly. Patches of bare skin on the animals' bodies twitched convulsively, their bones threatening to poke through the loose skin that hung from their gaunt frames. Only the steam that rose from their bodies indicated that the skeletal caricatures were alive.

The old man inserted his foot into a wooden stirrup and attempted to hoist himself onto the back of one of the horses. His wife pushed and shoved until he was at last on the bony creature's back. He slumped forward. The body postures of man and horse signaled defeat. The woman tied the trade goods into a bundle, lashed it to the packhorse and with her leading, they headed into the whirling snow. Their figures blurred, emerged for a moment when the snow eased, then faded into ghost-like shadows lost in a white mist.

As their figures dissolved, dusk pulled in about the trading post. Almost simultaneously they were replaced by another shadowy form. Charles wiped his eyes to make sure of the vision. In his mind's eye, he could see it plainly now. It was the old Blackfeet again, but this time as Charles remembered him at the height of Many Hawks' manhood, in 1867.

He was mounted on a fine spotted pony. At his throat he wore a bear claw necklace. His long black hair draped in front of him, one-half carefully combed and parted, the other half braided and wrapped with a strip of bright red cloth. He wore a white doeskin shirt, buckskin leggings with porcupine quills dyed blue, yellow and red arranged in colorful patterns and a pair of beautifully beaded moccasins. In his hands was a long-stemmed pipe with a giant-sized bowl made from green stone. Across his horse's shoulders was the white robe.

Charles wiped his eyes again. The ghostly figure was gone. He shook his head, brushed the snow from himself, stepped inside the warm room and lit a lantern. The white robe still lay on the counter. The trader stroked it and reflected again upon the scene, as it had been when he first came to Montana in 1866. He had been a young man then, only twenty-two years old. In those days the streams still held beaver and the plains were crowded with buffalo. Of all the tribes that roamed the plains, Crow, Sioux, Cheyenne, Kuteni, Assinibon, Snake and many more, the Blackfeet were the richest and most respected. Their warriors were feared then and their favor sought, even by the white man. But now, a short twelve years later, even the proud Blackfeet were humbled. Where would it all end?

He picked up a corner of the white robe and let it flop against the counter. Charles walked slowly to a sheet metal stove at one side of the rectangular room and poured another a cup of coffee. He passed a hand over his eyes. The coolness of his palm was refreshing and he drew his thumb and forefinger across his closed eyelids. He pinched the digits together and slid them downward until they came together at his upper lip. He tugged at his lip several times while he turned things over in his mind.

Charles couldn't shake the depressed feeling initiated by his encounter with the two old Blackfeet. It clung to him like an oppressive weight. He felt tired, old. He shook his head in an attempt to dispel the mood, but it dropped over him like a shroud. His feet dragged as he went to his desk. On it, shoved into one corner was a small rectangular box with one corner burned away. The trader slowly opened the lid and the tinkling sounds of a Viennese waltz filled the air. He closed the lid and shoved the box back to the corner of the desk. He breathed deeply and stretched his arms. The coffee had cooled and he tipped the cup and emptied it. He felt better now. He ran his fingers through his hair, then pulled a pipe from his pocket. He stuffed it full of tobacco, and lighted it with a splinter from the stove. Puffing meditatively, he watched the smoke rise toward the ceiling. It was dark outside now and the storm had increased its fury. A harsh wind slammed against the log building. A wolf howled, another took up the call and soon the night air reverberated with the lonesome sounds.

The trader rose to his feet, went to the stove and stuffed it with several chunks of wood, then returned to his desk. His thoughts returned to the past. It had been a long time since he had thought of Many Hawks and the white robe. He glanced at the fur. Glowing softly in the lantern's light. The white buffalo robe had played an important role in his life and now here it was in his possession. He wondered if Many Hawks would be alone and drunk one of these times and fall from his horse and freeze to death like so many others had lately.

Although he didn't often dwell on things that happened in the past, lately he found himself doing it more and more. Like that time in Denver with Ruby. Why should he be thinking of her now? Not that he didn't think of Ruby now and then. How could he help it?

But why the same dream of her over and over? A person would think that after seven years, some things would be forgotten. Ruby McIntyre. He sighed deeply. Wonder where she was now? Did she look the same? An image of a young woman drifted across his mind. Her supple body moved gracefully toward him, arms outstretched in greeting. Her long blonde hair fell about her shoulders and her hazel eyes smiled at him. Her dress was taut with the soft swell of her breasts. Ruby, that beautiful woman of his past. Did she ever think of him? Would he ever see her again? She had been sure that fate had meant them for each other, and in a way it had. It was strange the way fate worked. Take the way he and Fred Deiber had met at Gettysburg. He guessed that there wasn't anything certain in this life. A log shifting inside of the stove thumped and returned him to his surroundings. He glanced at the counter and the robe.

Light from the lantern threw shadows against the walls of the room. The white robe glowed softly. The wind throbbed as it whipped past the trading post. It was a soothing sound and Charles closed his eyes and leaned back in his chair. As often happened to him at such times, a verse from the *Rubaiyat* came to his mind. What was it the sage had said about Certainty?

> *Oh, come with me old Khayyam, and leave the Wise To*
> *talk; one thing is certain, that Life flies;*
> *One thing is certain, and the Rest is Lies;*
> *The Flower that once has blown, for ever dies.*

FIRST ED., XXVI

*   *   *

Young Charles was growing up rapidly. He would soon be seven years old. He had attended school for over a year and enjoyed every minute of it. Na-Ha-Ki was as interested in his progress as Charles. It had been her idea that she and the boy would learn to read together. They were both apt students and Charles was kept busy answering questions. It was a happy time for the little family. For the first time since Ruby had come to Montana, it seemed to Charles that his wife had forgotten the Ruby incident or forgiven him. Of late she had responded to him sexually more warmly than she had in a long time.

Young Charles loved to draw pictures and the walls of their quarters were covered with them. One of his favorite subjects was horses, especially Lightning Horse. He was drawing a picture of it now. He bent over his latest creation and attempted to draw a figure on the horse's back. He puckered his mouth, gripped his pencil in his fist and worked determinedly. Charles leaned over to observe his son's work. "You're doing a good job, Chuck. You want some help?"

Chuck shook his head emphatically. "No, I can do it myself. It's my picture!"

Charles smiled. "It sure is Chuck, but I'm trying to figure out who it is you are showing on that horse"

"It's Au-Ti-Pus. You know, the boy who was killed." Charles glanced at Na-Ha-Ki. She sat across the table from them, quietly sewing. She looked up when Chuck mentioned her brother's name. .

"When did you tell him about Au-Ti-Pus?"

"Last summer, he told Jeff and me. Am I old enough to tell me the rest of the story, Pa?" His gaze shifted back and forth between his father and mother. "I'm a big boy now, you can tell me please?"

Charles looked at his wife. She nodded her approval. "It is time for you to tell him. You are a big boy, Chuck." She reached across the table and squeezed their son's hand. Charles sat down in his chair and lit his pipe. Na-Ha-Ki moved to his side and seated herself on the robe by the chair. She rested her head against his leg. Charles stroked her hair as he talked. Little Chuck dropped his pencil, ran to his father and climbed into his lap. His father put his arm about him and the boy rested his red head against his father's chest. The fireplace crackled and thrust its warm radiance into the room.

"It was a long time ago when it happened, son. In fact, on the day you and Jeff were born was when it happened. Chuck turned his face to his father.

"Really?"

Charles felt Na-Ha-Ki stiffen, then relax as he stroked her hair. "There was a bad man who did not understand about the Blackfeet.

He was a soldier in charge of a place not too far from here." Chuck stirred in his father's arms.

"Did you know him, Pa?"

"Yes, his name was Captain Keener. One day he came looking for some horses that he said were stolen by the Blackfeet. When he couldn't find them he had his men surround the Piegan village." Charles took a puff from his pipe. "He and his men set fire to the camp and killed everyone in it. Your uncle Au-Ti-Pus was there and he was killed with the rest."

"Why did they kill the people in the camp when they were not the ones who stole the horses?" Na-Ha-Ki pulled away from Charles and spoke to her son.

"Because they were white men. They do not like Indians." Her voice trembled as she spoke. "They are women and child killers and dog faces."

"But Pa is white. So are Uncle Fred and Uncle Jack"

"But that is different. It is only the bad Whites who do not like the Indians,"

"My teacher is nice. She likes Indians," Chuck announced. "I don't like bad people. Why didn't you tell Captain Keener not to do it?"

"I would have if I had known about it. But when all of this was happening, you were being born, right here. I was helping Crow woman with your mother." Charles eased his son from his lap and onto the floor. "All right, its bedtime. Off you go."

Young Charles looked at Charles seriously. "Aren't you going to tell me about the time when you and Lightning Horse killed the white buffalo?" Charles glanced at the white robe Na-Ha-Ki sat on. "Was that the white buffalo, Pa?" Chuck pointed to the robe.

"Yes, son, but that's another story and it'll have to wait until another night."

"Father, do you think that I could ride Lightning Horse? You know, like Au-Ti-Pus?"

"We'll see, now off to bed." He kissed his son on the cheek and watched as he went with his mother into the bedroom. He leaned back and blew a puff of smoke at the ceiling. The boy was growing up fast. It was going to be difficult to try to teach him what was right. Some times it was hard to figure out why people did the things they did. Well, come spring, they would take a trip to the east. It would be good for the boy. He would meet all kinds of white people there. He hoped Na-Ha-Ki wouldn't have too many problems adapting to all of the different people and new things.

It was strange that the boy should ask about the killing of the white buffalo tonight. It had only been a week ago that Many Hawks and his woman had come into the post to trade for the white robe. He leaned over and picked up a corner of it and studied the white fur. His mind wandered to that day so long ago when he had saved Many Hawks' life. It had enabled him and Na-Ha-Ki to marry. Who would have thought that Many Hawks would wind up as a drunk? It had only been ten years ago that he killed the white buffalo. Wonder where he'd be in ten years and what he'd be doing. But as Jack always said, it didn't help to buy trouble.

The sound of the door to the boys' room closing aroused him from his thoughts. Na-Ha-Ki smiled at him crossed the room and eased herself into his lap. They sat quietly and watched the fire. It was low now and the room grew chilly. The wind whined and screeched as it whipped about the building. She pulled the robe about them and snuggled closer to him, then kissed him.

"I love my men, Big and Little Charles. You will not let our son ride Lightning Horse, will you?"

"Don't let it worry you. I know that horse and, who knows, maybe someday Chuck can ride him. We'll wait and see." He felt her stiffen and pull away from him.

"It'll be all right, I'll see to that." His mouth went to her ear. "Remember our lodge by the Marias. Maybe we ought to spend a week up there soon."

Her rigid body softened and she pressed against him. She stood up, took his hand and led him to their room.

*   *   *

Lightning Horse stood quietly while Charles saddled him. Na-Ha-Ki and young Chuck watched as Charles mounted the horse and rode it along the edge of the corral to the place where mother and son waited. He smiled at his son. "Climb up on the rail and get on, Chuck." The boy started to climb onto the corral rail, but stopped at his mother's words.

"No! I do not like this." She ran to her son and held him tightly. Charles dismounted and strode to them. Charles' mouth drew into a thin line. He pulled Chuck from Na-Ha-Ki's grasp and sat him on the topmost rail. He turned to Na-Ha-Ki and spoke sharply.

"He can't be a baby all his life. Now go back to the Post and tend to your own business. You think I'd let him get on that horse if I thought he couldn't ride it? He's been around horses since he could walk"

Na-Ha-Ki looked at her son, then at her husband. Young Chuck sat on the topmost rail of the corral rubbing the horse on its forehead. "You will take care of him?" she said.

"Certainly. Now go on, everything will be all right." His voice was softer now, gentle.

Na-Ha-Ki went to her son and squeezed him.

"I'll be all right, mother," he said. "See, he likes me." He rubbed the horse again. Na-Ha-Ki smiled at him and abruptly left. Charles watched her as she trudged toward the Post. Her body sagged and for an instant he thought about running to her and setting her mind at ease. If she felt that strongly about the boy riding the horse, maybe he ought to put it off until later. His thoughts were interrupted by his son's voice.

"Are we going to ride him,"

"Sure we are," he said. "When I get on, you sit in front of me." The horse laid one ear back when Chuck slid into the saddle in front of his father. Lightning Horse fidgeted about nervously, but soon settled down. Father and son rode him around the corral at a slow walk. "We'll do this for a while until he is used to having you on his back," Charles said.

"Can I ride him alone, now, Pa?"

"We'll see." They rode around the corral at a trot now with Chuck holding the reins. Charles reached around his son, grasped the reins and pulled the horse to a stop. "You ready to try it alone?" he asked.

"Sure, Pa. He likes me, I can tell."

"Well, I guess now is as good a time as any." Charles said. They dismounted and Charles led the horse to the fence and held his head while his son eased himself onto the saddle. Lightning Horse switched his tail and laid one ear back, then followed Charles as he led him around the corral several times. They stopped and the horse stood quietly, his ears cocked forward. Charles smiled and nodded his approval. He handed the reins to his son and stepped back.

"He's all yours, son. Go ahead." Charles smiled and flicked the reins. Lightning Horse started forward then jerked his head down. Charles sprinted toward them. The horse gathered itself together and hurled himself into the air. Chuck grabbed the saddle horn and clung tightly to it. His face was pale. Charles watched as the wild animal jolted into the ground. His front hooves swung in an arc, narrowly missing Charles' head. As Lightning Horse reared and twisted about in a circular motion, Chucks' fingers slipped from their grip and his body flew through the air and slammed against the corral fence with a sickening thud. His head snapped backward against a post and his body slumped to the ground.

Charles raced across the corral and knelt beside his son. He cradled the still body in his arms and rocked back and forth, dumbly. Chuck's cap had fallen off and his red hair glinted in the sunlight. His father groaned and rocked back and forth again.

At last he staggered to his feet, with his son still clutched in his arms and walked slowly toward the Trading Post. Na-Ha-Ki ran toward them. She clutched her sons' outstretched hand and leaned over him, crying his name over and over. The child lay still in his father's arms. Jack Taylor opened the door and Charles walked blindly past. He laid the small body on the bed and stared at him. Na-Ha-Ki pressed her mouth to the boy's and cried his name. The pale face against the pillow did not change. Charles pushed Jack aside and walked from the room.

His face was grim. He lifted his rifle from its place on the wall and strode to the corral. Lightning Horse raised its head and looked at Charles, his ears cocked forward. Charles lifted the gun, sighted carefully and fired it. The horse stood for an instant, then fell, shuddered, and lay still. Charles stared at the gun, dropped it, and turned away.

*   *   *

Na-Ha-Ki lay across the still body of her son. She lifted her head, stared at him, then turned away and buried her face against the breast of her son. Charles went to the bed and touched his wife. She pulled away. He clasped and unclasped his hands, then silently left.

*   *   *

Crow Woman studied the figure of the mother beside the mound of earth. .

"It is the way of our people. She will be all right. I will stay with her if she needs me."

Charles tried to ignore the dull ache that tore at his guts. His entire body felt as if it were carrying a heavy weight. He sighed, then walked slowly away. If that was what she needed to do, he supposed he ought to respect her feelings. If only he had paid attention to her wishes sooner, their son would still be alive.

Charles recalled the image of Chuck as he sat on the top rail of the fence, rubbing Lightning Horse and speaking to his mother. Would he go all through all of his life with that scene in his mind? He groaned. Moving, keep moving. That was the answer. When he moved somehow things were better. The rhythm of his motion seemed to help.

Fred and Jack watched their friend as he trudged down the trail. "He's taking it pretty hard, Jack."

"Don't know what we can do, Fred. That's the hardest part, not knowing what to do. Doesn't seem to be any way we can be of help to him. Blames himself."

"Nothing but time will take the hurt out of things. It doesn't ever go away, but time seems to blunt the hurt some."

"Charlie's been like a son to me." Jack shook his head as he watched the slowly moving figure of his friend. He breathed deeply and wished there were something he could do or say that would ease Charles' burden.

*   *   *

Na-Ha-Ki was still beside the grave of her son, with untouched vessels of food and water beside her. Three days and nights had passed but she made no move to leave the grave. Charles re-arranged a blanket about her shoulders. He knelt beside her, trying to shelter her from the wind that whipped at the blanket. He gently tucked it about her, but she ignored him. A low keening wail from the distraught mother permeated the air.

Charles gently shook her. "You can't stay here any longer. You must go with me." Na-Ha-Ki stared at him blankly, then threw herself over the mound of dirt. Her keening wail was at a higher level now, pulled up from far within her. Charles stood by helplessly, then made his way through the gathering dusk toward the Trading Post. Jack met him at the door.

"Any luck, Charlie?"

"No. Hasn't touched anything for three days. Refuses to move. Got to fix a better shelter, it's getting cold. Can't get her to move."

"I'll give you a hand." Jack said.

They gathered tools and materials and quickly built a crude shelter over the grave. Na-Ha-Ki crouched under it, oblivious of their actions. She rocked back and forth as small moaning sounds came from deep within her. Charles wrapped another blanket close about her. He was dimly aware of Jack's voice.

"Come on Charlie, you need to take care of yourself. She'll be all right for tonight. Crow Woman will stay with her. This is the way of her people."

Charles nodded numbly, touched Na-Ha-Ki, and followed Jack.

*　　*　　*

At the Post, Jack poured a glass half-full of whiskey and handed it to Charles. "I know you don't use the stuff much, but it'll help you sleep. I'll wake you up if we need you." Charles meekly accepted the drink, quickly downed it and collapsed on the bed. He awoke several hours later. It was as if it had all been a bad dream. Charles sat up and it all came back to him...the rearing horse, the frightened face of his son, the dull sickening smack of the small body against the post, his sons' red hair glinting in the sun. Charles buried his head in his hands and groaned. He quickly rose from the bed and hurried to the grave on the hill.

Na-Ha-Ki still huddled under the shelter. Her blanket had slipped to the ground. She was quiet. The food and water was untouched. Charles held the water jug to her lips, but she turned her face away and stared dully at the grave. At last Charles placed both arms under her, lifted her into his arms and carried her to the Trading Post and laid her on the bed.

Na-Ha-Ki's face was hot and her breathing quick and heavy. Crow woman knelt beside her sponging Na-Ha-Ki's face with a wet cloth. She stirred and moaned, then lay back. She moved her head from side to side. The fever rose. Her breath came in rasps and over and over she muttered their son's name and flung her arms about wildly. At last she lay back exhausted.

Through the rest of the day and the following night, her fever continued. Toward morning she stirred, her eyes opened. She coughed and looked at the man bending over her. A noise sounded in her throat. Charles' hand went to her brow. It was cooler now. He bent over her and listened. Suddenly he pressed his ear to her chest.

Nothing. He lifted her arm and then placed it carefully back on the bed beside her.

Charles straightened and stood for a long time staring at her, then crossed his arms across his chest in the Blackfeet sign of love.

Charles kissed Na-Ha-Ki's cheek and quickly left the room.

It was over.

*   *   *

Charles stared at the graves of his wife and son. The ache that tore at his insides seemed as if it would consume him. He had to do something. Move, that was it, move. He turned abruptly and went toward the Trading Post.

Jack and Crow woman watched as their friend strode away with the white robe over his arm. "Wonder where he is going with that?" Jack said.

Crow Woman shook her head silently.

"Guess he'll be all right once he has his cry out," Jack said. His face was furrowed. His wife remained silent. Crow woman knew that Jack didn't expect her to answer and it helped him to have someone to talk to. They watched Charles turn a bend in the trail and disappear from sight.

Charles' walk was rhythmic and steady. As long as he kept going he didn't have to think. He began to count, one, two, three, four . . . one, two, three, four . . . The heavy robe over his arm slipped and for the first time he became conscious of it. Charles stopped and stared at it dumbly, then asked himself, what was he doing? He shifted the robe to his other arm and resumed his pace. The steady rhythm soothed him and he resumed his count, one, two, three, four..., one, two, three, four, shift the robe. Charles was unaware of his compulsive behavior and had no idea of how far he had gone from the Trading Post. It was nearly dark and in the dusk the white fur stood out plainly. Suddenly Charles realized that he was tired. He eased himself to the ground and rested his back against a tree. The tearing ache inside of him returned and he rose to his feet and he turned back toward the

Trading Post. It was better now. As long as he kept moving he could manage. He stroked the fur with his free hand and slowed his pace. Charles knew now what he had to do. He stopped and stared through the night to the east. It was completely dark now, but his feet felt the trail in front of him as he returned to the Trading Post. He would leave, keep moving until the ache inside of him subsided. It was all he could do. He would take the white robe with him. He would go first thing in the morning. Maybe after a while he would come back when the ache left him. He slowed his pace and stopped. The ache returned. Move, move on and keep moving. Somehow the white robe was a part of it, too. Well, he'd keep going until the answer came to him.

Charles stopped again and examined his feelings. The ache was still there, but duller. Maybe being tired helped. He shifted the heavy robe to his other arm and moved toward the Trading Post once more. The robe's heavy weight on his arm was comforting.

* * *

He was through packing. The only things he was taking besides clothing and food was the robe and the music box. All that remained was to say his good-byes. Charles looked around the Trading Post one last time, then picked up his pack and strode to the packhorse and lashed it firmly in place. His gaze went to the hill and the mounds there. He walked to them and stood silently. His mouth drew into a line and he wiped his eyes with the heels of his palms. Charles crossed his arms over his chest and abruptly turned away.

Jack and Fred stood in the doorway and watched him as he approached. "Charlie, I hate to see you go," Deiber said. "When you expect we'll see you again?"

"Don't know. All depends. You take care of the business, now."

Suddenly Jack's hand shot out and grasped Charles'. "Keep your top knot on, you hear me?" Jack's brow gathered into three furrows above his nose and he looked intently at Charles.

275

Charles' hands fidgeted with a strap on his pack. "I don't know what to say. Thanks for everything. I'll write." He walked quickly away without looking back. His packhorse trailed along behind him. Suddenly he was aware of a small figure beside him. It was Jeff Deiber. Jeff's face was distraught and tears stained his brown cheeks. "Uncle Charlie, Uncle Charlie, please stay . . ." The child's anxious voice projected itself upon Charles' consciousness.

Jeff tugged at Charles' trouser leg. Charles stopped, picked the small boy up and held him in a tight embrace. His voice was soft, gentle and reassuring. "It's all right, Jeff. Uncle Charlie will be back, but he has to go now for a while." He wiped the child's tears with his handkerchief. "Now your Daddy and Uncle Jack will need you to help run things while I'm gone. Think you can manage?"

Jeff quietly nodded. "Will you bring Chuck back with you?"

"I'm afraid not, son." Charles paused and looked back at the Trading Post where Fred and Jack stood watching them.

"Now you go and be a good boy and help your Daddy and Uncle Jack."

Charles lowered Jeff to the ground, hugged him, and then gently pushed him in the direction of the Trading Post. He waved to his friends, then wiped his eyes, blew his nose and turned away.

The men watched until he was out of sight. "Wonder what is going to happen to him?" Deiber said.

"Don't know," Jack said.

"Funny the way he carries that white robe over his arm," Deiber said.

"He'll be all right after a while. I hope so. Time has a way of healing things."

*   *   *

The force that impelled Charles to make the long trip from Montana to Colorado pushed him blindly onward day after day, mile after mile. After the first long weeks of his journey some of the numbness passed and he carefully examined his part in the tragedy of the loss of his wife and son. Over and over the sickening thud of little Chuck's head against the corral post, Na-Ha-Ki's stricken look, and the events that followed the death of his son played through his mind.

*   *   *

When he arrived at The Wayfarer Hotel in Denver, he was unsure of his next action. Adding to his confusion was the city itself. Denver had changed remarkably in the eight years since Charles had last seen it. It was now 1878 and new wealth spurred on by the gold and silver mines of Central City, Leadville and Creed was evident everywhere he looked. However, The Wayfarer Hotel looked much the same. He entered the lobby and purchased a newspaper, sat down on a couch. He scanned the paper as he tried to compose his thoughts. There was no one in sight except a man behind the counter. A sudden impulse to leave and not look back crossed his mind. After all, he thought it had been eight years since he had last been in this place. Charles folded the paper, took a deep breath and walked slowly to the counter. The clerk looked quizzically at the white robe over Charles' arm. "May I help you sir?"

"Yes, can you tell me who is running the hotel?"

"What do you mean, run?"

"Well, the owners, The McIntyres, I used to know them a number of years ago."

The man hesitated for a moment. "I guess that would be Miss Ruby's parents."

"Mr. and Mrs. McIntyre are dead, Miss Ruby runs things now." The man eyed the white robe quizzically again.

Suddenly Charles was more sure of himself. His posture straightened as he looked directly at the young man behind the counter. "If you have a room, I'll check in and freshen up.

The clerk pushed the register toward him. "Second room on your right, at the top of the stair. Jimmy will take your things." He banged a bell on the counter and the porter, Jimmy, hurried to the desk. "Please assist Mr. Tucker with his things to room 223." he said.

Jimmy grasped Charles' pack and reached for the white robe. "No, I'll manage it," Charles said. He pulled the robe from the boy's grasp and followed him to the room.

The clerk pulled the register back toward himself and studied it pensively. "Charles Tucker, Fort Benton, Montana" it read. He glanced at the empty stairs where the man and boy had gone. Montana? The clerk cupped his chin in his hands and thought for a moment, then pulled a sheet of paper from a drawer. The pen made a drumming sound as he tapped its butt end against the counter. He started to write, crumpled the paper and tossed it into a basket against the wall. Well, it was none of his business, but there was something unsettling about this man, Charles Tucker. That heavy white buffalo robe was strange. Would be interesting to know who this man was, though.

The dining room was nearly empty when Charles entered. The hostess looked at the clock, then hurried over to the waiting man. "We were just closing the dining room, Sir. However, if you don't mind sitting at one of the tables over there," she pointed to a small table by the kitchen door, "we could serve you."

Charles smiled, "I wouldn't mind at all. Place hasn't changed much," he remarked as if to himself. He smiled at her and went to the table she had indicated. When he'd finished his meal, Charles leaned back and surveyed the dining room. He sipped his coffee and listened to the chatter of the waitresses as they went about cleaning up the rest of the room. The food had been excellent and for the first time in weeks he was relaxed. A feeling of warmth and satisfaction engulfed him. He sipped his coffee reflectively.

A waitress busied herself refilling sugar bowls. As she filled the bowl on the table next to him, she spoke to an unseen person in the kitchen behind Charles. "Be busy around here next week, Miss Ruby getting married and all."

Charles stiffened, listening intently.

And Still the Wind

"Yeah, most everybody in Denver will be here," The sugar bowl clinked as she replaced it and moved on to the next table.

Charles shoved himself away from the table. Hurriedly he placed some money on the table and strode toward the entrance. The hostess intercepted him. "Everything all right, Sir?"

"Oh yes, thank you. The dinner was fine. I left enough to cover it, I believe." The tall man pushed past her and was gone.

"He sure headed out of here in a hurry. Good tip, though." The waitress looked thoughtfully at the money and shrugged her shoulders.

The doors swung back and forth after her, making a soft rhythmic sound as she passed into the kitchen.

45-JEYS

EPILOGUE

(Upon this Chequer-board of Nights and Days;...) LXIX

Denver, North Platte, Council Bluffs, Chicago, Rock Island, Milwaukee, Detroit, Erie, Buffalo, Scranton, Philadelphia, New York, Atlanta, New Orleans, Baton Rouge, Albuquerque, Los Angeles, San Francisco, Salt Lake, Helena, Great falls, Boise, Denver, Sioux City, Fargo, Denver, Council Bluffs. The rhythm of steel wheels on steel rails had a soothing sound. Move, always on the move, that was the answer. After a while the cities fell into a pattern. Year after year, mile after mile, city after city, they blended in his mind now until it was hard to separate them. One looked the same as another, their people's faces alike.

The years passed, and the face of the country changed. Where the Indian had ridden free and unhindered, fences now blocked the way. Long horned cattle roamed where once the buffalo had grazed. Endless miles of wheat glinted golden in the sun, and in Montana, still the wind. It turned windmills now that pumped water into tanks where cattle and horses drank. Telegraph poles stretched across the country to the far oceans. Where it had taken weeks to send a message, it now took but an instant.

The year was 1910, the city, Council Bluffs, Iowa. Lou McMahan watched as a tall, white-headed man angled across the railroad yards toward him. The man carried a pack in one hand, and thrown over the other arm was a white robe.

"Howdy, Pop."

"Hello Lou, how have you been?"

"All right, all right, and you?"

"Fine, fine. You got anything heading west?"

"Sure enough, in about an hour. Freight is making up over there." He pointed to an engine with a string of cars moving slowly through the freight yards. "Come on over to the diner and have a cup of coffee and say hello to Maggie. She'll be glad to see you."

"Sounds like a good idea."

"Where are you going now?"

"Denver. Got a gal named Miss Ruby expecting me." They headed toward the diner and went inside. Lou pushed his empty cup across the counter then turned toward Pop.

"Ain't none of my business, Pop, but a fellow gets curious about such things. How come you don't ride the passenger, it'd be more comfortable. The way you tip Maggie, I know it ain't the money."

"You sound like Ruby!" Pop answered. He laughed shortly. "It's a long story and I'm not sure it's all that interesting, but there's times it makes sense."

Maggie leaned across the counter and grasped Pop's hand. "You see a red-headed boy named Joe on your way, let us know about him, will you?"

Lou patted Maggie's hand and added, "Not likely, but we think he got on a freight heading west a while back. His folks are looking for him. He's kind of special to Maggie and me." Lou coughed. "Big for his age, 14 or so, and likeable. Worked for Maggie," Lou blew his nose and coughed again. "Like a son, he was."

Pop placed his hand over Maggie's. "I can see he was special to you folks. You can never tell, I might see him. Red hair would make him easy to spot."

"Well Pop, I think she's about ready to leave. That sixth car back has some straw in it and ought to be comfortable for you."

"Thanks Lou, see you around. Keep your top-knot on."

"Sure enough. You too, Pop. See you when you come through again."

Lou watched as Pop tossed his pack and the robe into the empty car and pulled himself in after them. When Lou returned to the diner, Maggie shoved a wedge of pie across the counter and refilled his coffee cup. She came around the counter to sit beside him. "He's a nice old fellow. Funny how he comes through every year about the same time, talking about going to Denver to see his Miss Ruby." She shifted around to face Lou. "Do you think there really is a Miss Ruby?"

"I wouldn't be surprised if there was. Some say he is a painter. Comes East every year to sell his stuff to the rich folks. Rides the passenger train all dressed up. Comes back on the freights. Goes all over the country. There are lots of stories about him told by the railroaders." Lou sipped his coffee and cut a piece of the pie with the edge of his fork before continuing. "Some say he used to live in Montana and was married to an Indian princess. Had some sort of tragedy in his life. Don't talk much about himself."

"Seems strange, him wandering all over the country like that, carrying that white buffalo robe. Must be more to it than that." Maggie paused and gazed out of the window across the yard toward the car that held Pop Tucker. "I'd like to meet that Miss Ruby sometime. I bet she would be something to see."

Lou placed his arm around Maggie. "You women are all alike with your romantic notions and all." He squeezed her and continued, "Well ain't much we can do about it, love, we got problems of our own without taking on the whole world's troubles. Pop Tucker seems happy enough to me."

Lou paused and looked out the window and waved as the freight moved past. Its caboose lights winked out of sight, two orange globes in the dusk. A long whistle and the train picked up speed. "Wouldn't it be something if Pop and Joe did run into each other. I bet they would be good for each other."

"What did you say?"

"Nothing, Maggie, just talking to myself again," Lou said.

The train wheels clattered and thumped as they settled into a steady rhythm. Pop settled back into the straw, pulled his pipe from his pack, stuffed it full and lighted it. The train's motion was soothing, but the air was cool. He pulled the robe around him and puffed the pipe, first to the four directions, then to the sky and to the earth.

His mind turned to the *Rubaiyat of Omar Khayyam*. A verse ran through his head over and over.

> *'Tis all a Chequer-board of Nights and Days*
> *Where Destiny with Men for Pieces plays:*
> *Hither and thither moves, and mates, and slays,*
> *And one by one back in the Closet lays.*
>
> VARIATIONS 1859; XLIX

Thoughtfully, Charles looked to the northwest and crossed his arms over his chest in the Blackfeet sign of love.

Ψ Ψ Ψ

AND STILL THE WIND is the first of a series of stories that chronicle the saga of Charles "Pop" Tucker and the transformation of the old West. FAIR WIND THAT BLEW is the second novel that introduces fourteen year old Joseph James, who has run away from home believing he has killed his brother. The year is 1910, when Joseph's and Pop Tucker's paths cross.

221